The FOURTH GUARDIAN

Books by Ronald Anthony Cross

Prisoners of Paradise
*The Fourth Guardian
†The Lost Guardian

*denotes a Tor book
†forthcoming from Tor

The
FOURTH GUARDIAN

Book One of The Eternal Guardians

Ronald Anthony Cross

A Tom Doherty Associates Book
New York

THE FOURTH GUARDIAN

This book is printed on acid-free paper.

Edited by James R. Frenkel

A Tor Book
Published by Tom Doherty Associates, Inc.
175 Fifth Avenue
New York, N.Y. 10010

Design by Lynn Newmark

Library of Congress Cataloging-in-Publication Data

Cross, Ronald Anthony.
The fourth guardian / Ronald Anthony Cross.
p. cm.
"A Tom Doherty Associates Book."
ISBN 0-312-85634-2
I. Title.
PS3553.R5725F68 1994
813'.54—dc20 93-45302
CIP

First edition: March 1994

Printed in the United States of America

0 9 8 7 6 5 4 3 2 1

The FOURTH GUARDIAN

Preludes

Prelude 1

A CITIZEN OF THE SENSES

IT HAD STARTED out for Marcus as a typical day. True, it was marked *dies nefastus* on the Roman calendar, which made it an official day off for virtually every citizen of the Eternal City and meant that all of the courthouses and major businesses would be shut down. But then, with all those birthdays of dead emperors and even live celebrities piling up, it had got to where more than one day out of every three was an official holiday these days.

Marcus woke up early, as always, quickly dressed, washed, and ate a morning snack: a small bowl of sweetened porridge. Then he went out to the closest barbershop and got a summary of thc latcst ncws, while having his face scraped clean of whiskers. He prided himself on going to a public shop instead of keeping a live-in barber, as so many of the richer noblemen did. But the truth was simply that he always enjoyed getting out of the house and onto the streets of Rome. The streets were where the action was.

While drowsing off in the barber's chair he tossed around a few ideas about how to spend the holiday. There were always the chariot races, of course: they were rumored to have booked some really splendid drivers and horses for the old Circus Maximus. The races at the newer Circus, the one that Caligula had built on the Vatican, had been degenerating as of late, and those in the know were avoiding them and steadily frequenting the old Maximus.

Then there were the gladiatorial combats: but Marcus, as was the case with many young noblemen nowadays, was part of a conservative backlash, and viewed the games with distaste.

No, the games were out. The chariot races also. Finally he decided to spend the entire day at the baths, exercising, bathing, and flirting with the pretty young girls. In the afternoon he could wander around outside in the garden for a while, and perhaps later on he would stroll out into the city.

Rome would be dancing with life tonight. Her streets, markets, gardens, and porticos would be teeming with entertainers: clowns, jugglers, conjurors, fortune-tellers, snake charmers—you name it. People would be singing their songs, reading their poems out loud, and dancing their dances. Not to mention the gaudy display of thieves, pickpockets, whores, and other such riffraff.

Quite pleased with his plans, Marcus tipped the barber lavishly and headed for the nearest baths on foot.

By the time he arrived at the baths of Caracalla it was closing on noon. He had given in to the mood of the city and stopped off at a wineshop along the way for a few goblets of hot wine and water and a snack, enjoying as always the rowdy, low-life atmosphere of such places. Now here he was, deliciously woozy, wading into one of the cold baths in the frigidarium. The pleasant cool water shocked him awake.

A multitude of volatile Romans were singing, splashing, whistling, and shouting at each other, their raucous cries echoing off the walls of this absolutely enormous building, so big that, in fact, today being a holiday, it was quite possible that fifteen hundred noisy people might all be taking baths here together, while across town at the baths of Diocletian one might even encounter more than three thousand bathers sporting in the waters all at once.

In other rooms, men and women were playing ball, steam bathing, massaging and being massaged, practicing gymnastics, and who knows what else.

And men and women were bathing together. Emperor after emperor had applied various pressures to break up this risqué habit, all to no avail, thank Venus!

Right now, Marcus was flirting with two lovely nubile teenage girls with glistening wet bodies and glossy dark wet locks of hair falling over their eyes and foreheads in charming disarray.

They kept giggling and splashing each other in a delightfully abandoned manner, all the while sneaking looks at Marcus.

Catching their eye, Marcus made an obscene query, using his forefinger and making a circle with the thumb and forefinger of his other hand.

Still laughing, one of the girls shouted an insult back at him. Over the general tumult, he caught the words "prick" and "too small."

Children nowadays! If he were their parent he would give them a spanking for their impudence they would never forget. He was carefully savoring in his mind's eye the delicious vision of himself delivering this punishment when he heard his name being shouted out somewhere amidst all the uproar.

"Marcus Tibullus, over here." Marcus frowned, scanning the mob for this intruder into his fantasies, and was not too displeased to spot the lean figure of that old warhorse Gaius Melissus waving at him from the banks of the frigidarium. Wherever Gaius showed up, Marcus reasoned, his lovely wife Drusilla was likely to put in an appearance. Nubile teenagers forgotten, he scanned the baths surreptitiously as he headed toward Gaius, hoping to catch a glimpse of the man's wife au naturel.

"Drape a towel around that erection and follow me," Gaius commanded cheerfully. Somewhat peeved, Marcus climbed the steps up out of the cold bath and beckoned to a public servant for a towel. The middle-aged Gaius was probably leading him to one of the warmer baths or perhaps even a steam bath, he supposed. Older people, Marcus believed, needed warmer water.

But such was not the case. Gaius Melissus led Marcus through several rooms of baths and down a long hallway, to a door which led to a flight of stairs, and then down to another large room below the main baths.

"I didn't know this room existed," Marcus said as Gaius latched the door.

"Nor does anyone else, save a few of us. Members of our club. You've heard of us, of course. The Knights of the New Dawn. I'm sure you know Opimius there, and Domitius Gallus." Marcus clasped arms with the men in greeting. Three of them he knew and two more he knew of, but two of them were total strangers. One was a young knifeblade of a man, thin and quick-looking as a ferret, who at the moment seemed preoccupied with impudently staring at Marcus with his large, dark eyes; eyes that you couldn't see into, but at the same time eyes that watched your every move with calculated cunning.

"This handsome brute is Corbo, the gladiator, no doubt you've heard of him. Sometimes a Thracian, sometimes a retiarius, always victorious."

The man smiled a cold expression of some inner amusement, shared only with himself. "Anything but a myrmillo," he said. The men guffawed. "You're too skinny," one of them shouted. "The armor alone would trip you up and smash you down on the earth. Thumbs down, for certain." More laughter.

Marcus looked more closely at Corbo. A real killer, he thought. A Thracian was a gladiator who fought with a curved slender scimitar and a very small light round shield. The retiarii fought only with trident and net, while the myrmillone Corbo had jested about wore heavy armor.

Few gladiators were gifted enough to fight as both Thracian and retiarius and survive. Both styles demanded great skill and speed, while the myrmillone relied more on brute strength. They usually won.

Marcus found himself held in fascination by Corbo's gaze, as a bird is caught and held by the gaze of a snake. He could read nothing there. Nothing at all. Not a hint of life or emotion. Yet he had the strong sensation that some omen, deeply important to him, lurked there waiting to be read. Mocking him. The others noticed the two young men staring each other down.

"By the gods," tough old Gaius shouted, "the boys have fallen in love with each other. Which one, I wonder, will wear the sword in the family?"

Marcus reddened as the hearty laughter of the men drowned out all of his protests. Corbo merely smiled and looked away. He had no doubts as to who would wear the sword.

"No need to get all red-faced and wrought up about it. Many of our most powerful generals and emperors have had a taste for the exotic. Why, some of those long-drawn-out bloody campaigns abroad, I've had to sheathe the old sword in a few unusual scabbards here and there."

"Gaius never was one to turn away from a pretty young boy's backside," one of the men jibed.

Marcus was still doing his best to be heard in protest above the laughter. He longed for a conservative turn of life, back to the pure values of the early republic. Simple dress, simple foods, no buggery.

Of course there had been his affair with young Lucullus last year, but that was over with; he had outgrown that sort of thing.

After what seemed an interminable amount of time, the men recovered from their fit of ribaldry and Gaius introduced Marcus to the old Greek, Theseus.

"Not *the* Theseus," Marcus quipped, much to everyone's amusement. Every other Greek seemed to be named after some legendary hero or god.

"No, I'm afraid I'm just an ordinary man," Theseus said in a low, oddly toneless voice.

"Oh, he's ordinary, all right," Gaius wisecracked. "He's as plain as barley stew. Speaking of which, he's applied his talents for cooking and brewing toward mixing you up one of his special concoctions, eye of toad, old hound's bladder, pigs' farts, that sort of thing."

As Gaius was jesting, the old Greek was carrying over a goblet of what looked like red wine on a lovely, ornately decorated tray.

Marcus was dumbfounded. He had heard very little about the Order of the New Dawn, but it was obvious to him that he was being offered membership in it.

He smiled and graciously accepted the goblet, but all the time his mind was wheeling and dealing, adding up the pros and cons. He knew only of the Knights of the New Dawn that it was a secret society of conservatives, military men mostly. He was surprised they were asking him to join. But he knew two things for certain: (1) it would be dangerous for him to do it, and (2) it would be even more dangerous for him not to.

He accepted the goblet with both hands. It smelled like red wine. "I am honored. My father would be honored if he could only be here to see this. Most of you were his friends. And when I say 'friends,' I employ the word in its old Roman republican spirit, from the old days when friendship was sacred. I toast you, my friends."

It looked like red wine, smelled like red wine, and it even tasted like red wine, but it was not red wine. It was red wine and something else. Something else very potent.

The men were now sporting noisily in the bath, but Marcus was lying down on a mat alongside them, dazed and dizzy, staring up at the gorgeous ceiling. The patterns in the marble and tiles were beginning to move and weave and pulsate with life. What had they put in that drink? He sat up and tried to study Theseus' features, certain that the answer was there. But he couldn't make them come clear. They kept shifting through a myriad of subtle alterations and mood changes. Queasy, he lay back down again.

Gaius had explained the rules and goals of the secret society to him as he lay there waiting for the drug to come on. Only everything was all confused now.

He remembered Gaius telling him the latest anecdotes about the Emperor's silly, disgusting behavior. And there was something about the Greek, Theseus, something important—but he had forgotten what it was.

At first, the patterns in the marble and tile had come to life for him, more glowing and beautiful than ever before. At last he understood them. Everything about them. They were . . . no words. There were no words for such mystic beauty.

But now, suddenly, everything began to age and crack and crumble apart. Everything was rapidly becoming dust. This was the truth. The ultimate and only truth. Disintegration.

All the great buildings, statues, all the fame, the glory that was Rome, were rapidly and constantly crumbling into dust. To be blown away by fierce winds. And years would go on and on relentlessly until everything he knew and cared about would be forgotten.

And worse. He himself would die, would crumble, would be blasted into oblivion. No—not *would be*—was *now*. He was dying right now.

His body convulsed in agony as he struggled with all his strength to fight, to stay conscious. It's no use, he thought, they've poisoned me. And when finally he gave up, it was as if he and the whole world he knew, and himself in it, imploded into an ever-diminishing colorless void.

While he was out, he babbled strange things about someplace he called "America."

"Of course I've heard of it," Gaius was telling the others. "It was somewhere in the Atlantic Ocean in ancient times. Sank into the sea, didn't it?"

"No. No, you old warhorse, that was Atlantis. America is a land in the far north, covered in mists and smoke. You can't get there from here." Everyone laughed.

Only the old Greek listened attentively to the young man's muttered ramblings and said nothing. Finally, noticing his silence and the seriousness of his concentration, Gaius climbed out of the bath and joined him alongside the feverish, sweating, thrashing body of Marcus Tibullus.

"Well?" he asked, putting a hand on the old Greek's shoulder.

"He's the one," the Greek said simply.

From the pool, the gladiator, watching them the way a ferret watches mice, smiled his tight little smile.

Afterward, drowsing beside the bath in the private room where they had left him to recover, the visions Marcus had experienced churned through his mind over and over again, but the meanings always just eluded him. After an eternity, he heard the door open, close, the latch fall into place, and then the giggles.

Could this be another vision? he wondered as Gaius' luscious wife Drusilla, flanked by the two teenage girls he had been flirting with earlier, glided toward him on bare feet. How could this be?

Drusilla brought him another goblet of wine while the girls, giggling and sporting with each other, disrobed.

Was all this part of the initiation? "Drink," Drusilla commanded. Then she too began to disrobe.

Marcus drank the wine and lay back to watch the girls undress. Almost immediately he felt a delicious warmth shimmering through his body, quite different from the effect of the mind-bending drug the old Greek had given him. As he watched the two teenage girls, now completely naked, engage in lascivious, teasing kisses with Drusilla, a slow inexorable lust overwhelmed him. Still, he just lay there, agonizingly hard, and waited, until suddenly all three women turned and rushed over to him. Almost voraciously, one of the girls slid her lips over his penis, teeth scraping the edges of the swollen head, while Drusilla lowered herself down to a squatting position, offering her slippery wet vagina to his lips. He wasn't sure what the other girl was doing. For the next hour or so, it was simply impossible to keep track of who was doing what to whom.

Later on it became clear to Marcus in just what a web he had, through no special action of his own, enmeshed himself. Just by buzzing around.

"I'm on your side, Marcus," Drusilla crooned in her breathy voice, teasing him with a quick stab of her tongue in his mouth. He tried to capture it, but she rolled away from him, laughing. She had dismissed the girls and latched the door behind them.

If Gaius catches me in here with her, he'll kill me, Marcus thought. But this turned out to be the least of his worries.

"I'm only trying to save your silly young neck, Marcus. Gaius and the old Greek and the rest, they're doomed. There's nothing we could do to save them. Don't you see, we have to save ourselves. Each other.

"And oh, Marcus, when all this is over we'll have such good times. I'll never be jealous or possessive. Why do you think I brought the girls in? I saw you ogling them in the bath. And I wanted to please you. No one woman can please a man as well as three." She laughed charmingly.

"What do you want me to tell you about the Knights of the New Dawn?" Marcus tried cautiously.

"Not I. I don't want to know anything about it. I'm just a go-between. It's the Emperor who wants to know. And he will know, Marcus, whether you tell him, or someone else tells him. That's why you have to save yourself."

She rolled back over and playfully nipped his ear. "What? Ready again, so soon?"

Marcus didn't know exactly what Drusilla, or the Emperor, or both, wanted out of him. But he knew two things for certain: (1) it would be dangerous for him to do it, and (2) it would be even more dangerous for him not to.

Prelude 2

A CITIZEN OF NOWHERE

ELENA AWOKE, NOT knowing where she was. Or even who she was. Which was par for the course for anyone living with the old man, she figured.

But over the years she had resourcefully put together a system for figuring out the pertinent information. Simple—first you looked over the sleazy hotel room (or in this case, adobe hut). Sometimes you could latch onto what you needed to know from this action alone. But if nothing in the place rang a bell for you, the next step was to remember in detail something that you had done the day before. What language had you spoken, by what name had you addressed the old man? The rest (country, state, city, etc.) would follow quite naturally.

Nothing to being a sorcerer's apprentice, you see? Nothing in more ways than one. Take the old man, for instance. At first Elena had thought there were a lot of things about him. Things that could be understood. Fastened onto.

He was (she had thought) an old man, about seventy years old, a Mexican named Sanchez. A brujo. A sorcerer. The wielder of an amulet of power. One of the Four who guard the world. A man who lived an exciting life. An important man. A man in control.

So, as soon as he had made the offer (just astonishing

everybody), Elena had jumped at the opportunity to escape her miserable family life in Zacatecas.

She had seen it like that. And for a while she had lived it like that. The two of them had traveled around Mexico, stopping here and there at the old man's whim. As soon as they settled into their hotel room, or shack or whatever, the word would mysteriously get out, and then the people would pour in to see the old man about their various problems, large and small. Mostly he would spend the afternoons listening to their complaints and offering what seemed to Elena to be odd, perhaps even useless, suggestions (e.g., "No, you're addicted to smoking, all right. There is no way out for you. Nicotine is the most deadly drug known to man. But why Kools? You want to smoke Camels—no, no, don't deny it. That's the kind of guy you are. So for God's sake if you're going to be addicted to something, smoke what you want to smoke, understand? Stop worrying about cancer. You've got to die some way or other, anyway. You know the guy in all those Camel ads? You know, the pictures in the magazines, billboards? He's got a black moustache and he's all dressed up in khakis and he's always in Egypt or someplace like that? Well, see, you can tell that he's not afraid of nothing. What the hell does he care about cancer? Do you see?—You smoke Camels and you *are* that guy.").

All this time he would have Elena assisting him. Which meant either writing things down when he told her to — (Later, these notes were invariably thrown away. "Who are they for?" Elena had asked. "Why, for you, Elena," the old man had answered) — or perhaps he would request Elena to bring him some object or another. But most often she was required merely to sit there and nod affirmatively whenever he would ask her, "Isn't that so, Elena?"

In the mornings they would rise early so Elena could practice her meditations; or if the mood were upon him, the old man would instruct her in the art of wielding the mystic stone. Which consisted mostly of just sitting there, holding it in your hand, letting it get the feel of you ("Not letting you get the feel of it, see?"). Finally, all this excitement would be climaxed by some totally unfathomable statement from the old man. Such as: "I don't think the little stone likes you, Elena, but then, who does?" This inevitably would be followed by a truly unique fit of laughter. (The old man's laughter was more like a dry racking cough, or perhaps a fit of sneezing, than laughter.)

The stone itself, one of the four, was a small black piece of what looked to Elena suspiciously like ordinary obsidian, set in a funky old copper amulet, with a chain to go around your neck. Named Yawtlée.

"Yawtlée," Elena had exclaimed, dumbfounded as usual. " 'Yawt' as in 'Yaght' and 'lee' as in 'lay'?"

The old man nodded.

"Why do you call it Yawtlée?"

The old man opened his eyes wide and gave her his classic expression of astonishment.

"Because that's its name, Elena, of course."

Then they would pack up and go somewhere else. Seemingly at random. Sample:

Elena: "Why are we going somewhere else?"

Old man: "Because it is time to go somewhere else."

Elena: "But why is it time?"

Old man: "Because of the signs."

Elena: "What are the signs?"

Old man: "My slightest desire to leave is the most important sign."

And on and on.

Elena: "Is the stone alive?"

Old man: "It is more than alive, Elena. You are alive. It is awake." Another fit of laughter.

Elena: "Are you 'the Four who guard the world' because you have the stones, or are the stones special because of your power?"

Old man: "No, no, the stones do it all. You know, Elena, how they always say the clothes make the man? Well, that is true, unfortunately, with that sort of man. With us brujos, it's the stone that makes the brujo. Big improvement." Fit of wild laughter.

So this was what life with the old man meant. Even the time when she had volunteered to hold the stone without waiting for him to suggest it, even the weird event that followed, unbelievable as it was, she could manage to add onto her picture of life with the old man.

First he had stared at her with mock astonishment again (this seemed to be his favorite expression). Then he had blinked and said in his high, dry voice, "Elena, you volunteered? Let me ask the little stone." Closed eyes, then blink, wide open. "No, the little stone is playing hard to get now. Tell me, Yawtlée, what do you want Elena to do this morning?"

And just like that, a doorway had appeared in the middle of the room. Or at least, what the old man called a doorway. An opening in the air, as if to a cave or a tunnel, emitting a smoky yellow light. It had seemed to Elena that she could see things moving in there, but she wasn't sure.

"The only way to know," the old man whispered, as if telling her a secret, "is to go inside and look around."

Elena noticed that her mouth was open, closed it, and swallowed. Then she said, "Could I get hurt in there?"

The old man suddenly waved his hand and the doorway dissolved. Then for a while he just looked at her, shaking his head. Finally he said to her, "Elena, what a dumb question. How long have you been alive now? Twenty, twenty-five years? Surely you must know by now that you can get hurt or killed anywhere at any second. That is precisely why we have no time here to ask dumb questions, or to hesitate. Now you must go back to holding Yawtlée and apologizing, clearing your mind of Elena. Perhaps he will forgive you. Perhaps not."

Elena swallowed again. "And what if he won't forgive me?"

"How would I know?" the old man said with a smile. "Perhaps you might get hurt or killed even sooner."

So that was life with old Sanchez the brujo. Weird, far-out, but at least in some ways predictable.

Then one day, without warning and without giving any reason, the old man had informed her that they were moving to Louisiana. He had reserved two tickets for Mr. and Mrs. Patroli.

On the airplane she had noticed the change. The total change. He no longer dressed like a Mexican, combed his hair (what there was of it) like a Mexican, or spoke English with the same accent. Oh, there was still a touch of an accent, to be sure, but now it had a definite European tinge to it.

"You," she gasped, "you're not a Mexican?"

"No, of course not," he said. "I only sometimes pretend to be a Mexican, or a European, or an American, for the benefit of other people. People like you. People who don't understand what things are real, and what things aren't."

"But you told me about your childhood in the jungle."

"Not real. A chimera in my mind." He whispered the word "chimera" and gestured fluidly with his right hand. He used his trick of opening his big round eyes wide to emphasize certain words. It made him look, thought Elena, very much like a bird. One of those little owls. "I am a citizen of nowhere," he said gravely. "And you, Elena? When you are not pretending to be Mexican, then what are you?" He did his owl eye trick again. This time on the word "pretending," which he drew out elaborately.

Exasperated, Elena remained silent. Suddenly the old man rapped her sharply twice on top of the head. "Knock knock," he said, "who's there?"

Still, stubbornly, Elena refused to speak.

"For once," the old man informed her, "you got the answer right. But only through luck." Then he had laughed and howled until tears were in his eyes, and Elena had thought he was going to choke himself. Serves him right. She remembered that people on the plane had smiled to see the innocent old man having such a good time.

And so that was the end of life with the old Mexican brujo Sanchez and the beginning of life with faith healer Patroli. Wandering around the States. Then for a short while it had been France and Spain with Señor Gomez. And now back to Mexico again.

So, so much for habits—none. And so much for roots—none.

There was no way to get to know the old man or predict the old man, or even—she intuited, although she would have been reluctant to admit it even to herself—to ever understand him. All you could do was keep your eyes open and watch everything he did all the time without tacking the past onto it, because, as he had taken great pains to point out to her, the past was a chimera. So she had learned something after all, though she wouldn't have thought of looking at it that way.

But living with the old man was like living with a cobra: you had to keep on your toes every minute of every day and night around him. And Elena was only human, and sometimes she had to rest.

Which was why this morning she almost missed out on what was to be the turning point of her apprenticeship, the turning point of her whole life, perhaps even the turning point of the whole world.

Prelude 3

A CITIZEN OF INDECISION

ONE MORE TIME, one more time, Brice kept goading himself, sweat pouring down his body in rivulets—nay, veritable rivers of sweat were pouring down his manly body, all 5′ 7″, 130 pounds of it. Brice O'Conner was pumping iron, at least his latest version of it. It sometimes seemed a cruel stroke of fate to him that he should be doomed by his mercurial nature to change everything about himself, including diet, hairstyle, dress, college major, and exercise combination, at least once a month, while his brother Conal—well, Conal had it made. Had always had it made. Would always have it made.

On impulse he put down the weights, thump, which nowadays consisted of two lightweight (twenty-five-pound) dumbbells with which he executed a series of high-repetition exercises, preceded and followed by a few push-ups and pull-ups. High repetition, but not so high as last month, when he had been doing Heavyhands. "Properly done, Heavyhands exercise can be safer than other forms of aerobic exercise," the instructions in the box containing the pretty little red weights had insisted. But prancing around and flailing his arms about until near exhaustion four times a week with two-pound weights in his desperately clenched fists had somehow wrecked his left shoulder joint.

So now his new routine: a few standard exercises with light weights and high repetition, but slowly, easy on the shoulder, and no rest in between sets. Well—almost no rest.

Now, for instance, something had caused him to put down the weights, and move over to the open window, and look out into their lovely backyard upon his brother Conal the Barbarian. Which was a joke, because if there was anybody in the world who was not a barbarian, it was Conal.

Lucky bastard's got it made, Brice thought to himself again as he watched his older brother practicing his tai chi form, or rather, one of his tai chi forms (he knew about six different ones), on the raised, bright red wooden platform. The platform and the koi pond in front of it, along with the Chinese landscaping, made their backyard beautiful, eerie, haunting even. But by itself it was incomplete; it needed the slender figure moving gracefully across the platform in slow motion, performing the ancient Chinese exercises, to complete the picture.

Conal was doing a Yang form today, Brice realized, but one of the northern versions, instead of the southern ones you usually saw demonstrated. The arm movements were wider and more sweeping, and mostly the form was executed from a lower posture. It was probably excruciatingly difficult, he realized; he had had just enough experience with tai chi to know how hard it could be, moving low and slow on your bent legs like that, but you'd never know it from watching Conal. He made it appear totally effortless as he glided casually through the form, long hair and beard flowing in concert with the loose flapping black Chinese costume he wore.

Fascinated, as always, Brice watched him complete the form and start another. This one was a fast version of a southern Yang form, the movements small, brisk, and very, very quick; but nevertheless, as Conal did them they were totally fluid, each movement circling into the next without a hint of a break in the flowstream.

Brice decided to give himself the day off, left the weights where they were, and wandered out toward the backyard. Maybe later he'd pump the exercycle or jog a few miles around the junior high school track down the street. Maybe not.

By the time he got outside, his brother was working on yet another form. Maybe a Wu form, Brice wasn't really sure.

No question about it, Conal had it made. Older, taller, handsome, maybe even beautiful, with his long flowing locks and beard, and his elegant graceful movements. And if that weren't enough, it was obvious to Brice that his brother performed all of the other roles in his life just as effortlessly as he performed his tai chi. Conal had even lucked out namewise. Conal and Brice, the O'Conner brothers. Bricey O'Conner, for Godsake.

And then Conal had always known just what he had wanted to do. Tai chi, meditation, and strict vegetarian diet. That's it. No booze or drugs. No struggling through college, shifting agonizingly from drama major to psychology, and then to English lit, as Brice had done. In fact, Brice had never even come close to an idea of what he wanted to do in life. Except sometimes, when he was playing the guitar and singing some of Dad's songs or maybe one of his own compositions and something magic happened, and suddenly the guitar was playing itself, and he wasn't really doing anything at all, but only was a part of . . . call it the act of creation. Times like those, he felt certain that was it, and then the moment would fade and he just couldn't be sure, and he had to be sure. So he went to college in the winter, jumping from major to major, and then taught guitar and gave a few concerts in the summer. A schizophrenic, he thought. Whereas Conal, Conal was truly at one.

"Thought you were pumping iron there, big fella. Or were you just pumping the old one-eyed worm? Your right arm looks a lot bigger than your left these days, Bricey boy."

"Oh, screw you," Brice shouted back at his brother, trying to keep the delight out of his voice. It made him feel great just to have Conal notice him at all.

"Christ, I hope you go on one of those wimpy tai chi sex retreats up north this summer. I can't stand to see you waving around out in the garden like a fucking flower or something. If the neighbors ever catch a peek over the fence, they'll call the little men in white to come and escort you to where they all dress and think like you do."

Conal pivoted elegantly and gave Brice the finger in a beautiful slow-mo gesture.

"Seriously, I wish you'd quit slinking around me in slow mo all the time. Real men don't move slow. Didn't the Chinese tell you that?"

"Back to the iron, you miniature Schwarzenegger terrier. This time why don't you pound your pud with your left hand for a change? Even up your arm size. My brother, the body beautiful, two big arms and one little, beat-up, worn-out pecker."

Back to the iron, Brice echoed to himself as he headed back into the house. Or maybe the guitar. Christ yes, I've only got nine days till that concert at Arnie's. Maybe I should be hitting the guitar more.

The school year was over and now Brice was making the shift to summer again. The complete shift from schoolwork to guitar practice. Soon he was rummaging through the old sheet music in the den.

" 'The Power' by Calvin O'Conner," it said. But there was nothing there—no notes, no words, just the instructions typed in the middle of the page: "Play what you will shall be the whole of the law." Just another of his father's crazy jokes.

Christ, he thought to himself. Maybe I should just forget the guitar and go back and do nothing but work on the weights for the rest of my life. Simple but fulfilling. He pictured himself five-foot-seven and 200 pounds of muscle, four feet wide.

Sighing, he began to tune the gorgeous old Martin D45 that had once upon a time been his father's guitar.

1

HECTOR VILLARIJO'S GROCERY store was one of the high points of the backward village of Tres Águilas, the old man liked to say. "It is magic. This store is too small to have anything in it but some fruit, beans, and a couple packages of tortillas. Yet you can find anything in it you want. Look at these panty hose, Elena. Or here is a fine little stapler."

But Elena was not impressed: Hector's Mercado did not seem particularly small to her for a town the size of Tres Águilas, a jungle village a mere sixty miles inland from Acapulco. Elena and the old man were residing in one of the white adobe huts (there was no other kind), waiting for something; the old man had not bothered to inform her what it was. And meanwhile, visiting such points of interest as Ruben's pool parlor and Hector's market. One of the surprising facts she had discovered about Tres Águilas was the size of it. Nothing but white adobe huts, but so many of them. There must be thousands of people living here in this prehistoric dump. Why?

"I can't even understand why anyone stays here," Elena had said. "What are they doing here anyhow?"

"Tres Águilas?" the old man asked with an exaggerated air of astonishment. "This place is sacred. Many years ago, some people were lost in the jungle. Suddenly they saw an omen. A great eagle. It flew over them and circled and flew away to the south. For one day they traveled on in that direction. At the end of the day, they saw two eagles that circled and flew away, this time southeast. The next day they traveled southeast. On the third day they saw three eagles. The eagles circled and circled. Finally one lit in a tree behind them, one lit in a tree before them, and one to the side, making a circle with them inside it. They divined from this that they were to stay and build their homes here. Sure enough, they found a river." (He was alluding to the muddy creek that ran through the center of the town, and was the only landmark you could recognize among the identical white adobe huts.) "They hunted animals for food and grew crops." (The animals they hunted must have been snakes, lizards, and spiders, Elena conjectured. They were the only living creatures she had ever spotted here outside of the morose-looking villagers, who actually wore guns in their belts, and their mangy dogs. As for crops, Elena had never seen any evidence of farming.)

"So they named the village 'Tres Águilas'—'Three Eagles'—and that's why they stay here. It's sacred to them.

"Also, they grow a lot of Acapulco Gold marijuana, to sell back in the city." He laughed out loud at the punch line. "Sure, this is where they grow it all. I guess those eagles were potheads, you know?"

So that was why the men wore revolvers in their belts and appeared so taciturn all the time. It was a whole village of pot smugglers who hid their crops in the surrounding jungles and sneaked out to them at night, and of course had to defend them from each other. Delightful!

And everyone stoned all the time. Of course that was it! When she complained about this to the old man, he merely shook his head in amazement at her naïveté.

"Everyone's stoned all the time everywhere, Elena, if you haven't noticed. They are stoned on martinis, beer, wine, whiskey, tranquilizers, sleeping pills, aspirin, Excedrin, Nyquil, Alka-Seltzer, cigarettes, cigars, coffee, Coca-Cola . . ." His voice trailed off. "I could go on forever. They're so stoned on aspirin they don't even know when they've got a headache. They go around with a terrible headache acting like they're okay.

"In short, Elena, I'm the only one I know who isn't stoned on some kind of drug or other, and I'm stoned on magic." Besides, he pointed out, people stoned on alcohol tended to be dangerous and impulsive, while people stoned on pot tended to be relatively harmless fuckups. He preferred being around potheads just as long as he didn't have to depend on them.

So this morning, when the old man announced his daily trip to that eighth wonder of the modern world, Hector's market, Elena had pleaded a headache and stayed home. Even though the old man had informed her several times that it was her sacred obligation to accompany him everywhere and observe very carefully everything he did or said, he did not now raise any objections. "I'll get you some Excedrin at Hector's," was all he said.

Outside, he first studied the skies, as he always did. Clouding up, very unusual for this time of day, this time of year, here. Big foamy-looking clouds with grey underbellies, moving in fast. He discerned in them the shapes of a goat, some kind of great cat—perhaps a tiger—and a crow. Then he began to walk down the dusty street, letting those shapes play around in his mind. His theory was that after the first three figures you had enough to work with, so now he paid no further attention to the clouds.

Ordinarily the three figures would fall into place immediately in his mind, pointing out a myriad of subtle connected meanings, but today, for some reason, his mind was sluggish. Maybe I should get some Excedrin for myself, no? Elena and I can split a bottle, kill whatever sensitivity we got left. He chuckled at that, brought his thoughts back to the three figures he was attempting to divine.

But it was no use. Today he just could not interpret. It's surely going to rain, he thought, very strange indeed.

About halfway to the store, a large shiny black crow dropped out of the sky and landed in the dirt road in front of him. Angrily it cawed at him in its raucous voice. It cried out three times, then it flew away, driving itself on its long loose wings.

The old man didn't need a sharp mind to interpret that. It was bad news. A warning. Whenever a crow cawed at you three times, it was a warning. You were in some kind of danger.

He continued on down the road. A crow had been one of the figures in the clouds. The crow in the clouds had been the crow that had come to warn him. But the tiger and the goat— Was he the goat? If so, who was the tiger?

In the grocery store, was it his imagination, or was something wrong with Hector? He seemed more morose and preoccupied than usual. Was he just stoned?

The old man pushed a shopping cart down the first aisle. He had carefully memorized the setup of the store, as he always did, and could tell you exactly where every item in the store was. Still, he would push the cart up and down each row, and observe carefully the position of every can of fruit, every item of hardware, as if it were a painting in a museum of fine art. Grocery stores were places of power for him.

In the third aisle, halfway down, he pulled up to a stop, leaning on the empty cart. He was feeling strangely enervated, and achy. His thought flow seemed disjointed and uneven, as though bits and pieces were being removed that would have made sense of the whole. Maybe I do need Excedrin, he thought. His gaze was blankly riveted on a row of colorful packages of dried beans, rice, millet, barley.

Suddenly, with a chill, he realized what he was staring at: El Tigre kidney beans, a picture of a snarling tiger on the label.

The crow was warning me about the tiger. This tiger. Then I must be the goat.

Outside, lightning flashed, thunder followed, and after a brief pause, it began raining hard. The old man could hear it battering the roof and flailing the windows, but almost as if it were taking place at a distance, in some other world.

His viewpoint of the market was altering, stretching, and forming into something entirely alien. A large square of cold blue light shimmered into existence up ahead on the floor; it swirled and then started to clear up a little. Brightened up, and now the old man could hear a deep pounding, steady and menacing, as if someone were playing a drum somewhere far away.

And yet he could still see the regular everyday portion of the market as well. It was as if two worlds, entirely different, were superimposed, each upon the other, simultaneously struggling for dominion.

Over me, the old man thought. He had no doubt whatever that a powerful occult attack was being waged against him, and that he must quickly prepare to meet the brunt of it.

A young housewife and her four-year-old child were pushing a cart with a few cans in it down the aisle toward him. The mother's movements were languid and slow, as if she was not quite awake. From time to time her head would nod.

"Señora Martinez," the old man called out to her, wondering if she could see what he saw, the tear in the fabric of their world. "Señora Martinez, it would be better if you took Juanito and got out of here, now. Do you understand?"

She smiled a bland dreamy smile at him. "Nobody

can leave this market until you're dead," she said calmly. Now there was a huge flash of lightning followed by deafening thunder, and the lights went out in the little store. Señora Martinez' heavy tired face glowed in the macabre blue light, which seemed to partially illuminate the entire market.

The old man nodded. "Very well then, it would be best if you take Juanito back to the main desk, lie down on the floor under the counter, and stay there until this is over."

She nodded, her eyes vacant, fixed on something vague and far away. "I understand," she said.

"Will you tell the others to do the same, please? Will you do that for me? It is going to be very bad here for a while."

She nodded again. She was smiling, but two narrow trickles of tears ran down her cheeks. She turned her cart around and slowly headed back the way she had come. "Come on, Juanito. Let's go lie down for a while."

Juanito's small monkeyish face wore an expression of anxiety, but he was too young yet to figure things out. "I don't want to take a nap," he shouted. "I don't have to. I'm too big."

"You go with your mother. Now." The old man's voice was strangely sweet and soft.

But Juan shut up and went with his mother.

The old man hurried past them down the aisle to the end and then turned toward the checkout counter. In the eerie glow, he could just make out the shadowy forms of a few slow-moving shoppers already starting to gather in that area.

Suddenly a squat muscular figure darted out of the next aisle and menaced him with raised arms. In the pulsing blue light, the old man could barely make out something gleaming metallically in the figure's hand. Then he could see it clearly, as the light momentarily intensified.

Hector, the too-friendly little grocer, was brandishing one of his hammers.

"Well, Hector, I was just wondering where you have some chalk here. I know you have it, and normally I would remember exactly where, but my mind just . . ."

"You can't leave here." Hector waved the hammer.

"Leave here?" The old man laughed wildly. "I have no desire to leave here. All this is just for me. Why would I leave? Can't you see that something incredible is happening here? Do you think I would leave before it is over? Before I've understood it? Finished it? No, you can put your hammer down, Hector, I won't leave until this affair has ended, whatever it is, and you can put that in one of your corncob pipes and smoke it."

The figure lowered the hammer.

"The chalk, Hector, where is the chalk?"

"Aisle 5. At the very end, miscellaneous hardware supplies."

"Why don't you go over there to the counter with your friends and wait for me there? You see, this really doesn't concern you, Hector."

"I can't," the heavy little man said in a stubborn tone of voice, "I have to guard the store."

"All right, Hector, fine, you guard the store."

Ignoring Hector, the old man walked briskly to Aisle 5 and headed straight down to the far end. When he reached the area of the swirling blue light, he paused, observing it carefully. It was starting to seep underneath and actually through the shelves, causing the rows of items to appear unreal, as if they were a series of projected images, but it seemed to be mostly overflow here at this end of the store. The old man walked on through it, found a box of chalk, and walked back through again, feeling nothing more than a slight chill.

But by the time he got back to the center of the store, which was Aisle 3, the reality of the square of blue light was clearly taking over, and the store appeared to be melting away. A pit about six feet square had opened up in the floor and it was from this pit that the blazing blue light and the slow pounding of the drum emanated.

The old man got down on his knees in front of it and began to rapidly draw a circle around it with the chalk. As he reached the sides where he should have run into the shelves of canned goods, he found that he seemed able to move through them by concentrating on the pit in the floor. Whether or not this was an illusion, he did not know, or trouble himself about. He just finished the circle and then began to sketch a few peculiar geometric designs along the outer edge of the circle he had drawn, trying to ignore the fact that the light was rapidly glowing brighter, that the drumbeats were pounding in his ears. Elena, he thought suddenly, you should be here. What an irony to study all those years and now to fail me and fail yourself through one careless gesture. Then he caught himself and focused his thoughts back onto the chalk drawings he was working on.

It couldn't be her report card, could it? Didn't she always get good grades, figure out just how to approach each teacher with such precision that she had almost automatically, in every class, assumed the role of teacher's pet? This couldn't be her report card. But it was. Mama was weeping and carrying on about how now Papa would be driven by his sorrow to do—terrible things. Elena was afraid to picture what they might be, but she knew that they would include drunkenness and beating Mama: they always did.

Suddenly she was outraged. "You can't blame it on me, Mama, it's his fault and your fault, but you can't blame it on me."

Her mother's sad, lugubrious face hovered over her, teary-eyed and self-pitying as always. "But you know you are to blame, Elena. You've studied all those years, and now you've failed him and failed yourself, all through one careless gesture."

She waved her finger in Elena's face. "You should be here."

Hands plunged out of the wall, reaching for her.

Elena awoke and sat up on the couch. The lights were off and rain was pounding on the roof.

She had been just lying there, suffering from a dull headache and general lethargy, when she had suddenly dozed off. And dreamed that awful dream. What was it? Something about school and her parents, already rapidly fading from her consciousness. Couldn't have been important.

But she was still feeling anxious from the aftermath. Almost without noticing what she was doing, she put on her rain poncho and went outside.

The rain felt cool upon her face. A large black crow sat on the low adobe wall that encircled their hut, oblivious to the downpour.

He cawed at her and flew away, and disappeared into the rain. The echo seemed to hang in the air for an unnaturally long time, superimposed upon the pattering of the rain.

Suddenly, without understanding why, she wanted to find the old man very much. Confused images of her drunken father flickered in and out of her consciousness as she rushed through the rain.

When she arrived at Hector's Mercado she encountered a puzzling enigma. Hector's was closed, and the lights were out, but she could see inside to some degree, around the edges of the large, mostly opaque front window. A weird flickering blue light was emanating from somewhere inside, and she could just make out a few shadowy figures moving slowly around in it. Like sleepwalkers, she thought.

She pounded on the door. After a bit Hector answered, glaring at her with a fey expression on his chubby little face. He was holding one of his hammers.

"Go away," he said in a sullen tone of voice, so different from his usual obsequious manner. "You can't come in here. Go away now, or I'll hit you with this hammer."

He slammed the door in her face. Chills ran up her spine, causing her to suddenly wrap both arms around herself and shiver in the rain. But it wasn't from being cold.

It was obvious that something was very, very wrong here, and for a moment Elena was paralyzed with fear. This was her chance. Now. Her one and only chance to pack it in and run away.

Because she wasn't meant for anything like this. She was, she realized, a coward. She had gotten into this weird relationship with the old man precisely because she was afraid of everything, and so had searched out magic in order to make her life run smooth and trouble-free down that long highway clear to the end. Not to expose herself to the terror of the unknown.

In her mind's eye she saw herself running away, felt the immense relief. Then she stopped shivering and opened her eyes and saw that she was still there. She took in a deep breath and held it. Then she let it out and began pounding on the door again. After a long time the door opened and Hector stood in the doorway, looking crazy as ever, holding his hammer.

"I told you to go away," he growled.

"But I only want to buy a hammer," Elena stammered. "That's all. Just sell me your hammer and I'll go away."

Hector, never bright under the best of circumstances, appeared to be totally at a loss in this situation. He scratched his head and repeated dully: "You want to buy this hammer?"

"Why not, this is a store, isn't it? Here. Here's twenty thousand pesos, that ought to be plenty."

"But I can't sell you this hammer."

"Why not? You can get another one inside, no? Twenty-five thousand pesos."

Hector was still shaking his head. Elena smiled at him, what she hoped was a disarming, easygoing smile: "Here, hand it to me for a moment and let me have a look at it. I'm not even sure it's the kind I need. Has it got those little prong gizmos on the back to pull out nails?"

Elena held out her right hand casually and Hector automatically placed the hammer in it.

"Feels just about right to me," Elena said, and belted Hector square in the middle of his forehead with it. Hard.

Hector reeled, then sank down to his knees, then spilled over onto his stomach, holding his head in his hands and moaning.

Elena considered hitting him again, but she wasn't sure how hard you could hit someone with a hammer without killing him, and although Hector wasn't totally unconscious, he seemed to be in some borderline twilight zone, mumbling and moaning to himself. Clear out of the action.

Elena stepped gingerly around him, through the doorway, and over to the checkout counter. "Where's the old man?"

A woman she didn't know pointed over to where the icy blue light was coming from. "Dying," she said.

"You don't know the old man," Elena snapped back at her. Then she was rushing over toward the light, and toward the sounds. An immense low pounding, that she had noticed and yet not noticed, that seemed to be growing and swelling all the time. And the old man chanting in some forgotten language.

When she got there what she saw was this: the old

man was sitting cross-legged on the floor in front of a large chalked circle, holding his amulet out in his right hand.

Within the chalked circle, impossibly, a pit had opened up in the floor. The blue light was pouring out of it. There appeared to be a ladder or something like a ladder that went down, and something immense and brutal—something from another world—was trying to climb out of the pit.

Elena ran over and automatically kneeled down beside the old man and took from around her neck the little pouch with the herbs and blue-jay feather and the few pebbles that the old man had told her were her objects of power, then she held them out toward the pit in both her hands. Automatically she began to repeat the otherworldly mantra with him, over and over.

The drumming gradually grew louder and louder. Now she realized what it was: the creature's feet pounding on the ladder as it climbed to meet them.

Suddenly something like a huge round stone, ebony black and shining in the blue light, emerged from the pit; feverish eyes glowed yellow, and now the creature smiled a hideous wide grin, showing the enormous sharp teeth of a carnivore. In a deafening roar of triumph it shouted a name that Elena had never heard before and tried to reach the old man with its massive taloned claws.

But something about the chalk circle held it back. It could not break out. But as the creature began to struggle, roar, and thrash about, it became obvious to Elena that it was only a matter of time until it did.

Meanwhile, the old man's chanting shifted into longer and longer strings of alien words, which somehow became easier for her to follow. And as she chanted with him, she found herself descending into a trancelike state of consciousness where the chanting was almost automatic. Where the store fell away and nothing existed except the creature, the pit, the blue light, and the chanting. Time ceased to flow. There had never been anything else. There never would be anything else.

And now a thing was happening that, had it not been for her trancelike state, would have thrown her over the cdgc of tcrror.

The old man continued chanting steadily without a break, in his eerie forgotten tongue, and at the same time, he was whispering into her right ear in Spanish. And somehow she was able to follow his chant with her own voice and listen to what he was saying, at the same time.

"I can't hold this creature, Elena. Not for much longer. It is more powerful than anything I have encountered outside of the ally of the yellow cloud. I once swore I would never use Yellow Cloud again because he is too powerful, too much of a drain on my system. That is why I have tried, in vain, to introduce you to him. I am old now. I may not live through this. But I have no choice. We have no choice. You must stay behind and hold the creature here on your own. You must hold your mind steady and repeat the mantra I give you now, over and over without faltering. If your mind wanders, he will rip your life from you, as well as destroy the rest of us here today. Good luck!"

A new layer of icy cold fear flowed over Elena at the mention of Yellow Cloud. She hadn't thought it possible to add any fear to the terror she was already experiencing, but leave it to the old man. He had taken her with him on his visits to that terrifying world twice before. He had taught her to call up that particular doorway to that particular world. Obviously, he had been waiting for her to volunteer to go in there on her own. Well, he would have quite a wait for that one, she thought. She could feel herself trembling like a rabbit, hear her teeth clicking.

And now, behind them, Elena felt rather than saw the shimmering outline of that doorway superimposing itself on the rear wall of the market.

A sickly golden light filled in the outline, and Elena caught a whiff of something sweet and unidentifiable on the hot damp air that wafted to her from the new doorway.

She allowed herself to turn her head only once, for an instant, and she caught a glimpse of the old man moving slowly into the awful, familiar golden light. There was a hint of steam, and decaying foliage, and she thought she heard the cries of alien birds and animals, as distant as a dream: his form dissolved.

And she was alone. She jerked back around: the creature was smiling at her, a malevolent smile. Then she felt the force of its mind: it was like a tidal wave of static, ugly and discordant, tumbling her thoughts away from her like leaves in the wind.

She kept repeating the mantra.

Now the creature roared again and thrashed against the invisible barrier until she was sick with fear.

She kept repeating the mantra.

Had she been here forever? Alone? Always alone? Nothing existed for her except the idiotic meaningless words she repeated and the creature endlessly struggling to break out of the pit.

It was staring into her eyes now, and suddenly she caught glimpses of its icy blue world. Giant creatures locked in death struggles, blasted by freezing winds.

She kept repeating the mantra.

And then, not sure if this was another vision or reality, she saw a figure moving somnambulantly around her and toward the beast in the pit. Juanito's mother, smiling, arms spread wide.

Elena kept chanting the mantra.

Now the woman crossed over the chalk line. Bellowing in triumph, the demon gathered her into its arms and with one enormous hand engulfed her head. A loud sizzling popping noise, and the woman's legs and arms danced frantically, puppetlike. She screamed once, a short burst of indescribable agony, and then went limp.

The creature threw her body away from it as a monkey discards the empty shell of a nut it has eaten.

The body smashed off of a row of canned goods and fell, its legs and arms twisted at impossible angles, eyes wide and staring. All of her hair was burned off, and the skin of her head was scorched black. Elena could smell her burning flesh: she lay smoking among cans of vegetables.

Elena kept saying the mantra.

There was nothing else for her except saying the mantra. Only now she sensed that it was hopeless. Somehow, taking the woman's life had infused the creature with more power. It seemed to have actually grown, and Elena could feel it pushing harder and harder against the barrier, and grinding at her mind.

Her head throbbed with pain, and suddenly she was aware that without knowing it, she had given in. She was not saying the mantra, she could not open her mouth.

With a scream that actually caused her to clamp both hands over her ears and keel over facedown on her belly, the monster reached across the chalk line for her.

She saw its enormous black hand, open and rushing at her, when suddenly she was aware of someone else shouting.

The hand withdrew. She looked behind her to see the old man moving toward them. A sickly phosphorescent yellowish substance floated behind him, swirling about his shoulders: the cloud partially enveloped his head. It made her ill to look at it. She closed her eyes tight and just lay there, still with her hands over her ears, trying to pass out. But she could not.

She opened her eyes a crack to see the old man drifting slowly but steadily toward the pit, and suddenly, as if it had caught the scent of prey, the yellow cloud swirled off his shoulders, its phosphorescent tendrils streaming out to the huge black creature. For one moment she saw them struggling on the edge, the beast bellowing in pain and rage now, enveloped by the living cloud, and then both of them toppled backward, into the pit. There was a huge clap as if thunder had gone off inside the store and then a blaze of light and then dark. And silence. It was over.

For a while she just lay there listening to someone weeping in the dark, wondering who it was. Then she realized that it was her.

She sat up. Her eyes were growing accustomed to the dark. She could just make out the form of the old man lying on the floor. He was breathing too heavily.

Suddenly the lights came back on. Elena screamed. She had forgotten about the corpse, partially buried in cans of tomatoes.

"Elena," someone was whispering, "you've got to help me to get up. We've got to get out of here."

The old man was so weak he could barely walk. And Elena was hardly at full strength. But somehow she got him up and on his feet.

The people were still crowded around the checkout counter, including the dead woman's little boy.

"You won't remember anything that happened here, do you understand?"

"We understand," Hector murmured.

"Señora Martinez was struck by the lightning."

"Yes," Hector said in his dead voice, "that must have been it."

The old man paused for a moment, and though it obviously pained him to do so, he knelt beside the young boy and put his hand on the child's head.

The boy's shrewd dark little eyes seemed to be following every movement, evaluating.

"Your mother is dead, Juanito, do you understand me?"

"Yo comprendo; I understand."

"Your life is over. You must start a new life. This can ruin you, or this can save you."

"It can ruin me or it can . . ."

"I am going to tell you something important at this moment, because this is a moment of power for you."

He whispered something. Elena could not hear what it was. The boy's expression gave nothing away. Then the old man gestured for Elena to help him back up to his feet. The effort made him wheeze like an asthmatic.

When he got his breath back enough to speak again, he said: "Remember, you have not seen us today. The store was struck by lightning."

Hector nodded; the somnambulant shoppers mumbled agreement, their eyes a million miles away.

"They will be all right," the old man told Elena later, when they had completed their painful journey home in the rain. "It is only a matter of time. Their thought patterns were altered into quieter forms, as with hypnotism, or certain drugs. In time, they will always work their way back into their normal patterns again. This is true of the effects of drugs or hypnosis, or shock."

"Some people say drugs can permanently alter the mind," Elena said.

The old man laughed in a choked whisper. "Those people are wrong," he said.

After what seemed hours of struggle, Elena got the old man back to their adobe hut and down onto the mattress on the floor. She sat beside him on the sea-grass rug, legs crossed.

"You are obviously too sick to talk."

"And yet I must talk. Many things must be said now. And you must help me by asking the right questions."

His eyes were closed. In the candlelight, he looked very old.

"What happened back there?"

"Yes," he sighed, "that's the right question, all right."

His eyes opened a crack. Sometimes they seemed to Elena to glow with some unnatural force, wild and glittering, like the eyes of a hawk. He looked like he was dying, but the eyes . . .

"I was attacked by one of the Four. It had to be one of the Guardians. Only someone who wields an amulet could control a creature that powerful. But there is another possibility which could prove even more tragic for us, Elena. Perhaps there are two of them. My feeling is that it might take two of them working together to control such a force. Hopefully, I will turn out to be wrong here." Fat chance, Elena thought, but did not say. "Now you must let me rest," he continued wearily. "But first, tell me what you saw, in complete detail, no matter how insignificant it may seem to you. Leave nothing out."

When Elena had finished talking, the old man broke out in choked-up laughter again. Although it obviously hurt him, he apparently could not hold back his outbursts of humor.

"You saw a huge black creature with blazing eyes, like a demon? How perfect."

"Well then, what did you see?" Elena snapped at him.

"I saw nothing. I merely referred to it as a creature for convenience' sake. But it is not really a creature; or rather, it is a creature of power, invisible, unformed. Another world opened up, and I was attacked by an immense power, or rather I would have been, had we not contained it locked up at the entranceway, while I went for my most devastating ally. That being was, like my ally of the yellow cloud, only raw concentrated power. You can't see power. You sense power with your spiritual eye, but your orderly mind tries to show you an image to make it seem less alien to you. So you projected onto it an image of a huge black demon.

"Long ago, too long for me to remember when, my

mind gave up the human trait of protecting itself in that manner. As must yours, if you hope to someday wield an amulet."

Elena felt as if a cold wind had momentarily tickled her neck.

"And what do we do now?"

"Ah, there's the question. In a sense, the attack failed. Thanks to you, Elena. Without you I would have lost. You showed a tenaciousness I would never have expected of you. In the world of magic, endurance is everything.

"But in another way, the attack succeeded. The creature did me no harm, but I was forced to use a terrible power from a world I hoped never to have to return to. Seeking out and controlling the ally of the yellow cloud has drained me. I am very, very old. Too old to withstand the feedback from the yellow cloud without suffering damage. My life force is at an ebb. I may recover. I may not. Who knows?

"Meanwhile, I came to this village for a purpose. The stone in the amulet is, you might say, a battery for occult power. Over the years, it runs itself down, like any battery. Whoever attacked us here knows that I came to this village to replenish the stone, in one of my special places of power, a lake which is a juncture of several worlds.

"Now the stone is drained of power, as I am drained of power. And I cannot replenish it. You must do it for me."

Elena nodded, her stomach twisting at the thought.

"And it must be done right away. You see, Elena, this attack—" He rose partially up, gasped in pain, and lay down again, as if to emphasize what he was going to say next. "It had to happen. I always knew that it would happen. That sooner or later, one of the Four who wield the stones would want to wield all the stones."

Elena swallowed. "Why?"

"Because he or she, or more likely they, are no longer

satisfied to guard mankind from chaotic forces. They want to control history."

"Would that be so wrong?" Elena questioned, visualizing the moronic and hostile current world situation.

"Yes, it would be wrong. Humans must be free to learn how to live with themselves peacefully or to blow themselves to bits. The choice must be theirs. If they make the correct choice, life on the face of this earth will change beyond recognition. They will evolve beyond what we now consider human. If they make the wrong choice, they will simply end."

For a while both of them sat in silence. Then Elena said: "How can you expect us to live in peace, if even the Four cannot?"

The old man laughed, choked, and coughed. "Be better than us," he said.

Elena thought about that.

"Where is this lake?" she said. "Perhaps we can get you—"

He cut her off with an abrupt wave of his hand. "It is a few days' journey through jungle. Very arduous. And it must be done with all possible speed. Oh, there will be no more magic for a while. They will be drained by the attack they just made, as was I. They will need time to recuperate, and they will probably need to replenish their stones also.

"But what is to stop them from hiring thugs to physically steal the stone now that I am too weak to defend it? No, you must take the stone and you must be swift. I will draw you a map, but you can't handle this on your own. I am going to give you a phone number to call, and you must let Quinn take charge of these affairs. They are more along his line of expertise than yours."

He scribbled a number on the piece of paper she had handed him.

She had heard of Quinn. He had been famous among the inner circle as the old man's strong right arm. But she had never met him. Either the old man had no use for muscle anymore, or Quinn had retired. He had been before her time.

"What if he won't come?"

"Oh, he'll come, Elena, like a cat goes after a bird. It's just in his nature."

"What if . . ." She paused.

"Yes, go on."

"What if he's too old?"

The old man burst out laughing, choked on it, and lay there breathing hard.

"What if they come after you?"

"I believe they will follow the stone. But as a safeguard, early tomorrow morning, before you leave, you must move me to Garcia's house. I will wait it out there. Now I have to rest. Leave me alone. But before you go, here, take this."

And there it was. She held it in her trembling hands. A small, black, plain-looking stone in a copper setting.

"Too old," she heard the old man chuckle as she went out the door, heading for Ruben's pool hall to use the telephone, "then what about me?"

2

WHAT'S GOING WRONG now, Elena wondered, or maybe I should be asking, what's going right? They had been traveling fast and hard for two days through a part of Mexico that Elena had never known, a part that didn't seem to know itself, for that matter: first it would be thick jungle, then sudden stretches of semi-desert, a couple of low mountains, and then back into jungle again, all of it hot: deadly relentless heat that wore on you every moment of the day and then wouldn't let you rest at night. To top that off, she couldn't read Quinn well enough to tell if he was lost, semilost, or knew exactly where he was going.

The crude map the old man had drawn meant nothing to her, even in conjunction with the official map that Quinn used with it. She simply had no idea where they were. Did Quinn?

And now she was certain that something else was up. After dinner, if you could call beans and tortillas dinner, Quinn had sent the skinny Indian, Jorge, the one he seemed to set the most store in, slinking back the way they had come. Now Quinn was lurking at the outskirts of the camp waiting for him while the rest of the men sat around eating more beans, cursing the bugs, and smoking grass.

The fact was that Elena didn't like Quinn, had no

faith in him, and perhaps as a result of that, she just couldn't read him at all.

He was a fairly tall man, very lean and muscular, quite attractive, she thought, in a strange old-fashioned brutal manner. His hair was clipped short in a crew cut, and he was sporting a three-day growth of beard. His eyes were narrow and rather close-set, and his nose strong and a bit large. Not that much older than her, really, except for those eyes. His lips were a thin line, set in a tight, fixed manner that seldom changed, and gave him a tough, determined look. But the shape of his head was beautiful, with his perfectly round skull, small sharp chin, and high, finely carved cheekbones. Everything about him was lean and quick and ferocious looking, like one of those brutal dogs he was dragging along for some unknown reason.

Now, as she moved noisily through the underbrush to where he was standing, he made no move to acknowledge her at all.

"I have to talk to you." She looked nervously back toward the men.

"Okay."

"Look, do you really know where we're going, or are you just stringing me out?"

"If the map the old man drew is true, we're okay. If the map is off, we're lost." Then he permitted himself a smile, just a slight tightening of his lips.

"We're okay. Remember that mountain off to the right this morning, big round one, with the long narrow crooked spike rising up alongside of it? Sanchez told me to watch for it. We're okay. In fact, we should be very close."

Sanchez? Then Elena realized that he was referring to the old man by the name he used in Mexico. It had been a while since she had thought of him like that. Too many names in too many places. He was just "the old man" to her.

For a while she couldn't find anything to say to Quinn

and they just stood there listening to the insects, birds, and the raucous bantering of the men. Then one of the men began to sing a mournful country complaint. His voice was ridiculously sad and deliberately drunken. It seemed as if everything grew suddenly still; even the insects stopped their weird mechanistic noises to listen to the fool.

Then she saw Quinn's body tense and a moment later she heard the very slight sounds of someone moving in the underbrush. A shadow glided over to them.

"They're there, all right," Jorge whispered, looking from Quinn to Elena and then back again.

"How many?"

"I couldn't get close. They got dogs. I didn't want to take the chance."

Quinn nodded. "Right. Okay then. We're almost there. Let's wait till we get to the foot of the mountain. The lake's only an hour or two from there. We'll move on them then. Right?"

"If you say so," Jorge said without conviction. "But I don't know about Carlos," gesturing toward the hulking, drunken fellow who had been serenading them a few moments earlier. "That guy's a brute."

"He's right," Elena said, "they're all a bunch of brutes. I don't know what you hired them for, they're a lousy crew. They couldn't find their way home from the local bar, let alone . . ."

"And they're pissed about the dogs," Jorge interjected. "They say you treat dogs better than men. Those mules carrying all that fancy dog food, and you wouldn't let them carry any whiskey. I think it's mostly the heat and all. But they're bad men, Quinn. I think you're going to have trouble with them."

"Especially Carlos," Elena threw in, glancing nervously back toward the camp.

"Well, I didn't hire them as guides or Boy Scouts."

Elena looked puzzled.

"I hired them to fight. We're being tracked by someone. I don't know who, or how many, but they must be good. They don't get too close. But they don't lose us."

"They got hounds," Jorge said. "They're tracking you with hounds."

Quinn smiled. "We'll take care of that tomorrow. When the time is right. As for this scum"—he nodded toward the men—"the meaner their mood, the better."

Quinn started back toward camp, then apparently changed his mind and stopped again.

"Okay, maybe you're right about Carlos. I'll take care of it. Actually, that should be amusing if you care to watch." He grinned his tight grin.

My God, he's over the hill for sure, Elena thought. He's boasting to us because he's scared. Because he knows he no longer has what it takes for this kind of work. Who has? she wondered.

Back at camp, Quinn paused to study the shadowy forms sitting around the campfire (even in this heat) joking and drowsing.

Then he found the one he was looking for.

"Get up. Right now."

Carlos got up. And up. If Quinn was tall, Carlos was a giant. A massive, hairy, muscular brute who towered over Quinn.

"Straighten up the gear, right now. Take care of the mules and, oh yeah, feed my dogs a little tidbit or two. I think they'd like an after-dinner snack. When you get through with that, I'd like you to stand watch tonight. Can't have some wildcats chasing off the mules, can we?"

In the flickering firelight, Carlos looked more like a gorilla than a man. He was now trembling in anger, unable to speak. Finally he managed to rasp in a strangely controlled whisper, "And why me, Señor Quinn? Why Carlos?"

"I don't know," Quinn said in his cold, disinterested

voice, "I guess it's because I'm prejudiced against faggots."

Oh God, Elena thought, suddenly very much afraid, he'll murder Quinn. And then what will they do to me?

For a moment the giant form just stood there. A high-pitched noise like the whine of a small animal escaped his lips, as steam escapes a boiling teakettle. Then he charged.

The two men met and grappled. It looked like Carlos had taken a hold of some sort, but then, miraculously, Quinn slipped away. Carlos followed him, raining a flurry of tremendous blows at Quinn's head. Quinn twisted and turned with amazing suppleness. He seemed to be riding the blows, rolling with them, but they had to be taking their toll. Why wasn't he fighting back?

Then the men moved by, through the firelight, and Elena realized what she had seen but had not accepted, because, well, it just did not seem possible. The blows weren't landing on Quinn at all. And he was smiling now! A broader smile than she had ever seen him smile before.

It wasn't a case of footwork, though he did circle, and it wasn't a case of outside fighting. Quinn deliberately fought close to the big man, apparently at home in the middle of the storm.

And he was using his hands, but in a way Elena had never seen before, nudging Carlos' elbows and shoulders, actually guiding the big man's furious assault aside, until, as suddenly as it had started, it stopped.

Carlos stood there breathing in great gasps of air, hands slightly lowered. Quinn reached out and cuffed him lightly on the cheek.

"No balls?"

Carlos charged again. This time he tried to shorten and straighten out his punches, sacrificing a little power in order to gain more accuracy.

But Quinn now increased his lateral movements and

the strange, guiding pushes to Carlos' elbows and shoulders, sometimes smothering the big man's punches before they got started. And when Carlos tried to kick, Quinn seemed to anticipate it so soon that his foot was pushing on his opponent's shin before the kick had even gotten off the ground.

And now Quinn was beginning to throw a few light, casual punches, almost like slaps. Carefully placed. Effortless.

And then suddenly, just when it didn't seem like anything could go wrong, the big man threw one last gigantic all-out effort: forgetting about shortening up and straightening out his punches, he just cut loose with a whirlwind flurry of looping hooks, and out of nowhere one of them connected, sending Quinn reeling, and then another spun him clear around the other way and knocked his feet out from under him.

The men were howling like wolves. This is it, Elena thought, drained of emotion as she saw Carlos kicking at the form on the ground, but no, the form rolled with the kick over backward and somehow up onto its feet.

And now it was obvious to everyone that the fight was almost over. For Quinn was steadily increasing both the frequency and the power of his blows. This increase was gradual but inexorable and effortless. His attack seemed to build automatically as Carlos' attack weakened. It was strangely logical in its appearance, as if, the opposite of other men, Quinn was tired at the start of a fight but grew fresher as it went on.

Finally, under a bewildering barrage, the big man just sat down, and held his head in his massive hands.

"No more," he said.

Quinn stalked away without saying anything. Elena could see him rummaging in his pack, then he went back over and kneeled down to Carlos. He was carrying a bottle of whiskey, which he handed to the beaten giant.

Then he turned to the men. "What a man. What balls. I've never fought anyone who hit that hard before. Everyone have a drink. Come on, amigos. Drink up. Tomorrow we may all have to fight."

Soon everyone was just a trifle drunk and exaggeratedly happy. Somehow Carlos had come out of it a hero, and at the same time, he would probably now jump off a cliff if Quinn suggested it to him.

As soon as he could pull himself away from the men, Quinn wandered over to Elena. "Better get some sleep," he said. "Tomorrow ought to be a busy day."

"What about . . ." She nodded back the way they had come. Then she noticed Jorge was gone.

"Jorge's keeping watch back along our trail. But they're not going to move on us now. They're waiting for something. I think they're waiting for you to do whatever it is you're going to do to the stone before they come after it."

"And you don't know what that is?" Elena said.

"No idea."

"Good. You just get me there. The less you know, the better." She frowned. "How long have you known they were following us?"

"From the start."

"How did you know?"

He shrugged. "I just know. Want to stay alive in this business, you just have to know."

He smiled again. She caught the subtle shift of expression in the bright moonlight: tomorrow would be full moon.

"Still think I'm over the hill? Don't think it was easy letting that clown hit me. I practically had to throw my head at his fist."

Quinn turned and walked back to the men. The singing and shouting went on half the night.

The next morning, despite the celebrating, by the time

Quinn woke Elena, the men were already at work, breaking camp. "It was only a token drink. I was careful to only bring one bottle," Quinn told her. "They're going to need everything they've got today. You too."

From here on out they traveled even faster than usual, and Elena noticed that Jorge hung back behind them all the time now. Somewhere approaching the noon hour, they were passing along the edge of a range of low foothills when Quinn dropped back to talk to her. "See those twin hills, the two small round ones? Well, that's it. You go back directly between them and you hit a larger hill. You go straight up it. You'll have to do some climbing, and you'll come down onto a small lake. That's the lake we're looking for, and tonight's full moon. We'll pull on past the two hills a ways to throw off our 'secret admirers' " (he smiled at this phrase) "and then we'll set up an early camp. Then we'll wait. If they don't attack us by late afternoon, we'll attack them: try to knock out the dogs, the guide, while you head up the mountain. Things work out, by the time you start back I'll be waiting for you about halfway up. Things don't, you're on your own."

Elena thought about it, wanted to shake her head and protest: No good. What if I miss you on the mountain? It may not be so easy to find each other once we're separated. I think we should stay together as long as we can.

But she said nothing. Mostly she felt relief at being out of the gun battle. On the other hand, what waited for her at the lake of power was hers and hers alone. And now it seemed irrevocably one more step closer and more real than before. She merely shrugged, and then said: "All right, if that's what you think is best. Just don't miss me on that hill."

"Sure," Quinn said, "just don't get lost up there and come down the wrong side of the mountain."

Later on they pitched camp and waited to hear from

Jorge. Quinn was going over the weapons with obvious distaste.

"It was my father's .30-30. A fine gun. You have to aim a little high and to the right. About that much."

The only decent gun they had was the fancy automatic handgun that Quinn wore on his belt. And that probably wasn't going to be of much use in this kind of battle.

In the end, Quinn appropriated the old .30-30 lever-action rifle that shot low and to the left; at least it was a known evil. Then the men settled down to cleaning and checking out the weapons, and the waiting set in.

Elena was frightened and angry in alternating waves. She had been frightened ever since that macabre spiritual awakening the other morning in the supermarket—no, even before, since that astral doorway had first opened up in the middle of that cheap hotel room—and now she was terrified of what she might encounter at the lake of power during the full moon: she had had enough of other worlds.

And yet she might as well cheer up, she mused; she probably wouldn't live to get there. (Quinn waving his old .30-30, "What a piece of shit. They've probably got automatic weapons, and if they do . . ." He shook his head sadly.)

Elena felt he was blaming her and the old man for not allowing him enough time to purchase automatics. But the purchase of illegal arms can take a while, and full moon had been only seven nights away. Still, you had to give Quinn credit. She had called his number, and two days later he had appeared, with Jorge in tow. By the end of the next day, they were packed and ready to travel with this motley crew and the two squat ugly little dust-colored dogs.

And now the fear of what she was headed into alternated with stabs of outrage: they wouldn't even give her a gun. "What for?" Quinn had said in a curt tone of voice.

"You either know how to shoot or you don't. If you don't, what's the point of tying up a gun? All you'll do is shoot yourself in the foot, or worse, one of us. Worst of all, maybe even me."

Sometime in late afternoon, Jorge came in, and it was clear that the waiting was finally finished.

"They were certain to send a man to look us over," Quinn explained to Elena. "We had to wait until Jorge located him."

"Where is he now?" Elena asked, realizing the foolishness of her question as she uttered it.

Quinn shook his head, not bothering to answer, and now Elena noticed that Jorge was carrying two rifles.

Quinn gave the .30-30 back to its rightful owner and took the new rifle from Jorge, a bolt-action gun that looked a little larger and heavier than the other rifles they had.

"Okay, this is it. Let's get moving before someone realizes that the scout they sent out didn't come back to report."

And then they were gone, only Jorge hanging back to pack up one of the mules for her.

"This is Pepe. He's mean as a snake, so don't rile him up. But he's strong. Lead him as far as you can up the mountain, then just throw his reins down on the ground like this. With good luck, he'll hang around close enough so's Quinn will be able to find him when he comes up after you. If Quinn doesn't show . . ." Jorge shrugged, and a few moments later was out of sight following the men into the jungle.

Time went by slowly for her, strangely enough. She seemed to be drawing the power to concentrate from the amulet, and her mind ignored the distractions of worrying about Quinn and the others, or what she was going to do when she came down from the lake. The amulet sensed the nearness of the power reservoir, or so it seemed to her. She could almost feel it pulsing with excitement. And for the first time, she began to wonder what it would be like to wear the amulet when it had full power. Soon she would know. Yes. Yes. Something seemed to whisper in her ear, drawing her up between the hills and up the base of the mountain toward the lake with surer and surer steps. Suddenly she felt a wave of sweet confidence the like of which she had never felt before. She couldn't fail now.

She found a fairly level place and left the mule there. She was just preparing to make the final climb when from far off, down below, she heard shots. There were several of them close together. Then all of a sudden the unmistakable stuttering of an automatic weapon. Jesus Christ, she thought, how do I find my way back?

A few moments later and she stepped on a rock that slid loose in the soft dirt and then she started to fall, only her other foot wedged between two rocks and twisted her ankle as she fell.

She felt a very sharp, severe bout of pain, followed by a brief period of relief. Then numbness, tingling, and another blast of pain, at first even more severe, which finally subsided into a dull steady throbbing. She managed to free her foot. How badly am I hurt? she wondered. Only one way to know for sure. She struggled up and tried to walk, or rather climb, on it. But soon she was back sitting down with her whole foot steadily throbbing and swelling. Her eyes filled with tears from the pain, and also from the unavoidable realization that this time she'd blown it all as badly as it could possibly be blown, because there was no way she was going up that mountain tonight.

Jorge motioned and the men stopped. "Right through there"—he pointed—"and we hit a clearing, their camp and those hounds," he whispered.

He looked to the two tan-colored dogs straining at their leashes. But they were silent, only whining a little in their eagerness. They knew they were going to fight soon.

The men had taken their time and circled behind the camp. Taking care not to get too close, they were now approaching it from an angle where they had a slight advantage in high ground. Nothing you could call a hill, just a gentle slope up the clearing to the edge of the jungle.

But now they heard an excited barking.

"Shit, the dogs made us." Quinn was fast loosing the stocky, muscular pit bulls, who were straining at their leashes.

"Kill," he whispered. And then the dogs were gone.

"Wait till the bulldogs hit. They'll be shooting at them. Jorge, you take out the guide if you can spot him. Let's go."

The men squirmed out of the brush on their bellies, over to the edge of the incline looking down into the camp. The hounds were barking like mad and two of the Indians were running around pointing rifles aimlessly into the jungle.

Suddenly the barking switched over to a high-pitched yelping; and raising up a little, Quinn caught sight out of the corner of his eye of one of the brutal pit bulls shaking a hound by the throat as if it were a rat.

At that moment he saw a small figure in white partially emerge from a tent, then suddenly jump back inside. That's my target, he knew instinctively, but got the gun up too late. That little dude was fast!

Quinn fired off several shots into the tent, but in his mind's eye he pictured the quick little man rolling and dodging across the floor inside. And at the same time, he was aware of the men down below blasting the bulldogs, and at the same time Jorge was shooting; and then from the side, Carlos and the other three stood up and fired into the men shooting at the dogs.

Three men were down and the bodies of the two pit

bulls and the hounds were strewn about, unmistakably dead, near the tent Quinn was firing into.

"I got him," Jorge said, meanwhile firing at the pack mules. Quinn, still shooting into the tent, saw one of the mules go down on its knees, then another.

But in his mind's eye he was still following the little man across the floor of the tent. Fast as a snake, he would probably cut his way out the far side of the tent and . . .

"Back off," Quinn shouted, but too late for Carlos and the men over to the far side.

Jorge and Quinn got down flat as the little man in white spun into view around the side of the tent and the distinctive chatter of a Sten gun rattled into the brush, blowing away Carlos and the others.

Then the automatic fire was pinning them down and it was all over because nobody was going anyplace, except that, miraculously, the big rowdy, Carlos, rose up from the dead, chest splattered with blood, and took careful aim, and either hit someone or came damn close, because the fire went his way, knocking him down for keeps, and then there was—thank God, or thank whatever you believe in—a pause, and Jorge and Quinn had squirmed backward into cover and were up and running away fast.

A few moments later and the two men stopped to reload, and counsel.

"You take them away and I'll go up the hill after her."

Jorge nodded. If he resented the probable death sentence, he didn't show it. He just kneeled down and levered a bullet into the chamber, reached in his pocket for a handful of shells to reload while he had a break. Both men were feeding bullets into the slots on their rifles with almost supernatural speed.

"I'm pretty sure I got the guide," Jorge said. "The dogs are down and so are two of the pack mules. I'll stay here and take a shot at them and then try to drag them off away from the hills into the jungle. Without their guide or dogs, I'll lose them, if the guy with that British Sten don't get me. That guide was a good man. My cousin."

Quinn nodded, turned, and ran off. Behind him he heard a shot, a pause, and then the rattle of the Sten. Good luck, he thought, you'll need it. —Won't we all?

About halfway up the mountain, Quinn almost missed Elena. He had decided to change his plans and follow her up to the top, regardless of how she or the old man felt about it, so they could go down the far side of the mountain together if they were being followed.

Meanwhile, he could tell that there was no way he was going to get the mule up that mountain, and so that plan was shot too.

Uncharacteristic as it may be, he thought, I've got to sit down and think.

"Shut up, Pepe," he said to the mule, who was fussing around pawing the ground and snorting, when he heard Elena call out to him from somewhere above and off to his right.

She had instinctively chosen the wrong line of ascent, headed off the main path, and fallen down and sprained her ankle. It wasn't a bad sprain, but it was bad enough. No one was going mountain climbing on it. In fact, now that it was fast growing dark, it was going to be hard enough to get himself up the mountain.

For a while they just looked at each other in exasperation. Then Quinn said, "Well, give it to me."

"I just don't know what to do," Elena said to no one in particular, tears spilling over. Quinn held out his hand, waiting, and finally she took the amulet off from around her neck and handed it to him.

He felt the power emanating from it at once. It reminded him of cocaine, which he had once tried, and then decided against using because of the false sense of confidence it gave him. He was afraid it would lead to mistakes. But this was more subtle than the white powder, more real.

Soon he was off again, moving up the mountain surprisingly fast. He had no idea what to expect at the lake, but he knew that if the old man said something would happen there, you could count on it.

What had Elena told him? There were other worlds, innumerable worlds, where strange forces and powerful beings existed. The lake was a connection between several of these worlds. During the full moon, part of it would be in this world, part of it in another. Or perhaps it would be in many different worlds at once. These connections between worlds were what magic was all about. Sorcerers sought them out, drained power from them, and stored it up in power objects. Only this amulet was even more special than that. This amulet was a piece of another world, a veritable superamplifier of power. He could feel that much, he didn't need the old man or Elena to tell him about it.

And now, as he started over the rim and headed down the gentle incline to the little lake, the sky was completely dark, and the moon was rapidly climbing in it. With a sensitivity he had never felt before, he could perceive clearly that he was entering another world. Would his perception have been sharp enough to have revealed this to him without the aid of the stone? Not likely.

The water of the lake glowed with a strange greenish light, and when he looked straight at things, their edges began to blur and move.

"Glance quickly from object to object," Elena had advised him. "When something starts to blur, move your eyes to something else and keep moving them around. If you let things change on you, you'll get lost in your visions and you won't be able to function anymore."

So he kept shifting his glance around, trying to keep

things solid, and now he noticed that some of the rocks glowed brilliantly with the same inner light of the lake. Suddenly he stopped dead in his tracks, breathing rapidly, pulse accelerating. He could feel the hair on his arms and hands standing up and flowing into the air like antennae. The back of his neck itched. Something alien and menacing was coming his way. He knew this with total certainty.

He dropped down flat on his stomach and lay on the earth among the shining stones, queasy with an inexpressible fear of the unknown. First there was a loud humming in his ears and then they popped and now he could hear it—an intense whining noise and the heavy rasp of breathing, coming closer and closer.

Quinn pressed his eyes shut and held his breath. For a moment he felt the creature hovering over him, sniffing and searching for him, a creature of horrendous power.

Then, abruptly, it moved on. He felt the hair on the backs of his hands and arms settle down and his heart slow back toward normal.

"Jesus, what was that?" he muttered to himself, rising back up to his feet and starting up again, only then he realized that he had been forgetting to shift his glance around, and now he was headed into a maelstrom of glowing chaotic colors. Nothing was recognizable, not earth, sky, or lake, only weird twisting, rioting shapes and colors.

Desperately he told himself, "Got to keep moving," and tried to take a few steps, and tripped on something, and fell down and hit his head on a rock or something, and the pain caused things to clear for a moment, because now he could see a little bit of his own world—a shrub here, a rock there.

He got up again and moved slowly, all of the time shifting his glance back and forth rapidly, trying frantically to rebuild the familiar world he lived in, when all at once, for a brief moment, everything came clear.

It comes and goes in waves, he realized—I had better make tracks while I can still see.

Once more, farther down the hill, he had to stop and fight to get back his vision of the world he knew. He tried not to think what would happen if another of those power creatures came hunting him. He wasn't certain if his heart would stand up under the awful strain again.

But then, once more, his vision cleared, and this time he made the lake.

Without hesitating, he waded into the shining green waters and almost at once he felt, with his strange new sense, the power flowing into the amulet. It was immense. And while he didn't understand it, or know how to use it, he knew without a doubt that he was dealing with powers beyond his wildest dreams. Why was I satisfied with so little before? he thought in a flash of sudden clarity. Cocaine and other drugs people took were a joke. This was what people were after. Black magic. The power to alter the world around you, the ability to control unknown, unknowable forces from other worlds. This was everything. And now that he had tasted of it, he would not be so quick to give it up again.

Mission accomplished, feeling strangely serene and fulfilled, Quinn lay down in the shallow waters and released himself into the world of inner visions he had been struggling to keep at bay.

At first he experienced strange and beautiful scenes that he could recognize and identify. At one point a lovely young girl with greenish glowing skin rose up out of the mystic waters and waded over to him. She leaned down and pressed her cool lips to his brow and whispered a secret to him.

Immediately, he understood everything. All of his worries flooded out of his mind: he could feel them zinging off, as if he were releasing an enormous charge of electricity into the steaming air. Tears of joy poured down his cheeks because in this state at last he realized the secret, and nothing else mattered. Nothing at all.

Finally the visions came faster, and at the same time grew more intense and alien. He no longer could interpret or understand anything he was seeing, hearing, smelling, or feeling. He no longer could remember the wonderful secret the green lady had revealed to him, but all that night as he visited a myriad of alien worlds, learning and forgetting the secrets of many universes, he felt the pulsing life of the amulet, protecting and pouring its power into him.

In the morning, when he came down the mountain to pick up Elena, even she noticed the difference, although she couldn't have described it.

When he had her packed on the mule and started down the mountain and she asked him for the amulet, he had smiled a different kind of smile than she had seen him smile before.

"You have a badly sprained ankle," he said. "I think it's best that I hang onto this little trinket for a while."

3

Dear Bruthie,

Having a wonderful time, wish you were here. Ha ha.

Seriously, Bruthie baby, sorry I had to leave early, but something important came up, and I had to rush off and find a girl before it went back down again.

Just joking, Bruthie. But you know I wouldn't miss your concert for all the tea in Humboldt County. (Get it! Tea. Grass. Sinsemilla. Humboldt County!—Ah well, it's hard when you're a genius to remember that everyone else isn't on the same ultra-hi-power wavelength.)

"I get it, for Christsake, I get it," Brice said out loud to the letter, "I just don't want it. It stinks! Get it? Sinsemilla—it stinks? And stop calling me Bruthie, it's Brithie."

Seriously, Bruthie, I know you'll knock 'em dead at Arnie's Guitar Saturday night. (The few that go to concerts at Arnie's who aren't already dead, that is.) Everyone will be hovering on the edge of their seats waiting to hear the latest version of "Freight Train." I've got an idea, why don't you play all forty of your

> own versions of that great old classic. Just one hour solid of "Freight Train." That ought to give you the most popular performance ever at Arnie's Guitar. (Just so you pick it so fast they can't hear the awful tune.)

Brice gave the finger to the letter. "I haven't played 'Freight Train' for years," he shouted indignantly. But he smiled to remember how, when first learning to fingerpick the guitar, he had gone through about ten different versions of that tiresome guitar-picker's favorite. Each slightly more complex than the last. Conal had always detested the song and complained loudly and often about it. In fact, Conal had never gone much for any kind of folk-style music, except for Dad's, of course. Dad's music was different. Outside of the beautiful little house, and a lot of money, the music was all they had left of their father. It was hard for them to listen to it as music: it was sacred.

> Seriously, I know you won't play "Freight Train" forty different times, and I wish I could be there to hear you try out some of those new jazz-oriented compositions you've been working on. I think Dad would have really gone for those. I just trust you won't chicken out and revert to Irish jigs, now that I'm not there to keep you honest. I really am sorry, Bricey, and you better believe me, if there was any way for me to make it Saturday, I'd be there.
>
> Don't want to get corny, but it really is peaceful and beautiful up here, and close to God God God and full of the Tao. And you know, waving around in slow mo, as you so sensitively describe it, among the pine trees, flowers, assorted ditch weeds, and gorgeous idle rich girls, can be invigorating.
>
> I've got some advanced students who are pretty good. (Mostly I'm teaching the northern kwang pin Yang form, and you know what a bitch that is to

> learn.) But we're getting in a lot of push hands and combat-oriented stuff. There are three or four guys, and one woman, who are pretty good, and of course Jerry, so I may come home with a few bruises, ha ha, just kidding, no one's about to push me over.

"Yeah," Brice said, "I know." He had seen his brother at push hands before, the sensitivity combat game of tai chi, where two people would push each other's arms around, try to sense a weakness in the other's balance and push him over. His brother so effortlessly tossed all his partners down on the floor as to make it seem like some sort of comedy act: he's up, he's down, he's up. He's down.

But Jerry, the owner of the tai chi school up north where Conal was teaching his intensive course, was supposed to be an expert. Who knows, Conal, maybe you *will* pick up a few bruises. Knock some humility into you, Oh humble son of the Tao. He turned back to the letter.

> But mostly what I like is the solitude: life just moves so much slower up here, there's never any urgency or pressure about anything. No noisy traffic or pushy jostling people (well, we brought up a few with us).
>
> I spend half of my lunchtime eating, and half of it feeding the gang of blue jays and squirrels that hang around the campgrounds. They actually get to know you, and what's weirder than that, you get to know them.
>
> I honest to God have learned to recognize a mangy little squirrel I call Bricey, and a nasty jay named Conal. I can pick either of them out from their friends due to their obnoxious personalities.
>
> But all and all, I already am getting a little edgy from all the quiet. Too fucking many trees: I keep getting paranoid about Ents. A week or so more and I'll probably be only too happy to settle back in with

the beautiful people, and just spend the rest of my days roller dancing up and down the Venice boardwalk to the greasy strains of rock seeping into my brain through my Walkman headphones.

See you soon, but probably not for another week.

Yo Bro,
Conal

There were sarcastic little X's all over the bottom of the page. Brice shook his head at it. "Horse's ass," he mumbled to himself as he took out the photo and looked at it.

Conal teaching tai chi to a small group of students on a wide wooden platform, surrounded by pine trees so rich and green looking you could almost smell them.

But something was bothering Brice about the photo. He couldn't quite zero in on what it was, but he had an eerie sensation that something was definitely wrong here.

He closed his eyes and tried to relax his mind the way he pictured Conal would have. But it was no use. Relaxing and trying were opposites; he saw this clearly, for the first time. So what do you do now, he thought, truly confused, give up?

He opened his eyes. He was sitting in their backyard in the shade of the tree and it seemed to him that he had never recognized what it was like before—sitting in the shade of the familiar tree on such a bright sunny day. Looking out at the shocking-red Chinese-style platform, the pond. The grass and flowers seemed unnaturally sparkling and bright. The whole scene, mingled with the homely act of reading the letter from his brother, seemed to take on a friendly timeless familiarity, as if it had happened before, over and over again, and at the same time as if it would only occur this way, now, and already was swiftly fading away.

He got up and put the letter in his hip pocket and forgot about the photo. It would straighten itself out in its own good time, he knew. Anxious not to drag the moment out and ruin it, he walked across the lawn, and without hesitating, went into the house and shut the door.

MORNING IN THE Azteca Hotel in Acapulco. Intense tropical sunlight filters in around the edges of the venetian blinds and the rich, heavy wine-red curtains. It begins to play with the shadows on the walls.

Elena stirs and turns restlessly, lost in the enormous bed, which is lost in the enormous bedroom, which is lost in the enormous suite.

And the Azteca is by no means a first-rate Acapulco hotel. One of the high-rises that looks down on Hornos Beach, but nevertheless not a first-rater. Elena, who had never been in a first-rate Acapulco hotel, or any other Acapulco hotel, had wondered what a first-rate one would have been like. "Too many fucking waterfalls," Quinn had said. "They've got waterfalls in the swimming pools, waterfalls in the gardens, and waterfalls in the lobbies. It'll drive you crazy after a while. Everything gets wet."

She had been stunned to realize he was joking. Quinn was joking!

"We don't want a first-rate hotel and we don't want a grungy fleabag. In the middle is always where they search for you last."

But Elena had been overwhelmed by the opulence of the honeymoon suite of this second-rate Acapulco hotel.

(They were Mr. and Mrs. Gunnerson, shy honeymooners from the States.)

And now, peripherally aware of the light playing with the shadows, the enormous expanse of bed and room, she is not asleep, but also not awake. Between the cool sheets, she dream-thinks and think-dreams about Papa, who sometimes becomes Quinn, or about Quinn, who sometimes becomes Papa.

"Everything's out of control," she is telling her mother. "How did I ever wind up going to bed with a killer like Quinn?"

Her mother pauses, hard at work as always, kneading flour to make flour tortillas (instead of the usual corn; it must be Sunday, Elena thinks). As always, sauces are bubbling in giant pots on the stove. Her mother has two small stoves, one for sauces and one for everything else. And if she's not cooking, she's got to be washing clothes, ironing, or struggling to control the kids. Elena has sixteen brothers and sisters. And Elena is the oldest girl (slave). Girl! SLAVE!

And so Elena is a mother of four by the time she is six and of five by the time she is seven. Mostly Elena takes care of the kids and Mama does the cooking—and Papa?

Papa gets different jobs. Hard work. Construction. Cowboy. Handyman. Plumber. Home repairman. Gardener. Gambling. Whoring. Gambling. Drinking. Street-fighting.

Elena remembers the thrill of mixed fear-excitement on the rare occasions when Papa's home for a while. A tall, whip-thin man with a terrifying expression. He's in the doorway now. She feels her heart pounding with fear, with excitement, with fear.

"Mama, it's Papa, he's . . . Oh, look out!"

For no reason, in her dream Papa slams her mother hard in the face, knocking her down on the floor. Oh God, her eye will be black and swollen in church. Everyone will know.

And she knows that's not right, because she's really an adult now, lying in bed in the Azteca hotel room, and she knows that there is always a reason; that two people make a bargain to ruin both of their lives; that victims seek out their punishment willingly and unerringly, as moths do flames; that her mother was two people: hardworking, cheerful, always open, and filled with concern for the children. Pure, even.

And for Paco, her husband, she was a different person: dull, sad, whining, cringing, complaining, always quick to point out to him every little mistake or flaw in his character, never supporting or feeling pride in his accomplishments. As Elena grew older, she came to understand that once her mother had the children, Papa had become merely a necessary evil for her to endure. She needed the punishment. And so at first they would go through a big elaborate argument until they finally managed to find the necessary momentum to drive Paco over the edge.

But over the years they had worked it out and refined it and actually even gone past refinement and made out of it a form of shorthand, so Mama could merely respond to Paco's scowl with a certain glance or gesture which contained all the necessary nuances for him to read out the rest of the argument, and arrive at the conclusion right then and there, and drive himself over the edge of his white-hot rage.

In the end, Mama had been triumphant, and transformed his bursts of violent anger into a state of permanent, animal-like ferocity. He had punished her viciously and constantly whenever he was home, the last few years. And then, finally, he had died.

They had called it a stroke, but by that time Elena had been seventeen, and she had known that her papa had blown his brains out with rage.

She could see in Mama's eyes, under the genuine grief (Mama cherished grief), the triumph. The ultimate triumph. And of course the punishment had never ended. If being married to Paco was punishment, being widowed was also punishment. (First he beat me and then he had a stroke and left me all alone.)

So that even now, in her dream, Mama is not a real person for Elena and does not hold her interest at all. Elena feels guilty about this, and Mama likes that. She is always more comfortable around guilt.

Her face is blurred in the dream. But was it not blurred in life? She is more of an elemental spirit than a personality. A few feelings—warmth, heaviness, remorse, guilt—a lackey of the Catholic Church, and all of the time pounding away at those fucking tortillas, stone-ground, handmade, one hundred percent healthy fucking tortillas, so that even now in the dream, Elena cannot even remember her name, and worse, doesn't care if she can't remember it, because—heart pounding—because Papa's home.

Or was it Quinn? No, that was wrong. "Papa, you've got to help me. You've got to talk to me. You never talked to me, Papa. Why didn't you ever talk to me?"

He smiles his wolf smile. (Quinn?) "I have never liked you, Elena. You were always too much in control. Calculating. Scheming. Keeping your ass on the top of the heap. I suppose you've got to be that way when you're the oldest child in a big family. But nevertheless, I never liked you, I never trusted you. You never needed no one but yourself."

Elena is crying now. "I needed you, Papa. I need you now. Everything's gone wrong. Everything's out of control now. I feel like things are all spreading apart, and I'm supposed to pull them all back together, but they're too far gone and spreading faster and farther. I took up the study of magic because magic means control, total control of everything on every level. There was a man who was a powerful magician. So powerful he must be able to control the whole world, I thought.

"Only since I've been with him, my control has started to dissolve, to slip away. And you know what, Papa, I'm starting to doubt I ever had it in the first place. Is control an illusion, Papa? Is it all a joke?"

Papa laughs a thin laugh without any voice in it. Like a dry wind. (Quinn's laugh?)

"And you're willing to do anything to get it back. Ruthless. Cold. I never liked you, Elena, but I'll tell you a secret. You'll never get it back. Never!"

Elena sat up in bed, eyes wide-open.

Quinn apparently had slammed the living room door, and now she heard his muffled footfall, heading for the bedroom.

Now he stood framed in the bedroom doorway, lean and predatory-looking, with an insolent tilt to his posture. A hard man. Trouble. Even now, in his usual outfit of ordinary Levi's and a loose flashy short-sleeved tropical shirt, he seemed strangely at home in the elegant, ritzy hotel room.

He nodded at her. "Better get up. We've got to get out of here today. They're onto us already. Don't ask me how it happened so quick. They may have had informers all over the city waiting for us to show, as a precaution in case they missed us. I don't know. That little snake in white is the one. I could sense it. He'll stick to us like glue until he gets what he wants or we get to him. Anyhow, they're here. There's a man downstairs in the lobby and a couple more outside.

"We'll have breakfast in the hotel coffee shop. I've arranged to meet with someone there."

No more reaction to her nude body or their previous night of lovemaking than that. Elena nodded.

"Where's the amulet?"

Yesterday when they had rented the room, Quinn had

gone out for a few minutes. He probably hadn't even had time to leave the hotel, she thought. That night, when they had made love, he had no longer been wearing it.

"There's no need for you to know," Quinn said. "I can't carry it on me. So I stashed it. The fewer people know where, the better."

She nodded, but it was not an affirmation of what he'd just said. It was an affirmation of what had been hammering at her all night, all morning, all week. Things were blowing apart faster than anyone could push them back together.

Downstairs in the café, a nervous-looking little man carrying a briefcase sat down at the table next to theirs and ordered breakfast.

Quinn took a small envelope out of his pants pocket and slid it into the middle of a folded paper napkin.

Then he went over to the man's table. "Pardon me, our cream seems to have soured, can I borrow yours for a minute? I'll bring it right back."

"Sure, sure, *seguro, por su puesto,*" the nervous little man muttered.

Quinn poured some of the cream in his coffee. Spilled a little down the front of the container, and put the napkin containing the envelope under it to blot up the cream. When he returned the container, he returned it with the napkin and envelope.

"Sorry," he said, "I spilled a little."

"That's all right," the man said.

As they continued eating their breakfast, the man had pushed his briefcase back toward their table. When he got up to leave, it was still sitting there.

What's that all about? Elena wondered. No need for you to know, she answered herself. Thanks, Papa. Quinn. For making it so simple for me.

Back at their room, Quinn made a quick check of the outside of the door. The small piece of Scotch tape was still across the crack toward the bottom where he had left it when they had gone to breakfast. But as he had explained earlier to Elena, that trap was a red herring, they were meant to find it: that was merely to put anyone breaking into the room at ease.

Once inside the room, he went immediately to the dresser drawers in the bedroom and got down on his hands and knees searching the rug, didn't find what he was after. Then, slowly and carefully, he opened the top drawer. A small broken-off piece of a wooden matchstick that had been wedged in the side of the top drawer fell out on the rug.

Quinn smiled his wolf smile. (Papa?) "They found it and put it back, but, of course, they didn't know where to put it. They put it too high up. I had wedged it in the bottom corner. So—they searched the place."

He didn't bother checking the rest of his traps, but immediately set to work unscrewing the telephone receiver.

Elena licked her lips. Play it cool, she thought. "Hadn't you better check the amulet and make sure they didn't find it?"

"Right," he said. Then he went in the bathroom and shut the door. Soon, he came out again.

"No," he said. "It's still there." But he was smiling that mean smile, that "you'll never ever figure me out" smile of his. Was he putting her on?

A few minutes later, fidgeting around, watching Quinn crawling around on the rug or climbing up on top of chairs and tables, sweeping the place for bugs, Elena said, "I've got to go to the bathroom."

"No doubt," Quinn muttered, busy unscrewing a ceiling light fixture. But he ignored her as she disappeared into the bathroom, locking the door.

When she came out, he was screwing a light switch back into the wall with his small pocketknife-screwdriver.

"Well?"

"I couldn't find it. I looked everywhere and couldn't find it. I even looked in the toilet. I still couldn't find it."

"That's the idea," Quinn said, folding up his pocket-knife and stuffing it back in his Levi's pocket.

"Okay, it doesn't look like they bugged us. Come on over here. Just the same—" He turned on the TV loud, then spread the briefcase on the low coffee table and opened it.

"Ever use one of these before?" He pointed to the two ugly hypodermic needles in the case. "Well, I'm sure you understand the principle. Just don't break it off. Don't be gentle about it, just stab it in—the plump part of his shoulder will probably be the most accessible—and shove the plunger down fast. Don't worry about air bubbles. If he gets an air bubble that's his tough luck."

Elena nodded: "What is it?"

"Damn if I know. I just asked the guy for something that would knock someone out, and do it quick, and preferably not kill him. He's the chemist."

"And who is it for?"

"The guy downstairs in the lobby. Look, Elena, I'm going to level with you. These guys are good. Or rather, one of them is good. We're never getting out of here unless we take him out. All the way out. I've got a plan. It's a bit ragged around the edges. But I like to leave a little room for improvisation. I work best that way." He told her his plan.

Elena just sat there stunned. A little wild? A little ragged around the edges? My God, she thought, he's a raving lunatic. And there is nothing for me to do but go along with it. No way out at all. Even if I just give up everything, and run for it, the guys downstairs will get me. They didn't find what they were after in our suite. They won't find it on Quinn, and I don't know where it is, but they won't believe that.

"Okay," he said, "let's go."

On the way down to the lobby, Quinn chatted and joked with everyone who got in the elevator. Everyone went along with his clowning, and the women responded to him by grinning, slow, deliberate eye contact, and shifting on their feet, opening their stances toward him. Body talk. Come-on.

He's high from all this tension, Elena realized. He was made for this. He's clear in another city from me right now. A city where all the hotels and walls and air are made up out of violence. And he loves to breathe that air. He's hooked on it. Solid. Till the day he dies.

Out in the lobby, when Quinn pointed out the big man in the chair reading his magazine, Elena began to shake. For a moment she was shaking so much she almost dropped the rolled-up newspaper with the hypodermic needle wrapped up inside it.

"I don't think I can do it," she whispered to Quinn.

And then he wasn't smiling anymore. And his cold steely grey eyes opened up and locked onto hers. Suddenly she realized she was more afraid of him than of them. This fear gave her confidence. The shaking stopped.

"You'd better snap yourself out of it, baby," he said. "You know, you're not just along for the ride."

Stung, Elena slipped her hand inside the newspaper and got a proper hold on the hypo.

Quinn restrained her for a moment with a hand on her shoulder until the people in the elevator with them had time to filter out and the lobby quieted down a bit.

Then: "Let's do it," he said. And started off toward the main entrance.

Quinn's plan was to hold the man down in his chair while Elena put him out with the hypo, right there in the main lobby of the luxurious high-rise Azteca Hotel. Then drag him back to the elevator ("People don't see anything they don't want to see. We'll tell them he's drunk") and take him up to their room. Then Quinn would get out of him the whereabouts of the man in charge of their operation. ("A small man in a white outfit. Very, very quick.") Quinn did not say how he would get this information, but Elena guessed that it would not be pleasant. And then when he had it, Quinn would simply go there and take the man in white all the way out of the game for keeps. Once they had got rid of him, she and Quinn would come back here and pick up the stone. Home free.

Elena considered it the plan of a madman. Nevertheless, here she was, holding the hypodermic inside the rolled-up newspaper. Watching as Quinn strolled past the man in the chair, toward the door, to divert his attention. And now she was moving toward him, astonished that she was doing it, shakes gone. Steady as a rock. Wide awake. So wide awake. The fear had deepened and gone beyond fear into a kind of sizzling intense alertness. My God, I'm high on it too, she realized.

The big man overflowing the big overstuffed fifties-style wing chair in the lobby liked to think of himself as not so much a man, but a bear. A grizzly bear, to be exact. Even when he had been just plain Pedro, the scrawniest little kid on the block, the one that all the tough kids pushed around for kicks, the kid who had to endure all the insults, black eyes, and stolen lunch money, that grizzly bear had been inside him alive and growing.

So that he wasn't surprised when at age fourteen he had sprouted up and out.

And he had been ready to do everything humanly possible to facilitate the process: push-ups, pull-ups, heavy weights, anything to pump himself up. Not that he was one of these body-beautiful guys like Arnold Schwarzenegger, far from it. Big chest, big arms, big legs, big gut. So that when he finally hit upon his preordained profession, and they asked him his name, his response had been automatic. "I am the Grizzly Bear," he had said, launching his career as perhaps Mexico's biggest, meanest professional wrestler ever, in a field where every man was big and mean to start with. He had mangled men with his famous grizzly-bear hug, both in and out of the ring, and he was afraid of no one. Not even that scrawny little dude named Smith who had recently hired him, and who for some odd reason seemed to inspire fear in every man in Acapulco. No, the Grizzly Bear feared no one, and everyone feared the Grizzly Bear. Which was why he was so astonished when the whip-skinny guy he had been keeping an eye on from his chair suddenly turned around and walked over to him and put his puny hands on Pedro's massive shoulders as if to hold him down, and someone stabbed him in the shoulder with a needle.

Holding her breath, Elena leaned over, and, letting the newspaper fall where it might, jabbed the needle into the meaty portion of the giant's shoulder and quickly but calmly depressed the plunger. Somehow, the scene had acquired an otherworldliness about it that made it seem as if she were merely observing her body, or perhaps even someone else's body, do it. In her mind, she had been almost certain the needle would break, but in reality everything went as smooth as silk. She remembered to breathe again. Mission accomplished.

For a moment these images seemed to hang there suspended in time: Quinn leaning down, hands on the giant's shoulders, and she holding the needle, the newspaper on the tiled floor, and the startled woman in the bright red dress, mouth open, staring with unbelieving eyes at what she was seeing here.

And then things broke loose. An eerie loud roaring sound rumbled out of the giant's throat as he reared up and partway out of the chair, swinging his massive arm around and knocking Elena clear off her feet and down on the tiled floor. The woman in the red dress shouted,

"Stop—you can't do . . ." and was moving toward the two men struggling in the chair, so that Elena reached out impulsively and caught one of her legs, just to hold her back, and suddenly realized it was all or nothing and jerked her leg around with all of her strength so that the woman tripped and went down to her knees and then spilled over onto her hands on the hard tiles.

Grunting, Quinn shoved the wrestler back down in the chair. The giant's eyes did some funny drifting up under his eyelids and then he slumped back down.

Good, he's out, Quinn thought, and he was already turning his head toward the two women struggling on the floor when suddenly, emitting another chilling roar, the Grizzly Bear surged up out of his chair again, brushing Quinn aside as if he were a fly, and charged across the floor blindly, staggering, to be sure, and half fell onto the front desk, terrifying the young check-in clerk, and scattering the register, fancy pen sets, and telephone off onto the floor.

Mumbling to himself, eyes closed, breaking out in sweat all over, Pedro clung to the counter trying to hold himself up. A moment later and Quinn tackled him from behind, and gripped him around the shoulders and tried to drag him away from the desk. Fat chance!

"Ayudame—help me," Quinn shouted to the clerk. "He's having a fit. Help me get him down flat on his back."

Meanwhile, the woman down on the floor struggling with Elena twisted over on her back and kicked at Elena's head with her right foot, trying to free her left foot.

The kick, landing on Elena's head, hurt, but not enough to make her let go. She grunted in pain and twisted the woman's foot hard, causing her to twist back onto her stomach again. And now Elena scurried up her back and got a handful of dark hair.

But the woman she was fighting with, a rich vacationer from Beverly Hills who spent a lot of her spare time, of which she had a plethora, practicing tennis, running, and aerobicizing her pampered body, was no pushover, and soon they were rolling over and over, pulling hair and punching whenever they got the chance.

Now Quinn and the young day clerk managed to break Pedro's grip on the counter, and pulled him over backward onto the floor, where they landed hard, with the clerk getting the wind knocked out of him and Quinn somehow ending up on top.

Pedro was obviously stunned out of his mind from the drug, but he would not quite go unconscious. His eyes were rolling around crazily in their sockets and he was sweating and mumbling to himself, but he was still struggling.

Now a few spectators were materializing from various corners of the lobby.

Two young men got up enough courage to pull the two women apart and get them up on their feet, where they made vain nervous efforts at straightening up their hair and clothes, spitting vile curses at each other.

"Help me," Quinn shouted, "he's having a fit." Several men helped Quinn hold Big Pedro down while Quinn attempted to smother him with a sweater someone had handed him ("to keep him from biting off his tongue").

At last the drug took its toll and the Grizzly Bear's struggles lessened to a few spasmodic quivers, and finally stopped altogether. Quinn just sat there straddling him, breathing hard, trying to figure out what in the hell to do now.

Elena had meanwhile edged her way over to the chair and was surreptitiously scanning the floor for the hypo, while her sparring partner was babbling to the men who had separated them about what she had just seen take place.

The used needle had rolled around behind the squat heavy chair, but lucky break, it had not rolled far from it.

Elena managed to kick it underneath the chair without anyone noticing what she was doing. She leaned on the chair, out of breath. "That bitch is crazy," she said to the men's questioning glances. "This man was having an attack and we were trying to help him when this crazy bitch jumped on me." The two women started yelling at each other again when they first heard the wail of the siren.

Jesus Christ, Quinn thought, someone called the cops, or an ambulance, and for the first time in history they get here like lightning.

Already the guys in white, along with a crowd of onlookers, were pouring into the hotel.

"I don't know, the guy was having some kind of attack or seizure, all I did was hold him down."

The two young men in white rolled their eyes at each other and grimaced comically.

One of them was listening to Pedro's heart with a stethoscope while the other had pushed back his eyelids and was peering at his eyes.

"Some seizure," he said. Both of them chuckled. They knew the effects of drug OD when they saw them, which was every day. "He'll be okay; let's get him on the stretcher. Anyone know what he was taking? Okay, let's go. Jesus, what is this, a man or a hippo?"

They were still wheeling him out the front door when Quinn became aware that he was flanked by two big grim-looking men wearing lightweight summer sports jackets. Both of whom had their right hands in their pockets. The shorter, heavier-set one leaned close to whisper to him.

"If you think we won't shoot in here, try us," he said in English.

The other nodded, smiled. *"Es la verdad."*

"What now?" Quinn said, more to himself than to them. Would they risk shooting in the hotel lobby? Quinn was too tired to figure anything out. His mind had just plain short-circuited.

"Now we go to visit an old friend of yours out at La Condesa Beach. We were supposed to hang around outside in the streets and just keep an eye on things, but after all the fuss you made here—well, I think it's time for a visit."

Quinn tried not to notice where Elena had disappeared to. He had no idea what she would do now. But she must have caught on to what was happening to him because he had glimpsed her drifting off with the crowd that had gathered.

"Christopher Smith," Quinn said out loud. He had blown it all. An ambulance, for Christsake!

The stocky man managed a grim smile. "Ah, you recognized Mr. Smith?"

"I caught a glimpse of him. Anyone that small and that fast has to be Christopher Smith."

"Well, Mr. . . ."

"Just 'Quinn.' "

"Well, Quinn, unfortunately for you, your guess was correct."

Outside in the car both men were laughing so hard there were tears in their eyes.

"There was Big Pedro thrashing around on the floor, and this dude is stuffing a sweater in his mouth," the stocky man was explaining to the driver of the car, in English. Now the driver of the car began to laugh too. " 'He's having a fit,' he says, and, and—oh Jesus—the ambulance guys are standing there with their mouths down to here, trying to figure out what in the hell is going on."

A few minutes later, when he had regained enough control of himself to speak again, he said to Quinn: "Believe me, you've been out of it too long. You should have stayed out."

Don't I know it, Quinn said to himself.

Elena had allowed herself to drift outside with the crowd. Her mind was seething with thoughts, ideas, and battle plans, most of which were more insane than what she and Quinn had just gone through.

Luckily, her sparring partner, in what was left of the red dress, had headed either to one of the hotel rest rooms or more likely back to her own room, to try and repair the damage Elena had done to her hair, dress, makeup, and ego. Elena had practically torn the dress right off her, and given her a bloody nose.

Elena, on the other hand, hadn't fared quite so badly in the free-for-all. Partly because of her more informal attire: navy-blue short shorts, red T-shirt, and Nike running shoes.

She wasn't bleeding, and pretty much all she had to do was to get her long straight hair back out of her eyes and tuck in her T-shirt in order to blend in with the crowd. On the negative side, however, her right eye was throbbing dully and this was accompanied by a dry itching sensation. And of course her face was puffing up a bit where she had been kicked or punched, and she was still favoring her left ankle, the one she had sprained on the mountain, enough to give her a noticeable limp. But this kind of roughed-up look was common in Acapulco: maybe she had just fallen off her water skis, or got stoned and dived off the table she was dancing on in her bikini last night.

Her first inclination was to ditch Quinn and just let them have him. With this thought in mind she was searching out one of the ubiquitous taxis to complete her getaway. Then she could come back later and go over the room until she found the amulet and . . .

But too many things were wrong with that plan. Surely when they didn't get the amulet out of Quinn, they would be back at the hotel room waiting for her. And besides, she wasn't sure she could find the amulet anyhow.

She had already tried, and they had also. Something was really wrong there, and only Quinn knew the answer.

The final deciding factor was the old man's advice to "let Quinn handle it all."

No, there was really no choice to make. She had to follow Quinn and try to help him in any way she could, and if any chance came her way—improvise! Lots of luck.

A taxi correctly interpreted her preoccupied aimless movements and pulled up to the curb, so when Quinn and the two men in sports coats came out and got into the Buick parked illegally in front of the hotel, she was already in the cab. But what a taxi. The seats were covered with imitation zebra skin, and the steering wheel was some small red plastic custom job. A set of enormous fuzzy dice hung from the mirror. And the driver!

"Can you follow those guys getting in that blue car there and not lose them?" she asked in Spanish, feeling quite foolish.

"Wow, man, real cool, baby," the cabbie answered in English. "The caper is in."

"On," Elena suggested.

"Qué?" He swiveled around to face her. A wild-looking, very slender young man with delicate lovely features. Too lovely. He was wearing, Elena noticed, eye shadow and mascara. But still, he was an extraordinarily handsome young man with a thin straight nose, generous fleshy lips, and the huge dark eyes of a Gypsy.

"On," Elena repeated. "The caper is *on,* not *in.*"

"Wow, great, man, you speak American. I you main man. I no fail you, baby. Thirty thousand pesos and I all yours."

Elena felt for her wallet in her back pocket and was relieved to find it still there. Grumbling to herself in Spanish, 30,000 pesos for Godsake, she peeled off three 10,000-peso bills and dished them over to him in advance, as was the custom here.

"Please speak only American like me," he said. "Okay, man, here we go."

The Buick pulled away from the curb and merged into the stream of slow, heavy, noisy traffic, followed closely by Elena's taxi. And it's supposed to be the off-season, Elena grumbled to herself.

Soon they passed the Hornos Cine, proudly proclaiming, *Gigi y Flaming Pistols.*

"That's where I get American," the cabbie explained. "Great movies. *En inglés.* Hey. You want go with me? Don't worry, I fag, but I can screw woman too. Especially sexy dame like you. Hey, you make *uno* eye black."

"Getting a black eye," Elena corrected. "Don't lose them, please." Acapulco was noted for its crazy cabdrivers, and the area around La Condesa Beach was noted for its gay swinging atmosphere, particularly East Condesa, but this—I had to get this for a cabdriver?

"How, lose them? Only guys in Acapulco wearing jackets."

He himself was dressed in shorts and a black T-shirt with a pocket in it.

Despite his lean, delicate look, there was a loose, almost catlike quality about his movements. He sprawled back in the luxurious zebra-skin seat and goosed the gearshift with the shiny red knob as he downshifted and then geared up again with every slight fluctuation in the traffic speed.

At the same time, he darted in and out of lanes, honking his horn and, it seemed to Elena, barely avoiding accidents, yet keeping just the right distance behind the blue Buick. All this was so effortless that from time to time he would turn around and talk to Elena for a while, driving with the car on automatic pilot, she imagined hopefully.

Now he fumbled in his T-shirt pocket with his right hand and fished out a package of Camels. One-handed, he expertly tapped out a cigarette and lit it with the car lighter.

"Mind if I *fumo?"* he asked, after the fact.

The husky pungent odor of strong marijuana filled the taxi, causing Elena to choke.

He handed the joint back over the seat to her. "Acapulco Gold," he said, "the best in the West." He smiled a languid smile as Elena furiously waved it away from her.

"Sí, I could have good time with you, sweetheart. I'm DC/AC. Completely. Don't to me, matter what. American ladies and gents loves me."

Then, as the grass took effect, he lapsed into Spanish and began to chatter aimlessly about his life.

Elena no longer paid any attention to him, only occasionally interrupting the wild wheeling and dealing going on in her mind, to make certain he was not losing the Buick.

"Don't worry, man, everything cool," she was constantly being reassured.

Suddenly she was jerked out of her thoughts by the realization that they were stopped.

Up ahead of them the Buick was parked at the curb in front of a small cantina. "La Cucaracha," the sign said. Neon signs in the window advertised the availability of Carta Blanca, Corona, and Budweiser.

"What do we do now, baby?" he asked her, still toking on the joint. "Rup them out?"

"Rub. Rub them out," Elena corrected, and couldn't keep from smiling. You couldn't help but like the guy. Christ, the marijuana smoke must be getting to me, Elena thought.

They were parked in the bus zone, about half a block down from the Buick, and they watched as the men in sports coats got out of the car and, Quinn between them, headed into the cantina.

"They got rods," the cabbie observed. *"Cómo se dice?"* He tapped his pocket.

"Pocket," Elena said. "They've got rods in their pockets. Look, what's your name? *Cómo se llama?"*

"Speak *inglés,* please. My name Chackie."

"Jack," Elena nodded. "Okay, Jackie, can you get me a rod?"

He shook his head.

"I can pay for it."

"No way, man. Guns—*cómo se dice?*—guns are very hard to come by in Acapulco," he continued in Spanish.

"Can you get me some kind of weapon, Jackie?" Elena's head was throbbing now, and suddenly she found herself on the verge of tears.

"How much *dinero* have you got?" Jackie asked her.

She dug the money out of her pocket and handed it all over to him. He sifted through it expertly with his long dextrous fingers.

"Christ, *señorita,* you expect to get a *pistola* for this? You can't afford even a Boy Scout pocketknife."

Almost all of Elena's money was in her purse in the dresser drawer in her bedroom back at the Azteca Hotel.

Elena pushed her fist into her mouth and tried to talk, but only a strange stuttering noise came out. Tears were spilling from her eyes and down her cheeks, and her right eye was swollen almost completely shut and was now beginning to itch agonizingly.

In a gesture of almost unbearable tenderness, the cabdriver reached out and touched her cheeks with his delicate fingers.

"Lágrimas," he said softly, rolling out the lovely Spanish word for tears.

"Okay, let's not cry. Let's see what we can do between the two of us," he said in Spanish. "Friends?"

She nodded.

"Now, what kind of weapon do we want?"

"Something to kill men with," Elena sobbed.

"Sure. *Por seguro.* What other kind? Okay, if we can't get a gun we can get a *cuchillo*—a knife. Can he use a knife? He looked to me like the kind of man who can use a knife."

"Who?" Elena asked.

"The man those two gangsters with guns in their pockets herded into the cantina, who else are we talking about?"

Elena said nothing.

"Get out of the cab and wait here. And don't worry, I'll be right back."

When she got out of the cab he reached out the window and took her hand in his. "Amigos," he said.

The tears welled up again, and suddenly he batted his long sultry lashes at her over his huge dark eyes, and his expressive features lapsed back into his habitual loose crazy style as his speech shifted back into English again.

Only, was it Elena's imagination, or was there something serious hidden underneath the gaiety and exuberance? Something she would never get to know or understand?

"Later, alligator," he said as he roared off into traffic.

"On the moon, baboon," Elena answered, more to herself than to him, as she stood helplessly on the curb, wondering if she was ever going to see him again.

La Cucaracha cantina had a certain ambience, a sort of gritty down-to-earth workingman style that was rapidly becoming rare in swinging Acapulco. Tough, stringy-looking guys in weather-beaten straw cowboy hats sat around the bar sipping Carta Blanca, while sad *charro* laments wailed from the big old-fashioned jukebox in the corner.

Cowboys, Quinn thought. Cowboy music here, or in the U.S., always consisted of losing, losing, losing. Horses and bulls were always throwing guys off and stomping them. Gunmen were shooting them down too young. Good-looking girls cheated on them, over and over again. Everything was always going wrong for cowboys.

Quinn's thoughts were punctuated by a weird yipping cry from the box, whether issued from man, woman, or beast, Quinn couldn't tell.

Christopher Smith gestured to the bartender; apparently a prearranged signal, because the bartender in turn said something to the men at the bar that Quinn couldn't hear, and the five or six tough-looking *charros* immediately drank up the remains of their beer and left.

The man called Smith now folded his hands in front of him on the table and seemed to give the impression of a businessman acting chairman at a board meeting. He said: "Before we begin, I would like to direct your attention to the bar."

The bartender held up a double-barrel sawed-off shotgun for Quinn to see.

"Just so you will know it's there," Christopher Smith said. His voice was neither low nor high, but the brisk efficacy with which he handled his words, and the easy elegance of his sentence structure, gave to it an almost royal air that went well with the rest of him. A very small, neat, aristocratic little man with a narrow aviator's moustache, and a high, intelligent-looking forehead. In his white tropical suit, he rather reminded Quinn of the young David Niven.

Quinn glanced at the shotgun, and the bartender, apparently out of fussiness, put it back under the counter.

Quinn perked up a little. The shotgun was one mistake, and putting it under the counter was another. If the bartender had known Quinn in the old days, he would be keeping it on top of the counter with the safety off and one hand on it.

But the shotgun was a typical case of overkill if Quinn had ever seen it. If things got to boiling the way he hoped they would, there was no way anyone was going to get off a shot out of a 12-gauge double-barrel without hitting at least two of the three men seated around the table with Quinn. In the long run, Quinn figured, if he could get close enough to Smith, the bartender would just waltz around waving the gun and never have a chance to pull the trigger. It was a small thing, but it cheered him up to see that mistakes were being made here.

He took a sip of the beer; it had a sharp clean tang to it. Somehow, it tasted delicious to him (my last beer?).

The box vibrated as a group of sorrowful *charros* spouted out a series of climactic wails and the record went off. It was dead silent.

Apparently that was what the little man had been waiting for. He held up the gun and holster that had been removed from Quinn's belt.

"Excellent choice, if I may say so, which of course I may. A Browning Hi-Power P-35 (loaded with 9mm hollow points, naturally) in a Bianchi Askins Avenger combat holster. I must say, I myself prefer the Snik."

Quinn realized vaguely that the little man was alluding to a small fast-draw breakaway holster. He had been totally unaware that his own holster was called a Bianchi Askins Avenger combat holster. Quinn's theory was that going through life amassing such knowledge was merely cluttering up your mind with trivia, and that sooner or later such cluttering would cause the mind to trip at a crucial moment, the way cluttering up the floors of your house might cause your feet to trip if you had to move in a hurry.

He knew, of course, that his pistol was a Browning Hi-Power P-35, because he had found it necessary to sort through the maze of facts about automatics vs. revolvers. And then, once you narrowed it down to autos (which any intelligent gunman obviously would, because (a) they fired more times without reloading, (b) they reloaded faster, (c) spare clips were also easier to carry and get to in your pockets than bullets, and (d) being flat, automatics were easier to hide under your clothes and get out again in a hurry without snagging on something), then you eliminated certain autos for obvious reasons, and one of the few you were left with was a Browning.

When Quinn had found out he was heading for Mexico, he had arranged over the telephone for his man Jorge to pick up a weapon for him. He had specified a Browning in some sort of small, easily concealable holster. But he had given a list of alternate choices, most of which he would have considered satisfactory.

Yet the truth of the matter was that he knew very little about handguns, and considerably less about holsters; nevertheless, he knew a great deal more about both of them than he wanted to know. But Christopher Smith, ah, there was a subject about which he could never get to know enough.

With an elegant little flourish, Smith popped the handgun back into its holster, laid it down on the table in front of him, and dipped his hand under the table and back out with his own gun in it. Fast. Very, very fast.

"I myself prefer the Smith & Wesson Model 59," he said in his pleasant but slightly pedantic manner.

This interested Quinn. He had long ago labeled that model Smith & Wesson unacceptable. The safety on an S&W had to be pushed up with your thumb to fire the gun, as opposed to the Browning, which must be pushed down: pushing up was an unnatural movement out of synch with your draw, and definitely had to slow you down.

"How do you get the safety off?" Quinn asked.

Smith smiled a superior little smile. "I haven't had the safety on since I purchased it."

Quinn was a trifle jolted to think of this wild little gunman, fast as a snake, tooling around the world wearing an automatic pistol without the safety on. And no doubt he'd also had the trigger action lightened up to a hair trigger as well, as Quinn would have done with his had there been more time.

Quinn was smiling and shaking his head, without realizing he was doing it.

"As you can imagine, I can get it into play quite fast enough that way," Smith added unnecessarily.

"Yes, I can imagine that," Quinn said cheerfully. "In fact, I had a taste of it back there in the jungle. You were using a Sten, I believe. Certainly impressive. I was wondering about Jorge. Did you get Jorge?"

Smith looked ruffled. A frown rippled across his features and instantly was gone again.

"Let's not waste your remaining time discussing lackeys. The important thing is that I got you, and I'm going to keep you, until you tell me where it is. Either in pleasant surroundings here in this charming little cantina or, if you insist, a few hours later, in some sleazy hotel room, tortured and drugged out of your mind. The choice is entirely yours."

Quinn had another leisurely sip of beer, taking care to make all of his moves slowly and explicitly so they would not be misinterpreted. Smith, he had noticed, had not put his own pistol back in his holster, but instead had set it in his lap (no holster was quick-draw when you were sitting down). There he sat with a 14-shot auto lying in his lap with the safety off. Always off! Maybe I'll get lucky and he'll make the wrong move and blow his own pecker away, Quinn thought.

"I hardly see any reason for you to smile, Quinn," Smith said, his voice getting a little petulant.

"I like it here," Quinn said. "As you said, it's a charming little cantina. What's the hurry? What's the rush to get me doped up and tortured? Why don't we enjoy the ambience and talk things over like gentlemen?"

"There's really not that much to talk over, is there?

Still—" He too savored a long sip of his Dos Equis beer.

Quinn felt that although he was momentarily in a hopeless fix, he was gaining valuable information about Christopher Smith. Had things been reversed, Quinn would have had Smith drugged and tortured to the point of total submissiveness as fast as he could hustle him into some quiet hotel room. He would have made it a point not to have said an unnecessary word to him. But then, Smith was a member of the new-generation gunmen. And they generally tended more to talkativeness and gentlemanly gestures.

Quinn knew that the only thing for him to do was stall: keep Smith talking. He already had learned three valuable things about Smith that might come in handy:

1. He talked too much;

2. He apparently hadn't got Jorge; and

3. He had an automatic pistol lying in his lap with the safety off.

If I could get my hands on that baby, Quinn thought.

"You're smiling again, Mr. Quinn, and I can't help but wonder why."

"Quinn is my first name."

"Quinn what?"

"Quinn is my only name."

The two men watched each other warily from across the table and utterly ignored the thugs sitting on either side of them. The burly bartender polished glasses, careful to keep an eye on the proceedings and keep within reach of the sawed-off shotgun, though he felt certain, from his knowledge of men, that the tall gringo would cause no trouble. You learned to judge these things. That man was whipped. There was no tension in his slender form, no rebellion in his mannerisms, no fire in his glance. Gringos! Only a loose and easy resignation to his fate marked the man's expression. No, that gringo was finished. One could be certain of that. If only they could play something sad on the jukebox, some *macho charro* songs. Ah, well. But still, he kept reminding himself to keep track of what was going on at the table.

Outside in the streets, Elena had just given up on Jack the hack for the thousandth time within the short space of half an hour when a taxi—no, his taxi—pulled up to the curb across the street and double-parked. The door flew open, and Jackie hopped out, carrying something in a small brown paper bag.

He made his way carefully, with a skill that spoke of long experience, through the aggressive Acapulco traffic. He only almost got run over twice.

"Over here," he gestured to her as they moved into the alley in between buildings. Oblivious to the people walking by, he took out a narrow, wicked-looking dagger with a round black handle, topped with a silver eagle's head. He slid it out of its leather sheath and showed her the double blade that tapered to a point.

"Pretty good, man. Steel—how you say—too soff? But for onetime killing, okay."

Looking her over, he shook his head. "You don't even got belt?"

He took off his belt and, sliding the sheathed dagger onto it, he fastened it around her waist with the dagger in the back, with a solemn air of ceremony. His waist was so small the belt actually fit her when he fastened it in the last hole.

"Just make sure you facing them." Then he smiled and snapped his fingers. "I almost forget," he said. He picked the bag up from the ground where he had thrown it and fished up a pair of cheap dark glasses. "For you shiner," he said, carefully sliding them on her face. "Better.

"Okay, you wait here a minute. I know the girl who works this joint."

He went through the alley and disappeared around back. Time hung motionless in the heavy air. There was a pungent smell she could not identify that was making her sick. It seemed to her that it was the smell of death. Her death.

Then he was back again. He said, this time in Spanish: "Very well, it is all arranged. If you get out of this alive, you owe me money. I had to promise to pay her. Too much! Now go and slip in the back way. She'll give you her apron and let you take them the beers. She doesn't know what's going on. I told her you were in love with the gringo and would give anything to meet him. She thinks you are going to smuggle a love note in with the beer. When she sees the dagger, and the look on your face, she'll know I lied. But she'll probably not have nerve enough to back out. Besides, I promised her a lot of money, and Maria likes money. Good luck. I'll be across the street in the cab with the motor running. *Buena suerte.* Good luck, man, to both us. We need it."

And he was gone. Her heart was pounding so much she wondered if other people around her would be able to hear it, and she was sick to her stomach with fear; but I'm getting used to it, she realized, astonished. She began limping toward the back of the building.

"Oh, I probably never was as fast as you," Quinn was saying to Smith when he noticed the girl coming out of the kitchen carrying a tray with four bottles of beer on it. Which was odd, because the bartender had been serving them.

"Then what was it that made you so highly thought of?" Smith asked him. "Because you were thought of as simply the best, you know. When I was coming up I heard so many stories about you. Come on, what quality was it that made you stand out from the others?"

Quinn shrugged. Suddenly he realized that the girl was Elena. He tried not to look at her.

"I wasn't the fastest or the strongest or the best shot," Quinn said, trying to distract Smith from Elena.

She was balancing the tray with one hand and gesturing behind her back with the other. Quinn nodded, still not looking at her: she had something for him behind her back!

Then the bartender was shouting at her, and the tall American hood who had escorted Quinn to the cantina was up out of his chair and Smith was saying calmly, "Elena, do join us. Put the tray of beer quite carefully on the table and keep both hands touching it. Frisk her, Danny."

Elena did as she was told, and the tall American named Danny patted her down for weapons. "Jesus, will you look at this pigsticker," he was saying when Quinn rose up in one smooth movement, snatched a beer bottle off the tray, and with his other hand lifted up the table and surged forward, slamming the table into Smith's stomach before he could get his gun off his lap. In the same movement, Quinn threw himself on the top of the table across at Smith.

The gun went off under the table. Whether it had fallen on the floor and gone off on impact or Smith still had hold of it and was firing it under the table, Quinn couldn't tell, because the beer bottles and his own gun were all hitting the floor at the same time.

Diving across the table on his stomach, Quinn grabbed out at Smith's hair, instinctively ignoring everyone else until he got to Smith, but with his uncanny quickness Smith tossed himself sideways out of the chair just as Quinn reached for him.

Squirming over the table's edge, Quinn saw Smith slithering under the table. Obviously the gun had fallen out of his lap and he was going for it.

For a moment, stunned by the speed of the two men, Danny just stood there holding the dagger. Then he woke up and went for Quinn, getting ahold of his shirt with his left hand just as Elena rose up and, still hanging onto the tray, whipped it into Danny's face, hard. It made a loud metal clang. Then again. Danny let go and went down.

Quinn felt himself slip free and threw himself off the top of the table. He just managed to catch hold of Smith's foot, and jerked him back out from under the table a little ways, but couldn't tell whether Smith had got the gun yet so he twisted the foot around as best he could with one hand and slammed the beer bottle down on his knee hard. It made a loud cracking noise and Smith yelled, and the gun went off again, which meant he had it now, but it missed.

And now, stunned with pain, Smith was squirming around onto his back to get off a better shot at Quinn, but this gave Quinn an even better angle at the knee so he hit it again. And Smith howled. And suddenly Quinn was on top of him under the table and everything was too late for Smith because the beer bottle was coming down hard on his head, and there was nothing he could do to . . .

Elena, realizing that her job was to stall the others while Quinn went at Smith, had caught the short Mexican before he got out of his chair. But he was too strong. He blocked off the tray she was using as a weapon and surged up. Closed with her and got ahold of her.

The bartender was, as Quinn had predicted, hopping about waving the shotgun around, afraid to pull the trigger.

"Push her away, Shorty," he was shouting over the racket. And either Shorty heard him or somehow got the picture, because he pushed her and sent her sprawling away from him.

She looked helplessly over toward the bar, to see the

huge brute of a bartender glaring at her down the twin muzzles, tightening on the trigger.

Quinn grabbed up the Smith & Wesson and snaked out from under the table on his belly with the gun in both hands. He put three bullets into the bar, shooting so fast that the noise was blurred into one noise, and shooting so close that you could have put a playing card over the holes in the thin wood paneling. The bartender swiveled and blew a huge hole in the wall, then went down for keeps.

Quinn stood up, knocking the table over, and Shorty, who was just getting his gun out, got off a shot at him, but shot too soon and, amazingly, at that close distance, missed him completely.

Quinn twisted around and fired off a shot into Shorty's chest while Shorty twitched and shot wildly over Quinn's shoulder, but stayed up on his feet, so Quinn shot him again, but he still stayed on his feet, grimacing in agony, trying to get together the strength to squeeze the trigger. So Quinn shot him twice more. Tough guy. But nobody's that tough.

Meanwhile, Danny had got up off the floor and punched Elena in the jaw. She went down. And he got out his revolver in a hurry and was sighting it in on Quinn when Elena spotted the dagger on the floor right next to her. Gift from the gods. She grabbed it up, scrambled up onto her knees, and slammed it into Danny's thigh. Danny screamed and struck at her with the gun, forgetting all about Quinn for the moment. The moment was all there was. Quinn spun around and shot him three times, and now Danny forgot about everything, forever.

Elena tried to stand up, but fell back down again. Her head and jaw ached where she had been hit by Danny's fist and gun, and she was very dizzy. For a moment she had thought it was over, but Quinn twisted around and dived down on the floor again, holding the gun out in front of him, and slid around the edge of the table (which was tilted up on its side) on his belly, at the same time trying to calculate, unsuccessfully, whether or not the gun he was holding was empty. It felt empty. But Quinn figured it might still have a shot or two left in it.

But Christopher Smith was out of the action. Nevertheless, as Quinn rose up to his feet, he kept the gun trained on Smith, whose eyes were open but unfocused. The little man in the no-longer-immaculate white suit was sitting propped up against the table, where he had apparently pulled himself before giving up and passing out again. A thin trickle of blood ran down his forehead, which was swelling rapidly, and his left leg was out straight in front of him but had a funny angle to it. Quinn was surprised that he had been able to break it with the beer bottle, but then the angle had been just right, and the bottle had been full of beer.

Quinn went back to Danny's body and picked up his revolver from the floor, figured out how to get the safety off, and went back over and aimed it at Smith with his right hand, hanging onto Smith's automatic with his left.

Suddenly Smith's eyes came into focus; he started to mumble something, but stopped when he saw Quinn leveling Danny's gun at him. He closed his eyes.

What I had was grit, Quinn realized, but didn't say it aloud. He didn't like to give anything away. He just squeezed off the shot and finished Smith.

Then he wiped Danny's gun free of prints with a napkin off one of the tables and walked over to where Danny lay sprawled out in what seemed an unbelievable amount of blood on the floor. He carefully placed the gun in Danny's hand.

Next he wiped off Smith's S&W with the same napkin. And holding it by the barrel with the napkin, walked over to Smith and carefully closed the dead man's hand around it. Then he crumpled up the napkin and stuffed it in his pants pocket.

Good, he thought. Good and simple. Too simple, but cops like things too simple. They'll love it. Let them figure out who shot who, Quinn said to himself, they'll surely come up with something. He knew, of course, that it would be easy for them to see past the deception if they wanted to. But they probably wouldn't want to: it was all wrapped up for them and tied with a ribbon. He doubted if they would throw that away.

Then Quinn found his own gun, still in its holster on the floor, and stuffed it in his belt without bothering to fasten it on.

Elena was up and about now, somehow. She looked like she had been through exactly what she had been through. But she was on her feet.

"Come on, let's get out of here."

He kept seeing Smith look at him and then close his eyes. Endgame. I hope when they get me, I go out with my eyes wide-open, fighting with everything I've got.

Elena staggered ahead of him, back toward the kitchen. He noticed, strangely enough, that her limp was getting better. Maybe all the exercise is good for it, he thought.

Just before he followed her through the swinging doors, he checked out the room one last time. Everything looks okay, he thought, but the ambience is ruined. The whole place is shot full of holes and covered with blood, and everybody in it is dead.

But in the kitchen they found the waitress, Maria, down on her hands and knees under a table. On top of the table were three plates of tacos she had been preparing. Strangely, the smell of them made Quinn feel hungry. But he knew better than to eat anything for a few hours, until his stomach began to settle back down again. Elena was leaning over against the table, head down, apparently sick and dizzy.

"Wash your face in cold water in the sink, over there. See if you can quick get off some of that blood."

Somehow, unlikely as it seemed, Quinn hadn't gotten any blood on him at all.

"Listen," he said, dragging the waitress out from under the table and pulling her firmly to her feet, "what is your name?"

"Maria."

"Do you know who I am, Maria? Quinn? Have you heard of Quinn?"

"Yes, Señor Quinn," she whined in terror. "I have heard stories of you. Bad stories."

"Then you know what I'll do to you if you tell anyone anything about this."

Already someone was pounding on the front door. "Let's get out of here—the back door. Maria, you didn't come to work today. The boss told you to stay home. Big meeting. Understand?"

"Yes. Yes, I understand, Señor Quinn. Men's business. *Por seguro.*"

Outside in the alley, Maria broke into a run, away from them.

"She'll talk," Elena said.

Quinn shook his head. "They won't want her to. The cops have got it all sewed up, and they're not about to let anyone tell them something to open it up again. Besides, she knows she'll look like an accomplice to the cops. She knows too much. She talks and she gets it from every angle.

"But even if she does talk, so what? By that time, we're out of here. Don't you realize, Elena, we're home free? We did it, Elena. You and me."

And suddenly it hit her full force. Could it be true? She was swept with a giddy exhilaration: home free?

They followed the alley and came out a few buildings

down, crossed the street, and Elena guided Quinn to the taxi, which was still waiting there.

A small crowd had gathered in front of La Cucaracha, and a man was pounding on the door. People were shouting in Spanish, but already, as they sat in the taxi and watched, the crowd was rapidly dispersing. Finally everyone went about their own business. Someone blowing off firecrackers, or maybe even shooting off his gun inside a closed cantina. Big deal.

Elena realized that it was not going to be discovered now, but later, perhaps even tomorrow.

When they got back to the hotel, Elena had Jackie wait in his cab again. She intended to pay him handsomely.

Quinn told her to go through the lobby as briskly as possible because of the scene they had been involved in earlier today. My God, had that only been earlier today? It seemed like a year had gone by in the last few hours. But no one said anything to them in the lobby, or in the elevator up to their room.

Home free? The possibility was becoming a reality in Elena's mind. Everything had been breaking apart, falling out of control, and Quinn—had Quinn pulled the pieces back into place for her? It was too good to be true. She couldn't quite get herself to believe it. Still—it was looking better and better.

When they got inside their room, Quinn immediately sprawled out on the couch, totally relaxed. But Elena remained standing. She was afraid that if she once sat or lay down, she would collapse.

"The amulet?" she asked cautiously.

"Of course," Quinn said. "The bathroom, look inside the water tank in the toilet."

"I already looked there," Elena said suspiciously, but not sure what she was suspicious of.

"You didn't look close enough," Quinn said. Was it

her imagination or was there the slightest hint of mockery in his tone of voice?

She went immediately into the bathroom and took the lid off the toilet tank and set it on the toilet seat. She was vaguely aware that he had followed her in there, and was standing just behind her.

"I don't see anything," she said, completely puzzled.

"Look again."

Now she leaned down with both hands on the sides of the tank, peering into the water. Everything looked normal to her. She was aware of a slight stinging sensation in her right hip—insect. She turned around to see Quinn holding the empty hypodermic needle, but that couldn't be, because . . . Then she remembered. There had been two hypos in the kit—one for the man downstairs watching them in the lobby, and one for me!

"Sorry," Quinn said, "I'm keeping it."

And so she had lost after all. She had stuck in there with everything she had, but in the end it had just not been quite enough.

Quinn caught her when she fell and picked her up easily in his arms and carried her to their bed. He stretched her out on it. She looked so lovely and sweet in her repose. Even if beat-up a little. Maybe even because of it.

"Sleep tight," he said aloud, unaccountably, "don't let the bedbugs bite."

Then he put her out of his mind, went over to the telephone, and asked for the Marleys' room, which, as he had ascertained when they first moved in, was the room directly below theirs.

The phone rang for a long time and no one answered. Good, nobody home. He was about to hang up when a man answered the phone.

"Mrs. Marley's residence?"

Yes, he was informed, but Mrs. Marley was downtown shopping and wouldn't be back for . . .

"Listen, Mr. Marley, that's why I'm calling you. There's been a very ugly incident involving your wife. Shoplifting."

"Shoplifting?" Marley shouted incredulously over the phone.

"I'd rather not talk about it over the phone, Mr. Marley. I think it would be better for all of us if you would come to my store right away, as fast as you can."

Quinn gave him an address that would be somewhere on the far side of the bay and hung up over his protests.

Next he went over to the closet and changed his gaudy tropical shirt for a fresh one just like it. He had to wear loose floppy shirts outside his pants, in order to conceal his pistol.

Then he went out on the balcony, leaned over the edge, and looked down. Too far down. They were on the fifth floor, and he had never liked heights, but then again, he had never been one to let his likes or dislikes interfere with his business.

Holding tightly onto the rail, he stepped carefully over it, stuck his foot back in between the bars, and followed with his other leg. He was now on the outside looking in.

Now, holding his breath, he moved his hands off the rails and onto the vertical bars. Then he slowly squatted down, sliding his hands down the bars.

Then, using a great deal more strength than his slender build implied, he lowered himself over the side until he was just hanging there with his hands clinging to the bottom of the bars to his balcony.

Controlling the little stabs of terror that kept welling up inside of him, he made himself look down.

He was just hanging there, over nothing, but the Marleys' balcony was right underneath him, yet more inward; if he dropped from here he would miss it and then . . . But he stopped himself from thinking that. If he could swing himself back and forth, let loose of his grip when the arc of his swing was far enough inward, he could make it onto the Marleys' balcony. He had done it before. The first time's always the hardest, he told himself. But he found it difficult to get started. What if his grip slipped loose? Jesus, he thought, am I just going to freeze here until I lose strength and drop off?

Again he forced himself to slowly and deliberately look down. And down. There it is, he said to himself, waiting for me. It's waiting for me at every corner, and sooner or later it's going to catch up with me. But not today. Not down there.

He tore his glance away and started to swing his legs back and forth.

Jesus, I'm actually going to slip off of here and go down, he thought to himself. But just then, he instinctively felt that it was the right time to let go. And he let go. It was the hardest thing he had ever done, but he did it, and landed, not in the Marleys' balcony, but onto the railing, knocking all the wind out of himself, and he almost went over backward and blew it after all. But not quite. He hung on and got his breath back, and climbed over.

They had pretty good locks on the outside doors here, but the locks on the balconies were a joke. Four stories up and who needed them? Besides, most people just left them open. As did Marley.

Quinn put his pocketknife back in his pocket as the door slid easily open under his touch.

Then he went into Marley's bathroom and fished the amulet out of the toilet water tank. Right place, Elena, wrong room.

At the door he checked the hall carefully before he exited. Even though he doubted that anyone was now watching his room, he felt better leaving from one floor down.

Downstairs, he avoided the lobby and made it out the back by going out the window in the men's room.

Outside, he got in another taxi, told the driver "Airport," and noticed Jack the hack was still parked out in the street waiting for them. Poor Jack. Poor Elena. Would the cops be after her for that scene in the hotel lobby? No way to know. Would Jack get curious and go up to their room, or would he just forget it and chalk it up to experience? Forget it, amigo, Quinn advised him.

One thing Quinn was sure of: he had the stone back around his neck. He liked the feel of it there. The feel of power. And I'm going to keep it, he thought. From now on.

5

King Neptune's Bar was a favorite of the college crowd. Connoisseurs of hokeyness, they considered it charming in its mundane pretensions. The walls and ceilings were a tangle of fishnet, corks, and other weather-beaten-looking ocean paraphernalia. Here and there you encountered a painting of a sad-looking mermaid with great tits and enormous eyes, and there was one of Father Neptune, gigantic, robust, and stupid as always, his expression strangely reminiscent of Bluto of Popeye fame. Bowls of free pretzels, one of the main attractions, were everywhere.

But tonight, late late Saturday night, Neptune's was practically deserted. Good, Brice observed, so much the better.

"Very dry vodka martini with a twist of lemon peel—shaken, not stirred."

The bartender, a tough-looking but soft-spoken guy with a constant expression of amazed irony, smiled at Brice and shook his head as if to say: I'm always ready for it, but they always get me anyway.

"Sure thing, Mr. Bond," he said dryly, and mixed the drink while Brice watched him.

Brice watched, but Brice did not see. He was still stunned, shell-shocked from the concert he had just given.

The bartender, whose name, Mike, was pinned on his white shirt, poured the drink, sat it down in front of Brice, and said: "S'matter, son, threat of nuclear war, or is it something personal?"

"Hey, I'm okay," Brice said indignantly, "and I'm not a kid. I'm 26 years old."

"I know, remember, you showed me your ID," Mike said.

Brice choked on the martini. "Jesus Christ." His expressive face wrinkled up humorously.

"You have to sip it," Mike said. "Look, why don't I get you a beer? You can get plenty drunk on beer, it just takes more time."

"How 'bout sweet wine?" Brice said, brightening up a little.

Mike grimaced at the thought of a sweet-wine hangover. "I recommend the beer," he said. "Here's one on the house."

He poured out a tap Budweiser with a head on it. Brice sipped it, made a small face, but drank a little more of it.

"Not bad," he said.

"Listen, let me give you some free advice," Mike said. "Getting drunk off sweet wine is the worst. Not getting drunk at all is the best. Everything else is in between somewhere. And I don't know what your problem is, but I know kids. What I mean is, you'll probably look back a couple of years from now and see this was all for the better, right?"

"What are you," Brice asked him, "a bartender or a social worker?"

"Both. It's a new field. Sociobartending, we call it."

Stand-up comedian, Brice said to himself as Mike sauntered off down the bar to wait on/psychoanalyze another customer.

But you're probably right. He had another sip of the

beer. Getting drunk isn't the answer, and in some strange way I get the feeling that maybe it *was* for the best. And suddenly he realized that the fact was that he didn't really feel so bad. He was just acting out feeling bad because he felt he was supposed to feel bad. Might as well let go of that, right now. He had another swallow of beer. Chuckled. Actually, the concert had turned out so terrible that it wasn't tragic, it was funny.

Talk about disasters. There were always two performances at Arnie's Guitar concerts. Each one played for about an hour, with a long break in between where you could buy homemade cookies and cups of coffee.

Although he would never have admitted it to his brother, Brice had already planned on chickening out of playing his jazz-oriented concertos for classical guitar. He knew what the crowd at Arnie's wanted out of him by now, and he was just too chickenshit to go against the grain.

To start with, he was Calvin O'Conner's son. Calvin O'Conner, world-famous rambler, gambler, drinker, folksinger and streetfighter, lover and loser. He was reputed to have written thousands of songs. And to have forgotten most of them.

They wanted Brice to play his daddy's songs. And Brice had planned to give them what they wanted. A few of Dad's songs, a couple of sweet slow cowboy ballads, and for variety, a couple of (forgive me, Conal) Irish jigs he had worked out.

Irish jigs were the latest fad at Arnie's, which was actually nothing more than a huge folksy guitar shop that gave lessons and Saturday night concerts. Everybody who could pick was into Irish jigs. So all you had to do was work out a couple for guitar and you were assured success.

That was before Kevin Kelly. Kevin Kelly had given the early performance before Brice's. He had done everything that could be done to the Irish jig, and then some.

He was one of the most fantastic guitarists Brice had ever heard, though what he was doing frittering away his talent playing, for Christsake, Irish jigs at Arnie's, Brice hadn't a clue.

The moment the man (boy, really) sat down and curled around his guitar in that sweet, sweet intimate posture, Brice had known. It wasn't even like playing the guitar, it was like singing, or better, like whistling or humming. Kevin Kelly's technique was so smooth, so effortless, that it transcended technique. And the eerie music just flowed out of that old Hummingbird guitar like waves of water.

Brice had been both intimidated and inspired by the performance. He knew better than to try any of his Irish jigs he had slopped together, and at the same time, he felt inspired to try something different. Something uniquely his, and his alone. He decided to go with the jazz concertos on the spur of the moment. He put away his father's guitar, got out the Ovation classic, and sent a somewhat apprehensive Arnie off to the back of the store to scare up a small amplifier.

And so, for a hushed and astonished audience at Arnie's Guitar, Brice O'Conner, the son of the famous folksinger Calvin O'Conner, had served up a solid hour of intimate complicated music on a classical guitar. Music that never seemed to make up its mind whether it was jazz, classical, or pop. Music so introverted it seemed to seep back inside itself. Music so quiet in its nature it was as if you were listening to someone's thoughts, or something floating below those. Music you could never whistle, hum, or remember. Music that came and went like the wind, leaving behind not so much as a trace of a shadow. Brice's music.

It wasn't that they had hated it, or been bored by it. They didn't know how they felt about it. There had been a polite—well, not quite that—sprinkling of applause, and a lot of coughing and stunned silence.

There had been one moment of high comedy his brother Conal would have appreciated, when one of the bewildered Los Angeles hillbillies in the audience raised his hand and asked if Brice would play "Freight Train."

"I'm sorry, I don't know that one," Brice had answered.

No, Mike the bartender was right, it had been for the best. He had come out of the closet tonight. —About time.

"I'll drink to that," he said, and downed the beer. "Bartender, *un otro, por favor.*"

"One glass of beer and he starts in speaking Spanish. Good thing you decided against martinis or you'd probably be communicating with your shoelaces by now."

Mike drew him a beer. "This one's not on the house."

He was about halfway through the beer when he noticed the fox sitting at the table with her girlfriends, making a lot of noise. There were foxes and there were foxes, as Conal, his combination brother and lifestyle counselor, had pointed out to him. But this chick was *the fox.* He couldn't believe she was here.

She had been in the audience at the concert, in the first row, no less, and it had been difficult for him to get into his music at first, because she had been *the fox.* Just his type exactly.

None of your California golden girls for Brice, this chick was small, slender, and elegant as royalty, with a thick mop of glossy black hair cut straight across at the shoulders, and huge dark mischievous brown eyes. Jesus Christ, she looked like Cleopatra.

And this was the best part. Not only was she a princess, but she was also and obviously a hippie, beatnik, flower child, or whatever you called them nowadays. That was what got him. Not just royalty, Bohemian royalty.

Right now she caught him staring at her, just as she

surely must have caught him during the concert, and Brice felt his face flush, and turned away.

Out of the corner of his eye he saw her getting up. She's going to the ladies' room, he thought. But no—Jesus Christ, she's coming over here.

She put her hand on his shoulder! She, the fox, put her hand on Brice's shoulder.

"Out of sight," she said.

Brice just sat there.

"The concert, that jazz you played. It was out of sight, man.

"Do you mind?" she said, climbing up on the barstool next to him.

"You liked it?" Brice was astonished.

"I loved it. All of it. Are you going to leave this?" She picked up the vodka martini.

"I . . ." Brice said.

She tilted the glass up and chugalugged it all down.

"Wow, vodka." She made a face.

"Listen, my name is Jane. My friends call me Mary Jane for short, ha ha. Joke."

"I'm Brice O'Conner."

"Well of course you're Brice O'Conner, I just told you I saw your concert. Your name was on the fucking billboard," she said in a sweet innocent voice.

"Don't say 'fuck' around me unless you mean it," Brice popped out with before he had time to be shocked with himself.

Mary Jane laughed. High but throaty: her voice was as luscious as the rest of her.

She put her hand back on his shoulder. He could have melted. "Seriously, I loved it. It didn't seem like that was the right place for it, you know. It was so intimate. Sexy."

Sexy! Brice couldn't believe it.

"Listen, do you want a drink? Can I get you a drink?"

"Let's not get drunk, okay? Really I hate alcohol. A

really lousy drug, you know? And besides, that martini, I'm already drunk." Velvet throaty laugh again. "Not really, but almost."

"Almost me too," Brice said.

"Do you want to go for a ride or something?"

For a moment Brice was almost too stunned to answer. Then he said, "I thought you'd never ask."

Mary Jane made a quick trip to the ladies' room while Brice settled up at the bar. On the way back she stopped off at her friends' table. Brice saw her handing something to one of her friends. It dawned on him. Her car keys. *Her car keys!*

"Was I right?" Mike asked him in a low voice. The husky little bartender's craggy features were as expressionless as ever, but now Brice thought he could detect a secret joie de vivre hidden there. In fact, all of a sudden, he could detect it everywhere.

"Were you right? I never saw anyone so right, my man. Merry Christmas." Brice gave him a five-dollar tip.

"Does this mean I won't get my Christmas bonus from you this December?" Mike quipped.

Outside in Brice's car, an ancient Chevy Nova, which, miracles of miracles, started up first try, they drove with the windows down because it was one of those perfect, warm Southern California nights. Early summer or late spring, Brice wasn't sure which one it officially was. But it was gorgeous, sumptuous, the cool breeze heavy with the scent of jasmine. And Mary Jane—Mary Jane smelled so good, sweet, fresh, with just a hint of some exciting mysterious pungency.

"What kind of perfume are you wearing?"

Mary Jane smiled, flashing white teeth, even, small, and delicate teeth, with just a hint of a gap between the two top teeth that gave her smile that charming touch of gamine.

"I never wear perfume. Or wear makeup. It's all just me."

She sat over close to him. Touching, in fact.

"Listen," Brice said, "I know you must be disappointed in the car. I've been meaning to get a Datsun 230ZX" (is it ZX or GT or SL?) "but I just haven't . . ."

"I just fucking hate sports cars," Mary Jane said. "I mean what the hell is driving anyway, a goddamn game? I can't stand to see a grown man crawl into a little red toy without any roof and race around like a four-year-old on his tricycle, dig?"

"I dig."

"Novas are my favorites, though. Dodges too. Funny thing I just now realized. Wow. Dodges and Novas are both police cars, right? Far fucking out. I never thought about that before. I dig police cars. Wow. That's heavy."

Brice noticed that she had something in her right hand. A cigarette—or? She had fished it out of her funky blue nylon pack.

"Listen, do you have someplace to go, or do we have to drive around town all night?"

"We can go to my place," Brice said. "My brother's up north and we're all alone. I mean there's no one there. We can go there. If you want to."

"All right." Mary Jane smiled a sly conspiratorial smile at him.

"Where's my fucking matches?" She fished around some more in her shoulder pack.

"Great. Wait till you sample this stuff. Humongous, as we say in surf city." She lit the joint.

"Listen, I—ah—I, ah, don't smoke grass," Brice stammered. He went on to tell her why. A couple of years ago at one of his concerts at Arnie's, someone had brought around cookies for everyone. Brice had been the only one ingenuous enough not to recognize from the taste that there was pot in them.

It had taken a long time for the high to come on. Maybe an hour. Then it had come on and kept coming on. At first he had liked it, but then he just kept going up and up until he couldn't possibly stand to get any higher. Then he'd get higher. After a while he was just miserable and he kept having the paranoid fantasy that he was forgetting to breathe. Or was it a fantasy? Jesus. If it hadn't been for his brother's calming influence, he felt certain he would have panicked.

Mary Jane listened to the story, holding in a toke of grass and trying to keep a straight face. Finally she choked and laughed.

"It's not funny," Brice said, but he was smiling too.

"Listen, you just took too much. It's easy to do that when you eat it. Besides, you can't tell how much you've eaten till it's too late.

"Believe me, Brice, you're not going to get paranoid on this, and if you forget how to breathe, I'll give you mouth-to-mouth resuscitation, right? Just trust Mary Jane and have a toke of this wonderful purple sinse and you're going to have a very good time tonight."

Brice believed.

"I better wait till we're home and all. Because of driving the car and . . ." He took a toke, held it. It didn't taste particularly strong to him. The other two times he had smoked pot it was harsher, he had choked on it. It's probably not strong grass, he thought. The thought heartened him. He took another toke.

He was entering wonderland. It was all so sweet. The smell of jasmine, the tender warm night air, the flowers and foliage. Nothing was really changed, but it was all so wonderful. It was his home. And Conal's.

They got out of the car, slamming the doors: there was even something pleasant in the crisp sound of that. There was something pleasant in everything! It was true. Christ, why hadn't he ever realized that before?

"This grass is wonderful," he said to Mary Jane. She laughed. Her laugh was like champagne bubbles, he thought, so effervescent, so delicate.

"Shh," she said, her lovely finger touching her lips.

"Shh," he agreed. "Come with me. I have to show you something. Here. Around the back."

"Oh my God," she said. "It's exquisite. It's just exquisite."

Moonlight filtered through the arbor, dancing, and in the koi pond the image of the fat white moon stretched and contracted as the water rippled. You could hear the sound of the miniature waterfall that cascaded off the rock into one end of the pond, and out here, you could hear the crickets calling out to each other frantically in the dark. The empty platform looked haunted. Awaiting . . . ?

Brice climbed up the steps onto it and started moving in slow motion through the common Yang form, the only one he knew.

Oh yes, yes, he thought, now I understand it. My body understands it. No wonder Conal . . .

"Tai chi," Mary Jane said. "Wow, you're great."

Brice stopped. "You ought to see my brother."

"Listen," she said, "believe me, sweetheart, those crickets are right. Let's go inside the house and get together. It's better than tai chi. It's better than everything."

And it was. It was so good. So true. So right. And not for the reasons he would have thought, not the thrills, not the climax. But the whole act. The ancient ceremony. The little bits and parts that now seemed to be broken up into a series of complete separate scenes. Perfect scenes. It was the pot, he realized, that allowed him this insight. Would it always be there for him now?

They took off their clothes matter-of-factly and lay down on Brice's bed. And now the pot was really coming on, surging, scaring him for a few moments every once in a while. It was so much stronger than any other pot he'd had, it wasn't even a similar high. He kept having realization after realization, his mind opening and opening up like a bird flying into an infinite blue sky.

And Mary Jane, naked, luscious Mary Jane, was straight out of the *Arabian Nights.*

She drew down his face to hers and they tasted tongues, slithering, exploring. All of his fears dissolved. The pot made this intimacy so natural—no, not even natural, but necessary. There was nothing wrong with this, he realized, all the religions were wrong. This was holy. This was what life was all about.

"Oh God," he said, "oh God."

"Don't just look at me, sweetheart. Eat me."

He crawled down between her legs, yes, she was right. That was what it was for. A delicious tart. He tasted it. Ambrosia. Food of the gods. He ate her. Slowly at first, and then faster and faster as she rubbed up against him and her juices began to flow. Sticky sweet. He ate her until she came.

Then he got up on his knees, and holding one of her feet in each hand he slid his penis slowly in.

"Oh oh," she cried out, and soon she was squirming and lashing her head back and forth.

And somehow the pot had given Brice a control he had never imagined before, in his limited sexual experience. He was in no hurry to get anywhere, this was it. The more he slowed down and observed, the deeper the joy. It was in the beginning and not the end of the act. The joy was to remain in the beginning.

And so he teased her and teased himself, holding her legs up over his shoulders and pumping slowly, and every once in a while stopping, leaning down to twine together their two searching tongues.

But finally he could not stand it anymore. She was too beautiful. Too lascivious. Too desirable. She was the only woman. All women.

Then he lay down flat on top of her and rubbed his body up and down against hers as they rocked and pumped together faster and wilder until, writhing and shouting out, their bodies and minds clear out of control, they came together. Now.

"Yes, that's good grass," he said later, when they could talk again.

When he came out of the shower, Mary Jane was not in the bedroom. Oh no, he thought, please don't be gone. But then he remembered, he had the car.

He found her in the kitchen. She was just closing the lid on the coffee.

"You're going to make coffee?" he asked, awed. It was 3:30 in the morning. She was such a strange bird. So beautiful and strange.

"Just checking the kitchen out," she said, and smiled her dazzling smile.

He would later not remember that he had thought it strange that she had carried her pack with her into the kitchen.

"Hungry?" he asked.

She shook her head.

"Let's go back to bed. To sleep," she said.

"Oh ycs," hc said. "Lct's do that." Arms around cach other, they moved back into the bedroom.

6

MOVING THROUGH THE orgy, he was almost painfully aware of the bright heady mix of colors and odors. This can't be real, he thought, it must be a dream. He pinched his arm; it hurt, but somehow the pain didn't feel quite genuine.

"It's the wine," the hearty familiar voice informed him. "It's dulled your sense of pain." Gaius slapped him on the back, almost knocking him over.

Maybe it's not a dream after all, he thought. Maybe it's just the wine, the drugs, the noise, the colors.

A jazz group was racing through that great composition, "Miles Ahead," up on a raised platform in the center of the enormous room. Why, that sounds like Coltrane, he thought, and sure enough there was Coltrane in a plain white tunic blowing everyone away on his great tenor. Surging as always into new, unexplored realms.

He didn't find it unusual that Coltrane would continue to do this even after his death, but something about seeing him in the tunic, and the mixture of jazz and ancient Rome, seemed disturbing.

"I didn't know they had jazz here," he told Gaius Melissus.

"Only the best. As you can see: The Train, Miles, and there's Clifford Brown."

Clifford Brown, dressed in a party tunic, took over from Trane and exploded into a piercing staccato runaway solo on his gleaming golden trumpet. His tone was even more gorgeous than one remembered. Of course, those were only records, recorded under poor conditions, but here he was in the flesh. Well—in the spirit.

"Hey, Gaius."

An older man and two ripe lovely Roman ladies reclined on a huge red velvet couch.

"Why don't you introduce him to one of my friends?" He winked, smiled a lascivious smile. Wrapped his arm around one of the young ladies' lovely shoulders and draped a hand over one of her bared breasts.

He sensed that Gaius and the other man were trying to distract him from something important, something he was on the verge of understanding, and he turned away.

The wine, music, food, drugs, and people were all swimming around in his consciousness, changing and shifting shapes like ghosts. He had to get outside into the fresh air.

But on his way to the door he stopped before a table with a common everyday lamp on it and stared, his mind finally focusing in on reality. It was his lamp! It belonged at home on his bedroom table. And this little fact was enough for him. Somehow it penetrated to where the other absurd incongruences could never reach.

"It is a dream," he said out loud. "A lucid one."

Then Gaius' arm was around his shoulder, so firm, so real.

"We were hoping you wouldn't find out. Why worry about it? Just accept it as a different form of reality, Marcus."

His name, "Marcus," woke him up another notch.

"But it's not reality. It's all crazy. Part of it is ancient Rome, part of it is twentieth-century U.S. Not exactly my idea of reality. Couldn't you have hired someone to check out the details for verisimilitude, like they do in movies?"

Gaius Melissus laughed. "You must be going to different movies than the ones I catch," he said.

"Don't you understand? It's made up out of your memories. Some of them are memories of Los Angeles, some are memories of ancient Rome."

"How can that be?"

Gaius shrugged. "Listen, don't get sidetracked. Theseus is waiting for you outside in the rose garden."

Outside, the cool air refreshed him. The roses were huge, magnificent, with sweet fruity scents.

"Another flaw," he said out loud. "They didn't have roses in ancient Rome. Or if they did, I'm certain they were little tiny ones without any scent. These huge beauties are quite a recent development."

"It's not so much a flaw as it is an improvement," the old Greek said. "Why not have the best of both worlds?"

"But why ancient Rome and L.A.? That's what I don't get."

Theseus smiled; his dark eyes glowed in the moonlight. Can eyes really do that? Marcus wondered. He wasn't sure of anything anymore.

"Because it's happening in ancient Rome and Los Angeles."

"Wait a minute, hold on there, old boy. You mean something happened in ancient Rome and then recurred in Los Angeles?"

"I mean that something is happening in ancient Rome and Los Angeles, simultaneously, now."

Stunned, Marcus knew, as you can only know in a dream, that this was so.

"How can this be?"

Theseus shrugged. "We're only human, you know. We keep trying to understand reality with our puny brains. Box it up. Control it. But we don't know anything. We never will. And yet we can't ever accept that. That is our tragic fate.

"And here is yours, my son." He held out his hands. The amulet was in them. The black stone glowed.

A terrible fear seized Marcus, so strong he experienced actual vertigo, as if he were suddenly caught in the middle of a whirlwind. His heart was pounding like a drum.

"Take it," the Greek insisted in a firm voice. "Take it now, and forever: it is your fate."

"No." Marcus held out his hands in a warding-off gesture. He squeezed his eyes closed so tightly it hurt his forehead. Wake up, he screamed to himself. You can do it. Now. You've got to wake up.

Heart pounding, mouth dry, and head throbbing, Marcus sat up in bed.

Still half in the dream, half awake, he was aware that someone was in the room with him. With them: he sensed the warm sweet body next to him, Mary Jane, still asleep. But Marcus—no, that was the dream, he was not Marcus, his name was Brice, and suddenly Brice woke clear up, mouth open to scream.

A strange man was in the bedroom. He had obviously been going through Mary Jane's pack. Now he stood up straight, spread his hands, and smiled sheepishly, like a child caught in a minor infraction. He was a tall, lean, dangerous-looking dude, clean-shaven with short hair.

Suddenly Brice recognized him. "Jesus Christ, Quinn," he said, reverting to his childhood nickname for his brother Conal, "you've cut off your beard and hair. You scared the shit out of me."

Mary Jane was sitting up next to him now, oblivious to the fact that the sheets were around her waist and she was not wearing any clothes. Still half asleep.

Conal smiled his sardonic smile. "Good to be home, little bro. Teaching tai chi can be a very rough business.

And I see you've been having a *hard* time while I've been gone, forgive the pun." He eyed Mary Jane with comic lasciviousness. Joke! But, Brice realized with a start, Conal had actually been going through Mary Jane's pack.

7

BY THE TIME Brice had regained his composure and gone out into the living room to talk with his brother, Mary Jane was up and moving around the bedroom, cheerfully singing some weird little tune to herself as she searched out articles of apparel from where she'd tossed them last night. She seemed totally unruffled from the experience of finding a stranger in the room. And Brice's big brother was already seated cross-legged serenely on the hemp rug, waiting in the living room with that dreamy tai chi expression on his face. The only one upset or shocked is me, Brice thought. Should I be? But something was wrong. Brice knew that. Did not know how he knew. But knew for sure.

"Welcome back," he said. "I guess."

His brother smiled suddenly, and it was his old sweet smile. "Hey," he said, "don't strew roses."

"You were going through her pack, Quinn. Just why were you doing that?"

His brother's smile faded. Not for the first time, Brice caught the tinge of sadness in it. The hint of loneliness and solitude hidden beneath the sharply cut, handsome features. Hurt. Secrets never shared. But, as always, it was only a momentary glimpse beneath the mask.

"Ah, Bricey, Bricey, Bricey me boy," he said in his

fake Irish accent. "It's your brother Conal you have here, and nobody named Quinn. Quinn has gone away, Bricey, and he's never coming here again."

Brice shook his head. "I never understand you, Conal," he said. "Which brings us back to the pack. What the hell were you doing there?"

Conal rose up from his cross-legged position, silent as a ghost, without using his hands of course, and put his hand on Brice's shoulder. Brice was startled by the contact. His brother seldom touched him, seldom touched anyone, he realized.

"You have to trust me, Bricey," he said.

"Damn it, Conal, *you* have to trust *me.* You have to tell me what's going on with you. Where you've been for the past . . ."

Conal held up his hands. "Whoa, you're losing me, little bro, you getting a case of amnesia here? Me. Conal. Tai chi class. Jerry's. Up north. Remember?"

"Bullshit," Brice shouted just as Mary Jane came out of the bedroom.

"Oh-oh," she said, "I'll get the coffee on," and headed into the kitchen, still singing her song.

"What's she singing?" Conal said.

" 'I Only Have Eyes For You,' I think," Brice said in a low voice. "Don't change the subject, big bro. You weren't teaching tai chi."

"I sent you a picture, for Christsake," Conal said.

"Yeah, sure you did, Conal. Something about that photo, though. First time I saw it I knew there was something wrong. Yesterday it came to me just as clear as a bell. Last year's photo, Quinn. Same people. Same hairstyles. Same mysterious tai chi expressions, for Christsake. Maybe a different photo, but the same class, right? So where were you really?"

And now, for a moment, Conal looked even sadder than before. Weary. Someone at the end of a road. And

Brice was sure that Conal was about to tell him something, everything, at last. But the moment passed.

"Ah, the mysterious Bricey," he said, "sees all, knows all, tells all. I am impressed. Your powers of perception are growing; someday soon they'll reach a new level where you won't have to ask me questions: you'll effortlessly divine the answers from clues too subtle for the rest of us to notice. The color of dust on my boots, the arrangement of tea leaves in my empty cup, the flight of a bird across the sky."

"You're not going to tell me," Brice said.

"I can't." Conal shook his head, and now for some reason put both of his hands over his eyes. "I need some rest," he said. "Christ, do I need some rest."

"So go lie down in your room," Brice said in a piqued tone of voice.

"Soon," Conal said, "but not yet, little bro. Not quite yet. I've got to get away from here, Bricey. Someplace quiet. *We've* got to get away from here. Together."

"I don't get it," Brice said. "How soon?"

"Right away. Just for a while, little bro, trust me."

Brice glared toward the kitchen.

"Take Mary Jane with you—okay. Fine. Hey, any friend of yours—but soon, okay, little bro?"

"You're serious. Okay, how soon?"

"No rush," Conal said. "We've got time to eat breakfast. Pack a few things."

"Right after breakfast," Brice said. "Just throw some socks and shorts in a bag, and Mary Jane—some socks, shorts, and Mary Jane, right, and we're outta here. Oh, she'll probably love that."

"Hey, with Mary Jane or without Mary Jane, you dig, little bro? Either way's fine with me."

"Well, sure, as long as everything's fine with you. Shit, are you kidding, Conal, or is this for real?"

Conal opened his sad eyes wide; the pupils were dark and bright, intense: that tai chi look was fading fast.

"Oh, for real, little bro. For very, very, truly real."

"Shit," Brice said. "I don't know what to do."

"Then why don't you start packing."

Mary Jane came into the room, and she was still singing to herself in her sweet little voice.

"No eggs," she said. But no one answered. So she just stood there watching them, feeling the tension between them. Still singing to herself, but lower by a notch or two, so you couldn't hear the words at all.

Again Conal reached out and took ahold of Brice's shoulder, squeezed: his slender delicate-looking fingers were like steel, Brice realized with a start.

"Bricey, do you remember the fort? The secret fort that nobody ever knew about but the two of us? What did we used to call it?"

The question was so out of context that for a moment Brice had the shocked sensation that Conal was losing his mind. And indeed, his eyes, with their glittering nervous intensity, gave Conal the classic manic look, awake beyond ordinary wakefulness.

"Yeah, I remember," Brice said. "Why?"

"Just remember," Conal said, "no why."

Then he turned to Mary Jane. "Ah yes, no eggs, quite a dilemma were it not for the invention of the supermart. Little bro here can run down to the corner—well, drive down—while you and I get acquainted. After all, we're going on a trip together."

"Trip?" Mary Jane said. "What trip?"

Brice cleared his throat nervously and said, "Conal and I have to go out of town and I was wondering . . . I wanted to know if you would want to . . ."

"Oh sure, I've got nothing to do but fucking follow you around wherever you go."

"I didn't mean it that way," Brice said. "I just . . . It's just that I just met you, I don't want to lose you, I . . ."

Mary Jane turned and stalked back into the kitchen. Brice turned to Conal. "Shit," he said. "Great. Just great."

Mary Jane came back out again. "Yeah, okay," she said. "You guys want coffee? Let's get going on the eggs, okay? I'm starved." Then she turned abruptly and disappeared back into the kitchen.

"It's going to be all right, bro," Conal said to Brice as he went out the front door. "Believe me, it's all going to be all right."

The coffee was too strong. But that was okay, Conal thought, wake me up. That was the way to stay alive, get through all this, wake up, wake up some more, and just keep on waking up. Don't miss anything. But he had the sensation he was missing something. He was standing holding the cup and sipping from it, while Mary Jane was sitting at the bright yellow Formica-covered kitchen table. She stretched and smiled. Luscious little thing, Conal thought. And now she got up and bounced over to the matching yellow-tile-covered kitchen sink and counter. The tiles were so bright they were gleaming, and Conal had a strange dizzy sensation that if he stared into them he would begin to see things. Secrets would be revealed. Secrets he did not want to know.

He averted his gaze and looked out through the double glass doors into the backyard. The pond, the tai chi platform. He calmed down a notch. Okay. It was all going to be okay. He turned back to Mary Jane. What was she doing fussing with the can of coffee on the counter—didn't she already have a pot on?

"Did you find what you were looking for in my pack? What was it anyway?"

Conal smiled. "You'll never believe it . . . a gun."

"In here," Mary Jane said, and took a small-caliber

handgun out of the coffee can. Probably a Beretta .32, Conal thought—Christ, I'm starting to think like Smith.

So he had missed it. He hadn't been quite awake enough, at that, and everything wasn't going to be all right after all. Think fast, he thought. Ask a question. When she answers, charge her while she's talking. Not much, but it's all I've got.

"Are my eyes open?" he said, not thinking what he was asking, but just trying to get off something fast.

But Mary Jane didn't believe in giving anything away. She just thrust the gun out in front and squeezed off a shot.

Conal felt it punch him and twist him around. Christ, he thought, and twisted back and threw the coffee cup, coffee and all. But something punched him again and then again, so that he never saw if it hit anything, and then he was staring at something amazingly bright and beautiful, sizzling yellow, and there was a mysterious ball of light in the center of it and the light glowed brighter and it was only for a moment that he realized what it was. He was lying on the floor staring up at the ceiling light in the kitchen. Then he forgot again and the light grew brighter and brighter until he let go and went into it.

Mary Jane, using the pretty bright-red-and-white-striped kitchen towel to wipe her prints off the gun, went over and looked down at Conal's body. "Yeah, your eyes are open," she said out loud. Then she began to sing, "Are the stars out tonight, I don't know if it's cloudy or bright. 'Cause I only have eyes for you . . . Quinn."

She tossed the gun on the floor. Kneeled down and, still humming, searched the body. No stone. "I thought not," she said to herself. 'Remember the fort we used to play in, little bro?' Well, let's just ride it out till little bro remembers. Take a little longer, that's all."

Still using the kitchen towel, she fished Conal's wallet out of his back pocket and took the money out of it. There was a lot of it. Good. Her M.O. was, always give the cops something obvious and they would always take it. She didn't know that had been Quinn's M.O. too. But she wouldn't have been surprised. Quinn had been good. He'd just been in the business too long. Hair was starting just to grey. Few grey hairs in this business is all you get, honey.

She tossed the wallet on the hemp rug in the living room and went into the bathroom, where she flushed the bank roll down the toilet. All the time she was moving fast. Little bro would be home soon. Too damn soon.

Opened the glass sliding doors looking out on the backyard. Peaceful scene, that.

"Yeah, they came in through the sliding doors," she said to herself, but aloud. Kicked over a chair in the kitchen. Remembered to toss down her own coffee cup. Fer sure! After all, she had coffee stains all over her blouse, and in fact it had been hot enough to burn, even though Quinn had missed her with the cup.

Tried to tear her blouse but couldn't. Damn. Found a pair of scissors in a kitchen drawer. Hurry. Got it started and then it tore. Kicked one shoe off—good touch.

Now comes the hard part. The part that separates the men from the boys. And Mary Jane from everyone else. Okay. Here goes.

She doubled up her fist and struck herself hard in the nose. Tears welled up in her eyes. Hard but not hard enough. Shit. She hit herself again, harder. Grunted. Good, blood. Once more. Plenty of blood. She dipped her hand in it and spread a little around on her clothes. Not good enough. She hit herself in the eye, once, twice, not too hard. Didn't take much to give yourself a black eye. She could already feel it start to swell. Hurry!

She went over to the wall and smashed her fist into it. Once, twice, until her knuckles were bleeding and her hand was swelling faster than her eye. Nice touch.

Strangely enough, she was crying out loud now. Like

a hurt little girl. Well, that was okay too, might as well get an early start.

One more pretty bad thing. Shit. Nothing for it, she suddenly bashed her head into the wall so hard it made her dizzy and for a moment she thought she was going to pass out. She had to go over and hold onto the table. The dizziness passed, but her head throbbed and suddenly she got sick and threw up, some of it on the sickeningly bright yellow Formica table, but most of it on her torn blouse. She was still leaning on the table, breathing hard, all bruised, swollen, and bloody, and decorated with her own vomit, when Brice came through the door.

He didn't say anything, or even drop the groceries, but just stood there frozen like a statue, mouth and eyes wide-open. At last Mary Jane let herself fall so that her poor aching head hit the table, and from the floor muttered, "Police, call police," before she closed her eyes and tried for some much-needed rest.

8

IT WAS JACKIE the cabdriver who finally dragged Elena from out of her very bad dream and got her on her feet and moving again. The only problem was that she emerged from one nightmare to find herself in another. The headache, dizziness, and other disorienting aftereffects of being drugged didn't help; she had to keep reminding herself this bad dream was for real.

"How'd you find me?" Elena slurred the words as Jackie dragged her up off the bed and got her started walking around.

"Finding you *no problema,* baby. You chust go where the action is. Beautiful woman, I say, only all—*cómo se dice?*—all punched up."

"Punched out," Elena suggested "or maybe beat-up."

"Yeah, and limping like a lame goat, black eye, I tell him.

" 'Chur,' he says to me, 'that's Room 525, just get her and her crazy husband out of this hotel, no charge at all,' he says. 'No more killing anyone in the lobby, but just you go straight on out the door. *Buena suerte* and *hasta la vista,'* right? *'Nunca, por favor.'* "

"Yeah, well, never's soon enough for me too," Elena said, or tried to say, because Jackie was now holding her head in the bathroom sink pouring cold water onto it.

When she went through the lobby, black-eyed, hair hanging down stringy and wet, limping, still obviously woozy so that she had to be supported by Jackie's arm, the poor clerk spotted them approaching and actually jumped back inadvertently away from the counter.

Jackie paused long enough to throw down the keys and remark calmly, "She too stoned to walk, man," and then headed for the door, suitcase in one hand, Elena in the other.

On the drive back to Tres Águilas, Elena passed out again and mercifully slept soundly, which didn't in the least interfere with Jackie's monologue, disguised as conversation. But when she awoke it was quite dark, and there were no streetlights here. They left the cab on the main street (if you could call that dirt road a street), and Jackie practically had to carry her to Garcia's hut, she was so exhausted.

Funny thing, Elena thought, is that after all I've been through here, what scares me the most is facing the old man. You never know what he's going to do.

What he did, strangely enough, was laugh. Not for the first time did Elena notice how much his laughter resembled the cawing of a crow.

Apparently reading her mind, the old man finished off his outburst by cupping his hands around his mouth and cawing. It was such a good imitation that it sent a shiver down her spine, and perhaps due to exhaustion, she felt the weird effects of it rippling through her and into Jackie's body, and then out the door of the hut, like a breeze.

"Did you have a nice trip, Elena?" the old man asked innocently.

And from time to time, she would have to stop in the middle of her account and wait for the old man to finish another fit of laughter.

"My God, Elena," he whispered in his hoarse voice, tears in his eyes. "He tells you to look inside the toilet and you know there isn't anything in there because you already looked, but you bend over and peek down inside while he stabs you in the butt with a needle. Have I got that right? But tell me, won't you, when he shot that dope into you, what did you see down in there?"

"I thin she saw Mickey Mouse down in there in a little boat," the usually silent Garcia threw in.

"I've failed," Elena said solemnly when the laughter died down.

"Are you dead, Elena?" the old man said in a more sober tone of voice. "No? Then you have not failed yet. Do you understand? None of us have the luxury of quitting here. We got to go on through this thing until we win or we die. So you did your best so far. But you got to do better. We all got to do better, and you know what, Elena?" He struggled up to his feet. Now he looked just like any tired old man in the candlelight. Except for the eyes. Elena shook her head, she didn't know what.

"That's just what we were going to do." He nudged Garcia in the ribs. "Only next time don't get so damn physical." The two old men broke into another paroxysm of raucous laughter.

Before long Elena and the old man were back in Jackie's cab, driving into the night.

"I know Quinn," the old man said in a soothing tone of voice. "I know Quinn, as I knew his father before him. His father was a good man too. I used him in much the same capacity as I used Quinn—a soldier. But not just a soldier. A general, or maybe an officer in the commandos." (Maybe a hit man, Elena said to herself.)

"When I say I know a man it means I know his mind, his heart. I know where he lives, where he'll go. But most of all, I know what he'll do when he gets there.

"This thing with Quinn doesn't surprise me that much. In fact, perhaps you will not believe me, Elena, when I tell you that I had considered the possibility that this might happen." (You bet I won't, Elena thought.) "Quinn is strong, smart, let him handle the responsibility of the stone for a while. Let him draw them after him while I rest and regain my powers. We'll have to keep an eye on him, of course. But no, Quinn didn't really do anything much more or less than I had expected him to do. It was you, Elena, who surprised me here." He shook his head in the dark.

After a long pause, just as Elena was drifting again toward blessed sleep, he said: "Quinn lives in Santa Monica."

"Santa Monica?" Elena, jolted awake, couldn't quite place it.

"The City of the Angels," the old man said.

"The U.S.A.? We're going to the U.S.A.?"

"Yes, Elena, we're going to the U.S.A. Hollywood, right? The world can be yours. The only thing you need is money. Lots of money. *No problema."*

"But you never have any money," she mumbled, drifting back toward blessed sleep despite herself.

"That's because I have never needed it," he whispered. "Go to sleep, Elena. You've done your best. Sleep now."

She slept. When she awoke, it was early morning in Acapulco, already getting hot. They were parked, the motor off. The old man was gone. Jackie pointed at a flight of stairs leading up a slope to a modernistic yet Spanish-style mansion. *"Dinero,"* he said.

And later, after a leisurely lunch in one of the airport cafés, when the old man paid Jackie off, to Elena and Jackie's combined astonishment it was in thousand-dollar bills. Twenty of them.

Jackie was so stunned he looked as if he were unable to close his hand on it.

"For what you did for us," the old man said, "no money is enough. When all this is over . . ."

"Do me a favor, man," Jackie interrupted. "Thanks for the *dinero,* but next time you in Acapulco, don't look me out—okay?"

"Up," Elena suggested wearily. "It's 'Don't look me up.' "

"Tha's right," Jackie said, "just forget I ever been born, and let me live to spend this *dinero, gracias."*

"We've already forgot," the old man said. And abruptly turned and walked away. Elena touched Jackie's shoulder, then turned and limped after the old man.

The sun was riding high in Acapulco, and it was, as always, hot. The kind of steamy, wet, unbelievable hot it only gets in the tropics. But by sundown they were already in the City of the Angels, driving a recent-vintage shiny black Chevrolet Caprice Classic off the lot, into the beginning of one of those delicious Southern California summer nights.

"Since you identify with being a Mexicana, Elena, I got you a big Chevy. This is America we got here, Elena, and Mexicans here are supposed to all drive big Chevys." More of his crow laughter.

Elena was now, apparently, already a citizen of the United States, and the proud owner of a Caprice Classic. Only according to all her new ID her name had mysteriously changed to Ellen O'Brian.

"Only I'm not a Mexican anymore, am I, old man? How could I be a Mexican if my name is Ellen O'Brian? Someone named Ellen O'Brian can drive anything she wants, *verdad?"*

"Why, Elena," the old man said in astonishment, "I do believe you're finally starting to learn."

9

BY THE TIME Brice got home from the police station it was growing dark, and it was not really home anymore, and with a shock, a small one like an aftershock to one of those famous California earthquakes, he realized that it would never be home again. It was not just that he was emerging from the day into the oncoming dark of a normal warm summer nightfall, it was as if he were wearily trudging into an unending tunnel of cold, lonely dark.

Earlier, talking to the police, or rather, mostly waiting around to tell the same brief story that he had already told over and over, to some new poker-faced bureaucrat, his past had begun to pour before his inner eye as if it were he dying here instead of his brother Quinn. (Yes, now that he was gone forever, Brice had reverted to thinking of him as he had known him as a child, as Quinn instead of Conal.) In the police station, Brice had feverishly and compulsively relived their childhood, both in between and during all the questioning, as if somehow that would keep Quinn alive.

But gradually, as the afternoon wore on, that process had slowed, the shocking vividness of the images had faded around the edges, the energy of grief had spilled out and out until his mind had entered into a kind of entropy. This is the end of the universe, he realized. When Quinn had died, a universe had died with him. Brice didn't understand this, but he knew unquestionably that it was true: the death of any man was a tragedy of such enormous, far-reaching consequences as to transcend the ability of rational thought to categorize it. *And we all must die.* Brice's mind and heart near burst with the realization of it. Then came quiet. Cold.

I'll sell the place, he thought. Move out of here. Quinn would have loved it. "Get outta L.A. before the big one hits or the gangs get ya." Looks like I'm going to make it, Quinn. Die somewhere else. Of something else.

Brice felt so cold and dead inside that he was surprised to feel the slightest surge of warmth when he was able to identify the slender figure waiting for him on the front porch: Mary Jane.

"Hi, thought you were in the hospital."

"They let me out," she said.

"Thought they'd have you all bandaged up."

"They did," she said, "but I took them off."

Brice looked past her at the front door. "What do I do now?" he said. And suddenly he began softly crying, trying to hold it in, but it came on, an inexorable wave of grief, until he finally just gave in and fell down to his knees on the front lawn, weeping in huge, heartrending sobs.

"What do I do now?" he said again, but you couldn't really understand what he was saying anymore.

Then he felt Mary Jane's arms around him. And it was small comfort, but it was comfort when he needed it most.

"You trust me," Mary Jane said. "You come with me." And yes, Brice figured that was the answer. Only something was missing, something needed to be done.

"Wait," he said. "Wait." And he got up and made his way around the side of the house and into the backyard, and up onto the wooden platform. Where he began to move in slow motion, through the form he had so often watched his brother glide gracefully through. And for the first time he could concentrate fully, see his mistakes, understand what he would have to do to smooth things out, get it right, like his brother had. I'll work on it till I've got it, he silently promised his brother. Soon as I get straightened out, that's what I'll do.

When it was over he felt a little better, but numb, still numb.

He was sitting beside Mary Jane in her car, watching her slam the five-speed transmission through its paces, phased out, when it finally dawned on him just what he was seeing here.

"I thought you hated sports cars?" Brice said.

"I do, believe me, I do. I hate to go out with guys who drive them. I can't relax. But I can't do without this monster. I drive like a maniac. I'd kill myself in anything else." She smiled happily.

It's true, Brice thought to himself as she whipped the killer Porsche around a curve, wheels squealing, slipping, and finally taking hold as Mary Jane spiked on the gas and ripped the little car back onto the straightaway.

In an astonishingly brief period of time they were in Malibu. As they turned onto one of the side roads that led off the highway toward the cliffs and beach, the big black Chevy that was following them was just barely able to keep them in sight.

"One thing I've got to tell you," Mary Jane said as she pulled in the driveway to her beach house. "I know it hurts to talk about it, but I think we've got to. What I told the police wasn't exactly the truth."

Brice was staring at her with wide, red, unblinking eyes.

"Well, it was the truth as far as it went, but it wasn't all of the truth. Those two guys who killed your brother, it wasn't money they were after."

"What," Brice said slowly and precisely, "were they after?"

"The big one with the moustache kept slapping me around while the little one kept asking me over and over, 'Where is it?' "

"Where is what?"

"That's what I kept asking, 'What?' Every time I said 'What?' the big guy would hit me again. I think he said something about a stone or a gem or something like that, but I'm not sure. I was pretty groggy and scared out of my wits. Does any of this make any sense to you, Brice?"

Brice shook his head. "No sense at all," he said, getting out of the car.

Shiny red Porsche, modern-style house on a Malibu cliff with a wall of windows overlooking the ocean. It finally came home to him. "You're rich," he said.

Mary Jane shrugged. "I've got what I need. I worked hard for it."

At the front door, with the key in the lock, she paused. "Listen, I've got the key to a beach I share with a few of the neighbors. It's very peaceful there. Let's go down and relax for a few minutes."

Brice looked puzzled. "It's dark."

"Trust me," Mary Janc said. "It'll soothe your soul. You'll see."

Her key opened the gate to a high wire-mesh fence, and from there the two of them silently descended a fairly steep path that led down onto the beach. Mary Jane stepped out of her sandals and they moved out to the edge of the water. It was another warm spring night, like last night. God, Brice thought, was that only last night? First the concert, Mary Jane, then the dream, then Quinn. That peculiar dream kept tugging at the edges of his thought, something about ancient Rome, a stone, like Mary Jane had said, a stone or a gem.

As if reading his thoughts, she said, "If you don't

know anything about the stone or whatever it was they were after, do you know where Quinn might have hidden it?"

Brice shook his head.

"You sure?" Mary Jane said, kicking the sand absently with her bare toes.

"What difference does it make?" Brice said. "What the hell difference does any of it make, anyway?"

"Yeah, maybe you're right," Mary Jane said. "Maybe it's better to just forget the whole scene. Let's go back, okay? It's getting cold."

It wasn't until they had crossed the wide expanse of sand and were almost to the path that led back up the cliff that Brice noticed the two figures waiting for them on the path.

One of them, a big guy with a moustache, stepped out onto the sand to meet them. When he came out of the shadow of the cliff, you could see he had a gun.

"Oh shit, it's him," Mary Jane said in a harsh whisper.

"Lovely evening," the man with the moustache said. "Thought we might have a little chat. But that's quite close enough. Hold it right there."

Without changing pace, Brice kept walking toward him.

"I said, hold it there."

Now the little man moved out of the shadows. He was pointing an enormous gun in their direction, obviously a magnum of some sort.

Brice just kept coming.

"I'll shoot," the big man said.

Who cares? Brice thought, but didn't bother to say, and now threw a wild punch.

The big man backed easily out of range and then stepped back in again and rapped Brice sharply on the head with the barrel of his revolver.

Brice went down. His head was ringing like a bell from the blow, and when the numbness faded a little, he felt something warm and liquid running down his forehead.

"I said stop," the big guy reminded him. "You would do well to listen to what I say."

The little guy snickered and said, "Yeah, that's right. Where's the stone, see? That's all we want. You tell us where the stone is, you get to live, see? Simple."

Brice got up. Wild swing, he thought. Quinn would be ashamed of me.

"Sure, I'll tell you where the stone is," he said, and threw a stiff straight right hand, taking care not to telegraph with either his shoulders or his expression. And this time he caught the little guy square in the nose, not hard enough to knock him down, but hard enough to make him bend over and put his hands to his face and say "Shit." In fact, hard enough to make him forget he had the big gun in his right hand, so that he accidentally poked himself in the cheek with the cylinder and said "Shit" again.

Brice was watching him with something like satisfaction when the big guy caught him on the head again. This time he staggered but didn't go down.

"I trust you're not stupid enough to try my patience again," the big guy said, "because I assure you I'll shoot."

"Yeah," the little guy said, "you better tell me where that goddamn stone is before I lose my . . ."

Since he was within reach and Brice had managed to hit him before, he swung on him again. Never change a winning game, as Quinn used to tell him. And what do you know, not only did he catch the little bastard square, but this time the guy went down.

But then a moment later, so did Brice. Head ringing, he sat in the sand watching the guy with the moustache pointing the gun at him, reading his grim expression. Okay, Brice thought, this is it.

He was vaguely aware of Mary Jane, who had been standing behind him, frozen with fear, suddenly taking a couple of quick steps and diving on the little guy, who was still down.

The big man with the moustache turned and pointed the gun toward Mary Jane, but apparently hesitated to shoot for fear of hitting his partner.

Suddenly there was a deafening noise, once, twice, so loud that at first Brice didn't believe it could be from a handgun.

But the man with the moustache jerked back and around and then twisted back, held out his hands toward Brice. But his gun was gone, and there was a dark patch spreading on his shirt. Then he crumpled and fell.

Brice twisted around to see Mary Jane and the small guy still struggling over the big gun. But Mary Jane had it, and now just as Brice helplessly watched the little guy grab hold of the barrel and try to wrench it out of her hand, Mary Jane made a huge effort and twisted it back and pulled the trigger and kept on pulling the trigger.

Brice struggled to his feet and swayed dizzily in the soft sand. Mary Jane was trying to say something, but he was still deaf from the gunshots; he pointed to his ears.

"Got to get out of here, quick," Mary Jane shouted. "Right now."

"Are they dead?" Brice said.

"You bet your pet bunny they're dead. Come on. Right now, baby."

And when they reached the top of the cliff, totally out of breath, and Brice headed for the front door, Mary Jane steered him toward the Porsche.

"All the way out of here. How do we know there's only two of them?"

Brice's head was still ringing when he got in the car, and Mary Jane kicked it over and threw it into reverse and spun out of the driveway and back out toward the coast highway.

The two corpses sprawled out in the sand waited until they heard the unmistakable throaty roar of the sweet Porsche motor way up the cliff, before they sat up. Better safe than sorry, they figured.

"I hope that red shit all over your shirt is catsup," the little one said. "I am starved."

"Ah, always the gourmet," the tall, slightly portly one with the moustache replied.

"Yeah, right," the little one said, "just as long as it's fuckin' food. Right? What do you think, it all went pretty good?"

"Yeah, I guess so," the big guy with the moustache said. "I still think she's a bit fey. What if I made a mistake and hit him too hard with the gun barrel?"

"Still," the little guy said, "it worked out okay. You can't blame her for that. Who'd have thought the crazy bastard would come out swinging, with a gun barrel practically stuffed down his throat?"

"She can improvise," the big guy said.

"Mary Jane's the best," the little guy nodded. "She knows what she's doing. All she's gotta do is hang in there. He'll take her to the stone, sooner or later."

"S'pose so. Still, I'd rather just beat it out of him."

The little guy snorted at this. Held out his hand to help the big guy up.

"Fat chance," he said. "Did you get a look in his eyes when he was doin' his kamikaze number on us? Tell you what, he don't care, see? Not anymore. He's had all he can take and don't care about anything anymore. You could beat on him until he was fucking bits and pieces and he wouldn't tell you shit, 'cause he just don't care."

The big man with the moustache looked piqued. "How would you know? You're so in love with yourself you get upset if your hair gets mussed."

The little guy snorted with laughter again. "That's how I know," he said. "I leave the guys like him to Mary Jane. Come on. Let's get out of here before someone comes to see what all the fuss was about."

"Sure," the big guy said, " 'Rich Malibu Citizens Rush Down to Beach at Night to Check on Gunshots,' the headlines will read."

"Yeah, you're right there," the little guy answered. "They're all boarded in up there, hiding out under their beds. Probably spend so much time there they got TVs installed under them."

Laughing and joking, the two men made their way up the cliff. And as they had anticipated, no brave rich Malibu citizens came rushing out in the night to apprehend them. But ten minutes later they passed a police car heading back the way they had come.

"At least they were brave enough to phone," the little man said.

"Tell you what," the big man with the moustache said, "let's celebrate. My treat. Nouveau French, Chinese maybe?"

"Yeah, sure," the little guy answered. "Anything's okay. We got the catsup on our shirts."

10

The Sea View Motel was almost as original as its name. And then there was the weather. Either the weather had suddenly devolved toward winter, or else the short drive out of L.A. and a couple of hours north was enough to cause a noticeable change of climate. And it was not for the better, as Mary Jane viewed it. Nothing much that was happening here was for the better. Ah well, Mary Jane said to herself, patience is my forte—well, maybe patience and ruthlessness.

She pulled the curtain and peeked out the window at the famous Sea View Motel's sea view. Cold and overcast. This was the third straight day of cold and overcast, and in more ways than just the weather. She scanned the beach for Brice, and couldn't find him. But he was out there, all right. Sitting in the sand staring out into the sea. Because that was all he had done since they had driven up here.

As soon as he had spotted this nowhere dump, he insisted they pull in and rent—get this—separate bungalows. No sex, because he was already in a confused state of mind and sex would only further confuse him. "How long are we going to stay here, while you—er—straighten out your mind?" she had asked him.

"As long as it takes."

Of course she knew what he was doing: he was behaving like he thought his supercool, tai chi, laid-back big brother would have behaved. Mary Jane always knew pretty much what anyone she was working on was thinking. Mind reading's my forte, she thought. Well—maybe mind reading and ruthlessness.

What got to her was that she couldn't tell Brice what his big brother was really like: a sort of samurai daredevil madman, when he wasn't busy being Brice's California-style easygoing big bro. Pretty easy to be laid-back when you returned from one of Quinn's little business trips alive. She knew that much from experience. Empathy's my forte, she thought. Well—maybe empathy and ruthlessness.

What also got to her was the motel room she was in. Jesus Christ, she could stand anything, but this . . . ? The dull 1950s modern-style boxlike room with the dull beige curtains and carpet, painting of sad-faced clown—aw, too bad, fella—and African lion (clown and lion?). The fucking coffee table with the ceramic black panther toting a lampshade on its back. Jesus Christ, let's play: "How Many Secret Agents Have Committed Suicide in This Room?" (Mary Jane liked to think of herself as a secret agent.) Mary Jane bets fourteen. —No? Too low? Twenty-five? Still too low?

Now it's time for the most interesting topic of the day: what time is it? Okay, Mary Jane, you go first. Ten o'clock. Wrong! It's fucking twelve o'clock noon. Wonderful, I've slept till noon. Brice was probably in the restaurant across the highway by now, eating one of those terrific gourmet lunches you got at Billy's Café. Maybe clearing his palate with a mouthful of diet Pepsi, right? Hell with him, just leave him alone until he comes around. And he will come around. Sooner or later they all come around to cute little Mary Jane. After all, patience is my forte—Jesus, now I'm starting to repeat myself.

Anyhow, there's nothing to do, so do nothing, right? Only question is, do I go back to bed or go out on the fucking beach and stare out into the fucking ocean? Mary Jane wasn't really that much of a nature lover; she went back to sleep. Perchance to dream, she thought, hopefully in Technicolor. But in fact, Mary Jane only dreamed in black-and-white, dull but cunning dreams as intricate as spiderwebs, where she struggled and won and struggled and won, but no matter how many times she won, she always found herself enmeshed in some other trying situation. Ah well, patience was her forte. Better be!

Meanwhile Brice was in fact just now settling down across the highway in Billy's, about to bite into a Billy's Big Boy. Brice smiled at that. He knew that if Quinn were here, he would surely be telling Brice, "My God, Bricey, whatever you do, don't bite Billy's Big Boy. You know how it is with that deviant-lifestyle stuff. One bite and you'll be out shopping for the ring."

Suddenly he registered fully the woman he had been staring at without seeing. The one at the next table. It was her, the drop-dead beauty he had seen in here yesterday and the day before. She obviously thought he was smiling at her. Yet she did not smile in return. She just stared straight into his eyes with those gorgeous green eyes of hers; there was something unnerving about the intensity of that stare. He wanted to tell her that you don't just stare at a stranger like that without any expression at all on your drop-dead gorgeous face, no no no, you smile or you look away. Or you smile *and* look away. But there she was with that "look into my eyes" approach. What do I do now?

Don't do anything, Quinn would say. Just bite your Billy's Big Boy and wait. Not only that, but don't do anything ever, until it's clear what to do. That was always Quinn's advice, and that's what Brice was doing. Nothing. But things weren't really clearing up all that fast. Should he go back and tell the police? ("Believe me," Mary Jane had advised him, "whenever you shoot two men full of .357 magnum bullets, you don't want to tell the police about it. As wonderful as L.A.'s Finest are, they might just decide to put you in jail for about a million years so they can let out some poor misunderstood rape-torture killer who's been in there all week, and still keep their quota full.")

Did that make sense? But even if it didn't, Mary Jane had saved his life, so wasn't it up to her to decide about the police? And what about the stone or amulet or whatever it was? Of course Brice had a good idea where it was. The old fort. Aunt Miriam's house. Brice smiled.

It had been Quinn's idea to build the underground fort, and it had been Quinn who had done most of the work, Brice having been just too young to have done much more than follow his older brother around and hand him stuff. But it was Brice who had enjoyed it the most. For him it had been practically holy ground. No little kid but Quinn could have accomplished it, so Brice had always considered it to be a symbol of Quinn's power. And even now, thinking about it was to realize that his brother had been a meteor racing across the heavens of Brice's life, lighting up the sky and burning out before it could touch the earth.

What other kid of fourteen would have spent a month digging out the enormous rooms and passageways? What other kid of fourteen would have actually saved all his lunch money and allowance (as well as his brother's) to rent the cement mixer, then spend day after day of vacation slaving to lay the cement floors?

Dad had been on one of his many trips, and there had been no one to help Quinn out. And the first batch of cement had been bad and Quinn had discovered that a wheelbarrow full of cement was too heavy for him to handle, and it had even rained. Nothing went right. But that hadn't stopped Quinn. In fact, nothing had ever stopped Quinn from the time he was born until four days ago.

The walls had been even more difficult. At first Quinn had thought that he could just paste the cement on the dirt and make a wall that way. Fat chance! "Okay," he had said to Brice, "we'll figure out some other way." And he had. Begging, stealing, and borrowing junk lumber from all over town, they had constructed a ramshackle sort of wooden wall a few inches in from the dirt wall, and then poured the cement in between. When it had hardened, they tore down the wooden wall and rebuilt it on the other side. It only took him and Brice two weeks. And it had been hell for Brice. Painful blisters on all of his fingers, dazed from the summer heat, and weary and bored, bored, bored. The only thing that had kept him going was his awe of his big brother's genius. The cement walls came up to within approximately a foot of the surface. And now, Brice figured, they were at a dead end. They needed wood and lots of it, good wood, not junk lumber. The plan had been to lay wood planks across the walls and then cover them up with tar paper. Then you covered it all in with dirt and let the weeds grow back. A year later and you could walk across it, kids could play on it, and never guess that right underneath them was a humongous killer secret fort.

"Only where we gonna get the money for the wood, Quinn?"

But Quinn had smiled that old devil smile of his.

"*No problema, hermano mío.* You know our bank accounts in the good old B of A?"

Brice had started to shake. "Dad will kill us." Dad had given both of the boys a small amount of money to open accounts at the Bank of America. From then on, a percentage of their birthday money and any other windfalls was to be deposited. The idea was for them to learn to manage their own money, take on a little responsibility.

"But Dad's not here. Alas, he's left his two waifs alone to forge for themselves, with only the slightest of assists from their somewhat addled Aunt Miriam, once too often, I fear. The boys, without the aid of an adult's mature judgment, are about to close out their accounts."

"But he'll kill us when he gets back."

"But by then," Quinn had said, "we'll have our fort."

That was Quinn, all right. Pure essence of Quinn. And Dad had killed them, or anyway done his best.

"I figure it was mostly you," Dad had said to Quinn.

"Wrong," Quinn replied, "not mostly me. All me. I made Bricey do it. Bent his arm up behind his back." (Which Dad must have known was pure Quinn bullshit.) "I did it and I'm glad. It was my money and I used it the way I wanted to. I'd do it again."

Dad had smiled at that. "Oh yeah, what if I don't go out of town?"

Quinn had smiled back and said, "Going out of town is what you're all about, Pops."

Dad had flinched as if he had been slapped in the face. And that had been pure Quinn, too. There just plain had never been anyone like him.

"You're crying."

Shocked out of the past, Brice realized that the knockout strawberry blonde with the huge green eyes had just sat down at his table.

She sure knew how to start up a conversation.

"Yeah," he said, "I always cry at lunch. It's Billy's big burgers, I think."

"I can believe that," she said, same serious expression on her lovely, lovely face. —No, add another "lovely," Brice thought.

"I hope you'll forgive me for being so blunt, but you're the most beautiful woman I've ever seen."

She stared into his eyes and said, still as poker-faced as ever, "So what?"

"So what?" Brice repeated. "Let's see, 'So what?' Well, how 'bout 'You're the most beautiful woman I've ever seen, but why are you sitting down at my table?' "

She nodded. Okay. "To eat lunch," she said. Wow, now they were really getting someplace.

Thick, straight, strawberry-blond hair, parted in the middle, thick and long, all the way to that slender waist, green eyes, and creamy pale freckled skin. Was that a slight accent? Where was she from? But you don't just ask a stranger where she's from, do you?

"Where are you from?" Brice asked her.

For the first time since he had seen her, she smiled, but it was an enigmatic smile, naturally.

"I'm getting confused about that myself. My name's Elena, or my name's Ellen O'Brian. I must be either Irish or Mexican, or maybe something else. Maybe I'm a citizen of nowhere. You're not crying anymore."

"I'm crying inside, where the burger is," he said. "But now comes the question of the day. What are you doing here, with me—besides eating lunch? What do you want?"

"I want you to come with me to my room, the one next to yours, as a matter of fact."

Brice was stunned. And somehow, even though he felt it should be, the surprise was not all that pleasant. Things were just happening too fast and too unpredictably for him to sort them out.

"Oh, for Godsake," Elena said, "I don't want to screw you, I just want you to talk to the old man."

"Great," Brice said. "Tell you what, Ellen, or Elena, why don't *you* get up and go talk to the old man, okay? You never know, it sounds like something I might want to do; so, soon as I figure out just exactly why, I'll be along. But why don't you just get up and go without me, for right now?"

"I'll give you three real good reasons," she said in that rich, low, husky voice of hers, and she reached across the table and took hold of his hand, sending something rather like a strong electrical shock through his body, down his spine, and on down through his toes. With her other hand she took hold of his index finger.

"One," she said, "because you want to know about the stone." Still staring into his eyes, she now took hold of his middle finger and said: "Two, you want to know about Quinn. And three"—she took hold of the next finger—"you want to know about yourself. And one for the road, here, a little bonus maybe." She took hold of his little finger. "You want to understand the nature of existence."

She let go of his hand, got up, and turned and started to walk away, without looking back.

Brice scrambled up and fished a crumpled five out of his pocket, tossed it on the table, and ran outside to catch up with her. She was waiting for the traffic to calm down so she could cross the highway. "So many cars," she said, more to herself than to him, "going so fast. All the time. Nowhere. Know what I mean?"

"Can the old man really do that stuff? I mean, reveal the nature of existence? I mean, come on, that's pretty heady stuff."

"You bet he can," she said. "That's what I like the least about him."

And when she had led him across the highway to the bungalow next to his (Mary Jane on one side and Elena on the other), damn if the old man didn't look like just the kind of guy who could explain the universe to you. He was so old. Long scruffy snow-white hair and beard, huge round heavily hooded dark, dark eyes. He looked like one of those gurus you see on the cover of those popular books: *New Age Yoga,* or maybe *The Dawning of the Aquarian Age.*

Now he laughed out loud. It was a loose raucous burst of laughter, but somehow free and beautiful. From it you knew instinctively that here was someone real, someone free of worries or inhibitions.

"What?" he said when he finally stopped laughing.

"Me worry?" More laughter. Then he said, "No, I'm nothing like those guys who write those books. I'm a man who has been cursed with power. Power enough to destroy the world or to save it."

"That sounds like it could be either a curse or a blessing," Brice said numbly, mind reeling with the new understanding that this man was reading his mind.

"No way," the old man said. "The only real blessing in life is to be left alone. To be ordinary. And that's not going to happen to me. Or to you, for that matter. Everything else is a curse of some kind; you just have to figure out what kind. In fact, you might say that enlightenment is simply the process of figuring out what curse you're under."

More laughter. "The funny part is that it should be easy, because you know what? You're the one who laid the hex on yourself, did you know that, Elena?"

"Gee, no," Elena said. "I don't know how I ever got along without knowing that."

"You're just lucky," the old man said. "Problem is that all of your luck is bad." More laughter. And the woman Elena looked absolutely furious, green eyes blazing. Brice got the feeling that this sort of thing went on all of the time between the two of them.

"In our sleep," the old man got in.

"Meanwhile, while there's a brief letup, let me tell you about the stone, and about your brother, Quinn. Would you like to sit down? You can sit in that squat ugly chair if you like. Or the bed. I myself prefer the floor."

So I noticed, Brice thought, but said: "No, just say what you want to say, so we can get this over with."

"I'm afraid you're going to be standing a long time," the old man said. And he then calmly proceeded to tell Brice the wildest, most incredible story he had ever heard in his life.

"You expect me to believe that?" Brice had asked him in an awed tone of voice.

"Belief doesn't enter into it," the old man said. "You know that it's true, because of your dreams. Because you know that they aren't just dreams, but something more. Something trying to reveal to you in a different way the same story I've just told you."

Brice swallowed. "How did you know about my dreams?" he said.

"Exactly," the old man replied, his wide-open round eyes gleaming.

All at once, Brice just gave up. It was as if all his defenses were blown, not so much by the old man's crazy story, but just by the bombardment of strangeness after strangeness pounding away at his armor of rationality. For that's all it was, was armor. A belief that the world was sane; and, like all beliefs, rationality was a fairy tale, a "don't you wish" sort of thing. The real world was crazy. Chaos, he thought. We never actually built an orderly world out of chaos, we only built the illusion of an orderly world. Sooner or later the insanity of the ground seeped through the illusion and shattered your precious dream.

"I prefer to think of it as mysterious," the old man said. "But insane will do just as well."

Brice had his face buried in his hands. He did not want to look into the old man's eyes.

"And you want me to accept that I'm a reincarnation of that guy Marcus that I keep dreaming about in ancient Rome, right?"

The old man said nothing.

"And what does that make you? A reincarnation of the Greek? Theseus?"

He opened his eyes and looked into the old man's, and held his breath waiting for the answer, afraid of what it might be.

"No," the old man said, "I'm not a reincarnation of anyone."

And for a moment it didn't register on Brice and he just stood there locked with the old man eye-to-eye, waiting. Then with a shock greater than any he had felt yet, it came home.

"You *are* Theseus," he stammered.

Now the old man broke out into another long, loose, whooping fit of laughter, and Brice turned and abruptly stormed out of the room, slamming the door behind him.

There was a roaring sound in his ears, like time rushing down a huge empty tunnel, life after life after life pouring on and on to build the world, flowering up ahead, only to crumble in the wake. On and on. Forever.

He was aware that Mary Jane had appeared from out of somewhere and was talking to him, but it just wasn't getting through. She looked angry to him, over some meaningless triviality or other: what was he doing in there, or why wasn't he talking to her, or something.

He managed to tell her, "Leave me alone." And went into his own bungalow and closed the door, and, groggy now, feeling like it was he and not the old man who was the poor guy who'd lived through almost two thousand years of the great human tragicomedy, he practically collapsed on the bed, where he was so groggy that it made him dizzy to have his eyes open. So he quickly closed them and rushed into the blessed oblivion of sleep, like time rushing down that endless tunnel.

Sleep—perchance to dream. Aye, there's the rub, all right.

11

HE WAS TRYING to dream, struggling to live out that other life again, so long ago, so far away. But he *could* bring it here; here, now. He was just stepping into it when something pulled him back out again.

He opened his eyes and for a moment he was still in ancient Rome, because it was like a scene from ancient Rome that greeted him.

The beautiful green-eyed Elena, with her creamy freckled skin and her shock of thick blond hair. She wore one plain silver bracelet on her left wrist, and that was all. Slave girl. She said in a rather lugubrious tone of voice: "It seems I'm going to screw you after all."

Panicked, Brice sat up. His shoes and socks were off, and he had not taken them off; that must be what had woken him up. Filled with the resolve to follow his original plan to remain celibate until his mind cleared (if ever), he tried to say something that would sound forceful, but all he could manage was: "How'd you get in here?"

She said, "I have my ways." Then quickly, "No, I'm just joking—you left your key in the door."

Brice tried to say, "I don't want this," but couldn't speak. Tried to think, "I don't want this," but could only think "Botticelli's Venus," and it was crazy but true. She did resemble that ridiculous, almost comic-book-style combination of the ethereal and the sensual. And she was alive. I do want to, he thought. More than anything, I do want to.

As if reading his mind, she smiled, for only the second time since he had first seen her, but even this smile was slight and rather sad, like the momentary vision of a lovely flower through mist.

"Let me take your clothes off," she said. And when she leaned down, he saw that one of her eyes, which were both masked by eye shadow, was slightly darker around the outside area than the other: My black-eyed limping Venus, he thought tenderly, as her mouth found his. But he didn't wonder at this. It seemed to him that everybody was bruised, beat-up, and wounded these days.

But we keep going, and this, this is what keeps us all going.

Mary Jane had initiated him into the true mystery of sex. Mary Jane and marijuana. They had opened the door for him to step outside of time and experience the act fresh and new, as if it were the first time. And he had wondered, not without some apprehension, if it was only the influence of the drug or of Mary Jane herself, and thus the experience would be a chain which would bind him to her, to it.

But here it all was again. Only this time it was even more wonderful and more unique. More that indescribable sensation of being just newly invented and yet at the same time primeval, ancient. More the sensation of a dance. The ultimate dance, the dance of which all other dances are only empty symbols.

Once, when she was on top, she floated down to him, showering him with her rusty golden hair, and she bit his lip, sharply, enough to hurt. Then sat up straight and, swaying like a palm in the breeze, staring down into his eyes, she said, incredibly: "I am the only woman. You are the only man."

Later he lay silently, luxuriating in the afterglow of

bliss, with his eyes closed, not realizing what she was doing until he heard the soft click of the door latch. When he opened his eyes, she was gone.

Back in the bungalow she shared with the old man, Elena gave her report. The old man was, as always, sitting on the carpet cross-legged, with his back against the wall, ignoring the two absurd little fat puffy chairs. As he had often pointed out to Elena, sitting in furniture was like walking on crutches: it was okay if there was something wrong with you.

"You seem disturbed, Elena," he said. "Why should you be disturbed?"

"I feel like a whore," she said in her low calm voice.

"No," the old man said, "you are nothing like a whore, Elena. Whores are simple people. Victims of their own simplicity. All a whore wants is some money and some comfort without having to go out into the world and struggle and fight for it. You, Elena, you want the world, and you are willing to do anything to get it."

"Not very sympathetic," Elena said.

The old man shrugged. "Whores are victims of themselves, as are we all, Elena. Did you enjoy yourself?"

"Damn you." Elena's face flushed with emotion, a rare display for sure, the old man thought. Her hands were balled into fists.

The old man shook his head sadly. "Elena, Elena, Elena," he said softly, "I am already damned. As are you. Human beings are such miserable fools. Why do you all make such a big deal out of sex? Any dog can do it. If I ask you a question, it is because I need the answer. Did you enjoy yourself?"

"Yes," she hissed. "Didn't you order me to?"

"Good." The old man waved his hands languidly in the air and nodded his head. "That's good. Did you get up on top of him and bite his lips and say" (here he parodied the voice of a woman), " 'I am the only woman; you are the only man' "?

"Yes, yes, yes, I did everything you told me, said everything you told me to, okay?"

And now it was Elena who was crying. "I don't understand any of this. Who's his girlfriend with the shiny red toy car? What are they doing here in separate rooms? What's her part in all of this, anyway?"

The old man shook his head. "You're always complicating everything, Elena. Like you complicate sex. The fact is we have no need to know who she is or what she is doing here with Quinn's brother. It is obvious that whatever control she has over him, if any, she has got by sex. You only have to look at her to know that. Whatever chains sex can forge, sex can break. And, hopefully, you have broken them for him. It's up to him now to deal with her."

"But what if he doesn't?"

The old man went into one of his laughing fits: Elena figured it was overdue.

"Then you didn't enjoy yourself as much as I told you."

12

IT WAS RAINING. Strange; that didn't seem quite right, yet Brice could plainly hear it. But something was wrong about the direction of the sound; it was not coming from outside. No, the sound of rain was coming from deep down inside his consciousness.

Brice seized upon this knowledge eagerly as a way to enter into the dream. *Listen to the rain.* It pattered down on the immense ramshackle apartment buildings, some of them towering six stories or more into the Roman night. In some of the first-floor flats, the living was easy, the tenants slept cozily, all warm and dry. But as you rose up into the higher stories, the smaller the flats, the lower the price, until you finally got to the top-floor hovels where the poor huddled together, some of them in windowless rooms, waiting for the roofs to cave in or a fire to break out. Listening to the rain or maybe watching it leak through the roof onto their shabby furniture.

And way up there at the top of the hill, the rain also pattered down on the rooftops of the houses of the rich, and on the low, wide, two-story mansion of Gaius Melissus.

But I should be inside, Marcus-Brice realized, and thus I wouldn't be hearing it like this, seeing it like this.

And so he was. He slowly drifted in between the

elegant twin marble columns into the elaborately decorated long straight hallway. And straight down past the many curtain-covered doorways, and outside into the rain again in the atrium. And on across the atrium, the rain pounding down now onto the glistening tile mosaic where Alexander the Great relentlessly played out his many campaigns. It splattered off of the statues of gaily dancing water nymphs and into the fountains and ponds.

And still Marcus-Brice drifted on, through the Corinthian marble columns and straight down the hallway, where up ahead the second, more elaborate courtyard awaited him.

And on, and into this second, even more elaborate outdoor courtyard, a veritable garden of thirsty bright flowers reaching up into the rain. Shadowy statues gesturing dramatically out into the downpour. Past the two men standing outside, heedless as the statues of the falling sheets of water; drifted past them and on toward the cacophony of noise in the far room. Yes, that was where the party was. But suddenly Marcus-Brice was drawn back toward the two figures standing outside in the rain, was snapped back toward them as if he were a ball on a rubber string. Yes, this was it: this was the essence of the dream!

There was a peculiar turning-inside-out at this realization, and Brice disappeared, and all that was left was Marcus standing in the rain facing the old Greek, Theseus. Staring into the old man's eyes. The eyes! Wasn't he supposed to recognize something about the eyes? He couldn't remember what it was. And they seemed quite unfamiliar to him. Just eyes.

"Should it be raining?" he said. "It doesn't seem to me that it was raining before."

"Oh, that was probably just a dream," Theseus replied. "Concentrate on what I'm telling you here. Concentrate on your destiny. The stone."

Marcus stared at the stone the Greek held out in his

hands, as if offering it up to the rain. Hardly an exotic gem, though. It was quite large. It looked like common obsidian, black, uneven, unworked, opaque; and yet, was it his imagination, or did it glow softly from within, from some unknown source of energy?

"No, I won't take it, I've decided that much."

The old man's expression was sad, knowing, enduring; but where was the loose cackling laughter? These sad Greek eyes tilted down at the corners; these were not the mocking owlish eyes Marcus had expected to find. Strange, he thought, I seem to be looking for something here, trying to recognize someone, but I can't remember who or what it is.

"You must take the stone," the old Greek said, "or we are all lost."

Suddenly Marcus remembered exactly where he was and what he was doing here. He had to get out. Now. Fast.

"I said no," he snapped, and brushing the old man gently aside, he rushed away from the party, across the courtyard and back down the long narrow hall, across the atrium and again down the long hall, until he was finally outside, running in the narrow Street of Mercury. Across the street and down the hill a short ways, he took shelter under the awning of one of the few ritzy shops that were allowed in this high-class residential area. Here he waited and watched until the small troop of crack Praetorian Guards that served these days as the Emperor's secret police passed by, heading up Mercury Street to the summit and Gaius Melissus' mansion.

I betrayed them, Marcus thought. Drusilla and I. But I had no choice, really. Drusilla would have destroyed them anyhow, and me along with them.

Now he could hear the shouts, though they were muffled by the rain and distance. Still, he could hear them.

They're not arresting them, as Drusilla told me they would. They're slaughtering them like sheep. Of course I really knew they would do that, didn't I? But why am I standing here? Shouldn't I be running from something? What is that awful pounding noise?

Suddenly the dream changed into a full-fledged nightmare, more a feeling than anything else, an overwhelming wave of raw horror emanating from his heart, for that awful pounding was his heart.

And he was running now, down one narrow street and up another, whatever it was close upon his heels. He turned off a narrow street into an even narrower alley. Plowed through the slippery surface blend of mud and other, unmentionable slime, sliding, skidding, sometimes falling to his knees, heart pounding, head throbbing in time with his racing heart. He wasn't even surprised when he came to the dead end. Terrified, but not surprised. He had been through it all before, and yet he searched frantically for some way to alter the awful scene, so desperately that he almost gave in to the compulsion to just keep on running and try to smash through the wall that blocked him off. Anything but turn and face the shadowy figure which had been relentlessly pursuing him.

But, as he knew he would, he turned and watched, with pounding heart more than with his eyes, that slender figure approaching him slowly and easily through the downpour. It was Corbo the gladiator, and he was smiling that mocking familiar smile of his; and even in the dark alley Marcus caught the glint of a dagger in his right hand, but now it flickered from right to left as he playfully tossed it back and forth.

Trying to sound brave, Marcus said, "I have one of my own." And took out his own dagger and held it out in front of him.

But Corbo's smile only widened, and he said, "So much the better, I always enjoy a fight."

So Drusilla had betrayed her husband Gaius with Marcus, and then Marcus with Corbo.

"She'll betray you too, you know," he said to Corbo.

"I won't give her the chance," Corbo said. "I'm not a weak fool like you, Marcus."

"There was nothing I could do," Marcus said, as suddenly Corbo caught the dagger in his left hand, darted in with astonishing speed, and lunged with it at Marcus' chest. Marcus fended it off desperately with his own dagger, and Corbo sprang back out of range as easily as he had attacked.

"Very good," he said. "You're quicker than I'd have thought. Where were we? Oh yes—nothing you could have done. I'd have taken the stone, used it against them; or should I say, against us. Of course I probably would have killed you and taken it away from you. But then, I'm going to kill you anyway. Aren't I?"

Another attack, this time the same as the last only right-handed, the lunge at the chest; only in the middle of the lightning-fast move there was a strange slow-motion pause, just as Marcus brought his dagger up to block, so that he missed. He missed, and his arm went high, and as smooth as ice, Corbo's lunge continued on through, only the angle dropped down low under Marcus' guard and the lunge finished with a jarring blow into Marcus' stomach, knocking out all his breath.

Even so, Marcus struck back, but Corbo effortlessly snared his wrist with his free left hand.

"Fast, but not that fast," he said.

Now Marcus felt the hot, biting, unbearable pain coming on stronger and stronger. Felt the strength flooding out of him with each beat of his panicky heart. Frozen with mortal pain, he could not move. The two men stood there in the rain, staring into each other's eyes. Corbo's opened wide; they were round as an owl's, with a cold, inhuman quality. Ironically, just as Marcus felt the last of his energy seeping out, he recognized what he had been looking for, there in the eyes of Corbo.

Then it was as if he fell inward through time, as if death were a meteoric ride into the future. The last thing he saw before extinction was the rise of a horrific city, all made of cold steel and concrete; the last air he breathed was thick with the stench of machinery; the last thing he heard was the plaintive wail of a distant siren, rushing frantically somewhere through the roar and whine of traffic, either to cure or to kill. Then whatever was left that was Marcus sizzled and went out forever, like a damp fuse.

Brice sat up in bed. "Jesus Christ," he said. Still dazed, he snatched up his pants and T-shirt off the floor and pulled them on, stumbled outside barefoot. Pounded on the door. Elena opened it, but he ignored her and went straight past her to the old man, who still sat cross-legged on the rug, the way Brice had left him.

"Jesus Christ," Brice said, "you're not Theseus, you're Corbo."

13

A LONG TIME ago," the old man said, "much longer than you can comprehend—for no one who hasn't lived through generation after generation and watched people grow, bloom like flowers, and then wither, who hasn't seen great cities sprout up like mushrooms, decay, and crumble into sand, who hasn't watched humanity surge ahead and fall back, surge ahead and fall back . . . anyone who hasn't seen this come to pass can't really understand what I mean by 'a long time ago.' —Where was I?" And now came the wild laugh, loose and ropy. "I am growing senile; God knows if anybody has a right to it, it's me, right, Elena?"

But Elena was simply standing there with her mouth and eyes wide-open; this was obviously news even to her.

"Ah yes," the old man continued, "Corbo. They used to call me Corbo; or rather, to be more accurate, they used to call this form by that name. The consciousness which then inhabited it was primitive, as primitive as yours or Elena's, but of a more powerful nature. Was it some unknown power of the stone which changed it, or was it merely the course of time? Frankly, I don't know. But there is nothing left of Corbo here except for a certain essential detachedness. You might call it coldness, Elena.

"There were four of us who, through the finely developed art of betrayal, wound up in possession of the stone. The same four as now.

"To start with, there was Drusilla; and through Drusilla, her lover and strong right arm, myself, then known as Corbo the gladiator. There was Popillius. He made his fortune organizing parties for the rich and famous in Rome. No theme was too bizarre, no ornamental birds or animals too rare to acquire, no taste in exotica too outlandish. He would supply you with delicate pale-skinned prostitutes from what is now called China, beautiful young boys from Cyprus, ridiculously complicated orgies of food you can't even imagine nowadays. They would just keep bringing it on, course after course: all the rich young ladies and gentlemen would excuse themselves politely from time to time and leave the orgy to throw up in order to make room for more. Luckily, being a gladiator, I was excluded from this most taxing form of enjoyment. Had to watch my figure, you know—no peacock tongues or quail's eyes for me, just plain barley stew. Know what they called us gladiators in those days? 'Barley men.' That was practically all we ate, thank God." (Still practically all he ate, Elena added silently.)

"Anyway, Popillius had started as a lowly pimp, worked his way up to one of the richest men in all of the Roman Empire. We needed him for his money.

"Then there was Germanicus. Ah, Germanicus—" The old man sighed and shook his head. "A German, yet a soldier in the Roman Army. A very successful one. And this is the ironic part: his victories in war were all bloody campaigns against his own people. His name, 'Germanicus,' was a cruel joke among the German soldiers; the original Germanicus was a Roman general who had dominated the Germans about three hundred years earlier. The grandson of Mark Antony, no less.

"His own German tribesmen were naming him after their most hated, almost legendary foe. But he accepted the nickname without complaint. I can't even remember what his real name was, if I ever knew it. A cold fish. But a great soldier. And we needed someone with strong connections in the military if we were to have any hopes of survival in this affair.

"But it was all Drusilla's idea, of course. We had the money, the connections, and we had the stone. Why should we give it over to the latest madman momentarily defiling the throne of Rome by calling himself Emperor? To hell with the Emperor, we decided to run for it. So we brought in the most famous gem cutter in all of Rome and had him cut the stone into four gems of equal size. He made a perfect job of it—and good thing, too, as this was to be his last."

The old man shrugged noncommittally. "I could hardly refuse to do the job I was chosen for, even though I always found it distasteful to kill men who couldn't put up a good fight, which, by the way, included almost anybody you could think of." Here he paused and smiled, shook his head, and then cleared his throat and continued.

"We already knew by then, as did most intelligent people in those days, that the empire was disintegrating and the future lay with the East. So we went east.

"Oh, I could tell you about the history of the stone after that, and all about the four who stole it. I could go on and on. But what I can't tell you is what came before.

"What is the stone? How did it get here? What is the extent of its fantastic powers? We tortured the old Greek, of course—not me, I had no gift for torture, we hired an expert, a man Popillius swore by. But the information we forced out of the old guy was utterly useless, as I knew it would be.

"According to him, the stone had been created by Hephaestus, the smithy of the gods. In ancient times it had been presented to the man who later passed it on to Theseus, by Hermes, the fleet-footed messenger. It was responsible, among other things, for the fall of Troy, the destruction of Carthage, the eruption of Vesuvius, and just about any cataclysm or famous event you could think of.

"I suppose nowadays it would have been handed to him by a lovely maiden with pale green skin, probably to commemorate his luxury cruise on a flying saucer.

"But do you know what's funny, Elena?" he said, turning to face his obviously flabbergasted apprentice, who was now down there sitting cross-legged beside him on the rug. "I am more likely to believe in those fairy stories now than I was back then. Don't you think that's funny?"

Elena, never known for sense of humor, did not laugh or smile, but just continued to stare as if she'd forgotten how to blink.

"Did you say something, Elena?"

"I don't believe any of it," Elena mumbled. "Not any of it at all."

"Well, that's fine, Elena. The less you believe, the better.

"You've already seen something of what the stones can do. Soon, I am afraid, you will see more of it. Your beliefs would only be superfluous baggage for you to discard.

"No, there's only one thing I really know about these four stones. Power. They store power. Power enough to open or close off doorways into other, unimaginable worlds. Power to hold things together or to break things. Power to keep whoever wields them alive for generation after generation. Power enough to have destroyed the city of Troy? I don't know, but I no longer doubt that.

"I was the one who broke up the group. From the start, I was well aware that it was only a matter of time until one or another of them decided my head would be better off somewhere else than resting on my shoulders. So as soon as I had no more need of their power or money to escape the wrath of the Emperor, I ran away from them. And stayed away."

For quite a while the old man sat quietly cross-legged on the rug, apparently remembering events, places, and people from a time so long ago and far away that Brice could not really imagine it.

Elena, who obviously was used to these bouts of silence, simply sat there, patiently waiting it out.

Brice walked over to the window and pushed aside the shade a bit with his finger and looked nervously outside, but saw nothing. A distant seagull was screaming, as if in pain.

The old man, though Brice did not know it, was deeply aware of him, his darting thoughts, his nervous habit of pursing his lips together, moving to the window and looking outside without really looking at anything. It was hard for the old man to associate the image of this small, quick, nervous young man with Quinn, who had been tall, still, and deep. Yet . . .

"You remind me of your brother, you know," the old man said softly. Brice laughed, a short bitter bark that sounded more like a cough.

"But it's true," Corbo insisted, "there is the same element—how would you say?—tenacity, steel beneath the surface. Like my Elena here, only with Elena, it's not hidden. With my Elena, as you can probably see, nothing is beneath the surface." More laughter.

"For the zillionth time," Elena said between gritted teeth, "I'm not your Elena."

The old man shook his head sadly. "How many times do I have to tell you, there's no such word as 'zillion.' "

"There is so," she hissed in rage. "I've looked it up."

Ignoring this retort, the old man turned back to Brice. "Where was I before Elena interrupted me? Ah yes, your resemblance to your brother. .

"These things don't happen by chance, you know?

There are rules of relationship, of reincarnation, very strict rules."

"Which only you understand, I'm sure," Elena threw in.

The old man shook his head. "Wrong again, Elena, there is nothing to understand. They are simply rules.

"Look, I don't know why, but individuals are not reincarnated, never. What is reincarnated are relationships between individuals, always more than one. For instance, your father and your brother: I have encountered them many times throughout the ages, always together. I know them like the back of my hand." He examined the back of his hand for a moment, said: "Whew, ugly devil," then, "Where was I? Oh yeah, your brother the warrior and your father the poet-warrior, always together. I take care to utilize them in the service of my stone. Yes, it's true, over and over again, the two of them, but never you. But I have always known that one day I would find you through them."

"But how could you have known that?" Brice interjected.

The old man did his owl-eyed trick again, staring into Brice's eyes and making him blink. "I am a modest man," he started in, causing Elena to hiss something Brice couldn't quite catch, "but my little stone has given me certain—how should I say?—sensitivities. When I first encountered the two men you have been experiencing as your father and your brother, I sensed their relationship with you, and I expected to trace you through them. By this time my little stone had pointed out to me that I had erred in—well—killing you. In fact, it communicated to me a strong desire that I contact you again. I felt sure that it would be right then and there and I was surprised to find that this was not to be the case."

"You mean you don't know everything?" Elena asked innocently.

"I know only what my stone wants me to know," the old man continued. "But I knew that sooner or later, they would lead me to you. I just did not know how much later." Another burst of wild laughter, and then, in a soft sober tone: "And you would have another chance to do whatever it is the stone wants you to do."

Brice nodded, as if he were understanding or accepting something here.

"Okay," he said in his high smooth voice. "Let's say all this is true; I want to know what exactly does the stone do. What it doesn't."

"Me too," the old man said, "and I've only had possession of it for close to two thousand years. I told you, it stores power. It slows the aging process."

"But if the stone kept you from aging, and you don't have the stone anymore, what's keeping you alive now?"

"The stone did not keep me from aging, it merely slowed the process down a lot. Now that it's gone I will probably continue to age, but at a normal pace. But that's just a guess."

The old man's eyes opened wide again, giving Brice the eerie sensation of being hypnotized by a bird of prey.

"What good are guesses? None of us really knows anything—Why? What? How? The stones are some kind of amplifier. They affect each one of us differently, according to our inner nature. No one can tell you exactly what it will do for you. Except that it will open doors into other, unimaginable worlds, and it will also close those doors. It will be up to you to find your place in those worlds. It will very probably slow the process of your aging and protect you from illness, and it will change you. That's for sure. But no one can say how.

"That's all I can tell you. You must take the stone and find out for yourself. The way we all have. It should prove a most interesting experiment."

Now the old man broke out into another of his fits of

laughter. This time he laughed until tears rolled down his tanned leathery cheeks, while Elena looked on with an expression of mixed revulsion and fascination. Brice knew what she was feeling. Exactly. The laughter died out. For a long time everyone just sat there saying nothing. Then Brice went out the door, slammed it behind him. They could hear him knocking crisply at what must have been Mary Jane's door, two rooms over. A few moments later and they heard the sound of a car starting up.

"He's running away," Elena said.

"Of course," the old man answered. "Go see if he's heading north or heading south."

After a while she came back inside again. "North," she said. "What do we do now?"

"Why, we shower. Eat a nice dinner at Billy's"—Elena grimaced—"get a good night's sleep. Then, tomorrow morning, we pack. We have a nice breakfast at Billy's"—Elena grimaced again—"then we hit the road, because what's our hurry, Elena? Because he's heading north to Jerry's tai chi school. He's doing exactly what his brother Quinn would do if he were alive. That's what little brothers do when their big brothers die."

1

THE BIG CHEVY shot down the highway through some of the most magnificent, lush scenery Elena had ever looked upon. Yet in her dreamy, hypnotized state of consciousness, none of it seemed real to her. It was just too much driving: you gradually drifted into a world where the only reality was the feel of the surface of the road through the steering wheel, the purring of the big V-8 motor, accompanied by all the little creaks, squeaks, and complaints of the body metal. The farmland, the trees, the skies, the lakes, rivers, valleys, and the sprinkling of quaint little towns, all seemed fake, like movie sets, rushing at you while you sat still and turned the steering wheel from time to time in order to straighten out the picture.

For the old man could not drive. Or perhaps, Elena thought, simply would not drive.

He had, though, to give credit where credit was due, insisted yesterday that they stop off at a motel and spend the night. "Take your time. They are probably already there. But let them get unpacked, settle in, then we show up. Get it? They're too exhausted to pack up and run off again. Besides, by now he knows that wherever he goes, I will find him. The stone will find him. His destiny will find him. So take your time. He most likely took the coast highway, as his brother Quinn would have done. Picturing himself staring at the sea and thinking romantic thoughts. But his cute little girlfriend probably drove the car. You know how she drives, Elena. It's supposed to be the scenic route, but I'll bet it was like scenes at fast-forward on a VCR."

"The scenic route?" Elena had said, astonished, having just recently emerged from quintessential scenic farmland into quintessential scenic pine forests. "How could anything be more scenic than this? All this green, it even smells green. Where do they get all the water?"

"You are right again," the old man said. "Even though I have been all over the world, it is hard to imagine anyplace more scenic than this. Sometimes I must admit that beside California, even the wonders of Tres Águilas pale." Of course he had laughed at this. Too loud and too long.

"It's a good thing," Elena remarked, "that you don't actually tell real honest-to-God jokes. You would probably laugh yourself to death."

But even with the easy pace and the good night's sleep, the long haul up the length of California on Route 5 was just too much for Elena. How could any state be so large and so varied? *Madre mía,* it seemed to her more like an entire country than a state.

Frankly, I am so tired of driving, she was thinking, and yet—she had the feeling that she could go over the edge somehow and just drive on forever.

The old man chuckled to himself and said, "Oh, Elena, Elena, didn't I tell you that it was just a little ways outside of Redding? Didn't we just drive through that quaint, old-fashioned little town that I told you was Redding? You remember, we drove around and around through those pretty little treelined streets and looked at all those quaint Victorian-style houses, and you said, 'We're lost.' And I said, 'No, Elena, we're not lost. Just you are lost. I merely wanted to look at these houses for a while and relax my mind, so I told you to drive here.' Do you remember that? Redding? What do you conclude from that?"

"We're almost there?"

"You're right as rain, Elena. As always."

"I don't know what's so right about rain," Elena said to herself. Her attention was drawn out the window and across a large field to what appeared to be a playground area of some sort. "What's that?"

"Looks like a grammar school or a playground. But it's so small and so shabby," the old man said. "I guess we must be heading into Evansdale."

Evansdale, Elena said to herself. My God, Evansdale.

2

TOO MANY THINGS were happening at once—some inner, some outer—for Violet to keep up with it all. One moment and she was aware of those two mean kids, Tommy and Timmy, the dimwit duo of twin Ts, as she liked to call them, approaching fast, ten o'clock high, determined no doubt to take over the junky little semideserted playground where she and her brother William had come to spend the afternoon. You'd think one playground would be big enough for four small children. Even this one.

But next moment, just as she was bracing herself for the onslaught of the terrible Ts, her consciousness was sucked out across the field and toward the highway and into the big black Chevy blinking across her line of vision and on toward town.

Violet was not aware that she was standing with her mouth open and eyes closed, swaying and moaning. She was not aware that just as the two Ts got within range she had shouted out, "Black death," and swayed and fallen on the hard concrete. She was only aware of feelings and impressions emanating from the vehicle. She was not aware of anything she mumbled or shouted, until she started to come out of her trance and the first thing she heard was the voice of Tommy—the big T.

"Shit, what's wrong with Violent?"

And then the patient, deadly serious voice of her brother: "It's 'Violet,' not 'Violent.' And I don't know what's wrong with her. Nothing's wrong with her."

Involuntarily, Tommy took a step backward. The calm confidence of little William's voice and expression always gave him a sudden jolt of insecurity. Especially he was bothered by the boy's big, slightly slanted eyes. Christ, didn't he have to blink like other people? The little fart had the disconcerting habit of fixing his gaze on your face as if he were reading what you were thinking inside there. And even though, to be honest, he looked less Oriental than his sister Violet, somehow he looked even less Caucasian than her—some other race altogether. From Mars, maybe. The supershort hairstyle added to it. The tiny little kid was just two big weird eyes. Tommy knew instinctively that he would need to bluster a bit to get his courage back. But that was no problem. That was the way he always behaved anyway.

"Sure, Wilhelm, you turkey, nothing's wrong with Violent, people always fall down and scream and roll around and . . ."

"She didn't fall down, I caught her. Well, almost."

Now the other T, Timmy's sullen voice: "What the hell difference does that make, Wilhelm? God, you're dumb."

Violet sat up. "It's not the car, it's the fog."

"What fog? Jesus, there isn't any fog. You're so crazy. You and your brother both."

Violet looked off across the field of oats waving in the cool mountain breeze, toward the highway. "The fog following the car." But there wasn't any fog. The sky was clear. "There will be," she said in a sorrowful tone of voice.

"Oh shit, you're so crazy, Violent. That's why they call you 'Violent,' right, Timmy?"

"Oh, right, right, right," Timmy sang. "So-o-o-o right. So-o-o-o crazy. Look at me, look at me, I'm Violent." He began to jump around with his eyes closed and shout: "Oh, the fog, the fucking fog, death, arrgh, the black fucking fog death of it all."

"You shouldn't say that word," William said soberly.

"What word, what word?"

"Oh, you know."

"What word? 'Fuck'? Why not?"

"People will think you're stupid."

The two Ts exchanged puzzled glances. Timmy said, "Oh yeah? Why?"

"Because," William said, "stupid people say that word."

Face distorted by rage and frustration, the big T, Tommy, shouted, "Oh, you dumb fuck, you're such a dumb fuck," and pushed William. The effect on the small, delicately built boy was more like that of a blow than a push, knocking him backward and punching some of the breath out of him at the same time.

Tommy and Timmy, though unrelated by blood, looked far more alike than did William and his sister Violet. Except, of course, that William and Violet were both half-Oriental. Tommy and Timmy, for instance, were related by attitude: a kind of stubborn, slow-witted anger; and it was this attitude which, pervading every aspect of their consciousness since infancy, had formed their bodies: thick-necked, thrusting angry faces forward, heavy bodies leaning aggressively into the beginning of a fighter's crouch. Sullen, dull-witted expressions, not so much unknowing as unwanting to know. Shut off. Unreachable. Unchangeable.

"Don't push him," Violet said, stepping in. But Tommy and Timmy were both so big. Too big, and even if she were their size, too strong.

"Or what, bitch?" Tommy said, pushing Violet and getting similar, if not quite so spectacular, results.

"That's right, bitch." Timmy joined in—as usual—rushing over and pushing Violet from the other side, catching her off balance so that she tripped and almost went down.

"You guys going to play basketball?" William said in his calm, straightforward voice.

Caught off guard by this weird unrelated style of conversation, the terrible Ts' expressions changed from angry, near violence to angry, puzzled, and suspicious—in other words, for them, ran the gamut of emotion.

William was pointing to the basketball they had dropped in order to attack him and his sister.

Still wearing a paranoid expression, Tommy looked at the basketball, then back to William, then back to the basketball again.

"That's right, dum-dum, I'm Magic Johnson. I'll bet you don't even know who Magic Johnson is."

"Or Michael Jordan," Timmy shouted. "Right, Tommy? Or I'll bet you don't know—"

"Shut up, Timmy," Tommy said angrily. Timmy backed up a step.

"Well, I think basketball is a dumb game anyhow," William said.

Not knowing what to say or do, Violet just stood there watching this. It was out of her control. She was scared but used to it. When William took over, that's all you could do.

"What do you mean, basketball is dumb? Basketball's America's national sport, and Magic Johnson is America's ambassador or something."

"And Michael Jordan is . . ." Timmy trailed off when Tommy shot him a look.

"So what?" little William said. "All you do is throw a ball through a hoop. Anybody can do that."

"Oh yeah? Oh yeah? Well, I'll bet you can't do it, you little dumb fuck."

"But," William said coyly, looking away from Tommy as though he were really thinking of something else, "you don't have anything to bet, do you?"

"I do too. I do too. I have more to bet than you ever will, you little dumb fuck. I've got five dollars right here in my pocket and I've got my own bank account my grandma gave me, want to know how much? Only a hundred dollars, that's all."

Which was sort of true. His grandmother had given him a hundred dollars to open an account with, but Big Tom, his dad, had borrowed it almost as soon as Grandma had got it in there, and of course had never paid it back. And the five dollars was money his mom had given him to use at the grocery store on the way home. In fact, he realized nervously, he was supposed to be home with the groceries already.

"Yeah, I've got five dollars too," William said, "but I'm supposed to buy groceries with it."

"Oh yeah?" Timmy broke in like the idiot he was, and said: "Lemme see your grocery list." Sometimes Tommy wondered why he hung around with that jerk.

"Come on, *Bill*iam, where's your grocery list if you're gonna buy groceries?"

Now it was William's turn to look puzzled. "I don't have a grocery list."

"Why not, fart breath? We got a grocery list, don't we, Tommy?"

"I don't need a grocery list," William said. "I can remember what Aunt Martha wants." Then coyly—"I can remember everything"—turning it around again.

"What do you mean, you can remember everything?" Tommy said, trying to sound angry but just sounding upset. Constantly changing directions of thought was not his forte.

"I have a photographic memory and I can remember everything. Everything I've ever seen and done. And know what?" He waited for the answer, and despite himself, big Tommy could not resist:

"What?"

"I can remember everything you've ever seen or done." Big eyes unblinking. Serious expression—was this a joke, or what?"

"You are one weird little dipshit Chink fart," Timmy said, shaking his head in awe.

Tommy went over and picked up the basketball, tried to dribble it behind his back, with the usual results, cursed, and then dribbled it back over to Timmy and the Baines kids. Christ, how did these two weird little half-Chink kids ever wind up with the name "Baines"?

"Too bad you can't bet your grocery money, Wilhelm, or we'd find out just who can throw the ball in the hoop."

"Yeah, yeah," Timmy cut in excitedly, "and who can't throw the ball in the ocean."

Violet, who had decided to stay out of it all and let William do the talking, nevertheless couldn't resist throwing in: "The ocean's over a hundred miles from here, dumbo. I'd sure like to see you try it."

"Oh yeah?" Timmy rushed over and shoved Violet again.

"I can bet the grocery money," William said.

Tommy stopped dribbling the ball and looked puzzled. "What if you lose, dumb fuck? Won't they punish you?"

"Sure," William said, and now, for the first time, smiled. But it was such a small smile with his tiny little mouth just slightly stretched up at the corners. "But I can bet it anyway, see?"

Over on the playground's shabby little basketball court, Tommy put on another frantic dribbling exhibition with the same disastrous results. Even Timmy looked a little embarrassed by his display of ineptitude. He was going to get good, though, Tommy figured, if his dad would only give him more time to practice instead of all the time do the chores, feed the horse, work on the fence, work out the horse, rub down the damn horse. People always thought it was a big deal his having a horse. They couldn't understand it was his dad's horse, a goddamn racehorse that his dad thought was going to win the goddamn Kentucky Derby or something and all it was, was work and trouble. In fact, he was supposed to be home right now, working it out, wasn't he?

"I'd like to see you shoot it from here like this," he said, and fired one off from just outside the top of the key, which missed not only the basket but backboard, rim, net—you name it. But it was heading pretty straight.

"Well, I hit it from there before, three out of four times, didn't I, Timmy? You remember?"

Timmy shook his head: "No, you didn't. I hit it once, but you didn't ever."

"Did too."

"Did not."

"Did too."

"Did not."

Interrupting their quarrel just in time, William said, "I can't hit it from there because I'm too small. I can't throw it that far."

Timmy and Tommy looked at each other in amazement.

Timmy said, "Why, that's what we're talking about, you dumb fuck."

William hefted the basketball in his right hand, obviously calculating its weight, then moved inside the key to the free-throw line. "I can throw it this far, though."

"Tell you what," Tommy said, knowing just how

difficult it was to hit free throws, "I'll bet you my five dollars you can't hit five free throws in a row."

William thought about it, then shook his head. "Ten," he said casually.

"Ten dollars?"

William shook his head. "Ten free throws."

Tommy and Timmy once again exchanged dumbfounded glances. "Oh, you stupid little . . ." Timmy started, and for once had to stop for lack of words.

The two Ts watched in further amazement as the little, odd-looking boy with the big eyes, standing sideways to the basket, pointed a finger toward it with his left hand, and balancing the ball in his right hand only, shot-putted it in a high arc toward the hoop. "Jesus, that's the worst shot I ever saw in my life," Timmy said in something like awe. Only it went in. Ten times in a row.

"You owe me five dollars," William said, holding out his hand.

Tommy slapped his hand hard. "Do not," he said. "Your foot was over the line."

"Wait a minute," Violet cut in, realizing that William was losing control here, "you guys can keep the money, we've gotta be getting back home."

Tommy pointed his finger at William. "You owe me the money," he said in an angry tone of voice.

"No," William said, backing up a step, "I don't think so."

"Come here, you little dumb fuck. I'm gonna pound the shit out of you and then take the five bucks you owe me." He moved toward William, pounding his fist in the palm of his hand.

"No," William said, moving another step backward.

Suddenly Violet must have decided what the hell, because she came charging out from behind her brother, throwing a furious barrage of punches at Tommy, who had to back off for a moment despite himself. Shit, he thought nervously, good thing she's not any bigger. For although Violet was bigger than her brother, she was still much smaller than either of the two Ts. And her punches were wild; Tommy was having no trouble blocking them. Still, her assault was so furious that right at first he couldn't find the chance to do much of anything but block punches.

Despite being weird, however, she was only human, Tommy figured; and sure enough, after the first brief surge she stopped all that wild swinging and tried to catch her breath, and Tommy got in a punch. It was a good one too, crisp and hard and square on the cheek, and it whipped her head back. If Tommy was lousy at basketball, he was good at fighting, like his dad. He loved to hurt and he had a natural gift for it. Could just charge in and wrestle her down at this point, he thought, but nah, play with her, torture her for a while first.

Suddenly a voice, low-pitched but almost superhumanly powerful, broke from the sky like thunder.

"Shame. Shame on all who do the work of the Evil One. For though you are little, you are old enough to choose. Do you know what the Evil One is?"

Tommy and Violet froze in the middle of their fight like statues and stared at the source of the voice, along with Timmy and William. At first Tommy couldn't make out who it was. The big powerful figure was standing with the lowering sun directly behind it so that all you could make out was the size, the muscularity, the whiteness of the hair, emerging from a blaze of light. Then he realized who it was: the crazy old Black man the town paid to clean up the playground and do other odd jobs and maintenance chores. Rufus. At least that's what the kids all called him.

"Do you know what the Evil One is?" Rufus (whose formal, christening name was actually Ruford) repeated. No one volunteered an answer.

"He is spirit, soul, just as God is—not flesh, you see?

Know how you feel when you doin' wrong, like right now, Tommy? Well, evil be made up of that feeling, you see? Only they is no separation. That just illusion. It ain't real. So that everybody all over this world doin' evil, they be creatin' the spirit of evil."

All the time he was talking he was moving toward them. He was so huge and powerful it was like looking up at a giant with snow-white hair and beard and chocolate-brown skin.

"But the spirit be alive, Tommy, don't you see? You be creatin' it, but it be alive. It want to be more alive, so pretty soon you be feelin' that way more and more often. You be hangin' around other people help creatin' it. Like you and Timmy. You see? Don't nobody see?"

The crazy old man put both hands to his head and swayed with passion. Somehow you could almost see the passion shooting through him like high-voltage electricity.

"Don't nobody see nothin'?"

Tommy and Timmy ran for it. Scrambling toward the far side of the playground where their bikes were.

"Forgot they basketball," Ruford said, staring at the ball. "Poor little lonely ball, just sittin' there by hisself. Tell you what, though. That boy, Tommy, he better off without it. Why, he couldn't throw the damn thing in the ocean."

Then, as if hearing Violet's silent objection, he added: "If he was swimmin' in it.

"Don't nobody understand me," he said again.

"You're drunk, Rufus," little William said with his usual candor. Violet held her breath.

"I do believe so," Ruford said, after some thought. "Been sittin' up against the handball court there, on the other side, havin' me some terrible cheap wine. It gots no ambience at all, but I do believe it get you drunk. Where was I? Oh, yeah. But you gots to understand this here, son. It's important, see. What it is, is that I drink because can't nobody understand me, not that it be nobody understand me because I drunk. You see?"

William appeared to be pondering the problem quite seriously. Finally he said, "I understand that, Rufus. But I do believe you drink too much."

Ruford laughed out loud. "Oh, you right there, and when you right, you right. Why don't the two of you scoot on out of here and let me get back to my work?"

As William and Violet ran off toward their bikes, Violet whispered to William, "Get back to drinking is what he means."

"He's not so bad," William said. "I like him."

"You like everybody," Violet said.

"Do not."

"Do too."

"Do not."

"Do too."

"I don't like Tommy."

"Well," Violet conceded, "you like everybody that's human."

Both kids laughed.

"By the way," William said as he kicked up the kickstand on his old Murray, "when you're fighting like that you've got to keep your elbows in close by your sides. You got to keep your chin down sort of into your shoulder and throw your punches straighter. I'll show you when we get home."

"Why don't you show yourself, you little nerd," Violet said in a sharp burst of anger.

"Why would I want to fight?" William said in a puzzled tone of voice. "Oh, and Violet?"

No answer.

"Vi?"

No answer.

"Lettie?"

"Yeah, what is it this time?" Shouting over the whine of the bicycle wheels.

"The ocean."

"Yeah, what?"

"It's only sixty-three miles to Eureka."

Violet's beautiful heart-shaped face scrunched up into an exaggerated frown. "Thanks," she said, "I needed that."

3

THE BIG BLACK Chevy that had inspired Violet's terrifying vision was now cruising ominously down the main drag of Evansdale. The only drag of Evansdale.

"I don't believe this," Elena said. "Three Gs—Gasoline, Groceries, and Grill? Ye Old Curiosity Shoppe Souvenirs, Curiosities, and Genuine Antiques, okay; but the Tavern of the Laughing Moon and School of Tai Chi? Is this a joke? I don't get it."

"Ah, Elena," the old man said. "Yes, it's a joke, and of course you don't get it. How could you when you're part of it?" And now, guess what? What else but another performance of his cackling laughter, which for some reason this time made Elena relax a little.

"It's just California, you see? It's all a joke, but at the same time it's very serious. It's like another dimension: an astral world. Or what you might think of as the formative plane. Whatever they do here, they do out of the slightest whim, and it's a joke, it's funny. They're all like potheads, see? But whenever they do something new, it is an initiation for the rest of America. No matter how silly it is, all of those sober, unhappy little New Yorkers will be forced into imitating it. Oh, they will hate themselves for doing it, but they will do it just the same."

"Do what?" Elena barked in irritation. "I never get what it is you're talking about."

"Do anything," he said in a patient, sober (for him) tone of voice. "Anything at all.

"Park there, Elena." He pointed to the parking spaces in front of Ye Old Curiosity Shoppe.

"For instance, say some crazy Californian puts wheels on a surfboard, and maybe even a little chair, and then he paddles around town in it. Other Californians see him, and then they get the whim, see, they can't help it, they just think, 'Hey, what would I look like if I did that?' and 'What would it feel like?' and 'What kind of clothes would I wear?' "

Elena pulled the car into a parking space and now sat there fascinated despite herself by the old man's crazy explanation of California.

"Pretty soon everybody in San Francisco and L.A. is out paddling around the streets on surfboards. They all wear special clothes and develop a special language for it—especially the men, because California girls won't go out with guys who don't city-surf, and we all know how desirable California girls are—right, Elena?" Another gust of dry laughter.

"Now it's on TV, see? *Sidewalk Surfers,* two young, tough L.A. cops who hunt down crooks and chicks on their streetboards. Every magazine has some kind of article about how this is the best thing for your poor little heart—right, Elena? The very best exercise. Poor scared pale little New York guy can't help himself. First he just gets the clothes and learns a few of the sidewalk surfer words, just to impress his girl. He tries to resist, but he just can't help it. Sooner or later, there he is, out there on those icy sidewalks, freezing to death, trying to control his board as it skids across the ice and plows through a crowd of helpless screaming New Yorkers who are too weak to jump out of the way and hurtles headfirst into an oncoming taxi, which could, but refuses to, avoid him."

"Jesus Christ, but you're crazy," Elena said, getting out of the car.

"I know, but I'm crazy like the Californians, Elena. I'm the kind of crazy that changes the course of the world."

Standing on one leg like a stork, he slowly raised the other until his knee almost reached his chest. Then he kicked the car door shut. Hard. Chuckled as though somehow the action had pleased him a lot.

"I'm the kind of crazy you will have to become if you want to survive."

The casual statement sent a shock wave through Elena. Yes, she realized, it was true. All these years she had seen it, but blocked it out. You could not wield the kind of power the old man did without being nuts.

He turned back to where she stood frozen beside the car. "Yet did you ever stop to think that maybe I'm the one who's sane, and all the rest of you, scuttling around in your narrow little boxes which you've constructed out of reason, trying to break out, but afraid to break out—have you ever thought that it's all of you who may be insane?" More laughter.

"Oh, come on, Elena, cheer up. I was only joking, we're all equally insane, okay? Shall we take a look inside Ye Old Curiosity Shoppe and maybe purchase a memento of our trip to Northern California?"

GEORGE BAINES MOVED slowly and majestically through the aisles of what he thought of as junk to the broad front window of his store. The central motivating factor of George's complex personality matrix had always been the urge to accumulate: it was at the center of everything he did; understand that and you understand George. But, of course, central to the urge to accumulate is always dissatisfaction with what you've got, so that George always thought of the many and varied curios he sold in Ye Old Curiosity Shoppe as junk, mistakes, errors of his artistic judgment, but always wanted more of them. On top of that, damn it, he really didn't want to sell them. But he had to.

So, typical with George's penchant for ceaseless accumulation of things, coupled with his dissatisfaction with what he already had, the store was literally brimming over with so many varied and unrelated objects that lack of a main theme was its outstanding quality.

Now, as George moved so slowly but elegantly through the aisles—for he was fat, of course, through the mechanism of accumulating more food fuel than he could use up—his mind was assailed with clouds of darting little nervous apprehensions, through the mechanism of accumulating too many worries.

At the window, he thought: I wonder what's happened to Violet and William, damn it, they're supposed to drop by here on their way to the store and they should have been here by now. Damn it, Cyril, how like you to have died and saddled me down with two kids. Half-Oriental kids. How like you to have floated through your life doing nothing except what you wanted to, to somehow manage to make a living as a poet—a poet? (tough job, but someone's got to do it) — then marry the most beautiful Chinese woman in the world, have a couple of kids, and then pop off for heaven taking her along with you for company. You always had to win. "Cyril"—why would anyone name one of their kids plain old George and the other Cyril, for Godsake?

In this manner George shamelessly carried on his war with his younger, more successful (at least in his eyes) brother, even after death. In fact, it could be put that George had accumulated so much even of his relationship with his brother and stashed it away in his mind that, in a way, his brother was alive, could not die until George died.

Now, looking out the front window of his "junk" shop, worrying about the kids, he watched with interest as an old black Chevy pulled into one of the diagonal parking spaces in front of his "shoppe."

Nice old car, he thought, coveting it, but at the same time wishing it were a 1949 Studebaker or . . .

For a while the people sat in the car and talked. But they were coming into his shop, he was certain of that. Tourists, he guessed, for though it was early in the season, the tourists were starting to pour in, and the weekends could be pretty busy. By next week, perhaps, or the week after, the town would come alive. And for a while, people would buy anything.

But as the two got out of the car, George changed his mind. The woman was stunning, absolutely arresting, you could tell it from here. And the old man? What an odd couple, George thought, really getting interested. Just then the old man did a very odd thing. At the same time as he apparently was chatting with the strawberry blonde, he casually raised up his right leg until his knee practically touched his chest, and rather violently kicked the car door closed. There was something about the simple act, the loose smoothness of movement, the absolute perfection of balance, the confidence, that made the gesture totally out of place for a man of such advanced age. For he was clearly very old: white hair, white beard. Furthermore, he appeared to be completely at ease, laughing, smiling, almost too much so, while the woman appeared irritated, even quite angry. It was obvious by her posture, the way she slammed her car door, glared at the old man. Odd and odd and odd, George thought as they headed for his store.

"May I be allowed to be of service—madam—sir?" he said in his low precise voice. The woman's eyes were mesmerizing, huge, green as a cat's. Cold. She gave off the aura of fury, but it was cold, calculated fury.

Suddenly, for no reason that George could perceive, the old man emitted a loud cackling burst of laughter, which somehow was as mesmerizing as the woman's eyes. It was like the crisp scream of a crow, George thought. More of a challenge or an ecstatic assertion of self than an expression of humor: I am. I am. I am.

"You are so correct," the old man said, startling George. "In your choice of objects for your curiosity shop, of course," he added, perhaps in deference to George's shocked expression.

Then he said a strange and wonderful thing. "After all, I don't read minds, do I?" More laughter.

"I . . . I beg your pardon," George stammered when the laughter had faded.

"You can only have it once," the old man said.

Meanwhile, the strawberry blonde shook her head in disgust. Her entire posture indicated total disdain. Not only was she not impressed, George realized with a shock, but she was used to this.

"You can only have it once," the old man repeated, this time clearly, carefully, emphasizing each word as if it were the most important thing in George's life. And this time the bout of laughter was so severe that at the end of it he was wheezing and his eyes were filled with tears.

"You simply must forgive the old man," the blonde said icily, "since there isn't anything else you can do with him." This brought more laughter, though now it was choked; and George figured he was finally pretty much laughed out.

"Oh, Elena," the old man gasped happily.

"Excuse me," George mumbled, "might I show you around my shop, Miss—er—Ms. . . . ?"

She stared (glared?) into his eyes, unblinking, and said, "I'm not a fem libber or anything—just 'Elena.' "

George blinked; she was still there. Elena? George simply could not do this. "Surely, if Madam would . . ." he stammered.

"I'm not royalty, either," she insisted. "Just a simple Mexican peasant."

Beyond any question of a doubt, George realized, this statement, delivered with such confidence, established a form of royalty in the woman which was far beyond her notion of royalty, for it could not be inherited or bestowed by chance, but only earned. And furthermore, only a few would earn it.

"You are correct," the old man said. "Again, in your choice of objects. I think Elena and I would just like to browse." He drew out the word "browse" as if it had some special hidden meaning, and opened his eyes wide. The round eyes of an owl. Hypnotic eyes. Every bit as unique and wonderful as the woman's, in quite a different way. Hypnotic eyes. Sorcerer's eyes, he thought.

He blinked, and the old man blinked with him. Only

somehow, when the old man blinked, it was slowly and deliberately, as if he were accomplishing something secret by doing it.

George blinked again and discovered that he was suddenly unaccountably drowsy. So very, very drowsy . . . If only . . . He closed his eyes for a moment—blessed relief—and seemed to hear a whispering from somewhere deep within. He could almost make out the words. But not quite, not quite. With a start, he opened his eyes again. The old man and the woman—what was it she called herself? Elena?—were somewhere at the back of the store. Had he fallen asleep standing up?

He could hear the old man talking in a soft voice. But for the moment, the words somehow didn't mean anything. Just chatter. Just sounds. Music, perhaps, or the whispering of the wind through . . . what? Curios—junk?

"I asked you if you would come over here and help us with something. I need some expert advice, see? And Elena here is not helping me out much. But then—that's Elena."

Still in a daze, George Baines moved slowly toward the voices. Even his vision seemed distorted, somehow reversed; it was as if he stood still while the little junk store floated past him. He did not deliberately focus on anything. But when one or another of his many objects d'art drifted into his tunnel vision, it was as if he had never seen it before: a small pipe in the form of a miniature toilet bowl, a covey of brilliantly colored baseball caps, expertly designed so that they would fit no one's head, T-shirts with slogans on them like "I couldn't afford Disneyland, so I went to Evansdale," drifted into sharp focus, astonishing him.

And when the little wooden plaque that boldly proclaimed "All our guests bring happiness. Some in the comin', some in the goin' " leaped out at him, he perceived it for the first time as profoundly true. That's the way to look at it, the only way, he thought, drifting on.

Then, without registering when the transition took place, he was standing between the blonde and the old man, focusing his tunnel vision onto the object which the old man held out in his hand.

A transparent ball, with a miniature country scene in it. A church—or was it a schoolhouse?

"Look at this, will you?" the old man said, and turned the ball over and then right side up again. It began to snow, of course.

But it was so realistic. So well done. And was it his imagination or was the scene growing? The outline filling in? Bushes, trees, moving in the wind. Light glowing from the schoolhouse window. He could actually hear the children singing inside. But the music had a lugubrious haunting quality. Like chanting. The old man was chanting in his ear. And someone, it must be the blonde, was whispering in his other ear; but no, it wasn't the woman, it was the old man, chanting in one ear and whispering into the other. In some strange, inexplicable, yet perfectly logical manner he felt himself being pulled in different directions. Pulling apart. His ears popped, and suddenly there were two of him, one of them standing in the shop with the old man chanting to him, and one of him in the country scene listening to the old man's soothing chatter. Suddenly he shivered, aware for the first time of the freezing cold, the biting pungent country air, and he snapped out of the body in the shop, and became—becomes—here now. I am here now, he thinks, terrified yet enthralled.

He is aware that the old man is asking him questions and that he is answering, but this awareness is diffuse, mixed in with so many other, more important, awarenesses: the cold, the fresh air, the gentle flakes of snow falling through the soft golden glow from the window. And the singing of the children, for they are no longer chanting, but singing in clear, high voices as sweet as the voices of angels. Singing about simple things, the things of childhood. Evanescent things which can never be acquired or captured or preserved. Things as elusive as the falling flakes of snow. Here. Gone. Here. Gone.

Suddenly George's ears pop and he finds himself back in his shop standing between the old man and the beautiful strawberry blonde. But it is as if a tremendous weight has been lifted from him. He feels as he felt when as a kid he had on his first brand-new pair of Converse basketball shoes, shiny white with the little red stars.

"Why, I could jump over the moon," he blurts out.

The old man begins laughing again, and it is beautiful and wild, sweet but shrill, definitely the call of a bird.

Suddenly the lovely vision of whatever it was George has just experienced closes itself up as if within a bubble, and spins away into the darkness of his unconscious; and, with a sharp piercing loss so poignant that he stumbles and the blonde has to catch him and support him for a moment, disappears.

"What happened?" George said. Then, his cheeks reddening with embarrassment, he stammered, "I mean I . . . I mean . . . I'm sorry, I'm not feeling . . . quite right."

The old man leaned forward and peered comically into his eyes, and once again blinked, and suddenly even the memory of the memory was gone. "You were remarking that you felt wonderfully—what was that word, Elena?—buoyant?"

"I . . . I said that?" The thought that he had been baring himself that way before total strangers unnerved George even more than the loss of memory.

"Effervescent, even. Right, Elena?"

Elena answered by throwing back her head, turning her beautiful jade-green eyes in supplication up toward heaven, and mumbling to herself in Spanish.

"From Elena that means 'Yes,' " the old man said.

"Hey, listen, you said you feel ready to play a game of basketball, you know that? Like when you were a kid with your new Converse shoes—right? The ones with the little red stars?"

"Yes." It just bubbled out of George. It was true. And for the moment he let go of his embarrassment, fear, and all other emotional baggage, and said, "Yes, I do feel like that, exactly like that. In fact, I think I'll close up shop early today. I don't mean to rush you . . ."

"No, no," the old man said, "we've got what we came for." He held up the glass ball with the country scene. And for a moment George felt a totally inexplicable stab of pain. Almost had to stop himself from reaching out and . . .

Let go, he told himself. And let go he did. The buoyant feeling returned, and now he felt so good he could hardly keep from laughing while they conducted business.

"Tell you what," he said. "You can have it for free."

"It's for Elena," the old man said. "Thank the man, Elena."

And while he was closing out the cash register, George Baines was simultaneously humming to himself and wondering what the odd couple was talking about outside on the front porch—watching them through the window.

"How in the name of God did you do that?" Elena was whispering to the old man, outside. "How and why?"

"The stone," he said in a faraway dry whisper. He was studying the skies intently once again. For some unknown reason. Probably he didn't know why himself, Elena thought. "Not a cloud in the sky, isn't that strange, Elena? Where was I? The stone, of course. All of its powers have not left me. And that was the first to manifest itself. It will probably be the last to go.

"I told you that each of the stones gave slightly different powers. Perhaps it was the stones, perhaps it was us—I personally believe that it was due to our different natures."

"If you don't know, who would?" Elena complained.

"How on earth could anyone ever know, Elena? Anyhow, the stones give each of us several quite different abilities, but all four stones manifest the two central powers: the ability to transfer visions or commands from our minds to the minds of others, and the ability to open the doorways into other worlds. The first is called 'The Control'; the second is called 'The Opening.' I was merely exercising the power of 'control' over him, in my own unique way."

"So now we know that Brice and that female are in town staying with Jerry, and that they hang out in Jerry's tavern every night," Elena said. "But why did you ask him all of those questions about his kids?"

"About his brother's kids," the old man corrected. "Well—I guess it's just because I love kids."

From inside Ye Old Curiosity Shoppe George watched the old man go through another fit of laughter, and even though he couldn't hear it, it sent shivers up his spine anyhow.

Later, when he went outside and sat on the wooden steps leading up to the front porch, looking up into the darkening sky, he felt the first tinge of sadness and foreboding. Yet even this somehow could not touch his buoyancy, could not infringe upon the here-now.

Raucous cries, and the kids appeared on their bikes—how exquisite, how perfect. For the first time it struck him full force, the wonder they were, the blending of races and philosophies, the Orient and America: the new man, the new woman.

The kids, shocked by the sight of George sitting on the quaint wooden stairway, pulled up fast, standing hard on the old-fashioned brakes and causing the bikes to skid up to a stop, with the awesome control of childhood.

This is the way to be, George thought; biologists who had pegged the prime of fitness to be twenty-four or so were sure wrong, the prime was eight to ten; everything after that was downhill. No wonder no one knows anything about health.

Violet appeared to be in the first stages of developing a black eye. He decided not to mention it.

"We're sorry we're late, Uncle George, we got hung up," she said nervously, knowing, of course, that Aunt Martha would have called George and told him when they were leaving for the store. Oddly, George said nothing, just stood there eyeing them, which made Violet edgy.

"Don't you want to know where we've been?" she said. And noticed to her astonishment that there were tears in his eyes.

"I don't want to know anything," George said. "I just want to be with you."

And suddenly, for the first time, he scooped them both into his arms, hugging them to him, causing William to let go of his bike so that it crashed in the street and he shouted, "Hey." For the first time, and sadly, so sadly, for the last time as well.

5

THINGS WERE NOT quite clear yet. But surely they would clear up, slowly perhaps, but inexorably (that was how Brice pictured it); like a river that had been muddied up by a herd of stampeding horses, things would gradually come clean again through their own natural movement. And that river was time.

Mary Jane, for instance, was not quite clear—she was desirable and she was exciting, and she was cute as a bug's ear, but Brice could not quite place her into the picture yet and understand what role she played. He needed more objectivity, and that would only come with time, quiet time.

His brother's friend Jerry was another matter entirely. Brice had no trouble in "seeing" Jerry for what he was. An enigma. On the one hand, you could never predict what the crazy hippie bastard would do; on the other, his heart was right there on the surface for anyone to monitor, as simple as a child's. You could never control him—he was his own man, for sure—but you could trust him. You had to trust him. Brice smiled as he remembered the way Jerry communicated with those two strange little Oriental kids: he hadn't had to get down on their level, or talk down to them at all; there simply was no separation in the first place.

Just yesterday the two little kids had come over to the Tavern of the Laughing Moon to ask very seriously if Jerry could play. Brice had had to take over Jerry's duties at the bar in order to facilitate the game. It had been difficult, even in Brice's enervated, confused, lost mood, to keep a straight face.

"Sure, got to be Follow the Leader," Jerry had proclaimed. "Don't tell me you kids ain't never played Follow the Leader—my God, it's the only way to play. To start with, you've got to choose a good shooter, but be careful, 'cause no matter what you choose, I'm liable to get it—you see?"

A short while later and Jerry and the kids were down crawling around the floor, underneath the table, shooting at each other's marbles. Jerry turned out to be very conservative about his marbles, primarily aiming not so much to hit either of the kids' shooters but to hide behind the legs of tables and chairs in the bar so as not to be hit.

Mary Jane, even Mary Jane, had observed this affair with openmouthed astonishment. Brice remembered vividly the disgusted expression of the guy who ran the gas station/grocery store combo, the father of that nasty little kid Timmy, as the man shouted out: "Jesus Christ, Jerry, you already lost all your marbles about a thousand years ago. Least you can do is try a honest shot or two, for Christsake."

"No ukingfay way," Jerry had answered. "I'm in this to win. And I intend to win." And in a way he had won. From Violet, who had carelessly shot her marble out into the middle of the floor and left herself open, entirely by accident—or was it?

Sure as hell, as soon as he had shot out of his cover and scored on Violet and taken her shooter, he had suddenly found himself way out there in open territory with no place to hide. Still, it only gave William one good, clear, but incredibly long shot at him. Just the one, right?

"Miss, miss, miss," Jerry had muttered under his breath. Brice had had to bite into his lip to keep from laughing. But William, his intense eyes blazing into Jerry's, had smiled calmly and said, just as clear as you please, "Oh, sure, Jerry—fat chance." And right then and there, all of them, Mary Jane, Brice, Jerry, and the gasoline-grocery man, Russell, realized that Jerry had been had. Right from the goddamn beginning, he had been had.

The boy's little whippet-thin form curled over his right hand. Something colorful and symmetrical as a star whirled and spun out onto the floor and . . . plink, Jerry's prize shooter, a lovely sacred ancient agate, was in little—what was his name?—William's hand. "Gee, that's too bad," Violet had said. "My shooter's not so good."

"That's okay," Jerry had answered, eyeing his lost aggie, "I've only had it since I was ten."

Then, even more audaciously, William had used Jerry's lost agate to lure Jerry into more games. Could he win it back? Fat chance, as William would probably have pointed out.

Brice had liked that, as he had liked most everything about Jerry's place, which despite the exotic oriental name displayed more of a California-style Zen ambience than anything else. It was impossible for Brice to figure how he made a living off of it, though. Even considering the few tai chi seminars he taught during the spring and summer—he was preparing for one right now, coming up next week—or the few students who came up from God knows where to take regular lessons in the long, empty, narrow back room with the huge eclectic assortment of swords and other medieval weapons covering the walls. For Jerry taught tai chi sword, tai chi stick, tai chi rope dart, tai chi weapons Brice didn't even know the name or purpose of, just as his brother Conal had. But that was just about the only thing Jerry had in common with his brother. Where Conal had been tall, slender, and elegant, Jerry was medium-sized and rather stocky—in fact, a little plump and soft-looking. Where Conal had exercised a spare and biting sense of humor, Jerry was pure hippie slapstick. Jerry was always laughing, clowning around, without the slightest worry as to whether he was the butt of the joke.

"Your brother was the master," Jerry had said. "No shit, the real honest-to-God old-fashioned master; I'm just a student." In making that statement, though, he had been like Conal.

The Tavern of the Laughing Moon itself, despite the promise of its exotic name, had turned out to be a rather simple, unadorned type of place: just a big dark room with plain wooden floors and a long horseshoe-shaped bar. There were rows of vinyl-padded booths along the walls and absolutely no paintings or ornaments of any kind. There was not even a jukebox. Brice was learning the art of sitting in the cool dark and slowly drinking a beer or two; getting used to the taste of beer, the feeling. Hanging out.

"You'd attract more people if you put in a jukebox," Brice had said to Jerry.

"I like the quiet," was the answer. Which had to make you laugh, because if there was such a thing as a moment of silence around Jerry, Brice had yet to experience it. Right now, for instance, Jerry was singing in a terrible twangy voice, which may or may not have been a parody of some popular country-and-western singer, his version of "San Antonio Rose." He knew all the words to this, as well as to other pop western ballads like "Ghost Riders in the Sky," and once started could, and would, go on for hours.

"For the love of God will you give up and buy a jukebox, or can't you at least sing something romantic for Junie-Bug here?" Russ, who ran the gas station and grocery store combo down the street, was in his usual corner booth making time with Big Tom's wife June. Since Brice had arrived here the duo had practically been permanent fixtures, and their flagrant illicit romance was one of the big entertainment features of the bar. Everyone, of course, was waiting for Big Tom to catch on, at which time the entertainment level would go way up for the amount of time it took for him to stomp Russ and/or Junie-Bug into stains on the wooden floor. For Big Tom, as the rumor went, was Big Bad Tom. And indeed, Tom was big and Tom acted bad, but Brice wasn't so sure. The couple of times Brice had seen him, he had reminded Brice of a big tough ten-year-old boy who had gotten bigger, yet never really grown up. But Brice supposed sheer size had to count for something.

The oddest thing about this whole weird little scenario was that Russ acted totally subordinate to Big Tom in every other way except for Junie. The two men seemed to genuinely like each other. Perhaps, Brice speculated, Russ felt that Junie was simply a reward he had earned by letting Big Tom have everything else in life.

Now Jerry reacted to Russ's request for romantic music by breaking into a huge overblown version of "What Kind of Fool Am I?" And when he was through with that, followed with "Smoke Gets in Your Eyes." Brice had the strange sensation that Jerry knew the words to every song, and could supply a parody of the proper voice to go with it.

It was difficult for Brice to relate this short stubby comedian to his conception of what image a master of tai chi should project. It was even more difficult for him to visualize the relationship between his suave brother Quinn and this little clown. He shook his head and had another sip of beer. And let the bittersweet memories surface. Quinn, my beautiful brother, the last of my family, forever lost. As usual, his eyes welled up with tears. And since it was dark in the Tavern of the Laughing Moon anyway, he was not at first aware of who he was looking at when he turned to see who had just come in through the front door, causing all the bells nailed on there to clang and jingle.

"Jesus Christ," Jerry muttered, "what a gorgeous chick. And she's come here for me. Just for me, I know it." He leaned over to whisper in Brice's ear. "Ya see the old dude with her there? He's really only seventeen, but she's fucked the life right out of him, and now she needs a replacement. Naturally she's heard about me and . . ."

"Shit," Brice said quite loud. "Shit, shit, shit."

Something about the old man, perhaps it was the aura of confidence, or the aristocratic posture, was enough to shut Jerry up for the moment. But immediately the old man put on his own comedy show by blinking open his incredibly round owl eyes and putting on a mock display of astonishment. "Tsk, tsk, tsk. Why, Brice, such language. Please remember there's a lady present."

"Just leave me alone," Brice said in a soft but furious tone of voice.

The old man shook his head; his expression was wistful. "No can do," he said.

"Oh yeah," Jerry said. "It can be done." Watching Jerry move out fast from behind the counter, Brice observed a weird change come over him. Jerry sighed, a sound like steam escaping from a kettle, and his facial expression, along with the muscles of his body, visibly relaxed. Even his eyelids drooped to a dreamy, half-closed position over his surprisingly large blue eyes. He half smiled: it was obvious that he had entered some sort of self-hypnotic state, as if the thought of a fight relaxed him. "Tell you what you can do," he said to the old man. "You can leave or you can die."

Then to Elena: "You, too, woman; I'd hate to waste a beautiful woman, but . . ."

Back in the far booth even Russ was getting interested. In fact, he even shushed up Junie-Bug, making her go "Oooh" and glare at him, but it was a cute glare. At last

I'm going to see this weird little dude do that martial art bullshit he teaches. Russ was already planning to deliver a report of the fight to Big Tom, who would probably want to kick Jerry's ass sometime just for fun, but wouldn't mind a little encouragement in the form of a scouting critique from his old buddy Russell.

But what he saw next was so strange that he immediately forgot all about Big Tom, and even Big Tom's wife. What was this?

The old man slowly and deliberately formed a fist with his right hand and held it up in front of Jerry. "The one," he said, "became four," and here he popped up four fingers, "to guard the four corners of the world."

Jerry's eyes popped open wide. His mouth opened and formed an "O." "You're one of the Four," he whispered in an awestruck tone of voice. "Jesus. What can I do for you? Anything. Listen, uh—the kids are okay. Nothing special or unusual there."

"Kids?" Elena muttered. "What kids?"

Brice buried his face in his hands and muttered "Shit" once again.

"Jerry is one of our helpers, Elena," the old man said, "but he was initiated into our organization by Quinn. He has never met me before. He has met Germanicus, though, who I believe goes under the name of Boris something-or-other these days. Boris—Kreig? Kruger?"

"Yeah, Kruger," Jerry said, still speaking in a whispery, awed voice.

"Boris," the old man continued, "has always considered himself rather a patron of the arts. Surrounded himself with artists, poets. Very sensitive.

"Ah, Germans." The old man sighed. "There's always that strange dualism to contend with. First they smash Rome to pieces, destroy all of its artwork, burn all the books, plunge the world into the Dark Ages, which, believe me, were aptly named. Then they spend the rest of their history trying to re-create what they so enthusiastically destroyed. Did you know that one of the Hapsburgs was the ruler of what the Germans used to call the 'Holy Roman Empire of the German Nation'? Mind-boggling if you'd seen what they did to the original in the first place. Where was I?

"Oh yes, Boris likes to surround himself with artistic types. Apparently he couldn't keep himself from putting on a little art show of his own for a few of his inner circle. To make a long story short, after the charming combination art party/debauchery was over and Boris was sleeping off the effects, one of his friends, a suitably mad poet, decided to give up poetry for power and ran off with Boris' stone. Well, the fool had no idea of the immensity of our organization, of course, and must have thought he could escape by running away to America. Boris immediately punished the fool and his wife rather severely. In fact, it was capital punishment. But it took him a while to locate the stone. The man had given it to his two children and sent them off to their uncle. Here. Evansdale. When Boris found them, I guess he figured they were too young to know what had happened. Anyhow, showing a little uncharacteristic mercy, he simply took back the stone and let them live and forgot about them.

"To him the whole affair had no meaning, except that art had betrayed him once again, maybe." Here the old man interrupted himself with one of his bouts of dry laughter.

"But for me it meant something else."

Now the old man simply stopped talking. For a minute or so Brice figured he was just resting. But no, he had apparently finished with his story. Even Russ and June, who had picked up their drinks and sort of wandered over, had difficulty in keeping themselves from screaming at him, "For Godsake go on with it."

But Elena, who had obviously had experience with

this sort of thing before, stepped in with, "What did it mean to you, okay?"

The old man nodded, and for once his expression was very serious. He held out his small hand as if he held something in it for them to look at.

"To me it meant that the stone had wanted to go to the children. To use the children. You see, Germanicus and the others, they think of it that they are using the stones. But over the years, I have come to understand that the stones"—he paused and widened his eyes—"are using us.

"I think, for instance, that my little stone, Yawtlée, is through with me. It is trying to go to Brice, here. If he will let it. But then again, if he won't let it, I think it will anyway." More laughter.

"What kind of crazy horseshit is this?" Russ muttered, but everybody ignored him. Even Junie.

"So I had Jerry sent here through Quinn. I set him up with this bar, here, so he could watch the two kids and wait."

"But you never told me what I was watching for," Jerry said.

"I never knew."

"Well, what do you want now?" Jerry insisted.

The old man laughed again. "I still don't know," he choked out.

"Well, how 'bout a beer?"

"He doesn't drink," Elena explained.

"Sure, a beer would be fine," the old man said—naturally. Jerry went behind the counter and poured a mug of ale and slid it expertly along the bar.

Meanwhile, Brice was just sitting there, watching and listening but mainly trying to scheme. He hadn't the faintest idea what to do in this scenario. Maybe nothing, he thought. What can they do? They can't drag me out of here and force me to find the stone, right?

The old man was going through one of his quiet spells. Brice noticed him staring into his beer with a strange intensity. I wonder what the hell he sees in there? he thought.

Across the world, someone sat holding a stone in the palm of a hand, staring into a bowl of water and chanting. Thinking: Yes, that's it, look into your beer. Curiosity is your weakness. Like a cat's. Two voices were intertwined here, two spirits, two stones. Each concentrating on a particular task. Trap him, one of them thought, but could not break concentration by saying it aloud. Open the doorway, the other thought-willed.

Back in the Tavern of the Laughing Moon, Jerry was saying to Elena, "Has he ever done this before? Jesus, what's happening here?"

"With the old man you never know."

But Elena was worried. The old man had done plenty of weird things, all right, but just staring into his beer and passing out with his eyes open was certainly a new one. They had carried him over and stretched him out in one of the booths. Closed his eyes.

"Maybe he's already drunk his beer psychokinetically and passed out on us," Russ said with what was for him an unusually sharp touch of wit.

6

AND NOW THE two voices chanting, the two faces reflected in the opaque blackness of the two stones. Across the world, yet also here somehow in Evansdale. You could almost feel their chanting hovering in the air like a living entity.

A crack opened up in the sky. A strange luminous fog spilled out of it, moving fast, pouring through the trees as if it were liquid. Spreading out in all directions.

And now something indescribable, unformed, glided out, something darker, more substantial than fog. Something that moved with a deadly purpose. Then another and another. Through the last fading light of day, they floated like shadows. Seeking.

A small brightly colored butterfly fluttered across the path of one of the shadows, searching for its place to settle in for the night. In an instant it was dead, and a bizarre transformation began to take place.

Ruford was already holed up for the night in the little playground equipment shack the townspeople pretended not to know he was sleeping in. After all, there wasn't any equipment these days. He was just finishing his dinner, which tonight consisted of three cheese-on-rye sandwiches that old lady Benson had given him for washing her raunchy old Ford station wagon, and he was thinking to himself about getting his act together tomorrow and going into town for a full meal, when the revelation came upon him.

He got up immediately and went outside, and into a luminous otherworldly fog, with a strange greenish underglow, as thick as the foam in a mug of beer.

"Praise the Lord, it's the end of the world," he shouted out loud in his stentorian voice. "'Bout fuckin' time, too," he added with a chuckle.

"Aw shit," he mumbled, shaking his head. He could actually sense the chanting underneath the fog, causing things, directing things. He couldn't hear it, but somehow he could sense it. Was it evil?

Well, damn it, this was it. He had been worrying about it, waiting for it, and at last, here it was. And strangely enough—and he never would have predicted this part—but now that it was here, all of his fears had dissolved. I done what I done, he thought to himself, and here I am, one way or the other. "Too fuckin' late to worry about it, right, God?" he shouted out loud.

With a calm that amazed him, he walked slowly out onto the playground eerily transformed by glowing fog. The light of day was finally fading out, but the greenish glow in the fog was brightening.

" 'And death shall have no dominion,' " he shouted, not remembering the poem, just the one triumphant line.

And now, walking into the mystic fog, waiting for the Lord to take him, it was as if all the passion for the fight drained out of him, was released into the fog and the underlying chanting. The fight between good and evil, black and white, negative and positive, yin and yang, all over with now. End of world. (In fact, that had been the world.) But to go beyond . . . ?

"Praise the Lord," he shouted. Something wonderful and magical was emerging from the fog, an exquisite symphony of color and shape, beyond good and evil. It floated toward him magically, not even bothering to use its wings.

Ruford held out his arms to it, and as it floated to him, gathered it into his chest.

It was an enormous butterfly shape, but not really a butterfly. He could see that, looking up into it. Looking up? He must have fallen down, because now he was on his back on the cool concrete, looking up at the giant butterfly creature perched on his chest. The shape was wavering, shifting a little, the colors kept brightening and then fading like a neon light. And the eyes! The eyes were not the eyes of a butterfly or any other insect.

At first Ruford had not noticed the stinging sensation, it had been so subtle. Like being pricked with a very sharp-pointed needle. Acupuncture, the thing was giving him acupuncture treatments. And the eyes—this was not a messenger of the Lord.

Alarmed, he tried to sit up. But could not, he was so weak. The thing fluttered its wings; and its eyes, its evil eyes, staring glassily into his—evil!

Shit, he was not beyond the struggle between good and evil. He was still alive and in the middle of it. He made another effort to surge up. But his head spun and he fell back down again. He was so weak that everything was spinning from the effort. He almost passed out.

The thing was draining out his blood. There was no doubt about that. And now he realized what the stinging, aching sensation was: he didn't have to look down to see that what he had thought of as the butterfly's long graceful limbs were actually some kind of tubes which were penetrating his body and sucking out his life fluid.

God sure does work in mysterious ways, he thought, and would have laughed if he could have; "mysterious" was hardly the word for it.

And yet even now, deep down underneath the horror of feeling his heart pumping the last of his life force out of him and into the giant butterfly of death, beneath the aching pain, was a field of deeply growing shimmering bliss.

I've done all I could, he thought, and now it's over. The only thing left to do is to let go.

And death shall have no dominion, he shouted to himself as he fell away into the rising bliss, and finally went beyond the war between good and evil, and the concept of time, and froze in eternity.

7

WHILE RUSS WAS busy courting Big Tom's cute little wife in Jerry's tavern, his drab, miserable wife Helen was home alone, justifying her existence, as always, by cleaning house. Alone, so alone. Working away, scrubbing her fingers to the bone, while Russ was off supposedly working at the gas station, but she knew, everybody knew . . .

And all the time she was working—well, not right now maybe, but she should be working, not just lying down here on the living room couch, head pounding, all alone in Russ's fucking little dream house in the country, trying not so much to sleep but just to forget that Russ was chasing after that shallow bitch June. Trying to forget that despite all the platitudes about motherhood, she did not like her son (what's to like?), forget that this was her life. (How could *this* be her life?) Just plain forget everything, when their dog Big Mike (named, no doubt, after Russ's buddy and idol Big Tom), who was supposed to be outside in the first place, but obviously wasn't outside, started to bark. And kept on barking and snarling in such a convincing manner that there was no chance to block it out.

"What is it, Mike?"

Big Mike seemed to be caught up in a dilemma about whether to be furious or whether to be afraid. First he would scuttle toward the kitchen door, toenails rustling on the scarred linoleum, snarling; then he would back off, whining, hackles up all the way from the base of his spine to the base of his skull.

Helen opened up the door. Jesus Christ, what was this, Mars? Why not? First the lovely move from Sacramento to the charming little untown of Evansdale; from there perhaps Russ had managed somehow to have the whole house (if you can call anything that small a house) picked up and set down on Mars.

But as she looked out the door and tried to penetrate the thick, clotted fog, which was, believe it or not, glowing with an icky green phosphorescence, she felt the stirrings of a strong emotion. Which was something she hadn't felt for a long time. Only problem was—that emotion was fear.

It seemed to her that she could see smoky shadows moving deep within the fog, but shadows of what? Shit!

"Who—who's out there?" she stammered, realizing from the sound of her voice that she was really scared here.

"Stay out of our backyard. It's private property," she called out in a stronger voice. "It's private property." The American dream, she said to herself. The American nightmare, she amended, and for a moment she even wondered seriously if she was actually asleep on the couch and dreaming this, it was so otherworldly. No such luck.

"All right, whoever you are (whatever you are), I've got a dog here. I'm turning him loose. I warned you.

"Get out there, Mike." Mike whined and backed off a bit, toenails scrabbling on linoleum. Then snarling and growling a little. Mr. Tough Guy, but in no big hurry to get out there and prove it.

"Hey, do your thing, big guy, or keep your mouth shut from here on . . ."

As if he understood the implied insult, Big Mike, who while no pit bull was nonetheless a big, strong brute with some mastiff in him, charged into the backyard. Helen slammed the door behind him. Where's Timmy? She thought suddenly, surprising herself that the thought would even enter her mind. (Whew!—motherly.)

Probably hanging out with Tommy, as usual. He'd be better off with Tommy anyway.

Wouldn't he? Locked the door. And burst into tears and actually started to scream, but held most of it in, when she heard big bad Mike's agonized fusillade of yelps, ending in one horrendous cut-off howl. Then silence.

Oh my God. Oh my God. She was crying. Trying to back out of the kitchen but unable to. She could not take her eyes off the doorknob. Would the doorknob turn? Oh my God. Oh my God. Phone, there was a phone in the kitchen. Right there next to her on the wall. Somehow she broke through her paralysis and jerked the phone off the hook. "Hello. Hello? Hello?" Dialed 911. "Hello, oh please, hello." Nothing but static. Loud static. A sea of static. It was like one of those seashells you held up to your ear and listened to the goddamned ocean. "Hello, I want to talk to the police, oh please, can you hear me? Hello. I want the police. I want to talk to Timmy." She let the phone receiver drop and it swung down and bashed into the wall.

"Timmy, you shouldn't be out after dark. You shouldn't be out so late," she sobbed out loud. He's only ten years old, she thought, and I don't even know where he is. Oh my God, he's only ten years old, he's just a baby.

"Timmy," she cried out. Then the thought—no, the certainty—emerged, floating up from the darkness of her unconscious as slowly and inexorable and clear as a dirigible floating through the skies: I, Helen Lewis, am going to die alone. And in terror. She screamed, this time really screamed.

As if in answer, something black and round began emerging from the lower center of the door, as if it were growing from it in slow motion. It kept on coming steadily, and suddenly Helen could make out what it was.

"It's a dog. It's a dog. It's a dog," she chanted hysterically.

And it was, insanely, the head of a dog pushing through the solid wood surface of the kitchen door. It looked like one of those advertisement photos of a dog or cat entering the house through a dog door. Only there was no dog door. There was no dog door!

Still trying unsuccessfully to force herself to back through the doorway into the living room, and still crying like a baby, Helen now started to pant. Which was not easy. Pant like a dog. Was it a dog? It looked like a dog, yet its features were fuzzy and indistinct. "Mike?" It looked kind of like Mike but it wasn't Mike, oh no, it wasn't Mike. It seemed to be having trouble getting through the door. Was it stuck there? Oh how funny, she thought, I should laugh. But she screamed again instead.

The creature seemed to be still in the process of forming itself. And it was looking less and less like Mike, and even, yes, terrible as it is, admit it, less and less like a dog. Its jaws were becoming bigger and more powerful, its neck thicker, its head and eyes smaller. It's as if, Helen thought, it had used Big Mike as a blueprint and now was improving upon the plans.

The thing was halfway through the door now, and Helen shouted, "Oh, what are you?" and suddenly broke the spell and ran into the living room, hearing the scrabbling of toenails across her kitchen linoleum. Just like Mike, she thought, he's wrecking my linoleum, and she plunged through into the bathroom and locked the door and backed up and backed up and fell over the side of the fucking little bathtub in that fucking little bathroom of theirs and hit her head hard on the wall and fell down, into the tub, which was wet on the bottom. Had she wet her pants? Oh, have I? Have I? Have I?

It was just a dream. Oh, please, just a . . .

Something began to emerge through the lower center of the bathroom door. Something that made her scream and scream and scream. And she did the only thing she could do and pulled the shower curtain. Would it emerge through the curtain the same way it had through the doors? Or would it just . . . ?

She tried to pray but all she could think of was "Our Father who art in heaven." "Oh, please, Father," she choked out loud, "oh please, Father who art . . ."

And when it finally happened, it wasn't the pain, but the terror that escalated past the point that any human could bear. For physically she was quite numb and could only watch herself being torn to pieces without really feeling what she ought to feel, but the sharp clear flare of panic was like an explosion that blew the humanity of her consciousness to bits. And the thing about it was that it only lasted a moment. And the thing about it was that it lasted forever.

8

ABOUT THE SAME time as Russ's wife was being eaten alive in her bathtub, Big Tom was outside with the two boys, walking down his thoroughbred racehorse, and only real extravagance in life, Dark Thunder; weird fog or no weird fog. Naturally little Tommy and his pal Timmy were supposed to have done this hours ago, and naturally they hadn't. So here he was. Leading the big lanky black gelding back and forth along the path that led from the house out to the little homemade corral and around the outside of the corral and back again.

Sure he had jumped Tommy about it; damn it, the boy needed discipline; but actually Big Tom liked to walk the horse down. It was a quiet time, after the both of them had run their races—at least the kid had got home in time (just barely) to work the racehorse out, which he had damn well better. But mostly the whole routine was . . . well, just routine. Little Tommy would bitch, but take the horse down to Ruckerman's stable, better late than never, where he was allowed to use the track to run Thunder. Then Big Tom would bitch that the kid never walked the horse down enough (which was at all). This would give Big Tom an opportunity to lecture about the importance of the big black expensive horse and what it was going to do for them (and little Tom and his friend Timmy an opportunity to roll their eyes at each other). That was all right. What wasn't all right was this weird, weird, glowing fog. Somehow it even made the landscape (what he could see of it) look alien and, yes, foreboding. It seemed to him as if he occasionally caught glimpses through the stuff of things that hadn't been there before.

"What causes it to glow, Daddy?"

"Microorganisms," Big Tom came up with, not quite sure what that meant.

"Sure, Dad." The kids had laughed, but it was uneasy laughter. Still, they seemed to be getting used to it—kids'll get used to anything.

He could hear the two boys up ahead of him on the path swearing at each other in their usual half-hostile, half-friendly manner.

"You're a fart."

"No, you're a fart."

"You're a elephant fart. PU."

"Goddamn it, don't talk that way," Big Tom said, causing both boys to guffaw in amusement.

Tom drifted back into *the dream:* Someday soon, he was going to enter Dark Thunder in one of these local races—no contest. And from there work his way up to the damn Kentucky Derby. He knew old Dark Thunder could do it. Then wouldn't everything change! The boys couldn't understand it. He hadn't reached them yet, but hell, they were only ten years old. One day they would see that all the time and energy (not to mention all of their money) he put into that racehorse was love. And that animals respond to love by giving their all. He had confidence that old D.T. could win the Derby. And he had confidence that the boys would one day come to understand this. But Junie—that poor, shallow creature would never understand diddly-squat. Junie just didn't give a lick about anything 'cept Junie. Well, that was all right. Big Tom could live with that. And he was too busy putting all of his positive energy into D.T. here to throw any away on Junie. She was a mistake, he figured. But no sense crying over spilt milk. Once Dark Thunder started really pulling in the big bucks, Tom would have to deal with her. Maybe toss her out on her cute little—no, by God, he'd give her a chance. That way it would all be on her shoulders. He would be able to live with it one way or the other.

Suddenly several things happened at once to snap him out of his constant dream and into the blazing reality of the now: Dark Thunder whinnied and reared. A dog, his dog Bart, howled an agonizing howl, cut off, and the two boys froze like hunting dogs at point, just visible in the path up ahead of him. Big Tom, using his strong arms to bring the horse down and keeping his eyes glued on the boys at the same time, felt the hackles rise up along the back of his neck and feather up both of his forearms. What were they staring at?

When the dogs came out of the fog and took them, it was all over in a matter of seconds. If they were dogs. Strangely enough, even while reeling under the shock wave of horror and revulsion, he noticed that what he was witnessing here was more like a shark attack than something that would be done by dogs: the enormous heavy jaws which opened too wide and closed with too much strength, the thick ropy necks and muscular shoulders, the absolute silence. Just before they hit they swiveled their heads sideways as would a great white shark.

"Tommy," Big Tom screamed, but it was already too late. Too late for everything. Dark Thunder was trying to rear again, and Big Tom jerked him down again, and thought for a moment of jumping up there bareback and running for it. But why?

"Oh, Tommy, I've failed you," he shouted out loud. Then he let loose the reins and struck the big racehorse on the rump. "Run, Dark Thunder," he said. And Dark

Thunder, who needed no coaxing there, was instantly gone, vanished into the eerie fog.

As the creatures came for him, Big Tom noticed that their features seemed blurry, indistinct. But not when they hit. When they hit him, everything about them was as solid as a rock.

He was a big strong man and he tried to fight, of course, but fighting was entirely useless. And because their attack was so devastating, he did not even have time to register what they were doing to him. When they tore him to pieces he did not even have time to feel the pain. And he did not even realize who it was doing all that screaming.

9

GEORGE BAINES WAS still under the glow of what had happened to him in his curiosity shop earlier in the day. But unfortunately, his wife Martha wasn't.

After her usual bout of dinnertime nagging (everyone always ate as fast as they could in the Baines household and got away from the table, which was part of Martha's territory), the kids settled down in front of the TV, but something was wrong with the reception tonight. All you got was hiss and dots. So the two of them retreated to their bedroom, safely out of Martha's reach, while George went out on the front porch for "a bit of fresh air" (to escape). But what was this? It was supposed to be night, but it was practically as bright as day, filled with clotted hazy chunks of fog. Glowing fog. He actually went back into the kitchen and fetched Martha. She peered out the front door cautiously, her perennially angry expression changed to one of apprehension.

"So what?" she said. "Fog, big deal!"

"But why is it glowing?"

"How should I know? I've got to get back to my dishes." In control as always, but her frightened expression betrayed her.

After she had gone back inside, George moved off the porch and into the fog a ways. What was this? It wasn't only the fog that was so unsettling, but what he could make out through the fog had an unfamiliar quality, as if somehow parts of some strange other world were being juxtaposed over the common everyday one he knew.

For a moment he thought he could hear distant screams, but they were gone before he could be certain. Total silence, and then a sound that set the earth trembling. For a second or two he couldn't place it, he was so disoriented, but he quickly recognized it for what it was: horse's hooves.

He walked around the side of the house, where he was shocked to see Big Tom's prize possession Dark Thunder whinnying and prancing back and forth alongside the rickety wooden fence that encompassed his backyard. The dumb horse didn't seem to know whether he was fenced in or fenced out.

"Here, boy." George held out his hand, but the horse snorted and shied away from him. Still feeling the effects of whatever the old man had done to him earlier this afternoon, George did something he would never have done normally. He decided to act on an extremely subtle intuition, no more than a fleeting feeling. As he was walking back around to the front of the house, he suddenly broke into a run, which was something he hadn't done for ages.

Breathing heavily, intensely aware of his heart pounding under all that padding that was in some mysterious manner him, George threw open the front door and shouted for the children. Catching the urgency in his voice, the two of them came running. And for the first time he thought with a start: these beautiful slender Oriental children are mine. Not my brother's anymore, he's gone. They're mine. It was a breathtaking thought. And since he was out of breath already, he could not speak to them at all, simply grunt and trot back off the porch and around the house again. The kids fairly flew by him, shouting happily, until suddenly the older of them, the girl, my Violet, George thought, pulled up with small delicate hand dramatically held against small delicate forehead and swayed as if she were going to faint. "Oh my God, the fog."

"Never mind that," George managed to gasp out, "you just do as I tell you and you'll be all right, understand?"

"It's Dark Thunder. Dark Thunder, Dark Thunder," William shouted excitedly, pointing to the horse, which was still prancing up and down along the fence.

"Exactly as I tell you, Vi. You two get on that horse and ride for town as fast as you can, you hear? You head for Jerry's and don't you stop until you get there."

"But there's no saddle," Violet whined, really getting scared.

"One of you hold him and the other one climb up on the fence. Get going."

"But how can we . . . ? He won't let us."

"You hear me, get going, the both of you, right now."

George held his breath. He had stopped running but his heart hadn't stopped pounding in his chest. And wouldn't now till it stopped for good.

Some plan, George thought anxiously, how could it work? It was just a wild idea, and like all wild ideas it simply couldn't work. The horse wouldn't let him near, then why would it let the kids? Please, he thought, oh please.

The horse shied away from William, who backed off and scrambled up the fence. "You do it, Lettie," he said to his sister. "He likes you. Everything likes you," he added in a coaxing tone of voice.

Violet looked uncertainly back at George. "Go on," George said in a breathy voice.

"Close your eyes," William suggested, "and hold out

your hand and think to him, kind of. You know you can do it, Lettie."

Violet, who was beginning to cry now, closed her eyes and held out her hand. And then George saw a wonderful thing happen. The most wonderful thing he had ever seen in his life. The big racehorse suddenly began to quiet down and then walked slowly over to the girl's outstretched palm and nuzzled it. Violet took the reins and maneuvered the horse over up against the fence, and somehow kept him there while William scrambled onto his back like a little monkey. Somehow she even kept him from bolting while she climbed the fence.

There was magic all around me all the time, George thought, and yet I never even saw it. I was like Martha doing her damn dishes right up to the end of the world. Like nothing's really happening.

"Hurry," he said in a low voice, careful not to spook the horse, which was spooked enough as it was.

And then they came out of the fog.

"Go!" he shouted. Dark Thunder reared; George felt his heart leap up into his throat; but somehow, some unbelievable how, William kept his seat, and the moment the horse came back down Violet leaped off the fence and landed on the horse's back behind William, grabbing him around the waist to stop herself, so that the both of them almost toppled over the side. But they didn't, they hung in there, and William, holding the reins, dug his heels in, and Dark Thunder surged forward as if shot out of a gun.

It was so close that the huge doglike creatures were left snapping their massive jaws on empty air.

William guided the big horse straight down along the fence and almost immediately out of sight. Where they headed from there, George couldn't tell. All he could do was pray they could stay on the horse. Of course, living in Evansdale, they had ridden horses before, but not thoroughbred racehorses, bareback, at top speed.

All of the doglike creatures had followed the horse off into the fog, but George knew there were more to come. And sure enough, he now heard Martha screaming from the kitchen. She died doing the dishes, he thought, amazed. And suddenly three more of those creatures charged out of the fog and leaped at him, catching him on the arm, side, and thigh, clamping down with their huge jaws and tearing off chunks. He went instantly numb and fell over backward. And as he fell he caught sight of an enormous butterfly floating out of the fog. Message from God, he thought feverishly, but what does it mean?

10

EVERYBODY WAS FUSSING over the old man in the corner booth: Jerry putting ice on his forehead, while Elena chastised him angrily, oblivious to the fact that he obviously couldn't hear her, and Russ and Junie offered up a steady stream of totally useless suggestions. Mary Jane had shocked everybody by stepping in and giving him a crisp couple of slaps on the face, then shrugged noncommittally when she noticed everyone staring at her in astonishment. Brice, who was the only one not involved, was off pacing up and down the front of the room talking to himself, mainly arguing whether the prudent thing was to just flat out run for it again, or to play it cool and pack up and slip out in the middle of the night. He would have to borrow Russ's truck or else take Mary Jane with him. Some argument. Fact was there was no way he was going to let Mary Jane get away from him. So it would have to be later tonight. That was when he first heard the screaming. Probably just kids goofing around, he figured. But why did it cause those chills to run up his spine?

He opened the front door and stepped outside. It was a cool early summer evening, just beginning. But it was the beginning of an evening the like of which had never been witnessed on this earth before.

"Oh my God," Brice said out loud, moving forward

to lean on the wood railing of the porch and staring off into the fog.

All of the shocking, mind-boggling things that had happened to Brice lately, combined with that numbness which seemed to have followed his brother's death, gave the effect of living within a dream. A nightmare. None of it seemed real somehow: for one thing, it was all happening too fast. As if he were on a treadmill racing into a fusillade of fake shocking scenes. He would no sooner identify what was happening to him than it was gone and something new and equally shocking was popping up. Thing was, that just like a dream, he was astonished by it, but he really didn't believe any of it. Part of the reason he had come up here to Jerry's was to sort it out and try to decide what he believed and what he couldn't buy.

Greenish fog, for instance. Glowing green fog? Glowing green fog was definitely not part of this earth as he knew it.

It was scary, yet it was quite beautiful. And what was that weird shape in the middle of the street, some kind of shrubbery? That just plain hadn't been there earlier today.

Farther down the street he saw a woman running frantically toward him. He stared openmouthed. Even at this distance he could tell that she had just plain run out of whatever shoes she was wearing and was now sprinting barefoot down the middle of the street. He had never seen a woman wearing a dress run that fast before.

But it was not fast enough. Creatures fairly flew out of the fog and brought her down. Were they dogs? They looked like dogs, but there was something different about the way they moved, the size of them, the awful ferocity of their attack. They were not dogs.

At the same time he spun around to the sound of horse hooves, saw the horse stumble and go down. For an odd, stretched-out moment of time it seemed to hang there like a freeze-frame on TV. The big black horse hanging in the eerie glowing fog, muzzle flecked with foam, eyes bulging, and child—no, there were two of them clinging desperately to the mane. And then, a slow-motion frame of the creature crashing like an airplane, another of those big dog-things clinging to one of its legs, and yet another attached to its flanks, crashing and breaking with the two kids tumbling through the air toward him, hitting hard, but the boy up first, jerking the girl up on her feet and both of them running for their lives directly toward him.

It was those two little Oriental kids, Brice realized. And they could run like greyhounds, thank God. Still, the only thing that saved them was the dogs' determination to rip the horse to bits. It was a big horse.

"Get inside," Brice shouted, holding the door open, and then, when he was inside too, and just getting ready to bar the door, he caught a glimpse of the woman, or some woman, standing outside at the bottom of the steps.

"Jesus Christ, hurry!" he shouted. And with astonishing speed she charged up the steps and through the door and into the Tavern of the Laughing Moon. Brice slammed the door and dropped the big medieval-style bar into place to lock it. Then he turned to see the back of the woman and the absolutely astonished expressions displayed by everybody gathered around the old man, who were all staring at her.

11

FIRST THE CRAZY old man tells his crazy story and goes into a trance, then the Baines kids come racing in through the door crying, obviously in a hysterical state, then that weird, weird woman floats in, moving in her weird, weird way, and stands there staring at them, while Brice bolts the door (to keep the customers out?). This night of simple fun and festivities at the Tavern of the Laughing Moon was getting to be a bit much for poor little Junie-Bug—and unfortunately it was just starting.

"I want to go home," she announced, which was the biggest mistake she ever made in her life. Zeroing in on the sound of her voice, the weird, weird woman twisted around and seemed to lock her consciousness in on Junie's form. She was practically pointing like a bird dog. And she was . . . Sweet Jesus . . . And she was drooling, drooling, and sniffing the air in an intense, exaggerated manner. And . . . and was this a dream, oh sweet, sweet Jesus, because she was like a woman in a dream because her face, her features, were shifting and stretching. Just kind of moving around a little. Now she began to make an awful whining noise, and hunched her body over; at the same time her face stretched horribly, her jaws bulged and erupted from the squashed-down structure of her skull. And with alarming, unbelievable speed, she sprinted across the floor toward Junie. Russ, who tried to get in her way, was simply swatted aside and clear off his feet as though he weighed no more than a feather. Junie tried to scream, but the creature's short little dinosaur arms clutched her tight and the huge dinosaur jaws were around her throat and . . .

Brice stood frozen behind her, stunned by what he was witnessing; no one in the place seemed able to move, and actually Brice was lucking out by being the one behind her because he could not see what the others were seeing: the woman-creature was standing over the lifeless body with the savagely torn throat, that used to be Junie, and it was chewing. Making slurping noises and chewing.

Almost at the same instant Jerry ran and vaulted over the counter to get behind the bar, and Mary Jane whipped open her purse, jerked out her automatic, dropped the purse, and clicked off the safety.

When the creature turned and ran after Jerry, Mary Jane shouted, "Hey, over here," and stood waiting with both arms out in front in the traditional modern two-handed shooter's stance.

The creature stopped at the sound of her voice and swiveled toward her.

Mary Jane squeezed off a shot and waited to see the result. The hideous head snapped back but there was no blood. For a moment the creature swayed and froze there with everyone watching, then seemed to come out of it, and crouched down, obviously zeroing in on Mary Jane now. Who said in that sweet hip voice of hers: "Okay," and squeezed off three more shots.

The creature swayed and froze. Brice could see some indescribable form of turbulence going on in the head, and then it came out of it again, crouched, and was just starting to charge when Jerry vaulted back over the counter carrying a razor-sharp two-handed Japanese sword, a katana. Jerry had studied tai chi for years with several different styles of Chinese swords and daggers, but when it came down to a real fight, there was no question that the Japanese made the best blades.

Now he ran at the creature in short quick little steps, holding the katana straight up over his head, and suddenly whipped it down and then around in a swooping horizontal stroke, swiveling his shoulders and waist to get his whole body behind it. It was not unlike a batter hitting out at a pitch.

And it was a home run: the blade cut cleanly through the neck and the grotesque head popped into the air, arched up and up, then finally fell and hit the floor and rolled. Strangely, there was no fountain of blood. But then, what wasn't strange here?

The Baines kids shrieked in unison and then scrambled under a table. Everyone else remained exactly where they were until the body fell.

Then Brice took a step away from the door toward the scene across the room. "Hey, listen. Jesus, will someone . . ."

Suddenly the body scuttled across the floor like an obscene crab, scooped up its head, and clamped it back on its neck again. Stood up. Swayed. All of its features were shifting and moving around uncontrollably now. Then, all at once, they solidified. It swiveled and turned toward Jerry, crouched over.

Jerry whacked its head off again, his short plump body moving in a loose effortless manner that definitely reminded Brice of his brother Quinn now. This time he kicked the head across the floor. The body scuttled after it again.

Suddenly the little boy William scrambled out from under the table, stood up and jerked the cheapo red-checkered tablecloth off the table, scattering silverware, napkins, and salt and pepper shakers all over the floor, and threw the tablecloth over the decapitated head, covering it completely. At once the headless body's motions became frantic and disoriented; it rolled over and over, swinging its arms and kicking its legs spasmodically like a frog.

Then it seemed to melt. It even made a sickening fizzing sort of noise. It did not melt into liquid, but into gas. Some sort of dark cloudy gas. You could actually see it pouring off the body, then floating up and through the ceiling.

Jerry looked down at William. The kid's face was bruised and streaked with tears and dirt. Jesus, he thought, you not only beat me at marbles, you beat me at everything.

"There's more of them outside," Violet shouted, emerging from under the table. "Lots and lots more of them. They're killing . . . They're killing . . ." Her voice broke, and she wailed and began crying in earnest.

". . . everyone in town," William finished for her. "Mostly they're like dogs, but sometimes they're like—"

"Shut up, everybody," Jerry said. "Listen to me. Everybody get in the back room, back of the counter there and through the kitchen. Russ, you carry the old man into the back room, and goddamn it, you women try to get him out of his trance some way—any way. He's what this whole thing's about—you dig? So wake him up if you have to beat him awake. You kids go with him. Brice, I want you to . . ."

Russ tapped him on the shoulder. His expression was the sullen expression of an angry little boy.

"I don't have to take orders from you. I'm gettin' out of here and back to my family right now, dipshit. And don't nobody try to stop me."

Jerry smiled up at the bigger man and said in a low voice, so that no one else could hear it: "Tell you what, you'll do exactly what I tell you to do, anytime that I tell you to do it, or I'll cut your useless fucking rednecked head off and use it for a bowling ball."

Without any pause he turned back to the others:

"Brice, here's the key to the pantry closet." He fished out a set of keys from the pocket of his loose-fitting trousers and threw it to Brice.

"Little one, it's padlocked. There's a big can of gasoline in there; I know I'm not supposed to keep it like that, just lug it in here. Get moving."

Everyone moved out fast, even Russ, who was carrying the old man as easily as one might carry a sleeping child.

"Bring the rat poison too," Jerry shouted as an afterthought.

Then he was alone in the dark room, guarding the barred front door with the Japanese sword. Would they come from the front? No real reason to think so. Yet the action was out in front. They were hunting people, killing people out there; God knows, whatever they were, wherever they came from, those mothers were predators. He decided to stay with the front door.

When Brice came back in lugging the five-gallon can of gasoline and the bottle of poison, Jerry said, without taking his eyes off the front door, "Get back in the practice room with the rest of them. Take one of the swords off the wall and guard the door. These Japanese ones are the best, but be careful, they're sharp as razors. I'll be with you in a minute or two."

Brice had no sooner disappeared than Jerry noticed the strange dark-colored bumps beginning to protrude from several places along the front wall and door.

12

THE BACK ROOM of the Tavern of the Laughing Moon existed solely in order to provide the tai chi instruction promised by the sign out front. It was simply a narrow room with an empty wooden floor. From the center of the long unbroken back wall hung a cloth banner with a red and black yin-yang symbol painted on it. It was the only form of decoration except for the plethora of swords, knives, clubs, even spears, on either side of it along the wall from end to end.

There were some mats stacked up in one corner of the room, so the two kids pulled one out and Russ laid the old man down, complaining, "Jesus, the old fart weighs a ton."

Elena and Mary Jane kneeled down, hovering over the old man and trying desperately to think of something to do. "Hey, wake up now," Elena said. "You hear me?" And Mary Jane leaned over and slapped him in the face again.

"Don't do that," William said in his clear, calm voice. "What's the matter with him anyway?"

Elena glared at him and said: "We don't know what's the matter with him, do we? Or then we'd know how to wake him up, wouldn't we?"

"Then we got to figure out what's the matter with him first, see?" William insisted.

Elena looked at Mary Jane, who looked back at her and shrugged.

"Know what?" William said in an excited tone of voice. "I'll bet he ate something that was bad for him, like a poison apple or something. Oh, not an apple, but like that, right?"

"Oh for Christsake," Elena hissed, and then emitted a stream of angry-sounding Spanish.

"Then how 'bout if somebody evil is doing this to him so all these monsters that killed my aunt and uncle can get him while he's helpless?"

No sooner had he blurted this out than his sister Violet began to cry again and William turned to her and said calmly, "Ssh, we can't cry now, Lettie, we just can't," then turned back again.

Mary Jane and Elena looked at each other and then at William. Elena said carefully: "Could be, kid. But how would he do this from far away?"

"He would have to use the mysterious power of the mind. Don't you think? I do. I think you got to, you know, fight fire with fire. My sister Lettie can do stuff like that, maybe. Can you—I forgot what your name is—?"

Mary Jane said, "Mary Jane—and no way."

"How 'bout you? I've never seen you before."

"Elena."

"Can you do stuff like that?"

Elena looked puzzled. "I don't know," she said.

"Goddamn it," Russ complained, "is everybody here crazy 'cept for me?"

"I guess that's a 'No,' " William said.

"I remember your name," William continued. "It's Brice, isn't it?"

Brice nodded.

"Can you . . . ?"

Brice held out his hand palm-out and shook his head furiously. In his other hand he clutched a Japanese sword similar to the one Jerry had kept behind the bar, only with a slightly shorter blade. He was plenty scared, and the sword didn't do much in the way of relieving his symptoms. He had almost thrown up when he saw what that thing had done to June out there, and he figured the only reason he hadn't was that all that adrenaline pumping through his system had sort of settled his stomach. He was still sweating profusely, and every once in a while he would suffer a brief spell of dizziness and almost faint.

He himself felt that none of them had much chance of coming out of this mess alive, and he was amazed at how rapidly the rest of them dissociated from their own impending doom. The two kids and the women were working away at the problem as if it were some kind of test in school. A lot of that, he realized, was due to the influence of William. In fact, Brice had the sensation that this eight-year-old kid somehow was controlling his own surging emotions and manipulating the others as well. For their own good, of course. Could that possibly be?

Russ, on the other hand, seemed to be too stupid to grasp the overwhelming danger in the situation. Didn't he realize what had probably happened to his wife, his child?

Right now, for instance, he had taken down a long narrow Chinese sword from the wall and was swinging it lustily about himself in the air with obvious pleasure. As if reading Brice's mind, he turned to him and said: "Timmy'll be okay, he's with Big Tom. Tom ain't about to let nothin' happen to those kids. No way. I figure Helen—that's my wife Helen—I figure she probably got in the jeep and hauled ass over to Big Tom's, 'cause she knows that's where Timmy is—see? Big Tom'll take care of them for me, see? You don't know him."

Then he turned and whipped the big sword through the air again and said: "Goddamn it, I got to get out of here, and that little wimp Jerry had best not get in my way, neither." But he didn't say it with much conviction.

"You have to hold hands," William was saying when Brice's attention returned to the group gathered around the inert body of the old man. They were all sitting cross-legged on the floor now. Except for William, who was actually pacing back and forth while giving instructions. Mary Jane sat a trifle apart from the other two, with an expression of what might even be detached amusement. Mona Lisa smile. If it was a smile. Nothing, but nothing, seemed to ruffle Mary Jane. Was it the unceasing "sense of wonder" calm of a pothead? Brice wondered, or something else? It struck him that she and Jerry were a good match.

"Why do we have to hold hands?" Elena said, infusing each word with exasperation.

"I bet you do," William said. "Betcha anything you do."

Violet took Elena's hand and looked up into her eyes. Elena visibly stiffened. "If William says we have to hold hands, we might just as well give up and do it. The little fart's almost always right about everything."

"Okay, okay," William said, still pacing excitedly. "Now, Elena, oh yeah, that's it, Elena you got to hold the old man's hand with your other hand."

Obviously resigned, Elena picked up the old man's limp little hand in hers, with the expression of someone picking up a dead rat by the tail. It struck her as remarkable that it was not even that much larger than Violet's. He seemed so small lying there now. But when he was conscious his presence was so overwhelming that you never really thought of him as small. And William was right about all of it. She could tell the moment her hand touched the old man's. She could feel the flow.

And Violet, too. She could feel the power, the consciousness flowing to her from Violet's soft little hand. It was quite different from the austere clarity that marked the awareness of the old man; more subtle. But it was definitely there.

The old man had been right: anyone whom the stones touched had been opened up so that power would be able to flow freely through them. Anyone, and that included Elena. She was still conscious of William talking, but not of what he was saying. He was a long ways away now.

"Close your eyes." She caught that, and was not aware that she had smiled.

13

AS IF EXPERIENCING an entertaining hallucination on some powerful psychedelic, Jerry watched in wonder as the heads of dogs began to slowly emerge from the front wall of his tavern. He was so entranced that for a moment he forgot totally about the danger involved. Then he started, and said: "Shit, you don't want to let yourself get hung up on the hood ornament of a Rolls-Royce as it crashes into you. Right, Jerry? Right!"

But the fact was that the weird and terrible experiences he had just gone through had opened up an entire new world for him. He was a soldier, as his friend Quinn had been. And through Quinn he had been hired into a secret mystical organization that paid him well. He had been told the stories about the Four Guardians who protect the world from myriad unseen dimensions and magic assaults. He had heard about the powers of the stones, and he had believed the stories to a degree, he supposed. But belief was not the same as firsthand experience.

And in fact, when he had helped Germanicus (the name "Boris Kruger" hadn't fit him half so well) hunt down the stone here in California, he had constantly searched the man for some sign of magic, of the impossible. But there had been nothing, just a tall blond Germanic man with an ambience of cold ruthlessness. So Jerry had gone back to half believing. But this—this did not only validate itself for him, it validated everything he had heard. The wildest possible stories.

"But hey, let's stay alive here," he said aloud.

Judging from the glazed expressions, the dogs were in some sort of trancelike state, caused, no doubt, by the effort of pushing themselves through the walls. In fact, everything about them was glazed, vacant: they obviously weren't quite here yet.

Good thing the primitive mothers didn't know what glass was, Jerry thought, or they could have just crashed through the damn windows. Thank God he had painted those opaque in order to darken the bar.

"Eat death, dog," he said out loud as he slashed through the head of one of them, accomplishing nothing. In fact, he noticed only a slight but even resistance, like slashing through a head composed of water. And there was a visible turbulence around the area for a few moments as it re-formed itself.

Holding the sword in his right hand, also holding his breath, he thrust his left hand into the dog's head and waved it around, trying to disturb the structure. No dice, though: he could feel it flowing back into place behind as his hand moved through, and all he achieved was a momentary bubbly turbulence.

How do they know to come in here in the first place? he wondered. Remembering the human version they had killed, the body scuttling across the floor to regain the head, he thought, They must have some kind of senses we don't know about. How could the body know where the head is? And hearing: he remembered how the creature had come through the front door, very directly, as if it knew what it wanted. Probably the old man, Jerry guessed. But the sound of poor little Junie's voice had distracted it. No doubt about that, they had all seen how it had whirled around and zeroed in on Junie the moment she spoke.

Okay, sound. Must be scent too. He recalled its sniffing the air. But none of these things explained the body homing in on its head. Okay, so some unknown sense was involved, but the others were there as well. And one thing for sure, if you can block the head off from the body, the whole works just dissolves and fizzles off into the air like the bubbles in a glass of champagne. As if its vision of itself is necessary to hold it together here in this dimension. Without noticing it, Jerry started whistling "You Go to My Head" as he went back over and laid down his sword in the little pile of resources he had gathered together, and took a mental inventory. Twelve-gauge double-barrel Ithaca shotgun and three-quarters-full box of Peters #4 shells. Maybe! —Yeah, he liked that idea. Whatever they were, they couldn't function without their heads, so what would happen if you blew the head to bits with a shotgun? Might want to try that one. And of course its partner from under the counter of the bar, my old but sharp katana, the samurai's trustworthy companion—don't leave home without it. Okay!

Rat poison. Rat poison? Well, what the hell. Jerry picked up the bottle and walked over to the mutilated body nearby. Too nearby. Poor little Junie-Bug. Remembering the hideous half-human creature crouched over her body, chewing away, he poured the bottle of rat poison all over Junie's body and face, spreading it out as best he could. Sorry, Junie, but what the hell, this way if they eat you at least you'll have your sweet revenge. Jerry couldn't help smiling at that. Shit, what a monster you are, he said to himself.

And the five-gallon can of gasoline. Package of matches. Now we're cooking. Maybe. Don't forget to add the maybe. Sobering thought.

Many of the creatures were now halfway through the walls: front legs, shoulders, and heads on the inside; hind legs, hind ends on the outside. Jerry had been waiting for this.

He figured that what was taking all the time here was changing their molecular structure somehow so they could push it through something solid as it made contact with them. That probably meant that what was outside was still solid. All right!

Jerry began sloshing gasoline all over the wooden wall, first taking care to splash it directly onto areas around the heads, which did not seem to notice it, then spreading it around. According to his theory, the creatures couldn't push through the wall any quicker than they already were doing, but could they back up any quicker? Or were they stuck in between? Only one way to find out.

Jerry took a paper napkin off one of the tables and crumpled it up into a ball, lit it with a match, and tossed it into the wall.

"Eat fire, dogs of death," he said out loud. A blue river of flame spread out and ran clear across both sides of the wall; the heads appeared not to notice.

Of course they weren't really dogs. They had altered the form of what he thought of as dog, made the head, jaws, and neck larger, compressed the skull area, legs, and body. But then, over a few generations so had pit bulls. With a little nudge from their breeders. The only difference was these guys had done it quicker and better.

No, these were not so much dogs as prototypes of the killer-dog image, the way Brice's brother Quinn had sometimes struck Jerry as the archetype of the tai chi master, instead of a student of tai chi as Jerry had been. Watching Quinn, so tall, slender, and effortlessly fluent in all movement, you had to wonder if he had been formed by the tai chi or if it had been invented especially for him.

Ah yes, yes, one of the heads was opening its mouth, and a high-pitched keening noise was issuing from it. It was the first sound Jerry had heard them make, and it didn't in the least resemble any noise ever made by any canine Jerry had ever heard. Surely the thing was in pain; and hey, too fucking bad, fellas.

Now some of the others joined in and the sound was horrendous, but it was music to Jerry's ears. And now he could see that some of them were slowly, oh so sweetly and slowly, drawing back into the wall, roasting their poor little doggie bodies and doggie heads, inch by inch.

"Burn, you motherfuckers," Jerry shouted happily, and then ran back and vaulted over the counter and tried the phone once more. Of course it had been the first thing he had tried it as soon as he had cleared the others out of here, but all he had gotten was static. And that was all he was getting now.

It must be, he reasoned, that not only was some part of another world juxtaposed over this one, but Evansdale must at the same time be partly infused into that world, at least enough so that electrical signals couldn't get in or out. He had gotten the same results when he had turned on the little radio which he also kept behind the counter: just static, nothing but.

Or maybe the damn green fog just plain blotted everything out. He had only caught a glimpse of it through the open door, but it had been enough. The picture of the two kids scrambling in from that glowing, custard-thick stuff, followed by that monstrous woman-type predator, would be forever implanted on his brain cells. Only forever might not be so long, the way things were going here.

The one thing, subtle as it was, that had really sent the chills racing up and down his spine, had been the clothing. The creature had re-created the woman's clothing but had not understood that it was not a part of her body. Therefore her dress, for instance, had not rustled or floated, or in any way moved independently from her. It had only moved in concert with her movement or not at all. It had been a small detail that probably no one had noticed but

Jerry, yet sometimes it was the little things that really spooked you. It had shook him up so badly that he had almost not got to the sword in time, which would have been good-bye Mary Jane—right?

And while he thought of it, Mary Jane was another one of those little things that spooked him. She was just too calm, too cool under pressure, to be a norm. No way. That babe was another predator of some sort. A soldier, like him and Quinn, only a soldier in whose army? Well, that would have to wait for later.

He gathered up the shotgun, shells, and old faithful, his katana, and headed back to join the others. If nothing else, at least he had struck a blow here. As a last thought he turned to the flaming wall in order to savor the sight of all those openmouthed canine heads keening in agony.

"Bad dogs!" he shouted, and then turned and ran out of the room.

14

FOR A WHILE Elena just sat with her eyes closed, feeling things. Sensations were very strong. Weariness; my God, how terror wiped you out. But she hadn't realized how exhausted she was until she closed her eyes. Sensations: the hard wood floor pressing up on her buttocks and calves; an annoying itch, which she could not scratch, in between her shoulder blades; the hand of the old man in hers, and Violet's hand. For a moment she could not remember which was which, and it seemed important to do so. But as soon as she turned her attention to it she was able to perceive the difference, and even as she allowed herself to merge with the fiery warm glow that was the essence of Violet, she felt the two of them drawn into the vortex that she knew without doubt belonged to the old man.

But did it belong to him, or he to it? After all, he was just an ordinary being, a bit of earth, up and moving about on the surface of mother planet. But this channel of awareness was a funnel of liveliness and energy that widened out as you went down it, and then opened up more and more, until finally it spread into an infinite ocean that was bliss. That was being. That was awareness.

She felt herself (herself-Violet) shimmering with joy. Indescribable, limitless joy, until she passed out.

And came to at the end of a dark tunnel, looking down into a room. She did not remember who she was or what she was doing, but she knew that it was somehow important for her to be here.

Gradually she became conscious of different objects in the room. Shadow forms at first; then she made the discovery that merely by directing her attention to them they would be forced to reveal themselves to her: this was the law of this level of awareness, and once she had discovered it, it would be at her command forever. She knew this to be true.

There was danger here. She sensed this clearly enough, although she did not know what from, or why.

Someone was chanting; someone was leaning over, concentrating by staring into a clear white bowl of water. And there was a chalk circle drawn on the wooden floor, with four burning candles placed directly opposite each other. The four corners. To guard the four corners. It struck her then that the Four Guardians were also four candles guarding the four directions of the earth. Fragile little lights that could be blown out by a mischievous gust of wind, yet lights which held back the darkness. Very small lights.

Suddenly the ominous chanting (or rather, her perception of it) swelled to fill the room, and spilled out into other dimensions, where she perceived it altering creation on a very subtle level. A wave of fear crashed over her: if the Guardians were only flickering flames against the darkness, what was she? What was she doing here? What could she hope to accomplish?

She opened her eyes to find herself sitting next to Violet in the Tavern of the Laughing Moon.

"I saw the room," Elena said in awe. "They were chanting something."

"Why were they sitting inside that circle?" Violet asked, lifting her long narrow lids slowly.

"It's supposed to protect them from psychic attack," Elena said. "I think that the circle is just a way of concentrating their attention, though."

"What's 'psychic attack'?" William piped in.

Elena grimaced and said: "Us, I guess. Big deal."

William waved his small hands excitedly in front of her face: "Don't you see? Don't you? That means we got to attack."

"What do you mean?" Elena said, puzzled, scared. "Attack how? With what?"

"No, no, if they made a magic circle to protect against us, that must mean we can hurt them, see?"

Mary Jane raised her hand. "Hey, permission to speak, okay? Yeah, permission granted. Thanks. Listen, this is wild, and I dig it all, but we had better haul ass here or we're all dead meat, you dig?"

"But attack how, who, and with what?"

"Will you shut the fuck up and do what the kid tells you?" Russ snarled. "Jesus!"

"Listen," Elena said to Violet, deciding to ignore the men here, "could you see who it was, how many of them inside the circle? It was more than one; I could tell that, had to be. One to control the old man, and at least one to open up the channel between worlds or whatever they did to let these monsters in. But was it two or three?" She held her breath: Don't let it be three, oh please don't let it be three.

"I couldn't tell," Violet said. "I think that's part of the reason for the circle. I couldn't really see who was in it. I think, for once, little Einstein here may be wrong and they aren't worried about us attacking them, they just don't want us to see them."

"So what?" William said, starting to get exasperated for the first time. "We have to attack them, don't we? Here, let me in here." He sat down and wedged his way in between Violet and Elena, separated their hands and put his hand in Elena's right hand and took hold of his sister's left.

"Okay, can you take me there?"

"Sure, of course," Elena said dryly. "Why not? Why don't you bring your friends?"

"You can't do this, Willie, can you?" Violet said, first sounding petulant, then changing to uncertain.

"Bet I can. Bet you I can if I try. Listen, though—remember, Violet, Elena, do bad things when we get there. Just do anything bad that you can, okay?"

"The kid's right," Russell said, pointing at them with his sword. "Kick some butt. —Shit, now you're driving *me* crazy."

Brice just ignored the proceedings, marching up and down with his samurai sword, guarding against what, from where? Oh God, please let me out of this, he kept thinking. I'm no hero. Just let me out. But he knew God better than that.

15

THIS TIME ELENA must have instantly passed out, or perhaps the whole process took place much faster, but it seemed as if she had no more than closed her eyes and moved into the presence of the old man than she was back in the room where all the chanting was emanating from the middle of that chalk circle. Cautiously she moved closer to the edge and tried to see inside, but everything was smoky and opaque. The chanting itself was marked by a deep underlying reverberation; Elena could not tell how many were doing it or whether the voices were male or female. Tentatively she tried to penetrate the edge of the circle, but could not. It was as if it were covered by an impenetrable dome.

As before, her self-awareness was confused on this level so that she did not remember quite who she was. Strangely enough, though, she was able to retain William's command to do bad things here. It was created of purpose—will, and will was what had brought her here.

"Show us things."

Elena did not know who said this, but knew that it was some part of herself. Someone she had merged with long ago and far away.

She directed her attention to a lamp sitting on a low chest of drawers in one corner of the room. At first it was fuzzy and indistinct, then it gradually grew clearer and clearer. The lamp was a sculpture of a black African woman kneeling and bearing a heavy tan lampshade on her weary shoulders. And it seemed to Elena that it was breathtakingly beautiful. "Break it, break it, break it." The thought welled up inside of her and the lamp grew clearer and clearer until suddenly it simply exploded. —Yes!

"Show me, show me, show me." It was a violent energy, mischievous, childish, and wild, and there were two of them, poltergeists. The word flashed up from somewhere.

"Here."

There was a shelf full of books, and after a moment's pause the books flew off the shelf one after another, flapping their covers frantically and flying through the air like birds. —Yes!

"Here."—Oh, yes, yes, a cupboard full of wineglasses of various sizes and shapes, and a decanter full of rich red ruby port, how beautifully they exploded, one after the next. Yes! And the light fixture and the lightbulb on the ceiling. If you're not going to use it, lose it! Smash, tinkle, yes!

And by now Elena was caught up in the wild ride, the children had the reins. "Show me! Show me!"

Suddenly Elena was aware that the chanting had stopped; a dark, powerful consciousness was turning toward them, searching for them.

"Show me! Show me! Break, break, break!"

"No, stop it, come with me. Now."

"No, we won't stop, we won't."

With a tremendous effort, Elena surged out of the room, dragging the two other presences with her, and raced up the ever-narrowing stream of consciousness, before whatever it was that was searching for them . . .

16

ELENA OPENED HER eyes. The old man was already sitting up on his mat. William and Violet yelled "Yeah!" and shook their right hands, which were clenched in fists. Then they slapped the palms of their hands together, and insisted on going through the procedure with Elena next, who rolled her green eyes up toward the heavens, but complied.

"Once again, you surprise me, Elena," the old man said.

"I had help," Elena answered.

"That's the part that surprised me."

Elena was giving him a rundown of everything that had happened since his awareness had been "captured," as he put it, when Jerry came in through the door carrying a shotgun in one hand and his samurai sword in the other.

"All riiight!" he said when he saw the old man. "But hey, listen up, we've got to get out of here, but pronto."

"It might be better if we holed up and tried to defend . . ." the old man was in the process of saying when Jerry cut him off.

"No way. For one thing, they can get through the walls; for another, I've—well, I set the place on fire."

The old man shrugged, there was no way to argue with that.

"Do you know what we've got here?" Jerry asked him.

"From what Elena has told me, we are dealing with simple predators. Predators from another world, but still, just predators, nothing supernatural. Apparently on their world they have evolved the ability to shift their shapes as camouflage. It would be easier to get close to their prey if they looked like the creature they were hunting, a wolf in sheep's clothing."

"Why do they so often choose dog if they can take the shape of anything?"

"Who knows?" the old man said. "Perhaps dogs are what they find here that most resembles their original form, or perhaps they find that form to be the most efficient for their grisly purpose. There are plenty of dogs here to choose from, maybe it's just a matter of what they encounter the most wherever they invade.

"But we only know two things about them for sure: One: that they have been here before: certainly all of the folktales about humans who change into animals are about them. It is interesting to note that then, as now, the preferred form was that of a dog, although most people in those days interpreted them as wolves.

"Two: We know that they are difficult but not impossible to kill. I think that now that Elena and the kids here have broken the concentration of our enemies, the connection between worlds has been lost. There won't be any more of them coming through. The thing for us to do is probably just make a run for it. Get the hell out of here and stay out. I don't think they will be able to survive in this environment for long. At least, I hope not. Let's make a run for the cars out front. Six adults and two kids. Let's try for the Chevy. We can all pile in there. Elena can drive."

Jerry nodded: "Can't you control them, with the stone?"

The old man shook his head. "They are probably too stupid to control. Otherwise whoever is behind this would have guided them right to me instead of just turning them loose on the whole town and holding me here."

"Can you handle a shotgun?"

The old man smiled. "I'm too good with a sword. That would be a waste."

Jerry nodded. "Right, me too."

"I can use it," Mary Jane piped up.

Jerry smiled at this. "Sure you can. How much you weigh—ninety pounds? Forget it, this is a twelve-gauge double-barrel. Brice?"

Brice was shaking his head furiously again. "Never shot one, I don't know anything about guns."

"Listen," Jerry said, "if you can play the guitar, you can handle a gun, right? It's hardly as difficult as mastering a Bach fugue, you dig?"

"Hey, whoa there," Russ broke in. "You bet your ass I can handle a shotgun. Gimme, gimme!"

Jerry looked him in the eye, then nodded and said, "Okay," and tossed him the Ithaca. "It's loaded, but the safety's on."

Russ took care of that: with a loud click, he thumbed off the safety and pointed the gun square at Jerry's chest.

"All right," he said. "Gimme some more shells and I'm outta here. And don't any of you try to stop me, either."

"Hey there, big dude," Jerry answered cheerfully. "*Vaya con Dios.* Go out there and kick ass, nobody's going to stop you." Jerry handed him a couple of shells he took from one of the big pockets of the loose nylon vest he wore. "Sorry, that's all we got."

"I gotta get to Timmy and my wife," Russ said in an uncertain tone of voice.

"Sure, fine, we understand here. Don't we, gang?"

As soon as Russ had gone out the door, Jerry handed

Brice some more shells from his other pocket and said, "Okay, so Russ has volunteered to run point for us. As was so graphically pointed out to all us good little soldiers in Nam, your points don't usually last very long. So you pick up the gun, remember to hold it tight against your shoulder, she kicks like a mule. Use the sights, it isn't as easy to hit stuff with a shotgun as you think; and one of the barrels is choked down a bit here, so here's what you do: First you squeeze the trigger that's farthest out, that's the open barrel. Then you squeeze the trigger behind it, that's the choked one. There'll be a lever by your right hand; push it over with your thumb and the gun'll break open, the empties'll pop out. Blow their heads off. Let's go."

Before they reached the back door they could hear the loud *thunk thunk* of the big gun, followed by Russ's scream.

And by the time they were out the door they could see two doglike creatures tearing his body apart, and a third form, with most of its head blown off, already starting to blur, lying in the luxuriant spring growth of grass and weeds, just beyond what was left of Russ.

Jerry came out the door and down the wooden stairs first, followed by Mary Jane, who quickly got down on one knee at the bottom of the stairs and steadied her handgun on the other leg.

"Any ammo left?" Jerry whispered.

"One more clip," Mary Jane replied.

Instantly at the sound of Jerry's voice one of the dogs charged and the other stopped chewing and looked around.

The first shot went high.

"Damn," Mary Jane said, took aim again, and caught the charging creature square in the head with the next two shots.

The dog staggered, stopped moving, and just froze there with a vacant expression on its distorted canine face.

Jerry knew this condition would only last a few seconds, but a few seconds was all he needed. He hoped. So he charged out there into the yard. But just as Jerry reached it, the creature came out of its stupor and jumped up at him. He crouched to meet it. The sword whistled through the air, and once again, with a display of astonishing accuracy, Jerry managed to lop off the head. But this time the momentum completed the attack, and the headless body struck Jerry hard enough to knock him off his feet. And sure enough, immediately the body scrambled off in an effort to regain its head. Meanwhile, the other pseudo-dog charged with astonishing speed.

"Hey, over here," the old man shouted from the porch. And it worked: the creature twisted around in the air and ran toward the sound of his voice. As always, it charged silently, without the slightest hint of the noises an angry dog would make, but as it came you could see its jaws swelling and enlarging. Unnerving, to say the least.

Still kneeling, Mary Jane shot once and missed, then shot again and missed. Then the creature was past her and sprang up at the old man, who was waiting with raised sword to meet it.

Unable to get enough room for any kind of horizontal sword stroke, he drove the blade straight through the middle of its head, splitting its skull neatly in half down to its snout and knocking it back onto the grass, where it scrambled to its feet and stood there trembling slightly. You could see the turbulence where its skull was healing itself.

Still shaking his head, as if someone were listening to his argument, Brice somehow gathered enough courage to jump off the porch and go for the shotgun. And at the same time Elena and the two kids ran off the porch and a little ways into the backyard.

Smoke was visibly pouring out of the shattered windows of the tavern now, and you could hear the crackling of the flames.

Mary Jane walked calmly over to the recuperating were-creature and pointed her handgun at its head. But when she squeezed the trigger the gun made a loud clicking sound.

"Damn." She ejected the clip and fished the last one out of her purse, jammed it in just as the creature started to move, and put a couple of bullets into its skull. It fell back and stood still, apparently martialing its forces for its regeneration trick.

Meanwhile Brice, who was moving faster than he had ever thought possible, had reached the shotgun, scooped it up, found the lever with his thumb, broken it open, and popped in two fresh shells just as Jerry, who was now up on his feet again, beheaded his opponent for the second time, only this time grabbing the head unceremoniously by the ear and tossing it toward Brice.

Brice remembered to use the sights on the shotgun and blew it away, but found himself sitting on the seat of his pants with his ears ringing.

"I told you to hold it tight, goddamn it," Jerry shouted.

The old man, who was now off the porch, was obviously amused to see Elena hacking away at the other creature, which was still standing there trying to heal itself. What Elena lacked in skill she made up for in ferocity, as she had practically chopped the thing into ground round without ever once hitting its neck.

"Stand back, Elena," the old man said, stepped in and surgically removed the head, then kicked it out into the yard, nearer to Brice, who had by now almost attained a standing position.

Brice took careful aim and blew it to pieces, this time managing to stay on his feet. Broke the gun, reloaded automatically. Though he was not aware of it, he was catching on very fast here. But no sooner had he reloaded than he saw Jerry yelling and gesturing wildly at something beyond him. And he whirled in time to see a scene so weird and so unanticipated that he was momentarily frozen by it, as if he were one of the dogs trying to heal himself of some injury. He just stood and stared as the enormous butterfly emerged from the glowing mist, heading straight for him. It was moving surprisingly fast, and though it occasionally flapped its wings, it was clear that this was merely something it did for effect, and had nothing to do with propelling it through the air at such speed. The eyes were enormous, not human eyes, of course, but then again, surely not the eyes of an insect. It was going to . . .

Brice came out of it, and now, getting the feel of the gun, he squeezed the second trigger, using the choked barrel to condense the cloud of deadly pellets, and blew the lovely thing's head off. Now the wings fluttered frantically and for a moment the bizarre headless lepidopteran hovered in the air, going neither backward nor forward.

Suddenly the figures of one, two—no, three more of the dog-type creatures ran out of the fog and began leaping up at the headless fluttering form. Instantly they had it down in the grass, tearing it apart.

Now two more canine forms appeared, and behind them Brice could make out even more shadowy, swiftly moving figures.

"Jesus Christ," he shouted, and then turned and ran back toward the burning building.

"Get back inside," he shouted, though the advice was obviously ridiculous.

The silent pack charged through the tall grass after them, and were at Brice's heels, when with a loud roaring sound the building literally exploded into flames. It threw off a shock wave composed of heat that practically knocked everyone off their feet.

Some of the dogs emitted that high-pitched keening sound that Jerry had observed earlier. All of them turned tail and ran away from the flames a short distance, then turned back around and edged slowly forward, some backing off again.

"They don't like heat," Jerry shouted. You had to shout to be heard over the roar of the fire. But the dogs weren't leaving. As Jerry led the group around the burning building to the front, staying as close to it as they dared, the dogs, keeping their distance from the heat of the flames, followed.

Both children were crying now, and somehow seemed to have fallen under the hand of Elena, possibly the most unlikely of the group to deal with them, as she now herded them after Jerry. The old man came next, followed by Mary Jane; and Brice came last, guarding their rear with Jerry's shotgun.

In the front of the building even the porch was on fire. The dogs were between them and the cars, and now it was only a matter of time before the flames died down.

"Shit," Jerry said, "there's no damn way out." Except one, he thought to himself.

"Okay, you guys, this is it. Elena, you got the car keys, right? Mary Jane, you and Brice get the kids into the backseat. Old fellow—you never did tell me your name—you get up front with Elena."

He held his faithful old samurai sword up straight over his head.

"Brice, you and the kids go first. Wait a bit till I get things going here. But goddamn it, don't you wait too long. You tell him when, Willie, all right?"

"Jerry—" William, still crying, held out his hand, but Jerry was already running along the front of the building and then suddenly darted right out into the pack of dogs.

One moment they saw forms launching through the air, distorted by the flickering of flames, and then Jerry went down.

And remarkably enough, came back up again somehow, sword whirling and spinning among the leaping shadowy forms like a living thing.

"Now," William whispered, and ran toward the big Chevy Jerry had pointed out. Everyone followed.

Not daring to look behind them, they all managed to scramble in and slam the doors, and Elena somehow got the key into the ignition and the car started.

"The lights," the old man suggested hopefully. But the lights did not frighten the dogs, only attracted their attention. And they did not even swerve to avoid the car, so Elena plowed right through them, and around what was left of Jerry, and out of town, fast.

"Thank the gods Elena never remembers to lock her car," the old man said.

Elena, saying nothing, simply bore down on the accelerator. Her face was covered with a mixture of sweat and soot. But I'm alive—somehow, she thought exultantly. She could hear the kids crying in the backseat, now that everyone else had quieted down. The big car was moving out pretty fast, thanks to the old-fashioned who-cares V-8 engine up front, but not fast enough to suit Elena.

"Come on, come on, come on," she whispered to the car, to herself.

"For goodness sake slow down a little," Mary Jane kibitzed from the backseat. "We can't hardly afford a car accident or a flat tire here, right?"

Of course she was right, but Elena just couldn't force herself to ease her foot up off the accelerator; as far as she was concerned it was glued to the floor.

It was just at this moment that the horse-type creature galloped out of the trees and charged the car head-on.

Somebody screamed, glass shattered. The horse actually flew up, smashed into the windshield, and was tossed back off the front again and onto the pavement, where it struggled to get up.

"It's getting up," Elena said, trying to restart the car,

which turned over and stalled, and turned over again and stalled, and finally just stalled.

"It's flooded or worse," Mary Jane said from the backseat. "Oh, shit!"

"The horse," the old man started to say, but Brice was already out the back door, taking aim, and click—wrong barrel, empty shell. The horse was just getting to its feet when the second barrel fired. Taking a lot of its head off, but not enough, apparently, as it stood there clearly and quite swiftly re-forming itself again.

Brice broke the gun, fished two shells from his pocket, and reloaded even quicker than before; but by the time he was ready to fire, the old man was already out of the car and hacking away at the horse's neck with the samurai sword. But you don't take a horse's head off with one sword stroke, not even with the finest blade ever forged. So, after what seemed to Brice an eternity of chopping away at the neck like a feverish woodsman at his favorite tree, apparently satisfied with the point he had reached, the old man backed off and yelled, "Shoot!"

This time Brice, sighting in on what was left of the neck and using the choked barrel, blew the head clear off, and the old man grabbed it by the mane and chucked it underneath the car. Immediately the body began to thrash and kick and then go through the now-familiar process of dissolving into a cloud of smokelike gas.

"Get out and run for it," the old man shouted. Elena was still trying to start the car, but it was obvious to everyone that the battery was dead.

They began running up the road, only by now, staggering was a more apt description of it.

"How far?" Elena gasped, without breaking stride.

"How would I know?" the old man wheezed. But it was all academic: up ahead familiar shapes emerged from the fog. One, two, then more.

Brice and Mary Jane took aim with their guns, and

the old man held his sword in a casual, relaxed manner very unlike Jerry's style. Yet you could tell he meant business.

"Very well," he said, "let's die like warriors."

The dogs charged. The shotgun went off and the handgun popped three or four times before Mary Jane used the last bullet in the clip, and then just kept going click, click, click. The shotgun roared again. In all the noise and confusion Elena could hear but not understand the sound of the swiftly approaching siren. It wasn't until the car hurtled out of the fog and the headlights hit the dogs that she realized what was happening.

The front doors flew open and two cops jumped out shooting, one with a shotgun, one with his revolver.

Whether it was the lights, the noise of the sirens, or just the confusion of attack from a new direction, the dogs whirled around and charged the two policemen.

And whether it was an intelligent intuition on the part of the cops or just plain panic, each of them ran a short distance away from the car, drawing away the dogs before they went down.

William was already sprinting toward the car, followed by the rest of the group. This time Elena piled into the backseat with the kids and Brice. And Mary Jane dived in the driver's side.

Their saviors had left the motor running. With astonishing skill Mary Jane whipped the car backward and spun it around facing the way it had come, jammed down the accelerator, and once again, siren still blasting, they were racing down the highway.

After a bit Elena noticed that the peculiar green fog was rapidly thinning out now. We're going to make it, she allowed herself to think for the first time.

"How are the kids, Elena?" the old man asked from the front seat.

She looked down. "They're asleep," she said, with awe in her voice.

"Me too," Mary Jane chipped in. "Sometime next year, maybe."

The old man chuckled. Nothing seemed capable of changing his mood.

"How about that?" he said. "Elena's charming new family is having a nap."

"Family, my ass," Elena snapped back at him. "Family nothing!"

Brice leaned forward and toward her around the sleeping kids. Even though it was dark, he seemed to be trying to make eye contact with her. His eyes, what she could see of them, were black gleaming spots of intensity. "You're wrong," he said. "Family is everything."

17

FINALLY, AFTER WHAT seemed like hours of hurtling through the night, imagining myriad varieties of possible forms that might rush out and attack the car (thank God they didn't have rhinos or elephants in California), Elena saw light up ahead. A slight glow, it was coming to them from around a curve in the road, and Mary Jane slowed the car and pulled up before the police barrier.

It wasn't until she was out of the car that Elena realized how beat-up she was, again! It was obvious by the way the policemen stared at her, wincing. She had finally had time to heal up from the old injuries, with the exception of the ankle, which still bothered her some, and in fact was quite sore from all the running she had just subjected it to, but now she had an assortment of new cuts and bruises. Her nose was bleeding and swollen, probably from bashing her head into the steering wheel when she had driven the car into the horselike creature; and she seemed to be more singed from the fire and covered with soot than the others. Why was it that Mary Jane, and all those crisp, slender, competent heroines she resembled, always escaped unharmed and managed to suffer only a charming degree of disarray?

"Gee, bet I look a mess," Mary Jane said, smiling, as

she stepped out the driver's side. "Hey, don't shoot, boys. It's me, Mary Jane."

"Don't shoot until you see the whites of her thighs," Elena grumbled, waking up the kids.

"Where are we?" Violet murmured sleepily.

"Where the road goes around that big bend," William said in his small clear voice, "about ten miles outside of town, about twenty-seven miles to Redding. Wouldn't you say, Mary Jane?"

"If you say so, sweetie." Mary Jane shrugged.

And why was Mary Jane able to drive a car like that? What the hell was she anyway, a professional race car driver?

As the rest of them emerged from the car, it became apparent that Brice also hadn't fared so well. He was obviously in pain from where the big shotgun had pounded his right shoulder, and like Elena, was bruised, beaten, and exhausted.

It struck Elena that Mary Jane was more of a match for the old man than she was. The both of them looking relaxed, calm, even slightly amused. Surely the old man would be better off paired with Mary Jane for an apprentice.

"Yeah, but I'm stuck with you, Elena," the old man whispered as he raised both hands over his head where they could be seen clearly, following the orders the policeman shouted to them through the megaphone.

For a few minutes Elena had been sure that on top of everything else they were going to wind up, children and all, down at the police station in Redding going through some local form of nightmarish interrogation. But leave it to the old man to put her fears at rest. "No, Elena, it's not the Redding police, it's the county sheriff's department." Great!

After a while the short heavyset officer who seemed to be the sheriff allowed himself to be persuaded by the old man to move off a ways from the others in order to talk in private. It seemed that the old man had some secret classified information that he would only reveal to whoever was in charge. Figured!

After a few minutes they rejoined the group, but a noticeable change had taken place in the little cop's demeanor. Whereas before he had looked angrily alert, verging on some sort of emotional tantrum or other, he now appeared at ease and sure of himself.

"I'm taking them into town myself, Guthrie," he announced to the tall saturnine officer who seemed to be his second-in-command.

"But, Sheriff," Guthrie tried to cut in.

"No buts, Guthrie, just do what I tell you. This is an emergency we got here, and there's just plain no goddamn time for explanations." He cupped his pudgy hand around his mouth and whispered, "Reds."

"Reds?" Guthrie whispered back, amazed. For a moment he had forgotten what Reds were. Did the sheriff mean sleeping pills? Then he had it. Russians! Jesus Christ, he had always known the sheriff was nuts: But what the fuck would the Russians be doing out here creeping around in the forest? Invading Evansdale? Jesus!

Reds just outside of Redding? Hiding in the redwoods? In his mind's ear, Guthrie could clearly hear the sheriff reminding him, as always, "How many times do I have to tell you that there are no redwoods anywhere near Redding? There is your Douglas fir. There is your sugar pine. And there is your incense cedar. But you have got to travel some before you come to the great California redwood forest." Guthrie's lack of horticulture knowledge had always seemed to infuriate the little sheriff. But, being a city boy and all, Guthrie figured, So what? Oughta be redwoods in Redding. Guthrie tried to keep from smiling here, but was not one hundred percent successful.

"You find this deplorable situation amusing, Undersheriff Guthrie?"

"No sir, of course not, sir," Guthrie said, trying to appear calm and collected, while at the same time wheeling and dealing inside his mind with all the options he could come up with here on such short notice. Reds in Redding? Goddamn it, come to think of it, wasn't the chubby little psycho always blathering on and on in that "I'm almost having a nervous breakdown" style of his about how you can't trust that evil bastard Gorbachev, who was just putting on an act, just leading us on until—until what? Until he could sneak a battalion of Russian commandos into the redwood forests, or spruce pine forests, or whatever the hell they were, and take over Evansdale? Let's see, probably got 'em to the California coast by submarine and then snuck 'em in on surfboards, right?

"I see you do think it's funny, Guthrie, but let me tell you one thing here which you had better take very seriously. You do exactly what you're told here, or you start sharpening up your sales pitch, real fast." (Guthrie had, once upon a time, in a distant city, been forced to earn a depressingly erratic living by selling home remodeling over the telephone.)

"Uh, sure, of course, Sheriff. But, I mean, just what is it that you're telling me to do here?"

"I'm telling you to do nothing till you hear from me. Maintain the barrier, but do not—I repeat, do not, under any circumstances—go beyond it.

"I'm personally taking these survivors back with me to Redding. I want to involve the police department in this one. It's about time I got together with Chief Browning for a friendly chat, anyway.

"You know, Guthrie, I been thinking, it wouldn't hurt our two departments to operate on a more friendly basis." (What!!! —Guthrie had to deliberately hold himself back from slapping himself in the face here and shouting, "Wake up!")

"And this baby, Guthrie, this baby is just too big for any one department to handle. Just how big—I'm afraid I can't tell you that just yet. But one thing I can tell you, Undersheriff Guthrie. Tomorrow morning when the sun comes up, we're gonna move on into Evansdale and kick us some Commie ass."

So he's finally flipped out, Guthrie figured, but was that good or was that bad?

"Might I point out, sir, with all due respect" (Sheriff liked that sort of jargon), "that it's against procedure for you to drive these people anywhere without backup? Why don't you take Bulkowski or someone with you? Let them do the driving, you're probably a little bit tired from all this—uh—responsibility, aren't you?"

"Listen, Guthrie, I understand what you're doing here, and I want you to know I appreciate it, see?"

The short stocky little sheriff put his arm affectionately around the tall, rawboned undersheriff's shoulders. It was all Guthrie could do to keep from leaping backward and throwing up his left arm to ward off the attack. Instead, he gritted his teeth and managed a tight-lipped unhappy little lopsided grin. In all his years on the force, this was the most out-of-character behavior that the sheriff had ever indulged in.

And once the sheriff had all of what Guthrie thought of as the suspects piled into a car, casually in front and back seats, with himself driving, and got the car started, he actually grinned and waved bye-bye to Guthrie. Stunned, mouth open, Guthrie and several other astonished officers waved back as the car rolled off into the dark, toward Redding.

"I've got some questions I need to ask you now," the chubby little sheriff said, glancing over at the old man, who was sitting up front by the window, with Mary Jane between them.

"No, Sheriff," the old man said. "What did you tell me your name was? Billy? Well, Billy, you must have forgot, but you already asked me all of the questions, and all of the answers were just exactly the ones that you wanted to hear. Do you see? All you need to do now is to go over it while you drive. You just ask yourself any question you want to, and then give yourself the answer you want, and that's what I told you. Do you understand?"

"Sure, that's easy to understand," the sheriff said in a cheerful voice. "Boy, that's just great. Why didn't I think of that?"

"Well, let's say you did think of that, okay, Billy? If I say so, then you did. How would you like that?"

Billy just smiled. Things just keep getting better and better, he thought.

"All right, fine, Billy, you thought of that idea. And do you know what else, Billy? You can make it easier to concentrate by blocking out everything the rest of us say to each other. You don't have to hear anything all the way to town. That way you can just think about all of your questions and my answers, all right?"

"Can I have thought of that idea, too?" Billy asked in a childlike voice.

"You did think of it, Billy. And you thought of lots of other wonderful ideas too, too many to even remember. But for now, with your permission, of course, I will count to three. When I reach 'three,' you will no longer hear anything we say until we reach town. Then you will drive all of us to a nice motel, all right, Billy? One, two, three."

The old man turned back around in his seat to talk to Brice and Elena. The kids, who were now awake again, were squeezed in side by side between the adults, and the girl was crying again.

"Why don't you sit on Elena's lap?" the old man said. "That way you'll have more room."

"Don't have to," she sobbed.

"Yeah, I know that, but here, lean over here close to me, okay? I got something to tell you, but I want to whisper it."

Suspicious expression on her little heart-shaped, tear-streaked face, Violet scooted forward, then stood up, holding onto the back of the front bench seat in order to get close to the old man.

"You're not supposed to stand up in the car," William pointed out.

After a short pause, the old man said: "Tell you what, William. It's all right to stand up in a car as long as it's a police car. So you come over here too.

"It's Elena, see?" he whispered in an outlandishly conspiratorial manner. "She's scared to death, you see? And she's the kind of person who just can't take care of herself, you know? She needs someone to take care of her, so I want you kids to stick close to her, okay? And believe me, Violet, I wouldn't ask you, but I know how bad she feels right now. Can't you please just sit in her lap just for now? Just till she goes to sleep?"

Still sobbing, Violet nodded and then crawled into Elena's lap and put her arms around Elena's neck.

William sat back down again and suddenly said: "Now what's going to happen to us?" and burst into tears also.

For a while the old man said nothing, then said, "You stay with us from now on."

Violet audibly sucked in her breath. And William, sounding as astonished as everyone else in the car, said: "Forever and ever, no matter what?" The old man did his owl-eye trick and then solemnly nodded. Till death do us part, Elena said to herself, and winced.

Even Brice's expression was that of pure amazement

at this announcement. Only Mary Jane managed to keep her cool well enough to answer. "Wow, instant family."

Having dealt with that matter, the old man moved on. "Tonight in the motel I'll arrange for transportation. Another car, I think. First thing in the morning we head back to Los Angeles. I've got further arrangements to make there. Brice, you can take the car then. I assume you have decided to retrieve the stone from wherever your brother hid it. Or would you rather wait around and test out whatever method of attack they decide on next?"

Brice buried his head in his hands and groaned. "My shoulder feels like it's been kicked by a mule. I wasn't cut out to be a gunslinger."

"You did fine, hon," Mary Jane said. "You just have to remember to pull it in tight up against your shoulder."

Still evading the question, Brice said: "I wonder just who they were really trying to kill, anyway, me or you?"

The old man smiled. "Of course they were trying to kill me. Why would they bother to kill you? In fact, they would probably prefer to have you alive so that you would lead them to the stone.

"But make no mistake about it: they would rather have me dead than have you alive. Their first choice would be to control all the stones; but if they could have me out of the way and my stone lost and forgotten for a while—well, that would be a very close second. They could just lay back and take their time finding it. After all, time is something they have plenty of.

"No, I was definitely the object of their attack. But they wouldn't have been too upset to have wiped out our whole little group here.

"Also, I would imagine they had an agent there in Evansdale, so there was some slight chance that whoever that was would survive the attack and come up with the stone. Not much of a chance, mind you."

"Who was it?" Brice said.

The old man shrugged. "What does it matter? Whoever it was is dead."

Mary Jane, a slight smile on her lovely little face, began humming softly to herself, some jazz tune Brice could almost but not quite recognize.

Brice shook his head wearily and said, " 'Dead' just about describes everybody in Evansdale these days. Shouldn't we feel guilty about running off and just leaving them?"

The old man shook his head. "What could we do? I managed to convince the cops here to stay out of town until morning. Did you notice the way those creatures reacted to heat? My guess is that they will have difficulty surviving the heat of the sun. Thank the gods it is turning summer here and not winter. Sure, maybe a couple of them will survive for a while. You see, these old folktales that your grandma tells you, they generally have some valuable truth in them somewhere—shapeshifters that can't endure the sun. No, I think most of it's over, at least for poor little empty Evansdale. Oh, I wouldn't want to go for a nighttime stroll in the woods for a while around there, but the worst is over. For them. For us, I am afraid, the worst is yet to come. Which brings us to the real question."

But the old man did not even ask the question. Merely stared at Brice and did his eye trick.

"Okay," Brice said, "I give up. I'll see if I can find the stone for you. But as soon as I get it, I'm handing it over to you, do you understand? Or no deal."

The old man nodded. "Sure, sure, fine, so tomorrow morning we head for Los Angeles. Elena and the kids and I will stay at a hotel while I set a few things up, and you can have the car."

William, who seemed to be half listening to what must have been a totally incomprehensible conversation, and at the same time nodding off to sleep, sobbing himself back awake from time to time, suddenly sat forward in the seat and said in an excited voice: "L.A.? Can we go to Disneyland?"

"Oh, for Godsake," Elena muttered, and stiffened up, jolting Violet back awake.

"How far is Disneyland from L.A.?" the old man said.

"Oh, for Godsake," Elena said again, even more emphatically.

"Hour," Mary Jane said.

"With you driving?"

"Half hour."

"Okay," the old man said. "I don't see why not. In fact, I think maybe that's a good idea. Sure. So, first thing, our friend Sheriff Bill here drops us off at a nice hotel in Redding, then forgets all about us and goes home. Gets himself some rest—right, Bill?"

Bill said, "Thought I wasn't supposed to hear anything."

The old man laughed. "Well, you can hear this, though, because when you drive home you're going to forget it anyway, see?"

"That sounds good," Bill said, turning to look at the old man. "Did I think it up?"

"Sure, sure you did, but keep your eye on the road, okay? Hey—both of them." (Bill was driving with one eye shut, here.) "Let's see, where was I . . . ?

"Oh yeah, so tomorrow we rest up. Sleep late. Take it easy, you know. Have a nice big breakfast. It will take me a little time to make some contacts with my people, arrange for a suitable vehicle. Then we hit the road. Straight on down to Disneyland. Some hotel there. Elena and the kids can go play around in the park while I take care of some business. Brice, you take the car and get the stone. What about Mary Jane?"

"She comes with me."

The old man nodded. "Fine. —And I know, Elena: 'For Godsake!' "

18

THE NEXT MORNING, waking up in the mundane little hotel room, with the dull country decor, was so disorienting that it was almost impossible for Elena to convince herself that any of the bizarre events of yesterday evening had really occurred. The same seemed to be true of the children, who were sleeping on cots. The old man, who hadn't been to sleep as far as Elena knew, had already gone next door to wake up Brice and Mary Jane, leaving Elena to deal with the kids—naturally!

"Where's my uncle?" William asked sleepily.

Dead as a doornail, Elena thought, but tactfully managed to refrain from saying.

"Just go in the bathroom and take a shower."

"Why do I have to take a shower?"

"Look, you both have to take showers because you both stink, okay? It's bad manners to stink."

Both children laughed happily, and Violet pointed at William and shouted, "You stink worst, so you go first. —Hey, a poem."

To which William answered: "You stink worse, though, Lettie. You stink worse than anybody."

To which Violet answered: "No, no, no. Boys always stink worse."

"That's right," Elena said. "So, as I was saying, William, you go first. Then you brush your teeth."

"But we don't have our toothbrushes."

"Then you just use your heads, okay? You . . . you rub your teeth with your finger like this—" Elena demonstrated. "Then you rinse your mouth out with water. Then you won't have bad breath. Well—not as bad."

Both kids laughed, although Elena certainly looked serious enough about it, and William went into the bathroom and then stuck his head back out.

"The shower isn't on yet."

"Well, turn it on."

He shook his head. "Would you please do it?"

Wasn't eight old enough to start your own shower—or was it?

"I want to see how you do it," he said poignantly.

But it was when they finally went outside that the real disorientation set in.

"Is this it?" Elena asked the old man, who was standing around staring off into the sky. For a while the old man ignored her and continued his scrutiny of the clouds. Then he blinked and glanced at the sleek, gleaming white Mercedes parked in their space. "Yes, that's it."

Elena walked around it, slowly, cautiously even, as though she were afraid of it. On the rear end was the insignia "560 SEL." She nodded. Then walked over to the driver's side.

Just then Mary Jane came out the door of their room, followed by Brice.

"Mary Jane will drive," the old man said, tossing her the keys.

Once they were seated inside, the old man explained, "I want Mary Jane to drive all the way. I know we would have more room in a van, but I want to get there fast."

To Mary Jane he said, "I'm sorry, I would have got a sports car, but with all these people . . ." He shrugged.

"Hey, okay," Mary Jane said, kicking it over. "Jesus, you can't even hear the fucking motor. All right, hang onto your heads."

But there was no need to hang onto anything; the big car was so smooth and so quiet that it was hard to believe you were tearing down the highway at over a hundred miles an hour, gobbling up the miles.

A couple of hours later and they were sitting in a small freeway off-ramp café many miles south, eating breakfast. Elena was sulking. "I still don't see why he gets a malted milk for breakfast." She pointed her egg-filled fork at William.

The old man shook his head. "Because he wanted a malted milk for breakfast, Elena. You see? Do you want one? No, because it wouldn't taste right for you. So you don't get one. You're stuck with eggs. But that's what you want.

"Just like with cars. You don't want to drive a Mercedes-Benz or a Porsche, Elena. You don't want to drive a hundred miles an hour, even if you think you do. You just want to tool along in a nice Chevy Caprice. That's your nature. There's nothing wrong with that. In fact, it's convenient. But just don't envy Mary Jane her Mercedes or William his malt. Just eat your scrambled eggs."

19

THE NEW BUT no longer white Mercedes slowed down in front of Brice's Aunt Miriam's house, and then pulled up ahead and parked farther down the street.

Brice was driving, while Mary Jane, who had chauffeured them all the way from Redding to Orange County, was now sound asleep in the passenger seat next to Brice.

They had arrived very late last night only to be turned away by the Disneyland Hotel, and had finally checked in at the Marriott for a few hours' sleep. But they had gotten up early, at Brice's insistence, and she was still exhausted from her long drive the day before.

When Brice had suggested that she recline the luxurious bucket seat and catch a nap, she had been unable to resist it. And she had slept all the way from Anaheim to Tarzana. Now the absence of movement of the car woke her.

"Where are we?" she sighed, rubbing her eyes.

Brice leaned over and kissed her on the forehead. "We're here," he said.

"Where's my purse?"

"I tossed it on the floor there."

Brice got out of the car and waited for her to wake up.

"Know what we had better do?" he said to her as she got out of the car. "Listen, I know this sounds funny, but my aunt's a weird old lady, and I'm talking really, really weird here. You just go around the back, the gate's always open, and there's some trees back there. Wait for me there, okay? I just want to check in with her and let her know it's me."

"You don't want your aunt to meet me," Mary Jane said incredulously.

"It's not that, but believe me, she's pretty old and pretty—well—strange. She might imagine we'd be doing something naughty out there in her own backyard."

Mary Jane shook her head, but she did as he asked. And it seemed quite a while before she nodded awake again and looked up from where she sat propped up against a walnut tree to see Brice standing over her, carrying a dull-yellow cushion and a flashlight. A cushion?

"Are we actually going to do something naughty out here in her backyard?"

Brice smiled his small bittersweet smile. "Yes, I think so," he said, and winked.

"It's over here," he said, moving through an area where the shrubbery was particularly dense, though most of it was dead and dried out.

"Ah, here it is." He removed a large dead bush and revealed a hole in the earth.

"You wait here," he said. "I'll be right back out with the stone. Then we can settle back and enjoy ourselves in the great outdoors. You know, fun, fun, fun in the California sun?"

Mary Jane looked around. It was a huge backyard. And furthermore, the nearest adjacent territory seemed to be a vacant lot. Guess you could get a little naughty here, she thought, shaking her head, looking at the cushion she was now sitting on.

After a while Brice's head appeared. He had a strange cautious expression, reminding her of a prairie dog checking out the terrain for predators. This was it, she realized with a start.

He emerged slowly and awkwardly from his burrow.

She stood up. "Did you get it?" Heart pounding.

He nodded. Held out his hand. It was . . . it was the stone.

Mary Jane took the little autoloading .32 out of her purse.

"Sorry," she said. "Toss it here."

Brice shook his head. "I don't think so," he said. "Thought that was your last clip."

"I lied," Mary Jane said, "I had another one." But now she was surreptitiously trying to hold the gun on him and at the same time fish around in her purse with her other hand. You didn't get to be as good as Mary Jane without being able to tell from the weight of your handgun whether it was loaded or not.

"I tossed it out the window somewhere on the freeway while you were asleep," Brice said.

Mary Jane's heart was really pounding now. Funny how similar were fear and elation. Winning and losing. Was she losing here?

"How did you know?" she said, trying to gain time.

"Are you kidding?" Brice said in an angry hiss. "How could I not know? Did you think I was that stupid? That vain? That you were that attractive? Nobody's that attractive, Mary Jane. Might as well drop that gun."

But Mary Jane hung onto the gun. It was still a weapon of sorts. A club. "I can still take you. I'm an expert in hand-to-hand."

Brice smiled. "I don't think so," he said. "I think you're just too small. But then, I guess we'll never know." He pulled up his big loose T-shirt, and Mary Jane saw with horror that there had been a revolver hidden under it. A big revolver.

"Aunt Miriam is a bit fey. I told you about that?

Likes guns. Isn't that weird for an old babe like that? Guns and cats. This one's her favorite. Gun, that is."

He took the S&W .357 magnum out of his belt and aimed it at her.

"Throw me the cushion."

"You're not going to shoot me?"

"Course not, throw me the cushion."

"Oh Christ, Brice, you're not going to shoot me. You couldn't shoot me any more than I could have . . ."

"Save it, Mary Jane," Brice said. "I told you I'm not going to shoot you. You just do as I say and I won't hurt a hair of your gorgeous head. But I need the cushion."

"What for?"

"For Christsake, Mary Jane, I'm going to hide the stone in it, okay? And then stash it back inside where it came from while I get in touch with the old man and figure out what to do with you. Now toss me the cushion."

Mary Jane tossed him the cushion. Brice caught it in his left hand and pushed it down over the revolver in his right hand, trying to smother any sound it would make. Then he thrust both hands out toward Mary Jane and squeezed the trigger. The bullet hit her high but hard, spinning her around. The shoulder, she thought, but couldn't be sure.

Play dead, she was thinking, but by then the second bullet hit her lower down and knocked her off her feet. And as the third bullet plowed into her she wasn't thinking anything at all.

"I lied too," Brice said, although she hadn't asked, and couldn't hear the answer. All that fuss about the cushion and it hadn't worked at all. His ears were still ringing from the reports, but then again, this was the San Fernando Valley, who cared?

Later, after he had dragged her body over and stuffed it down into the entrance to the fort and covered it over again with shrubbery that was as dead as she was, he had returned the gun to his aunt. "What were you shooting at?"

"Squirrel," he said. For some unknown and possibly unknowable reason, his aunt had always hated squirrels.

"Hope you blew the little bastard's brains out," she said with a smile.

"Oh, I did," Brice said. "Believe me, I did."

Later on, Brice found the old man alone in his room at the Marriott. He was sitting cross-legged on the thick red carpet, apparently doing nothing but just sitting there.

"Elena and the kids are enjoying Disneyland, and I finished with my business earlier. I've been waiting here to talk with you alone. Then we have to meet them in a few hours at—what do they call it? 'Pirates of the Caribbean'? Wherever that is. Show me the stone."

When the old man held the ordinary-looking black crystal in its copper setting in the palm of his hand, it seemed for a moment as though Brice could discern a charge of almost invisible blue electricity spread up and through his arm, but as soon as he caught sight of it, he lost the vision again, and decided he had probably just imagined it.

"Ah yes," the old man said, "this is Yawtlée. Did you know that the stone's name is Yawtlée? But the stone is yours now, or rather, you belong to Yawtlée."

Brice shook his head, but wearily.

"You fool," the old man said softly, "can't you see you have no control over it? We have no control over it? Don't you think I would rather keep the stone for myself? But the stone has chosen. And it has chosen you." He smiled. "For the moment," he added.

Brice sighed and put the chain around his neck and dropped the amulet inside his T-shirt. Out of sight, out of mind? Fat chance. "No way out," he muttered.

"The only way out is all the way in," the old man

amended. "And that's the way I have chosen, for all of us. The short dangerous way. The Roman way, I might add.

"Germanicus would not have understood it at all. Like all Germans, he likes to maintain a certain distance, a logic, about all his decisions. And Popillius also would not understand it. Popillius is at heart a pimp. And pimps have no nationality. They are the same everywhere. But Drusilla, Drusilla is a Roman. This move will not surprise her."

He stood up slowly and walked over to a small desk in one corner of the room, and selected one of several envelopes. Walked back over and handed it to Brice.

"Tickets," the old man said. "We're going to Hawaii. Luckily, we won't need passports, although I could have arranged for them. But it would have delayed us. I want to move fast. On the other hand, not too fast either. Everything must be"—he paused and performed his owl-eye trick—"exact.

"You will notice that the tickets are for a couple of days from now. We all need the time to recuperate, particularly"—owl-eye trick—"me. Besides, that will give us two more days to enjoy Disneyland. They always say it takes three days to fully explore Disneyland, no?"

Brice nodded wryly.

"And it will allow Germanicus, Popillius, and Drusilla just enough time to receive the messages I sent them and gather at the meeting place I have chosen. But not enough time to really get cooking. Besides, they can all keep an eye on each other until we show up, you see? And I'll just tell Elena that I couldn't get earlier tickets, because everyone in California is going to Hawaii, or some such ridiculous story. The children will be delighted."

Brice shook his head wearily. "Lie to Elena?"

The old man performed one of his fits of laughter. "The children delight in Disneyland. It's lying to Elena that delights me. And what is it that delights you, Brice?"

Brice said nothing. His expression said nothing.

The old man nodded as if he had been answered, and continued:

"I decided to leave your identity the same, so you won't need new ID. Elena, however, is now your loving wife, Mrs. Elena O'Conner. And the kids are yours as well. As you so aptly pointed out, family is everything."

"But why Hawaii, if it's okay to ask?"

"Sure, ask anything you want. It's because that's where our enemies will be. The ones who want to steal the stone. Well, I told you I like to do things the Roman way. We're going to lure them there and then go right to them and take their stones away. And kill them. At close quarters. Or we're going to die trying."

"Great plan," Brice said. "And we drag the kids along. What on earth purpose does that serve?"

"The kids have been touched by the stone. They have power, and we need all the power we can get. But more important even than that, the kids have a right. Germanicus killed their parents. They have a right to take their role in the main battle. To revenge."

"To revenge?"

"Hey," the old man said, "you said it, not me. Family is everything. That's the Roman way."

"They'll die."

"Probably we'll all die. Who knows? But one thing for sure: if we lose this one, those kids will die wherever they happen to be. You don't think Germanicus would let them live this time around, do you?"

"If it is Germanicus."

The old man held his small strong hand out, turned it over and then back palm-up again. "Popillius or Drusilla, I don't know. Maybe fifty-fifty. Maybe even both of them. But Germanicus I would bet my money on. One hundred percent."

"So we go to Hawaii," Brice said, "to fight it out at

close quarters, the Roman way. How do we know they'll be there?"

"Oh, they'll be there, all right. They have to be there. Drusilla owns a health spa on Maui. I've called an emergency meeting of the Four there. If it turns out to be Germanicus and Popillius, they'll have to show because they won't want to chance my aligning myself with Drusilla. If it's Germanicus and Drusilla—" He shrugged. "Same reason. Besides, I told you they don't think like me. They will be harboring the illusion that I might want to reason with them. Bargain with them."

"Why not?" Brice said.

"When they're dead I'll bargain with them."

Brice nodded. "So, what if it's all three?"

"Then we would have no chance no matter what we do, and we might as well get it over with."

"The Roman way?"

"The Roman way."

"All right," Brice said in a dull voice. "We go to Hawaii." Fact was that Brice didn't care all that much what happened these days. He felt sort of dead already.

"By the way," the old man said, "what happened to your friend Mary Jane?"

Brice said in the same dull voice: "She just dropped out."

1

HONG KONG: THE heavyset man with the neatly trimmed aviator's moustache and short-cut salt-and-pepper hair sat in the bow of the little boat slowly but surely cutting its way out deeper into the bay toward open waters. He drank in the sights and sounds of Hong Kong, not least of which was the snarling of the little diesel engine driving the bullet-nosed trawler he was sitting in.

"Alas, no more charming butterfly sails," he said.

"Too slow," the slender Chinese man sitting next to him replied. "Take all day get anywhere." He waved his hand outward to encompass the bay. "Plenty sails out there."

"Yes, that's true," the other man admitted. Hong Kong Harbor was still a lovely sight, with hundreds of ships of every size and shape churning the waters, sails of every design and color billowing in the breeze. Or rather, they would be billowing in the breeze if only there were a breeze. But the harbor was changing. More and more of the boats were run by noisy smelly diesel engines—like this one. The fishermen (who had lived here in this bay on their boats since the days of ancient Rome) were now fishing with synthetic nets, lines, and ropes, one hundred percent plastic. Many of them were even moving into the city, where the government was doing its best to provide jobs and education.

The man with the narrow moustache understood that all this change was necessary and probably most of it was for the better. Still, there was no denying that all over the world, as things changed toward the purely functional, charm was being lost. Sometimes the man wondered if any of it would ever be replaced, or whether human beings would gradually evolve into insectlike worker drones who would never notice intangibles like charm or grace or beauty. Well, he figured he would probably be around to see for himself.

"They've even moved the two big floating restaurants."

"Long time, no see," the Chinese sitting next to him said.

"Long time, no see what, Mr. Chan?"

"Long time, no see Hong Kong, Pop. Pop forget Hong Kong. Boats too slow. Boat people too stupid. City people too fast. Too hot. Too sticky. Everything in Hong Kong too much or too little. Pop forget."

"Well, I haven't been gone that long," Pop replied, smiling. But it was true, he had forgotten. A month in Hong Kong was like a year somewhere else. He had forgotten, for instance, that Mr. Chan despised the boat people, as had his relatives before him, and theirs before them, and on and on back into the period of history before the birth of Mr. Chan's savior, who strangely enough had been a Jewish carpenter some two thousand years ago.

"Why do you hate the Tanka, Mr. Chan?" Pop asked, knowing that it was a foolish question.

"Not only do I hate the Tanka, but also the Hoklo, do not forget the Hoklo. They are inferior, I believe, even to the Tanka." The Tanka and the Hoklo were the two tribes of boat people, but the vast majority were Tanka. Thus Pop had neglected to include the Hoklo.

"Do you know how they became the boat people?" Mr. Chan went on. "They committed a terrible act of treason. They were not fit to live on the Chinese soil, so in ancient times they were condemned to live on their boats forever. This is the truth." Mr. Chan folded his arms in a gesture of finality. I have spoken.

Pop turned and looked at the boat person sitting behind them steering the trawler. The skinny old man smiled a happy toothless smile. It obviously didn't bother him much. Was this the price you paid for charm?

Now the man cut off the motor and the boat slowed.

"This is it, Mr. Chan?" Pop said. He always wondered how they knew where they were. It was only a patch of water like any other.

"Mr. Woo will easily find us here. We are early. I have pointed out to you that we would be early. Did I not?"

"Indeed you did, Mr. Chan. But as you must know, I enjoy the luxury of being early. Of watching others arrive. Of relaxing and watching."

"Of being sticky and hot," Mr. Chan groused. "Yes, I am aware of this. As was my father before me. And his before him. Are you really a demon, Pop, who never grows old?"

Pop laughed out loud. It was the rich heavy laugh of a man who enjoyed his life.

"Well, your father's father was right about that, Mr. Chan. I am a demon, and don't you ever forget it."

"I would never be so foolish," Mr. Chan said. "Ah, look, I do believe Mr. Woo is arriving early also. How strange. But then, it is well known that Mr. Woo has no sophistication."

"And his father before him," Pop added.

"Exactly," Mr. Chan said, appearing pleased.

The other boat, another of the new, low, bullet-nosed trawlers, pulled up alongside alarmingly fast, but rows of old tires attached along its hull acted as bumpers, softening the collision to a muffled *thunk,* and an extremely thickset, muscular Chinese, dressed in what was obviously an expensive, finely cut summer suit, managed to climb aboard without too much loss of dignity.

"Mr. Pop, Mr. Chan, greetings. It is good to see you both in such good health. I see the hot sun does not bother you. Still, I cannot hope to understand why you always choose such an awkward—if I may say so—meeting place. Do you worship Tin Hau?"

Pop laughed again. Tin Hau was the ocean goddess whom all the boat people had worshipped since ancient times. However, this goddess had apparently once been a living person, because, as everyone knew, her birthday was on the twenty-third day of the third moon. And when it rolled around, all of the boat people would be out tooling around the bay in full fleet, many-colored sails, banners and flags flying, brightly dressed people all cheering, waving, singing, drinking.

"Ambience," Pop said.

"If I may ask without appearing ignorant, Mr. Pop, what is 'ambience'? Is it perhaps like tradition?"

"Yes, Mr. Woo, you might say that it is a tradition of mine to meet people in the same manner that I met their fathers before them. In the old places."

"If you will forgive me for saying so, Mr. Pop, I am a modern Chinese businessman. Surely you do not wish to insult my intelligence by suggesting that I would believe these foolish legends which you have spread about yourself."

"On the contrary, Mr. Woo, it is you who are ignorant," Mr. Chan cut in, "if you dare to say that my father and his father before him were not telling the truth."

"Gentlemen, gentlemen," Pop interjected just as the two of them broke into rapid-fire Cantonese, "let us remember the rules here. After all, Mr. Woo, you are a businessman and this is business. Let us keep it that way.

You may believe whatever you wish, but if you wish to do business with me you will follow my rules—Rule Number One being that you shall speak only English in my presence so that I can always be aware of what is being said."

This was one of Pop's many little jokes. The fact was that he could speak Cantonese, and most Chinese dialects as well, but preferred them not to know it.

"This man has insulted me," Mr. Woo grumbled.

"Mr. Chan, you will please apologize to Mr. Woo."

Mr. Chan looked sideways at Pop without any expression on his face whatever. Then he said: "Very well, I am sorry, Mr. Woo, if I have called you an ignorant fool, or that I pointed out that your mother enjoyed . . ."

"Enough, Mr. Chan," Pop cut in. "I add my own apologies to Mr. Chan's. May we now discuss business?"

"And get out of this sticky heat," Mr. Woo said.

"I will agree with Mr. Woo in that, Pop. I don't understand why you insist on being here at all. I can handle these affairs for you, as I have pointed out before, time and time again."

"Yes, it is true that you can, and do, handle a great many of my affairs here, and some in Shanghai as well. As did your father before you, and his before him (which you do not have to believe, Mr. Woo). But the reason I must be here to make these arrangements in person is—as Mr. Woo has pointed out—tradition.

"I will not sit back and watch my business grow without me. To do so would be to drain the benefits of their most important commodity, charm.

"Now, let us begin, Mr. Woo." Pop took a small notebook and pen out of the pocket of the elegant bone-white Panama jacket he was wearing. "Your benefactor, Mr. Lee, will need a large, comfortable place for his celebration. Not far from downtown, but not too near either. Am I correct?"

Mr. Woo nodded. "Yes, it is so. These are influential

and powerful men he will be entertaining, but they are also men who will quite probably display a great deal of crudity in their expression of enjoyment. They are"—he winced—"Japanese."

Mr. Chan just sat there, stiff as a board, mouth open. What were times coming to?

Pop smiled. "Very well, crudity is my specialty. They will need women, of course. I will arrange for my boat people to bring fresh ones in from the mainland. There should be at least two for each man?"

"These are Japanese," Mr. Woo said in a pensive tone. "I fear two will not be enough."

"Make it three each," Pop said, scribbling it down. "All young, white-skinned, beautiful."

"Better include some blondes," Mr. Woo added. "The Japanese sometimes like blondes." He shrugged.

"Sure, blondes are easy. And you, Mr. Woo, your preference?"

"Blondes also," he said, looking down at his shiny black shoes. Mr. Chan made a slight effort to disguise his expression of disgust.

"Let's see, fancy place, three women each, plenty of booze—all kinds. Big buffet-style dinner, steam bath, sauna. How 'bout a few exotic dancers to start things off, followed by a sex show?"

"Excellent suggestion."

"Young boys?"

"Perhaps just a few, just in case. I have found it better to be safe than sorry."

"Exactly, Mr. Woo. And what about drugs? All kinds? Coke, marijuana, 'ludes?"

"They have expressed a preference for opium, I am afraid," Mr. Woo mumbled. "You see, they . . ."

"Yes, yes, I get the picture," Pop said, shaking his head. "Opium—China; how utterly naive."

Both Mr. Chan and Mr. Woo now looked at each other with sympathy.

Pop smiled his elegant smile and said: "Acquiring opium hardly presents a problem to me. I'll make sure it's Colombian. Only the best stuff. You can tell them it was grown in the fields of Lantao or Tibet or someplace equally romantic and evocative." Pop shook his head and muttered: "Opium."

"The Japanese know little about drugs," Mr. Woo complained. To this Mr. Chan nodded fiercely in agreement.

Having completed the business arrangements for the party, Popillius felt the usual sense of fulfillment. A job well done. As to the party itself, he had long ago ceased attending these sorts of functions; he preferred the quiet life. His primary joy these days was fishing, and the silence that went along with it. But nonetheless, he felt a sense of accomplishment at being able to make it possible for this little group of rich Japanese businessmen or Yakuza or whatever they were to party themselves into a coma. Festival! They deserved it. They worked harder than other men, why shouldn't they enjoy more? Popillius may not have been Roman in the sense that Corbo was, but he was Roman enough to understand the meaning of festival. And to revere it.

In fact, the succession of debaucheries over which he had presided were blurred in his memory into one endless psychedelic orgy wherein the exotic guests changed costumes, bodies, and faces in bewildering array—a veritable kaleidoscope of flesh.

Parties in Rome, Byzantium, China, medieval England, Renaissance Italy, all the same, all different. But different only in the beginning, the opening gambits, the costumes, the music, the mannerisms, the choice of drugs; but when the clothes came off and tensions started screaming for release, the differences disappeared or perhaps even were transcended (yes, he liked that word). What was left was the true unity of mankind. And he knew how to deal with that. No, the other three, the bearers of the stones, had needed Pop from the beginning—despised him, but needed him, for even in mighty Rome, so many of the most important decisions were made by so many of the most important people under so much pressure from those universal desires.

Pop blinked his eyes, and the memory faded. What was that, heading out across the charming Hong Kong bay to meet them?

"Is that one of ours, Mr. Chan?"

"As usual, Pop, your eyes are the eyes of an egret."

Pop smiled at the image and allowed himself to think, If it had been a Roman party they would have wanted him to include egrets. He told this to Mr. Chan, who asked him, "To screw or to eat?"

Pop smiled. "Possibly both."

And later, when the message had been delivered and the little boat departed, Mr. Chan asked him, "But what does the message mean? It seemed no more than mere gibberish to me."

"It means," Pop said, "that instead of leaving from here for Shanghai, from Shanghai to Thailand, Thailand to Burma, and Burma to India, that I have got to fly straight to Hawaii and endure, no doubt, the awful music of the ukulele."

"Is there no way out?" Mr. Chan wondered.

For a long time Pop said nothing. Perhaps he was just enjoying the sights and smells and sounds of the harbor, and had forgotten the question. But after a long time he said in a sad tone of voice, "I don't see how."

2

JOHN D. BELLINGHAM did not know his way around Oslo, and thus was having more difficulty making his way to the rendezvous than he would have predicted. The two hours which had been allotted to him was turning out to be just barely enough.

He had started out this morning in an irritable mood, which was now growing rapidly more so. For one thing, the reason why he did not know his way around Oslo (or anywhere in Norway, for that matter) was that he did not like Oslo (or anywhere in Norway, for that matter). He considered the architecture dull, the food dull, and worst of all, the art (whatever there was of it) unbearably dull.

He could not understand the point in building a huge sprawling city with literally hundreds of miles of forest within it. A city within a forest, he could understand. But a forest within a city? He agreed completely with America's beloved movie star ex-President that when you've seen one tree, you've seen them all. And it had always seemed to him that mostly what one did in Norway (yes, even in the city, in Norway) was to admire trees. He had seen forests enough to know the awful truth: the hills were not, unfortunately, alive with the sound of music. They were the dead, dull, primeval past.

No, he had been convinced at quite an early age that

the glory of life lay solely in the spirit of man as expressed in the loftiest works of art and architecture. Everything else was looking backward into chaos.

But more than anything else, he was irritated at himself for being here in the first place. What in the hell was he doing here? It was so unlike him to go chasing off on what was so obviously going to turn out to be an utter waste of time.

He thought wistfully of the lovely, warmly lit skies of Italy. Everything was beautiful in Italy, the people, the skies, the architecture, the art; my God, the art! Even the goddamn clothes and bicycles, and automobiles. Even the goddamn shoes!

Or flashing Spain. He could be in the Prado right now. So why was he here? He relived the odd experience in his mind for what must have been the thousandth time, and tried to make sense of it.

He had been in a nightclub somewhere in Copenhagen. He did not even remember exactly where it was or the name of it.

The tall blond man had come over to his table and simply sat down. His bodyguard Joe had asked him, "You want me to toss him outside?" But it had been the stiffness of expression on Joe's face that had caused John D. Bellingham III to rise up a notch out of that rosy haze of drunkenness and carefully examine the man. What he had thought of before as tall was in actuality closer to immense. The man was perhaps only six-foot-five or six, and he was thin, but his frame was enormous, with extremely broad shoulders and big heavy bones. Huge hands and large blunt features. Short nose. Small, bright blue eyes hidden between the high cheekbones and broad low expanse of bulging forehead. Thick shock of straight white-blond hair. The man was certainly not handsome, but he wasn't really ugly either. Simply different, strikingly different, with a hint of cold brutality in his expression, or rather, in his lack of it.

Now the man smiled at him, but there was no warmth in that smile. "Tell him to go away or I will hurt him." This said in an utterly calm soft voice. Did John Bellingham detect a note of anticipation here?

"Joe, it's okay. Just move over to the bar for a bit. I'll be all right."

Why had he done that? It had been so out of character that even as drunk as he was, John Bellingham III had been unable to believe he was saying it. But it was what happened next that had really thrown him for a loop, that he kept running over and over in his mind as he would have a portion of a videotape where he could not understand what the people were saying.

"I will not waste my time," the man had said. (Yes, he had said "my," not "your.") "Allow me to introduce yourself. You are John D. Bellingham, one of the world's richest men. You do not really do much of anything, as your father already did it for you. You travel, and you collect art. You live for art. Am I correct in this?"

"Who—who are you?"

The man had smiled a tight, thin-lipped smile that was close to a grimace. "I am a person who can bring you"—he paused as if searching for the correct word—"absolute fulfillment, fulfillment beyond your wildest dreams. Tell me, do you prefer the paintings of the Dutch masters or the paintings of the Italians?"

"Quattrocento . . ." John started to say. "Tell me, what's this all about?"

"Ah, the Italians, just as I thought."

Was Bellingham mistaken, or was there a hint of sarcasm in the man's voice?

"As a matter of fact, Botticelli, the culmination of the search for perfect beauty, the holy grail of the quattrocento period."

The man actually rolled his little blue eyes. As foolish as it was, Bellingham felt compelled to go on trying to defend himself.

"I know that a lot of critics assign that position to Piero della Francesca, but . . . but the purity is not there. Not on the level of Botticelli. Just look at anything he's painted and you can't miss it. 'Beauty,' it shouts. It needs no justification or reason other than its own mysterious existence.

"Oh, I know, I know, Leonardo broke through the wall of idealism and into the open air of humanism . . ." He trailed off. It was obvious that he was making a fool of himself. Was the man understanding anything at all of what he was trying to say here?

"Listen, my friend, Mr. John D. Bellingham the Third," the man said in his calm low voice, "you have no need to lecture me about the Italian Renaissance. I was there."

Had he actually said that? Bellingham stared open-mouthed and tried to focus on what the man was saying now.

"You like Botticelli. Have you never wondered why he painted so little in the later part of his life?"

"Vasari . . ." Bellingham started to say, when the man cut in.

"Oh, Vasari, for Godsake, everything Vasari ever said about anybody was a lie, surely you realize that?

"Anyway, if you want to find out something no one knows, except for me, of course, about what Botticelli was exploring during the later part of his life, I will tell you how to do it."

He leaned across the table and handed Bellingham a folded piece of paper with an address on it.

Irritated but nevertheless intrigued, Bellingham found himself unable to resist taking the paper and unfolding it. A ticket fell out. "I have taken the liberty," the big man said, "of securing a small cabin for you for tomorrow night on the all-night ferry. It leaves here at five P.M., and it doesn't get to Oslo until nine the next morning. You should be able to sober up by then . . ." The big man paused and scrutinized Bellingham carefully, grimaced, and added: "Perhaps."

"See here—" Bellingham tried to interject.

"If you don't like the idea, just throw the ticket away, or give it to one of your drunken friends. Feel quite free, Mr. Bellingham. And don't worry about hurting my feelings. Fortunately, I have none.

"I would suggest, however, that you take the ferry. If you do so, and you manage to arrive at this address by eleven A.M. sharp (I will not wait), I can guarantee you that you will have an experience that will fulfill your whole useless life."

The man grinned his evil grin. Bellingham blinked.

"See here—" he stammered again. But the man simply pushed his chair back from the table and stood up.

"Are you a German?" Bellingham mumbled, again amazing himself with his own display of ineptitude.

But the man seemed to enjoy the inane question. He smiled his first real smile. "I am the only real German," he said, and walked out.

Which was why Bellingham was now here in Oslo wandering up and down streets with names like Uranien Borgveien, Bogstadveien, or Eilersundts Gate (at least every other street here was some sort of "Gate"), looking for an address, while suffering from the effects of a terrible hangover. No, he had not recuperated on the all-night ferry. Fueled by irritation, he had drunk more. And more.

What on earth was he doing here? Would he even have considered it if he hadn't been drunk in the first place? For the thousandth time, he almost turned back, tried to turn back but could not turn back. He had to know what he would find that would relate to those final desolate days of his beloved Botticelli. Then he would be furious. Then he would rage. Then Mr. . . . Mr. . . . Who? The man had not even given him a name. The only real German?

And when finally he found the address, miraculously it was just then closing in on 11:00 A.M. Had the man actually been able to compute somehow the exact amount of time it would take him to search out the place?

It turned out to be an ordinary apartment in an ordinary building, on an ordinary street, naturally. But to Bellingham everything in Oslo was ordinary anyway. After he had finished with this fiasco, perhaps he would celebrate by stopping off at a café and having an ordinary sandwich (Oslo's specialty) and an ordinary five-dollar glass of beer. (If the price of beer hadn't gone up, that is.)

He was thinking along those lines when the door opened (no need to actually knock, of course) and the man, looking even bigger and more rawboned than the last time Bellingham had seen him, appeared in the doorway.

"Ah, early. I myself am always early. As they say, the early bird gets the worm. Which, unfortunately, as I am certain you will concur, is often what us poor early birds wind up with. But today, my friend—I think you shall find that today will turn out to be the exception. Come in, come in."

"See here, the first thing—" Bellingham, trying to assume a more aggressive role, was instantly cut off by a wave of the big man's hand.

"Don't waste our time. What you want to see is in the back room there."

For the first time Bellingham noticed the room he was standing in. It was totally unfurnished save for one old-fashioned, comfortable-looking overstuffed armchair. The man went over and sat in the chair, and did not say another word.

Bellingham walked around him and went through the

door at the far end of the room. Through a hall, where another open door awaited him. It was another unfurnished room, except for one item. Only it wasn't a chair. It was a painting on the wall.

An hour later, when he came out of the room, he found the big man still sitting in the chair. Not reading. Not fidgeting nervously or glancing at his watch. Just sitting.

"It . . . What I just saw in that room . . . It just can't possibly be," Bellingham said.

"Don't you find it interesting," the big man said in his exaggeratedly ironic voice, "that he turned away from the more Christian-oriented subjects which occupied most of his later work, and returned finally to the robust pagan idealism . . ."

"It can't be," Bellingham insisted.

". . . of his youth?" the big man patiently finished his sentence. "I do."

"I'll have to return. I'll need art historians, technicians, my personal art adviser Jeremy Fisbes, for a start. If he finds no obvious flaws, then I'll . . ."

"But I will be gone, Mr. John D. Bellingham the Third, and so will the Botticelli. The verification will be your problem and not mine. I know who painted it.

"I will, however, make you this offer, and no other. Go home. And by home I do not mean the chateau in Switzerland, the villa in Portugal, the ranch house in Santa Fe, or the penthouse in New York, I mean home, where you came from, that overblown ostentatious mansion in the English countryside. A week from now you will receive a letter with the name of a man you have never heard of, as well as the number which goes with a Swiss bank account. You will deposit—oh, let's see—ten million dollars should be enough. If you do so, the painting will be delivered to you and you may do what you wish with it. Meanwhile"—now he glanced at his wristwatch—"I have an appointment."

"But I can't . . . How can I know . . . ?"

"Sorry, Mr. Bellingham, but I must rush you off. I have more important things to attend to."

For a while Mr. Bellingham just stood in the street staring at the door to the apartment building. Soon, true to his word, the big man came out, smiled and waved to him, and walked away. He did not seem in the least concerned about whether he would get the money or not. For a moment Bellingham could just barely hold himself back from rushing over and begging the man. Or perhaps attacking him. He didn't know what to do. It would be ridiculous to dish out ten million dollars to a stranger, but equally ridiculous to let an unknown work of Botticelli, possibly his last painting, just slip away from him; and for a mere ten million dollars. From him and from the world. (For in his heart he knew the painting was authentic.)

And yet, strangely enough, what bothered Bellingham the most was the nagging suspicion that had he answered "Raphael" or "Leonardo" to the man's question, he would have entered that room and found one of their paintings hanging there instead.

Finally he snorted and shook his head at his own foolishness. I'm already contemplating behaving like a dotty eccentric, let's not just go stark raving mad here. Let's just get home and try to figure out what to do about the Botticelli. One masterpiece at a time.

3

BORIS WANDERED THE streets for a while, looking into the eyes of the people, not at all sure what it was that he was looking for, but sure that he wasn't finding it. After a while he stopped off at the Studenter Lunden for a sandwich and a beer. This was the pressing appointment he had alluded to earlier, and in truth, he probably needed lunch more than he needed another ten-million-dollar bank account, but he had always liked to think of himself as a man with a great deal of foresight, hadn't he?

The Studenter Lunden (or Students' Grove) had always struck Boris as a sort of parody of a German beer garden. A tree-shaded park with tables, chairs (some of them under parasols), and promenades, frequented mainly by young people, it had everything but the soul of a beer garden.

Here students sat about chatting and drinking coffee or tea or soft drinks. No one was drunk, or gaily singing. With the price of alcohol in Norway, no one could afford to get drunk.

Boris had a hard time imagining how a people could invent such a dull way of life, and as usual wondered what he was doing here. What he was looking for. Germany? The Germans were no longer Germans, in his mind. Was that what drove him farther north into duller and more sterile countries?

Even when he was a little boy, the Germans had no longer been Germans. And that had been almost two thousand years ago. When he was eight years old, his tribe had migrated south and mingled with the more Romanized Germans along the Rhine. Grown soft. And he knew for a fact that if the tribes of German barbarians had destroyed Rome, it was only in their feverish attempts to become Romans. By the time he had worked his way up to an officer in the Roman Army, he had nothing left for them but contempt.

But he still remembered the early days. The cold hard days. The giant blond warriors that no man could stand against. The wolves. The snow. The pale-skinned, strong, brave women. The terror of battle. The drunkenness. The pillage and rape, all seen through a child's wide eyes, imprinted on that young unformed mind by searing cold flames of fear. It was the most alive he had ever been, would ever be. After that, Rome had been no more than a pleasant dream.

Oh, the ancient Aryan way of life was the best. Hitler had been right about that. Wrong about everything else, though. Boris had seen that from the start. The Jews, for instance, were not a problem. Any more than their religion was a problem. Nobody really believed that nonsense nowadays anyway. But by raving and ranting about it, *der Führer* had made them more important than they really were in the scheme of things. And he had also burdened the German people with a ridiculous cloud of guilt that they would probably never be able to crawl out from under. Split the German people in two. If you could call them Germans.

Boris had to smile at that thought. He remembered watching Hitler practically foaming at the mouth at an early rally, ranting about the glories of the Aryan people.

And he had been astounded to see the weak little body, the thin dark hair, the crazy eyes. Aryan? The man looked more like a Jew.

Boris forked over a small fortune in kroner to a pretty girl behind the counter at one of the shops, picked up his mug of beer and carried it over to an empty table with a shade umbrella blossomed over it.

By the time he had gone back for his third beer, the girl at the counter gave him a disapproving stare. "I hope you will not be driving," she remarked in Landsmaal, which was the new Norwegian, but which really was the old Norwegian before it had become corrupted by Danish. Nowadays it was popular and patriotic to speak it.

Amused, Boris deliberately answered her in perfect Danish, "Not yet, I am not yet drunk enough to drive, thank you."

Yes, he truly did not like Norway, or Norwegians, and really had no idea what he was doing here. Looking into the eyes of the people. Looking for a strength and unity and purity that had been the essence of Germany, but that had died long before Germany had even become a nation. Would he simply find himself moving farther and farther north, looking into the eyes of the people, not finding?

I'm more of a romantic than that fool Bellingham, he thought. Botticelli! Just the thought of that most romantic of the romantic Italians disgusted him. Botticelli—art?

Art was supposed to reflect the essence of life. The cruelty, the pain, the slash of the whip that woke you up. That was art. Botticelli was a fucking comic-book painter. And not even one of the best of those. He preferred Barry Smith if it came to that.

It was at this table, heroically downing another beer, that his friend Nils found him.

"I thought maybe I would find you here, Boris. Drunk as usual, I suppose."

"I am not drunk, Nils. As you know perfectly well, I do not get drunk."

"I sometimes think that you lack the necessary imagination," Nils said cruelly.

Boris said nothing, waiting. It was true in a way. In another way, though, Boris could have demonstrated the expression of an imagination beyond any artist's dream. For controlled imagination was the secret of all magical power. But "control" was the key word here. The same relentlessly developed control that would not allow him to get drunk. But no, he would not lie to himself, it was the stone that would not allow him to get drunk. Nothing more than that.

Nils tried to wait out the silence, staring into Boris' icy blue eyes, then gave up and said: "A message came for you. 'Very important,' he said. 'I don't know where he is, he'll probably be back this afternoon,' I said. 'You'd better find him,' he said, and just turned and walked away. Bastard. I should have punched him in the nose."

Boris smiled at this. The picture of Nils with his long golden hair and his luscious petulant lips punching someone in the nose was enough to almost make the big man laugh. Comic-book stuff. Botticelli should have painted it.

"Funny thing is, Boris, it's addressed to Boris Germanicus Kruger. Is your middle name really Germanicus? Jesus Christ, I guess you're lucky your parents didn't name you Sardonicus or something."

Boris' smile grew wide. "Germanicus is my middle, first, and last name, Nils."

Back in his studio, as he arranged carefully folded articles of clothing and packed them neatly into an army-surplus bag, Nils paced up and down, stopping to stare every once in a while at one of Boris' paintings. It was easy enough to see why no one ever bought the damn things and the poor fool had wound up so dirt-poor that he had to use an old army bag when he went on a trip. Jesus, why do I always get mixed up with losers like this? Nils wondered.

"You just got back here; I don't see why you have to go to Hawaii anyhow."

"I just told you, Nils, my Uncle Eddie sent me a ticket. We can't afford to upset Uncle Eddie, can we? Besides, it may be my only chance to experience a luau. A new artistic high."

Nils nodded grudgingly. Boris' Uncle Ed was the crazy who sent him beer money from time to time.

"Do you like it?"

Nils looked over from the painting he had been staring at to the bed in the far corner of the studio, on which Boris had carefully emptied out the drawers from the only other legitimate piece of furniture in the place. Jesus, Nils thought with fresh anguish, how could I have gotten mixed up with someone who lives like this?

"I said, do you like it?"

Nils reluctantly looked back at the painting again. The canvas depicted a gaunt old man murdering a young girl. A very young girl. The girl's mouth was open in an agonized scream. The knife was just now entering her belly. All this done in shades of grey. Except for the wound. Thing about it was, it was so very well done. So painstakingly rendered. Lovingly, one might say.

"No," Nils said.

Boris nodded. "You have restored my faith in my work," he said. "Now come here. I am through packing, and we have some time before my plane leaves."

Nils swallowed nervously and said in his high, petulant voice, "Do you want me to beat you?"

"It's not a question of whether I want to be beaten," Boris said, smiling that tight little smile of his. "It's a question of whether I need to be beaten."

IF "HAWAII" WAS a word for paradise in the average vacationer's vocabulary, to Elena it was merely a synonym for boredom. It was so much like Acapulco, and frankly, Elena had had enough of Acapulco to last her forever. More fucking waterfalls, she thought to herself, trying not to snarl at the voluptuous dream wench who was snaring her with a lasso composed of flowers.

And hot. Where Elena came from was hot and dry. With Hawaii and Acapulco you got hot and wet. Big deal. So where Northern California had impressed her in spite of herself, Hawaii had immediately left her cold. Or rather, hot. Wet hot.

And naturally they had no sooner landed than they were racing to get on another plane. It seems this particular island wasn't good enough. They had to fly to another island just like it. Maui (famous for Maui Wowie, right?). When all this was over, she was planning to go to some cold, pleasant country place with a few lakes and rivers and trees, and just cool out. If she were still alive, that is.

The edge of terror which she found it necessary to constantly blunt with sarcasm and condescension cut through once again into her consciousness, just for a moment. But a moment was enough.

I'm scared to death, she thought. I'm just so scared

that I can hardly stand it. I'm almost ready to scream. And if I once start to scream, will anybody ever be able to stop me? Why, oh why, am I here, doing this? But she really knew the answer. It was not a pleasant one for her to face. She was here because there simply was no way out. If she deserted the old man and ran for it, they would surely hunt her down and kill her later. As they would the kids. In the end there was no other course of action for any of them to follow, except to do whatever the old man decided they should do.

Jesus, I'm so scared, she thought. Is the old man scared too? She tried to empathize with him, but as usual had absolutely no success. How do you empathize with someone who's had almost two thousand years of experience and has been blessed with unimaginable powers? If he was afraid, he was certainly keeping it a secret.

Brice, in her opinion, wasn't afraid either. Not like her, anyway. She couldn't really "climb inside his head," but she could come a lot closer than she could with the old man.

Brice wanted no part of any of it, but it wasn't because of fear.

Part of it was the death of his brother. She remembered the intensity of his expression in the car the other night when he had said to her, "Family is everything." Was that what he had said? Something like that. It was hard for her to picture that he and Quinn were brothers. Make that, had been brothers. Yet she knew beyond any question of a doubt that Quinn had been the most important single element in Brice's life. The nucleus. The big brother. The winner. The father figure. Quinn death!

But it had not just been the death of Quinn, it was something else as well. Something Elena could not quite put her finger on had driven in the final bamboo shoot underneath the fingernail, the one stab of agony that had thrust him beyond the reaches of pain and fear. Where he was now. And whatever had happened to that bitch Mary Jane? Here today, gone tomorrow? I doubt it.

It occurred to Elena that she had actually had sex with both brothers. Had screwed the entire O'Conner clan, so to say. After years of celibacy, which had been all right with her, after the painful but limited experience she had had with men up until she had been "selected" by the old man for her "special role" in life. (If you could call someone hallucinating the head of a bird on your shoulders the process of selection.)

No, Brice wasn't scared. Not really, not like her. Brice was clear out of it. Cold, grim, it was as if he were somehow turning into his brother, now that his brother was dead. Wonder what ever happened to that little bitch Mary Jane? she thought again, but this time the thought was more intrusive. But if Brice isn't scared and the old man isn't scared, what about the kids? Those poor, poor kids, she thought, or were they? Sitting next to her in the rental car which, for a change, Brice was driving, the kids looked bright and alert and even happy. They were singing, for Godsake. Actually singing.

Where Brice had phased out of it all in one way—the guy with nothing left to lose, maybe—the kids seemed to have adopted a similar, yet different, form of constructive dissociation. Since the old man had given them all (except for Brice) their new IDs and told them the roles they were expected to play (they were all the O'Conners now: she the wife, they the kids, and the old man their grandfather—Corbo O'Conner?), the kids had somehow immediately managed to confuse their roles with reality. It was clear that to the both of them Brice was their father and Elena their mother, and most of all, the old man was their goofy but lovable grandpa. One big happy family! Oh, sometimes you could see the brief flash of fear as the memories wedged in, but most of the time they were playing the game. And while they were playing it, they were believing it.

They had actually enjoyed Disneyland. Elena could hardly believe it, but knew it was true. How could the mind of a child be so vulnerable, yet so resilient? Yet these were special children, as the old man had pointed out to her: children selected by the stones. Playing out their special roles in whatever game this was. Like herself, they had no choice in the matter. They had enjoyed Disneyland, and they were enjoying Hawaii. Children!

And that was another thing, of course: Hawaii was nothing very different to Elena, or to the old man. And even Brice came from Santa Monica. Hawaii was pretty much Santa Monica only more so. But the kids had lived in Evansdale for the last few years. Hawaii was probably paradise to someone from Evansdale. So you might as well enjoy it today, die in it tomorrow. If you lived that long. Elena shuddered and closed her eyes, but her mind would not rest. Swarms of angry thoughts patrolled it, on the lookout for fear. At least I don't have to drive, she thought.

Brice, on the other hand, welcomed the opportunity to drive the rental, which this time was a Chevrolet Cavalier. The old man definitely had a thing for Chevys. This one was a dusty brown color which he supposed was meant to represent gold. But it was a nice car to drive. And driving offered him the opportunity to get into a groove and put himself on automatic, which was one of the things he had always been an expert at. You couldn't get to be a good guitar player without it. So he had offered to drive the car, and now that they were out of the airport town, Kahului, and a ways out on Highway 30, he was tuning in. It was a scenic drive, naturally, offering cliffside views of the ocean at first and then winding down to the narrow valley (the Olowalu Plain, Corbo pointed out to them) where cane fields sloped up toward jutting, surprisingly high mountains. It was easy to phase out now. Corbo gave you instructions here as he did in everything else, so you could forget about where you were driving, and just drive.

And the weather was great, no question about it. Despite Elena's bitching, there were fresh cool breezes wafting all over the surface of this island. Practically like air-conditioning, only with soul. And he was wearing comfortable clothes; the old man had bought them all new wardrobes without the slightest interest in what they wanted to wear. So they all (yes, even Elena) wore shorts and ridiculously flashy Hawaiian shirts. Brand-new running shoes. Sauconys, to be exact, which apparently had been on sale. Leis of flowers. It was easy to forget and drive. Forget and drive. But sooner or later you had to remember two things. You had to remember that Quinn was dead. And Mary Jane. You had to remember the expression on Mary Jane's face. That final look. When all the wheeling and dealing was over, and the full realization settled in. Forever. Revenge was not sweet. Brice knew that for a fact now. It was not sweet, but it was necessary. In fact, now that it was over, nothing else was necessary. But was it over? Mary Jane had only pulled the trigger. Somehow this fact had not struck Brice until he had finished with Mary Jane. Until then his mind simply would not let anything else in. But strangely, the moment Mary Jane had bit the dust, it had come flooding in on him. The obvious that he had not seen before. He was in this all the way, just as surely as his brother Quinn had been.

After a while they came to a small town, and more ocean. The west coast now, Corbo explained, the town was called Lahaina and was only a few blocks deep and a couple of miles long.

They stopped off for lunch here, the kids exulting in malted milks with every meal, while the old man pretended not to know that this was an unusual indulgence. Elena bitched about it, of course, but only halfheartedly. Kids shouldn't be allowed too many sweets, she felt. And despite himself, Brice could sense in himself the stirrings of the same ridiculous nervous misgivings. For Christsake, the kids were liable to be dead by tomorrow. Maybe even tonight.

The thought chilled Brice. This might well be their last day on earth. Me too.

Back in the car, they headed north. The Cavalier was no Caprice, the old man pointed out to Brice, but the roads were narrow here, mostly two-laners. You had to make some sacrifices. Furthermore, he preferred the old Chevy Nova of bygone days, with the big eight-cylinder engine. He did not like front-wheel drive, but it had its good points. The Cavalier had a lot of room for such a small car, and he felt it was just about perfect for their needs here in Hawaii. But he preferred both the Caprice and the Cavalier over the Mercedes. It was unfortunate that he had been forced to rent it, but Mary Jane's nature had made it imperative. Mercedes-Benzes were inferior in every way to Chevys, he explained patiently, which he felt had an edge over Fords, although the new Ford models were definitely getting better. Mercedes-Benzes were ostentatious, greedy, and much too fast. It was definitely a mistake to travel faster than necessary. You might miss something. A form hidden in the clouds, the flight of a bird. Something important. (Brice did not have to look at him to sense him widening his eyes as he spoke, here.) In every way a Mercedes was too much. Used too much gas, cost a fortune to buy and a fortune to repair. Too fast. Too elegant. Too this, too that. And there was nothing worse in the world than too much of anything. Why, for the price of one Mercedes you could buy three Caprices. You could drive a different-colored Caprice every day.

When Elena tried to ask, in her typical acerbic manner, whether driving a different-colored car every day wasn't an overindulgence also, the old man had paused significantly, done his owl-eye trick, and said mysteriously, "Not if each color is necessary in order to complement the soul of the particular course of action you are following on that particular day. Do you see, Elena? No?"

After what must have been an eternity of driving through a lecture on automobiles, they entered yet another small picturesque town. The old man took time out from his lecturing to point out that this was Kaanapali, which meant that they were almost there.

Northward, Highway 30 took an inland climb. Down below them Brice caught glimpses of fancy condominiums and cottages lining both sides of a lower cut-off alternate route. Soon they were descending again, and now pulling into Napili Bay.

"We're almost there," the old man announced tirelessly, as he had before. As before, the children cheered and clapped their hands.

Finally Brice was instructed to turn into one of the driveways, underneath a sign announcing Napili Sunset Resort. The gravel driveway, mostly hidden by a profusion of rich foliage, led a long way up through that veritable jungle of tropical shrubbery and onto a wide parking area. The resort appeared to consist of one large building as well as several scattered smaller bungalows, also hidden amongst thatches of glistening green bushes, some of which bore huge red flowers of some sort. The huge parking area circled a large elegant fountain in the Roman style, complete with the statue of a sexy nude nymph pouring water from a jar which she balanced on her shoulder. "Drusilla," Corbo explained to Elena offhandedly, as if he were a tour guide. The whole place sang of wet tropical paradise, and by now the children were squirming in their seats.

But no sooner had Brice got out of the car than a man came out of the main building to meet them.

"Don't unpack yet," he informed them brusquely. "We've still got a ways to go."

Then circling the car to the passenger side and seeking out the old man, he held out his hand and said, "I'm Franco Giardo, I work for Drusilla. I was told to meet you here."

"I know who you are," the old man said. "I've seen you fight. You were good. Very good. I'm Corbo."

Franco smiled, it was a wicked smile. The man was not big, probably five-nine or ten, but was massively muscled. His small head, which sat on his thick neck, was finely formed, with beautifully sculpted features. His rugged beauty was only accented by the signs of battle, the broken nose, the scar across the jutting cheekbones under the left eye. The neck jutted up from heavy sloping shoulders, thick chest, thick biceps, forearms; everything about the man was thick, heavy, and packed with muscle. Yet he moved easily, confidently.

"I was too slow for the good ones. I could take a punch and I could bang, but I was just a hair too slow."

"For the ring," the old man said, "maybe. But in real life you don't have some referee to break you every time you clinch. You would have slaughtered Devons."

Franco's smile widened. "You know, I do believe you're right. Anyway, those days are long behind me.

"Listen, Drusilla and the others have gone on to what she calls the inner resort. Have you ever been there?"

The old man nodded.

"Yeah, well, I'm supposed to drive you up there. Only we've got a problem. I was only told to take you and your"—he looked at Elena amusedly and searched for the word—"your apprentice here. Nobody told me to take this guy or the two kids along."

"Well," the old man said, "I'm telling you now."

For a moment it was clear that Franco didn't take well to the direct approach that the old man specialized in.

He said nothing in answer, merely stood quite still, staring into the old man's eyes. But Corbo did not seem to mind, simply smiled and waited patiently.

"All right," Franco said, drawing the words out. "Before we get started I hope you don't object to being searched."

The old man did his owl-eye trick and said, "Would it matter if we did?"

Franco shrugged, a maneuver that caused the muscles that joined his thick neck to his massive shoulders to swell up to where it looked as if they might pop his head off.

First he methodically went through all their luggage, and when the old man suggested that the kids go play in the fountain, Franco interrupted this chore and thoroughly patted down the kids.

"Well, what do you think?" Elena snapped. "Are they carrying guns?"

But much like the old man, Franco merely seemed amused by her display of anger. "I don't think that anymore," Franco said, and went back to rooting through their suitcases.

"Interesting wardrobes," he remarked caustically when he had finished. "Nothing but Hawaiian shirts, shorts, socks, and underwear. I figured you for a class act."

"This is Hawaii," the old man pointed out.

Franco grunted. "Don't remind me." For Franco, Hawaii held all the charm and ambience of a TV sit-com. He thought of it as one enormous golf course with a few spas, hotels, and tennis courts built in, out of necessity. As to the climate, he figured what climate? Summer, summer, summer, followed by summer, could hardly be considered climate. Just as pretty, pretty, pretty could quickly grow tiresome to the eye. It was clear to Franco that somehow the ideas of eternal youth and constant summer were tied up in his boss Drusilla's mind, but naturally he kept his mouth shut about it. Still, what he would not have given to take a stroll once more down the mean streets of Chicago or Philly in midwinter when the streets were covered with snow and the air was that delicious icy cold. Maybe pick a fight, pick up a chick, catch some funky jazz or soul. There was no funk in Hawaii. At the thought of Don Ho, Franco visibly shuddered.

"Too cold for you?" Elena suggested.

"Hardly."

Through with the suitcases, Franco started in on the people, obviously enjoying the task when it came to Elena. "I always say, pleasure first," he remarked.

"What an original philosophy," Elena responded, but at the same time patiently endured the ordeal.

After Elena came Brice, then finally the old man.

"Jesus, good thing I searched you," Franco commented, holding out the little red Swiss Army pocketknife. "What a weapon." He opened the blade. "What balance," he said sarcastically. "I'll bet you could throw it across the room and pin your opponent's shirtsleeve to the wall, just as he was quick-drawing his piece, right?"

"Sorry to disappoint you," the old man said, "but I don't throw knives. It's an art I never bothered with. Not much of a blade here, but see, it's got both screwdrivers, a Phillips head and one of the regular ones. It's the Tinker model. I like it the best because it's so small and you'd be surprised how often you need a screwdriver to fix things."

Franco, looking interested, said: "Yeah? What do you fix with it, anyway?"

The old man looked surprised: "Anything. Do you want me to leave it here?"

"No, no," Franco said. "You may have to protect yourselves against a pack of fucking mongooses—mongeese? Or maybe you'll need to screw something, right, babe?" He winked at Elena.

"Babe?" Elena said incredulously. *"Babe?"*

"Well anyway, according to my expert opinion, you guys ain't armed. Except for Mr. Corbo here. Sorry about all this. But it's something the boss insists upon. Can't see the need for it myself, but . . ." He shrugged.

"Believe me," the old man assured him, "it's quite necessary."

"Whatever," Franco said. "Anyway, let's get this show on the road. Elena? I assume that you are Elena; Drusilla said you'd probably be with Mr. Corbo here. You can ride with me. You there—" (this to Brice) "you can drive your car and follow us up."

"Know why I asked you to ride with me?" Franco asked Elena once both cars had gotten under way.

"Because I'm so fucking beautiful?" Elena answered in her most sarcastic tone of voice. And when Franco said nothing, added bitterly: "Figures!"

Now they were definitely into mountains. Real mountains this time, on surprisingly hazardous roads, quite often with long patches unpaved. The air was cool and clean and no longer carried scent of the ocean. For about five minutes it rained violently, then instantly cleared again.

"These roads can be a bitch in the rain," Franco commented. "I hope your friend doesn't drive the Chevy off a cliff and kill everybody in it," he said cheerfully, smiling at the thought.

Soon they reached a turnoff, a narrow dirt road blocked off by a large, old-fashioned wooden gate and marked "Private Property—No Trespassing." Franco got out and unlocked the gate and held it open while Elena and Brice drove the cars through. Then he locked up and drove what must have been at least two miles up the winding road.

"We're here," he announced.

Elena, who was just nodding off, blinked awake and took in the scene. Charming little bungalows like fairy dwellings peeked out from hiding places in the shrubbery. A second look put things into proper perspective. The only reason the bungalows had looked small was the enormous size and profusion of the foliage. But the view straight ahead across the rustic old wooden bridge to the main cottage showed that the low sprawling Mediterranean style of architecture helped add to the deception; you could see wings on either side of each bungalow, barely visible, spreading out into the jungle of plant life and disappearing there.

A small but spirited stream rushed tumbling and twisting beneath the bridge. There were a few seminatural ponds or swimming pools—Elena could not tell which they were—and of course there were the omnipresent waterfalls. It was just beginning to get dark, an amazingly long-drawn-out process here in the tropics, and the air was surprisingly cool, but invigorating, spiked with a pungent odor which Elena could not identify.

"She usually keeps this place reserved for what she calls the 'inner circle' of her health spa," Franco explained to Elena and the rest of the group, who had gotten out of their car now and were approaching. "They come up here from time to time and do whatever it is you inner people do. I'll probably be heading back down with the 'outers' where I belong, soon as I deliver you guys, that is."

"I doubt that," the old man said. "Under these trying circumstances, Franco, I don't think she'll want you to go anywhere for a while."

"Yeah, maybe," Franco said, sounding unconvinced.

"Oh, I think so," the old man said. "I think you've just made the inner circle, at least for a while."

Franco led them across the bridge and down a small gravel path that led to the first and largest cottage, if you could call it that.

The door was opened by a woman, strikingly beautiful in the classical Italian mode. She reminded Elena a little of Sophia Loren, and it was only when they had stepped into the lighted room that Elena could detect little signs of age, the beginning of a delicate network of wrinkles at the corners of the long, heavily lashed eyes; at the corners of the sensuous mouth. Not much. As if she were just now beginning to be touched by the years. But certainly she had aged far less than Corbo, and also less than the other two men in the room with her.

"Drusilla, Popillius, Germanicus," the old man said, nodding. And for the first time Elena realized what she was in the room with here. Her expression must have betrayed her, for the big blond man smiled at her and said, "Yes, you are correct to feel awe; the Four who guide the world are together here for the first time in, oh, what must be hundreds of years."

"That's 'guard the world,' not 'guide the world,' Drusilla shot back. "Your ego's showing again, big boy." She rolled her lovely eyes.

She's so gorgeous, Elena thought unselfconsciously, but why does she look so young? Then Popillius comes next, he's almost as young-looking as she is, but not quite. The German looks older, fifties maybe, and Corbo seems to have aged the most. I wonder why?

"They insisted on bringing along this guy and these two kids," Franco announced in his usual brash style as Brice and the children came through the door.

"What is this?" Germanicus demanded. "I don't quite understand. Is this a family vacation or is this a meeting of the Four?"

"These people have been chosen by the stones," Corbo said in a tone of voice that suggested that he was patiently explaining things to a child. "They have been touched by the stones. The stones wanted them to be here. What could I do? I am only a servant."

It was clear to Elena from the way the other three Guardians looked at each other and shrugged or rolled their eyes that they were as nonplussed by the old man's mystical manner of thinking as she was. This surprised her. She had thought they would all turn out to be as weird as he was.

"You should not be a servant of the stones, old man," the German said in his cold, sarcastic voice. "They are just stones. You are a man. Perhaps even more than a man. The stones were made to serve you."

"That's not what Yawtlée says," Corbo replied.

"Who's Yawtlée?" the one called Popillius interjected. He was a medium-sized man with a stocky build and a British aviator-style moustache. He was quite handsome and looked rather like some old-fashioned swashbuckler movie star just starting to go to pot. He was the only man in the room wearing a suit.

" 'Yawtlée' is what he calls his stone," the German said with an obvious touch of scorn. "Would you please tell me why you call it that, Corbo?"

"Because that's its name," Corbo said, bringing on another series of eye rolls and shoulder shrugs.

"Germanicus?" Drusilla said.

"Fine with me. Who cares?"

"Popillius?"

"I've forgotten the question."

"The people Corbo brought along. Do they stay or do they go?"

A nervous expression crossed Popillius' handsome, jaded face. "Go, go, go," he said. "Sorry, but this is business. Important business."

"Up to me, then," Drusilla said. And then, as if registering the children for the first time, opened wide her mesmeric eyes and fixed them on William, who frowned and moved back a step. "Can I get you a drink?"

"Ginger ale?" Violet said.

Drusilla nodded, heading toward the bar.

"Cherry Coke," William said, seeing how far he could

push it. "Cherry lemon Coke," he corrected, after a moment's thought.

"No, it's only up to me," the old man said. "Otherwise, why would I have brought them if they weren't going to stay?"

"If you would just keep quiet, Corbo," Drusilla said, pouring the drinks for the children, "I was going to say, 'Yes, what difference does it make?' They can stay, but they can't come to the meeting. Tonight. Let's say an hour from now. Shall we make it dinner? Here?"

"Whoever put you in charge, Drusilla?" Germanicus groused.

"My man Franco can eat with the rest of you in your bungalow," she continued, ignoring Germanicus. "Afterward he'll be staying here with us too."

"Fine, fine, I should have brought my lovers along," Germanicus complained.

"Oh yes," Drusilla countered. "What an interesting spectacle that would provide."

"What about the rest of your lackeys?" he went on. "Surely one of them would enjoy presiding over the meeting, why don't you invite them to stay the night?"

Drusilla shook her head and muttered something to herself under her breath. "You are already starting to annoy me, Boris, and you've only just got here. There are only three of them, and the only thing they are going to preside over is dinner. As soon as they've cleared the table they will be gone. But you, Boris, I'm already starting to wonder here, when will you be gone?"

Boris smiled gleefully. "What a shame that Mother Nature had to waste all that cattiness on a mere female," he said. "But then, who else?"

"Here, here," Popillius interjected, "let's not get started off on the wrong foot like this. Let's keep our cool, as they are wont to say these days." But he looked rather uncertain about it all, and this wasn't exactly soothed by Corbo's burst of wild laughter.

"No, they don't say that these days," Corbo choked out, "They say—" Here Corbo began a long-drawn-out monologue of youth clichés acted out in the style of a ghetto youth, much to Pop's obvious aggravation and Drusilla's amusement. It was clear to Elena that these were the traditional roles they had played over the passage of centuries, Popillius the elegant, even conservative pimp, as a foil for Corbo's robust court jester routine. Drusilla obviously played the role of the delicious cheerleader they both courted, while Germanicus looked on, alternating his mood from icy rage to one of amused disbelief.

Drusilla handed each of the children their drink, and apparently totally over her brief fit of pique, playfully ruffled Popillius' hair.

"Pop the peacemaker," she said. "Listen, I've taken the liberty of having a sort of smorgasbord prepared for you people. I didn't know some of you were coming, but Franco always eats like a horse, so I made certain to order tons. All you've got to do is fish it out of that giant fridge in your bungalow. There ought to be plenty for you and the kids, Elena." She tossed Franco keys.

"Fine, me and the kids," Elena said through clenched teeth.

"You might as well go and get settled in, Corbo; come back here as soon as you shower, if you ever indulge in anything as mundane as showering, that is."

Corbo smiled. "Sometimes I meditate in waterfalls," he said.

Germanicus snorted. "Great, what do you meditate on in waterfalls?"

The old man looked dumbfounded. "On water, of course."

5

I WOULD MARRY you tomorrow for a honeymoon today, babe," Franco was earnestly explaining to Elena between enormous bites of a ham sandwich he had made out of a slice of ham that must have been an inch thick.

"Can't you just leave me alone?" Elena replied. "Please? Can't you just take your ham sandwich into the bathroom and just do whatever you have to do to it and then come back out and leave me alone?"

"Jesus," Franco said in awe.

"I don't get it," William said to Violet, who rolled her eyes at him. Kids!

"What about you, dude?" Franco said to Brice. "You her boyfriend? You object?"

"Only on aesthetic grounds," Brice said.

"Jesus." Franco shook his head. "You sharp-tongued devils." But smiled a big smile. His supreme confidence in his body made him hard to insult. If worse came to worst, he figured he could either screw you or punch you out. Effortlessly.

With Drusilla it had been the former. She had picked him up at a boxing match, of all places. Right after he had lost the big one to Sweet Pea Devons. He had been all bruised up, swollen eyes, nose, you name it. She had come right into his dressing room and—he savored the memory still—had sex with him right there on the dressing table. Luscious, luscious sex. Chased everybody out and locked the door. He hadn't even known her name. Jesus!

Afterward, she had offered him the job. And of course, bizarre as it was, he had snapped it up. Because he wasn't just another dumb pug. No way. He knew where he was headed from here in the fight game. And the way he was headed was down. Straight down.

So he took the job. What kind of job could he get anyway where they paid him $50,000 a year, no questions asked, as long as he didn't break training? And he hadn't.

Oh, it had been tough, all right. You had better believe it. If he had thought training for a heavyweight fight was torture, this new form of training was more like mass murder, himself being the multiple victims.

First had come the intensives in automobile driving: these had not been so bad. Except that they had taken up all of his time. They had been residence courses, all three of them, but in different places with different instructors. The first had only been a week long, and had taken place in Northern California. It was pretty much a jam-packed short course for aspiring race car drivers. All morning long you raced a Porsche like a maniac, around a track or through a slalom, with the instructor strapped in next to you, observing your effort. After lunch he would lecture to you about all the errors you had made, both in technique and in strategy. It had amazed Franco to find out that he did so many things wrong when he drove a car. Like most men, he had thought himself an expert. But it had turned out that there was hardly any aspect of his driving that the instructor would leave untouched: everything from the position of his hands on the steering wheel to the positioning of his seat.

Later on he was taken to several different racetracks and sometimes just stretches of highway, which he would drive and map out: where he would plan to apply the brakes, where he would slam on the gas to straighten out the curve, how fast he would head into the next one. All this, of course, subject to the instructor's icy professional criticism. He had learned a lot from that instructor. But he had learned even more from the long hours of hard driving.

But all that had been nothing compared to what the next course was going to put him through.

Three months in Arizona! Nowhere, Arizona. Why Arizona? He had no idea, but there it had been. Frantically driving through the heat and dust, race cars, touring sedans, ordinary cars, and even big limousines. It would have amazed Franco to know that his predecessors had been trained in chariots and on horseback. And at times, yes, even initiated into the mysteries of controlling camels. But thankfully the age of camels was over and now it was the age of limousines. So Franco had spent the greater part of the last month driving huge clumsy limousines as if they were Porsches, through all kinds of weird obstacle courses in the desert.

This instructor had taken quite a different approach. He had not spent so much time criticizing or offering suggestions. He had merely watched quietly, and then said, in his soft, detached voice, something like: "Good. Now let's try it a couple of times with the big Lincoln."

The third course had been the most exciting. It had actually turned out to be two courses in one. First a couple of weeks at combat training with a handguns intensive, followed by a defensive driving course for the chauffeurs of the rich. Both of these classes had been given at the same facility in Billings, Montana, and had evolved into a split shift for him where he spent the mornings trying to evade ersatz terrorists and kidnappers in a big limo, and the afternoons on the combat simulation shooting range. The driving course this time was a mere three weeks. But at the end of each three-week course the chief instructor would dismiss everybody and then say something like: "Franco, you are to stay on for another session, at your employer's request, of course. I don't want to nitpick, but I feel I must add that it seems to me from what I hear from Macay that you're getting a bit sloppy with your handgun practice. You are fast, he tells me, but you are just a bit loose. Might I point out to you that shooting a handgun, along with driving an automobile correctly, principally depends upon a certain tightness of mind. There is no room for passion, for sweeping gestures; everything must be controlled, and while you are performing one motion, you must be in the process of planning out the next. Control is everything. Thank you, see you tomorrow."

But believe it or not, this had been the easy part. Driving a car and shooting a gun were fun, fun, fun, compared to the brutalities of the hand-to-hand combat training which was to follow. And the kind of hand-to-hand training Franco was going to receive seemed to have more in common with the techniques of the Spanish inquisitors than those of the spiritual-minded Orientals he had heard about.

Every morning started with roadwork, seven to ten miles of it. Followed four days a week by weight training (it was here that he graduated from light heavyweight to a full-fledged heavyweight). The afternoons were split up into two parts also, the first consisting of kickboxing instruction, which included stretching and heavy-bag work; the dreaded second part was spent in full-contact sparring. This hurt. You wore padding and protective face masks, of course, but it hurt. Every day.

But Franco learned this fast. Besides which, as far as he was concerned the die was already cast: he had been a very good professional boxer, and he was short and heavyset. He would never rely much on kicking techniques, and his hand techniques were about as good as they were going to get. So he picked up a few simple but powerful kicks, and improved on his elbowing and head-butting maneuvers, for which he had been infamous to start with. And soon he was ready to graduate.

The way they graduated you here was this: One of his off days, when he wasn't scheduled for the weights, he was told to take an hour off and get some rest. When he returned he found the dojo empty, except for one man, noticeably shorter than himself, and he wasn't tall. A small man, and not nearly so heavily built as Franco. A strikingly handsome, slender—yes, even delicate-looking—man, with a black silky moustache, large very dark eyes, smooth coffee-colored skin, not a black man nor a white man. With the air of an aristocrat. Yes, that was it. Franco was to learn later that he was a Syrian. But that his mother was Moroccan and he had been raised part of the time there, part of the time in Syria. Part of the time in Egypt. Part of the time in Spain. But he called himself a Syrian for convenience.

Right now, he was just a small man in a judo gi sitting cross-legged in the center of the empty room, waiting for Franco to enter.

"Get ready to get your ass kicked," the man said simply, rising gracefully to his feet.

"Where's the gear?" Franco asked nervously, looking around for headgear or chest padding. Even the mats had been folded up and piled on one side of the wooden floor. "The gear?" Franco tried again. But the man had said all he was going to say, and now was carefully beginning to approach Franco in the circling manner of combat.

Okay. Franco settled in. If this little dude was testing him without safety gear, he'd better be prepared to fill out the report card in heaven. On second thought, hell.

Soon, though—much too soon—Franco found himself on the floor with the wiry little dude clamping some kind of exotic choke hold on him while he thrashed around trying to break loose. Six seconds later, and he was unconscious. He had only the vaguest memory of starting to throw a simple front kick.

When he came to, the little man, who was once again sitting cross-legged on the wooden floor, patiently observing him for signs of life, explained to him in his soft voice: "In the real world, grappling will always defeat boxing. It's simple: you could develop your footwork to the level of Sugar Ray Robinson, but once you're on the floor, what good would it do you?"

"Then don't get on the floor," Franco argued groggily.

"They have a game," the man, whose name, he later learned, was Achmed, said, "called 'football.' A man tries to run through other men. If the blockers keep the other men away, or if he runs fast enough to avoid them, he scores a touchdown. But if someone tackles him, he will go down. If a man is hit hard and low, he will go down. If you believe that you could be tackled and not go down, then you should be a professional football player. You would make millions. You would be the only ball player who could not be tackled.

"On the other hand, football players haven't been trained to throw or trip you. And they are trying to deal with someone who's running away. There is no man who can stay on his feet in a fight if the other man has been trained to take him down. Unless, of course, he outweighs him by eighty pounds, as you outweigh me" (this said rather scornfully).

"The real secret," he continued, "is to be trained in kickboxing as well. Just enough to be able to block a few punches or kicks, not much, mind you, but just until you can come to grips without getting hurt too bad. Once you do, the fight will quickly be over, as I have just taken pains to demonstrate to you."

"Yeah, great," Franco mumbled, sitting up. "Why didn't you just tell me?"

"Because I wanted you to understand just exactly what position you occupy in the real world of hand-to-hand combat. You're right up there with all those professional boxers, kickboxers, and masters of karate: at the beginning. You've had the preliminary course, and now you're ready to start. Before I'm through with you, you'll be able to choke someone unconscious inside of a minute, or if you prefer, break an arm or leg. Of course"—the little man smiled warmly—"you can always choke them unconscious and then break whatever you choose. That would be a perfect time to practice those flashy kicking techniques of yours."

And that had been the beginning of his real martial arts instruction. Only one year of it, but it had been one intense year. One year of nothing but running, weight training, and wrestling, except that it wasn't really wrestling. Everything in it was lethal. Or judo, except it wasn't judo. Nobody bowed or called anybody "sensei."

"We don't bow to anyone," Achmed had informed him. "We don't have to."

Then there had been a moment of silence. Achmed's expression gave nothing away. But sensing something, Franco waited.

"There is a man called the Shadow," Achmed said finally in a soft voice.

"Ninja?" Franco wondered. He knew that the word "ninja" meant shadow warrior.

Achmed shook his head. "Perhaps ninjas are named after him. He trained me, and my father before me, and others, many others, before him. He is the ultimate warrior. To him and only him do we owe our skills." He shrugged. "We sort of bow to him, I guess," he grudgingly admitted.

"To the Shadow," Franco said, trying to keep a straight face, "right."

And so the brutal training went on, and on. Only a year, but still, you had to wonder about his boss-to-be, Drusilla. She acted as if time meant nothing to her at all. As if she had forever.

Anyhow, he had gone through it all, and here he was, a mere chauffeur/bodyguard, but a chauffeur/bodyguard now making $90,000 a year. And a chauffeur/bodyguard who could kick anybody's butt. Yes—even you, Achmed.

In short, he had just about everything he had ever wanted in life, and in fact, a little more. Which was why he was only amused by the sharp-tongued green-eyed blonde and her snitty little college-boy boyfriend, if that was what he was. This whole weird situation with the four superpsychics or whatever the hell they were seemed as if it had been set up specifically for his amusement. But then again, in good old Maui two chickens fighting over a kernel of corn would easily pass for top entertainment.

Savoring the last bite of his ham sandwich, an inspiration struck him: thou shalt make another.

"Pass the ham, sweetheart, unless you'd rather make me a sandwich yourself."

Elena practically shoved it off the table into his lap.

"And let me give you some advice my dear old mother gave to me. When the iron is hot . . ." He leaned over and whispered to her what to do with it, loud enough for Brice to hear it. Now Brice and Elena stared at each other in disgust, clearly forming a bond under the pressure of this intense onslaught of macho vulgarity.

"And believe me, babe, this iron is always hot."

"Then why don't you . . ." Elena told him what she thought he should do with it, not bothering to whisper.

"In fact," Brice added, "you could try that on your dear old mother."

Franco merely smiled, and chewed. He knew the secret: all things come to he who sits and eats.

6

MEANWHILE, IN THE first bungalow, the one appropriately named "the Royal Suite," a different sort of dinner party was taking place. A fancy French-style dinner with all the trimmings was being served to the Four Guardians by two formally dressed servants, the sort that hover over your salad trembling, holding enormous peppermills. The only thing missing was the wine. It had been supplied, of course, but nobody was drinking it. For even though the stones would quickly counter the effects of alcohol, as they would any other poison, no one here was looking for even a momentary dullness of wit.

The Four themselves represented a strangely balanced discordance in the styles they represented. Pop in a grey three-piece suit which anyone could tell by the cut had set him back a normal man's monthly salary, even in Hong Kong, where he had bought it. His tie was one of those dull wine-red jobs that look like they belong wrapped around a Christmas gift under a richly decorated tree. The sort of tie that for some unknown reason is paramount to being well dressed. This understated elegance, along with his dapper moustache and suave, handsome expression, matched him perfectly with Drusilla, who was simply stunning in a black, low-cut gown. The only ornament she wore was her stone, mounted in an elaborate silver setting, quite different from Corbo's.

Corbo and Germanicus, on the other hand, had both dressed with an unconcealed disdain for decorum or the public eye, Germanicus with a certain artistic flair; while Corbo gave the impression that he had simply pulled on whatever was at hand. Both wore Hawaiian shirts, but the big German's was as lovely as a painting. In fact, on closer inspection, the pattern seemed to have been lifted from a Gauguin. The jeans were preshrunk and faded just to perfection. The shoes were the most expensive Adidas. Whereas Corbo's Hawaiian shirt looked as if it had come out of a bin at a Pic 'N Save discount mart. His shorts were hockey shorts which he had obviously found on sale at the same sporting goods store where he had bought his track shoes: glaring grotesque Saucony Gleems.

Everyone except Corbo was now working on the main course, *boeuf à la Bourguignonne,* which according to Popillius, who seemed to be the gourmet of the group, had been exquisitely well prepared.

Corbo, who had disdained his *salade Niçoise,* had zeroed in on one of the accompanying vegetables, baby lima beans, which seemed to be the only thing not swimming in some sort of rich cream sauce. He had pushed away the rest of his dinner and asked if he could have a bowl of the beans along with a piece of bread. It was this that he was just now finishing up.

"Would you like more?" Drusilla asked him warily.

"No. This is enough."

"Don't tell me," Germanicus said around a mouthful of beef, "that you've turned vegetarian, Corbo. I remember you from the arena. You had no mercy on man nor animal in those days."

"These beans are all that's necessary," Corbo said.

"Ah, what a sad, tired statement. Don't you think that sounds rather worn-out, Drusilla? Just what's necessary, our Corbo? Why, you always wanted everything, Corbo; the less it mattered, the more you wanted it. No, no, I'm convinced of it, my good man, it's not that you've attained some sort of moral enlightenment over the years, you've merely lost the energy to be bad. You've grown old."

"Everyone grows old," Corbo said, "sooner or later."

"But that brings up a point that I've been wondering about myself," Popillius interjected. "Why some of us faster than others? Why, for instance, does Drusilla appear so much younger than the rest of us? When we acquired the stones, we were all around the same age, except for Corbo, who was younger. And now . . ." He shrugged.

"Yes, why don't you tell us, Corbo?" Germanicus said, pointing with his fork. "You seem to have turned into the guru among us."

"That's very simple," Corbo said. "The little stones try to give you what you want. Drusilla is the most vain among us, Popillius the next, then Germanicus. I have no need to appear young."

"I do believe you are right for once," Germanicus said, pushing his plate away from him. "The stones will give you what you really want, whatever that might be."

"And what is it that you might want, Germanicus?" Corbo said softly. "That is the important question here tonight, isn't it?"

"What's all this about, anyway?" Popillius interjected. "Can't it wait until tomorrow?"

"You would have drunk your wine," Corbo said, "had you thought it could wait until tomorrow. No, it's all very simple. I'll tell you what it's all about. Germanicus here, or Boris, as he calls himself these days, is trying to kill me and take my stone. One of you, perhaps even both of you, are helping him."

No one was eating now. And in fact for a moment no one moved or said anything. Then Germanicus said:

"If that is so, then may I ask you, what are you doing here?"

"Several things," Corbo said. "For one thing, I would like to point out to the innocent one among you, if indeed one of you is innocent, exactly what's been going on behind your back. Do you think that when they are done with me that they won't turn on you? No, I'm afraid your only logical course of action is to join forces with me. Now, before it's too late.

"And then, I also feel I should point out to the guilty one among you the vulnerability of your position. Do you not realize what Germanicus will do with you once he's finished with the two of us? He wants it all."

Germanicus raised his great hand in a "stop" gesture. "Very amusing," he said. He looked as if he had just tried the wine after all and found it quite sour. "Don't you have any advice for me? I feel quite left out."

"No," Corbo said. "I'm afraid my advice to you would have to be to give up right now, and then I would let you live. But surely even you are too smart to believe that. So I have nothing to say to you. Drusilla?"

Everyone waited, watching Drusilla, whose lovely face appeared not quite so young as it had a few moments ago.

"I have no part in this," she said in a measured tone of voice. "And I want no part in it. I don't know whether it's true, or want to know whether it's true. I just want to be left alone."

Corbo turned slowly to the elegant man in the white suit. "Pop?" Popillius swallowed and then spoke. "Listen," he said, holding his hands out at shoulder level, "I don't know what's happening here. I don't know if any of this is true, or if the whole thing is just being made up by Corbo for some reason or other."

"That's right," Germanicus cut in. "How are we to know that you're not just lying to us?"

"Because," Corbo said, "we all know I don't lie."

"Well, then, I'll tell you something here, Corbo." The big German smiled. "It just so happens that I don't lie either. So I'll admit it. Yes, I want your stone. I need it. The world needs it. Give it to someone who will do something with it. Change things, use it. Someone who is not tired out."

"And?" Corbo asked.

"And I'll let you walk out of here alive."

"You're lying now," Corbo said.

Germanicus' smile broadened. "Yes," he said, "I suppose I am lying just a little."

"But your heart's in the right place, eh, Boris?" Corbo suddenly laughed out loud. It was a shrill and shocking sound in the quiet room. "Germanicus here is just a New Age hippie at heart."

Germanicus punched the table with his fist, but it was obviously an act of enthusiasm and not anger.

"Yes," he hissed, "it is going to be a new age. But not the one everybody is imagining. Not some weak, insipid, romantic goody-goody world where everyone will live safely and carefully in their government-supplied house eating their government-supplied porridge until they finally die of boredom. Quite the opposite, my friends, it's going to be a new age when finally the cream shall rise to the top of the milk. When strength at last will seize its reward. An age of courage and adventure. But you can't have courage, my friends, unless you have conflict. It is going to be an age of glorious conflict, and evolution, when the upward path of mankind shall be guided by the just power of the wielders of the stones."

And once again everyone was quiet. This time they were all staring at Germanicus. After a moment, Corbo, who was shaking his head, said, "Ah, there you have it: Germanicus, the world's first Nazi."

Once again Germanicus smiled. "Perhaps, in a way,

you are right again, Corbo. Perhaps I am a Nazi. But not in the crude, predictable mold that Hitler invented. In fact, I couldn't care less about the Aryan race. But the Aryan ideal, ah there you have another matter. And do you know what the Aryan ideal is? Let me tell you. It is no more and no less than a world ruled by the power of reason. Dominated by human thought. But it is a reason that has been sharpened by fear, that has survived conflict and been hardened by it as flame tempers a sword. It is the world ruled by a human mind which has conquered its own emotions and exists only to purify itself in further conflict. Always moving outward, farther and farther, to the end. Only there is no end, is there? That is the way I see the Aryan ideal.

"Ah, but I see I am boring you. I do have something else to say here," he continued. "Something of more practical interest to you, I'm sure. It's simply this. Popillius was correct. Tonight is not the right time for this. Tomorrow, after a good night's sleep, we will all—yes, myself included—find ourselves in a better mood to continue this discussion. I shot off my mouth, I admit it. But it was just talk. I'm sure we can all reach some kind of agreement if we put some effort into it. So let's postpone all this. Till tomorrow. All right?"

The big German stood and stretched and yawned, which was an awesome sight, and said, "No, no dessert for me, thank you," waving away the waiters, who were still hovering about, carefully controlling their expressions. "You see, in a way I agree with you, Corbo. Enough is enough, and more is no good. We just don't agree on what's enough. For dinner, or for mankind."

He walked out of the bungalow.

"Or for ourselves," Corbo added. Then he too stood up, and stared silently at Drusilla, who, strangely enough, held her hand to her forehead as if she were feeling faint. An odd, old-fashioned gesture, but easy enough to read.

She said, "Leave me out of it; yes, I'll have some of the mousse."

Popillius cleared his throat and said, "Yes, me too, dessert, and leave me out of it too, Corbo. Let's wait till tomorrow and see what happens then."

Corbo turned abruptly and without a word left the bungalow, with no more concern for decorum than had Germanicus before him.

7

EVEN THOUGH IT was not late, somewhere around 9:30, the children were already nodding out. Elena was trying to deal with them and at the same time toss a little sand on the fire that kept flaring up between Brice and Drusilla's macho bodyguard chauffeur. Brice didn't seem to have the common sense to be frightened. Perhaps he felt secure in his belief that Franco wouldn't really dare to physically attack one of Drusilla's guests, but Elena wasn't quite so certain herself. Somehow Elena had no difficulty picturing Drusilla leaning over the battered body of Brice, shaking her lovely head, and commenting along the lines of: "What a shame. I keep telling Franco to control that hot blood of his, but you know men. Honestly, I really do think he's getting better."

Yes, that sounded like the bitch, all right. Though Elena did not know her, she had felt an intense instant dislike of the woman. And since she had grown to trust more to her instincts as this horrendous ordeal wore on and on, she had already made her judgment. She would have bet anything she had at this point that Popillius was innocent, and that Drusilla and Germanicus were behind the attacks. Working together.

"I'm real sleepy," Violet said, and Elena felt a sharp

stab of pity as she noticed that the girl's cheeks were wet with tears.

During the day both kids acted as though they were on a vacation with their relatives. But at bedtime, the both of them automatically began to cry. Elena was not even sure if they knew they were doing it.

Poor kids must be so confused, she thought, against her will. She knew what it was like to cry yourself to sleep.

"Hey, yeah," Franco said, getting up off the puffy, brightly colored flower-patterned couch which he had somehow managed to spread himself out in and occupy totally, "not a bad idea. Nurse Bricie here will take you into the bedroom, tuck you in, and sing you a few lullabies. Elena and I have some important areas to explore out here in the living room, right, babe?"

Mercifully, the front door opened just then and the old man came in. Suddenly Elena was aware of her blood throbbing in her veins as she scrutinized the old man's expression for some sign of what had transpired at the meeting. With the usual results.

"How did it go?" she asked, surprised at the shaky quality in her voice.

"Drusilla will need you," he said to Franco, and then, in answer to Elena's question: "It went bad, Elena. Brice, help Elena get the rug off the floor. Quick. Elena, where are the suitcases? Get out the chalk and string. We'll need a small bowl of water, the four candles. William, would you bring me the salt from the kitchen, please?

"No, wait a minute, let me tell you something first. I didn't really tell you kids why we came here to Hawaii, but I got to tell you now. Violet, William, are you listening?" The children nodded, and William blinked sleepily.

"I mean really listening. You got to wake up here. You remember your father, your mother?"

Violet nodded solemnly, and William said, "I do

too," in an angry tone of voice, as if he had been accused of forgetting.

"I mean your real father and mother. Well, you know how they were killed?"

"It was an accident when they were driving a car," Violet said. Tears were streaming down her cheeks now.

"No, it wasn't an accident," the old man said ruthlessly. "They were killed because of something that your father took. A stone, an amulet. You know, you wear it around your neck? Black stone in the middle of it, like the stone Brice wears. Only different setting. You remember it?"

Violet shook her head.

"Well, your father was killed because of it. Because it was a stone of power. Do you understand me?"

"Like a magic stone?" William said in his cool voice.

"Yes, like that."

William shook his head gravely. "There isn't any such thing. I don't believe it."

"Yes, you do," the old man continued. "And what I'm trying to tell you is that the reason we're here, here in Hawaii, is to kill those people who killed your father. And your mother too. And your uncle, see?"

Violet burst out in a choked voice, "My uncle's not dead." She was crying freely. But William, who had started to cry too, had pulled himself out of it now, and was observing it all with his usual strange, detached expression.

"Okay, look then," the old man went on, "whether your uncle is dead or not, we've got to kill these people. Tonight."

"I don't . . ." William started to say.

"Listen," the old man said. "They are the ones who tried to kill us in Evansdale, and they are going to try again tonight."

"Those . . . those . . . dog things," Violet sobbed.

"They caused that, you see. With their powers. They sent those creatures to Evansdale. And they are going to try to kill us here tonight again. So we've got to kill them anyway. But you've got to kill them too, because they killed your parents, you see?"

"Revenge," William said doubtfully. "What good will that do?"

"Oh, it has to be," the old man said with conviction. "If you let someone harm your family and you don't take revenge, life is like a story that doesn't make sense. That has no right ending, you see? Our life, we're making it up. But it's like a story, it has to have meaning. That's the point of it. Family is the reason, the center that holds it all together. Family is sacred. But without revenge, family is no longer sacred. And your life wouldn't mean anything, you see?"

"But if we have to kill them anyway, why are you telling us this?" Violet sobbed.

"Because I want you to want to kill them, I want you to want it with all your hearts."

"Hey," Elena said, wandering over from the kitchen, carrying a bowl of water across the now-bare wooden floor, "let me ask you something for a change. How come all this talk from you about family, Corbo, when you don't have any?"

The old man blinked and opened his eyes wide for emphasis. "You are all my family, Elena," he said.

8

USING A POCKET compass and the string, the old man set the four candles an equal distance apart at the four cardinal points of the room, which was now cleared of furniture and rug.

"The circle has two purposes," he explained as he measured with the length of string (now folded in half) to mark the center between two diagonally opposed candles. "It is both for concentration and for protection. It is an ancient custom, and like all ancient customs is about ninety percent hogwash. But it has its uses. Particularly for beginners. When I start to draw it, you must all be silent and concentrate on what I am doing. Try to see it in your mind's eye as a dome, not a circle. A glass dome, see, which will go over your head. When you are in danger, concentrate on that. It will guide your powers to block off whatever is attacking."

"And just what do you think that will be?" Brice said, trying to sound unconcerned but speaking too fast. "More of those shapeshifters?"

"No, no, of course not," Corbo said. "You think they would loose uncontrollable carnivores like those here when they have to be here too? It will have to be something else entirely, but as to what . . . ?"

"Why are you so certain they will attack tonight, anyway?" Elena cut in.

"Oh, it will be tonight. As soon as they can initiate it, in fact. Before either Drusilla or Popillius can think things over or change their minds in any way.

"But if by some miracle of good fortune I am wrong and they do not attack us tonight, then we will attack them as soon as the circle is consecrated. So any way you look at it, it's just about to start. Now keep quiet and let me concentrate on the circle."

But he had no sooner begun to move the chalk than everyone plainly heard running footsteps on the gravel pathway and someone trying the door, then pounding on it.

"Let me in, it's Drusilla."

"Don't," Elena said in a clipped, harsh voice.

For a moment Corbo knelt motionless on the floor, considering, while everyone else stared either at him or at the door, from where they sat cross-legged on the floor within the circle of protection that he had just begun to draw.

Then Corbo sighed, put down the chalk, and got up and went to the door, opened it, and said simply, "Drusilla," in a resigned tone of voice.

"Corbo, I'm sorry . . . I'm so sorry." Drusilla moved into the room, where now, though the only light was that of the four candles, everyone could see that she was wearing some early signs of battle: hair mussed, face bruised, feet bare, fancy evening gown torn.

"I needed some time to think," she continued. "How could I know if it were true, if you were . . ."

"And now?" Corbo interrupted.

"They're using Franco, possessing him. I think it's Pop. He was always good at that sort of thing. I tried to take over control from him. But he's too strong. Franco struck me." She touched her bruised and rapidly swelling cheek and swayed, as if the thought that someone would strike her was so disorienting as to make her momentarily lose her balance. "He . . . he tore the necklace right off of my neck. He broke the chain. Took the stone. And I ran for it. He let me go. As if I didn't matter," she said, unable to conceal a note of rancor.

Strangely, the old man smiled. "But it was the wrong stone, wasn't it, Drusilla?"

"You knew?"

"Oh, come on, Drusilla, you would hardly be foolish enough to wear it under those circumstances. I know you better than that. And so should they. You can be sure it will dawn on them, and very quickly, that something is very wrong. Now, where is it?"

"Do you think they can tell if it's the real one, I mean using Franco like that?" Drusilla hedged.

"For Godsake," Elena snapped, "tell him where it is."

"Yes, I think they can see well enough through Franco's eyes. In fact, they probably already know. So where is it?"

Drusilla put both hands over her eyes as if blocking all this ugliness out, and mumbled something to herself in some other language. Then she took her hands away, and apparently having made up her mind in some fashion said: "Very well, I am forced to throw myself on your mercy, Corbo, if you have any."

The old man stifled his laugh for once, and hissing, gestured for her to go on. She sighed and continued.

"There's an electrical outlet in the main bathroom. Not the one up by the sink, but the one down low on the right-hand wall, practically at the floor. You unscrew it. It's not really an outlet, just a box that comes out of the wall. It's an amateurish setup, I know."

"I like it," the old man said. "Listen, you stay here. Elena: Drusilla will take charge while I'm gone. You help her prepare the circle of protection. I'll go after the stone."

Brice started to say something, but swallowed whatever it was.

"Old man," Elena said as he was turning to go out the door.

He turned back with an amused smile. "Yes, Elena?"

For a moment it looked as if she were not going to be able to spit it out. Then she said simply, "Don't believe her. Don't go."

"There is no choice," he said, and went out the door.

9

IN BACK OF Drusilla's cottage was a long rectangular swimming pool, lined with tiles. There was no diving board, no steps or ladders to distract from the simplicity of the strip of water, but instead there was a break in the low, tile-covered wall that bordered the edge of the pool farthest from the bungalow. This narrow breach came at the exact middle, only dipped partway down the wall, and was obviously intended to be used as a natural diving platform.

Keeping the wall between himself and Drusilla's bungalow, Corbo crawled to the gap in the center and then cautiously rose up enough to peek through it across the pool.

Straight ahead, across the pool dead center, was another statue. At first he could not make it out, even in the bright light of the moon. Then he recognized it, the owl-eyed Athena. The fierce goddess of victory in battle. How appropriate, he thought. On either side of the statue was an arbor covered with dark shadowy shrubbery of some sort, probably flaming-red bougainvillea, masking the two wings of the cottage. It struck Corbo not for the first time how little things really changed over the ceaseless passage of centuries. This lovely scene could easily have been an ancient Roman country villa. If this was the dawning of a new age, what was new about it?

No, he was convinced: in their essence, all things were timeless. Like this brightly moonlit pastoral scene. In fact, wasn't it too bright? How could this flood of illumination be a product of the moon? Almost at the moment that Corbo noticed this aberration, the sky brightened up another notch, and then his attention was distracted by a disturbance in the pool. As he glanced down, the water bubbled frantically, and suddenly a geyser spouted up out of the center of turbulence and settled onto the tiled border directly in front of him. Here it rose and fell, sizzling and frothing rather like a fountain of some unknown liquid trying to form itself into the shape of some creature or other, but unable to decide which one. Although it had no eyes, at least as far as Corbo was able to make out, it definitely seemed to be staring at him through the gap in the wall, as he was staring at it.

Gradually he became aware that it was whispering to him, but he could not make out what it was trying to say. Just as he could not really see it. It was not yet fully here, in this world. It was waiting for him to complete it: a water elemental, he realized. And as his own nature was that of fire, it was most likely to be antagonistic toward him. For a moment he thought of just ignoring it. Refusing to bring it into being. But you never knew. Elementals were information, and information, either positive or negative, could be useful. So he stared at it, watched it constantly change its shape, until it reminded him somewhat of a fat little pig. Laughing out loud, but muffling it so that it was more like choking, he guided the thing into existence on this plane as a pig with horns.

"Funny, funny, funny," it said, growing thinner and longer, but retaining its piglike nature. "What an old fool you are. How I'd love to rip your throat out. And who knows, perhaps I shall." It stretched out its arm, which sprouted a human hand full of very unhuman claws, toward him, but Corbo did not flinch.

"I cannot be harmed by such as you," Corbo whispered. "And I command you to tell me whatever you know that may be of service to me here tonight."

"You command?" it shrieked. "Command? Who are you to command? You couldn't even hold onto the stone. It ran away from you. Now you have no way to protect yourself, let alone command an elemental. I shall rip out your . . ."

"I have nothing to fear from you," Corbo said. "I may not have the stone, but I have wielded one for hundreds and hundreds of years. Some of that power will not leave me till the day I die."

The creature's face elongated, stretched, and twisted in excitement. "Tonight," it shouted triumphantly. "The day you die is tonight." It laughed hysterically and suddenly burst apart into bubbles which fizzed back into the pool.

Tonight, Corbo thought. I die tonight. Well, I suppose that's useful information of a sort, he said to himself. And stood up and made his way around the side of the pool. The back door to the bungalow was open. The lights were on. But it was obviously not the light from the bungalow or from the moon that was causing the sky to glow at the edges, giving the false impression of dawn. It was neither of those which had caused the waters of the pool to swirl and fizz. Or created the fleeting glimpses of unidentifiable creatures at the corners of his vision. He knew only too well the cause of it all: it was the side effects of the mystic stones in use.

Moving carefully but swiftly, he entered the cottage.

10

WHY DON'T YOU give it to me now?" Drusilla said, breaking the uneasy silence. She had just finished drawing and consecrating the large chalk circle, and they were all of them sitting cross-legged inside of it, staring at each other in the flickering light from the four candles.

"Not a chance," Elena said, answering for Brice.

Violet, who was rubbing her arms and nodding off, said, "It's cold in here." Which Elena realized was true, and was quite an unlikely situation for Maui this time of year, even in the mountains. And the skies outside the window were growing brighter. And brighter.

"Corbo said she was in charge," Brice said hesitantly.

"The old man is gone, and we may never see him again," Elena said, not really listening to what she was saying. "So we get to choose who's in charge. And we choose me."

"Nobody chooses you, you fool. Nobody except for you. Give me the stone. You don't have enough experience. I know how to use it. Just hand it here."

"I vote for Elena," William said. "How 'bout you, Lettie?"

"It's *really* getting cold in here," Lettie said. Then, as an afterthought: "I vote for you."

"Okay," William said, "one vote for me, one vote for

Drusilla, and two votes"—he held up two fingers to emphasize it—"two biggies for Elena. Who do you vote for, Brice? Drusilla?"

Brice smiled his furtive nervous little smile and reached out to touch Violet lightly on the cheek. "I vote for you," he said.

"Wow," Violet said excitedly, "that's the first time anybody's ever voted for me."

Drusilla, obviously with effort, controlled herself. "Children," she said under her breath, as if they were alien beings.

"Haven't you ever had any children?" Elena said. "For Christsake, you're practically two thousand years old."

"She's not that old," William said, and scrutinized her carefully. "But she's pretty old."

"What would you know about it?" Drusilla snapped. "I've lived out three lifetimes when the Roman Empire was still at her peak, when every grain of sand on the Mediterranean Sea was Roman soil. Just about the only big meaningful stretch of continuity this sorry world has ever known. It is true that I was forced to flee Rome to the East. But the East also was Rome. Everything was Rome. I lived on in the East through lifetime after lifetime while Rome crumbled apart bit by bit in the West. And finally even fell in the East. Then I lived through all the clumsy attempts to rebuild it again."

In her memory, flashes of Charlemagne being crowned Emperor in a ridiculously elaborate ceremony by Pope Leo III, at Rome, alternated with flashes of Napoleon being crowned by Pope Pius VII at Paris, a full thousand years later. Amazingly, she sometimes momentarily confused the two men, the two courts. They had both dreamed of recapturing the glory that was Rome, but Charlemagne was the one who had reinstated the charming custom of reading poetry to music—with a little nudge from Drusilla, of course.

"History!" She shook her head. "What you moderns think of as history is mostly a series of clumsy attempts to rebuild Rome. And do you know what? The United States did a pretty good job of it. Roman law, Roman religion. In some ways it even improved upon the technology, though not as much as you moderns would like to think. Hopefully, I'll even live through all of this, and maybe one day I'll see something that's not Rome, something new in the West. That'll be the day."

"But you've never had children," Brice said with sudden insight, "because you're afraid it will age you."

She shook her head again. Her lustrous hair billowed like a cloud in the steadily brightening air. "I had no choice in the matter. The stone keeps me young. But it won't let me have children. I think it's true for all of us. It's a small price to pay," she said, unaware of the tragedy lurking in the pun.

"Please listen to me, I'm trying to help you. All of you. But I can't unless you give me the stone. Can't you see, I'm the only one here who really knows how to use it?"

Elena shook her head. "No way. You know how to use it too well. I don't trust you. You say you're on our side now. You might even *think* you're on our side. But when things start heating up around here, really get to cooking, you're too self-centered. Too vain. I think you'll turn on us. Just like that." Elena snapped her fingers, making a loud cracking noise in the empty room, apparently, judging by her expression, shocking herself along with the rest of them.

"Hey, that's neat," William said.

The two women glared at each other. Brice took the chain from around his neck. And now held the stone in his hand. Not really knowing what to do with it.

Looked from Elena to Drusilla and back again. I

could just keep it myself, he thought. But that would be an ego trip. I don't know how to use it. I don't even want to use it. At this moment, he had a revelation. He wasn't really meant to use it. It just didn't feel right to him. Just a brief surge of insight, but he was certain it was true. And what about Drusilla? Was Elena right? Did Drusilla know how to use it too well? Want it too badly?

He leaned over and held it out to Elena, who—almost reluctantly—reached out to take it.

She breathed slowly, then for a moment did not breathe at all. She felt a warmth of exultation spread out through her body and beyond, but could not tell if the feeling emanated from her or from the stone.

"Ah, Yawtlée," she said, "at last you come to me. In all your power." Or is it that you come to me in all my power? she asked herself.

"Couldn't you feel it?" she asked Brice.

Brice shook his head. "I couldn't feel much of anything." He ran his slender, nervous fingers through his hair and said, speaking in that staccato, too-fast style of his, "Actually, I can't figure out what I'm doing here. I can't fight. I can't use the stone." His dark little eyes seemed to glitter in the weird luminescence. They reminded Elena of a raccoon's.

"You're here because Yawtlée wants you here," Elena said. Then she turned to face the others. "You stay in the circle," she said, and then walked confidently across the chalk line.

Instantly she felt an evil presence searching eagerly for and then finding her, descending upon her, viciously pressing down, so that she actually stumbled under the onslaught.

But now for the first time she experienced the protective power of the stone: it manifested itself as a bubble of heat, and she could feel it leaping up all around her like a conflagration, forcing that maleficent awareness, whatever its source (Pop? Germanicus?) to jump back, like some foolish child who had touched the flame of a match. And she was free to make her way over to the front window and look outside.

The sky was ablaze; sparkling from within. And it was now quite cold, much more so than it had been inside the protective circle. Even painfully cold. Had it not been for the protection of the stone, she would not have survived it, she felt. But perhaps this was merely illusion. Who could possibly know what was real and what was illusion anymore? *Not you, Elena.* She smiled. The thought was like a nudge from the old man.

As she watched, the scene outside the window shifted, altered, and rebuilt itself, and then continued the process, as if searching for the right world but not quite ever finding it. Like you, Elena. When suddenly the light blinked out. Just blinked out. Just died. And there was nothing outside the window at all. Not dark. Not light. Void. Indescribable void.

But then, after a measureless time of staring into nothing, Elena began to make out ominous figures forming themselves out of that nothingness. Tiny at first, they began to float toward the window, growing as they came.

Wordlessly she turned and walked back inside the circle, where immediately Drusilla began chanting forgotten words and moving her hands in some strange but somehow evocative pattern. Closing up the circle again.

Elena shook the children, who were nodding off, until they woke up again. "Now," she said simply. Their eyes blinked wide.

"Under no circumstances can any of us leave the circle from now on," Drusilla said sharply, "or it will shatter our defenses. Concentrate on the circle. Reinforce it with your thoughts." She closed her eyes for a moment, realizing for the first time how important it was to choose the right words here. Then she opened them and said:

"What you get here if you fail is not an F on your report card. What you get here is dead. Do you understand?"

Violet and William nodded maniacally. They either understood or thought they did. Who knows? And damn it, where the hell is Corbo? she thought to herself. Was there really any chance that he could get back her stone from Franco, or from whoever was controlling Franco, that is? Maybe, but she had her doubts. Too many of them. She felt that her only real chance in all this confusion was to stay near the other stone and wait. Perhaps it was her destiny to switch stones. Perhaps even to wield both. She would know soon enough, she thought as the front door swung open slowly of its own accord, drawing her attention outward into what appeared to be an endless, incomprehensible void.

11

CORBO HAD SEEN no signs of life within Drusilla's cottage, so far. So he moved on swiftly, yet cautiously, through the hallway and into the bathroom. More Rome, he observed, all this fancy blue tile, the Roman-style bathtub in the corner. The sink, even. He had never understood the Roman obsession to soak yourself in water. Scrub yourself. Anoint yourself with scented oils (soap nowadays), pat yourself with towels. Caress your skin with clouds of powder. Sprinkle secret parts of your body with perfumes. It all struck him as meaningless forms of worship, whether of the body or of water he was not sure; but then, his element had always been fire.

Quickly and quietly he found the outlet, got down on his hands and knees. Took the little Swiss Army knife out of his pocket, opened out the blade with the appropriate screwdriver, and removed the screws. Pulled out the box, and yes—let out his breath—the stone was there.

"How convenient. I always said, if you want a job done well, let Corbo do it for you."

Corbo looked up to see Franco standing in the doorway. The body was Franco's, the voice was Franco's. But the words, of course, were not Franco's.

"Germanicus," Corbo said, rising casually to his feet. "I would have expected you to mount the main attack, instead of allowing Popillius . . . Wait, ah, I see it. You don't want him to get control of two stones at once. You're afraid he'll become more powerful than you."

"Just hand me the stone, Corbo. And don't worry. You know what they say: Don't worry, be happy." Franco moved forward and held out his hand.

Corbo opened his eyes wide and said, "You can't move. You can't think. You can't even blink. You can't stand. Fall. Fall."

Franco lurched. But quickly regained his balance.

"No, I'm afraid I've already got too good a grip on the man. I'm in control here. Now, give him the stone. We may be able to come to an agreement after all. I have no reason to harm you once I get the stone."

"I'm not Drusilla or Popillius," Corbo said scornfully. "Do you think I don't know you better than that?"

"Which is why you'll be the first of us to die. You must let me know how you like it."

The body of Franco lashed out with a vicious left hook, but with an astonishingly smooth movement, the old man rolled his head away from the blow and moved back a step.

"No sucker punches, please," he said. "Even when you were in the ring, Franco, you always neglected to use your jab. Can you hear me in there?"

Franco took a step forward when suddenly, without the slightest warning, the old man tossed the stone to him, and he automatically caught it out of the air. Held it out in front of him and stared at it with a puzzled expression. "What the fuck?" he said. And these words were obviously not from Germanicus. "What's going on here?"

The old man stepped in swiftly, grabbed two handfuls of luxurious thick black hair, and rammed his head into the bigger man's face, jerked the head back, and pulled it in, head-butting him once again, splitting open the ridge of his cheekbone, and tried to bring up his knee hard and fast into Franco's groin.

But this was no amateur. And the pros don't stop when you stamp on their feet, knee them in the groin, or break their nose. The pros don't stop at all.

Franco grunted but managed to turn sideways enough to avoid the full impact of the knee, but staggered from it anyway. Dropped the stone and scooped the old man up in his arms, swiveled around, and smashed his body into the wall, once, twice, finally breaking loose those claws clamped into his hair, then carried him over to the ornate Roman bathtub in the corner and threw him in. Hard.

The old man's body smashed into the wall and the edge of the tub, and even caught some of the fixtures before settling inside, limp as a wet towel.

Was he dead or wasn't he? He sure looked dead. Thing to do, Franco figured, was bash his head against the edge of the bathtub and make certain. You had to be a good finisher in his book.

But suddenly he swayed, holding his head in both of his large square hands. He could feel that damn fool in there trying to take over again. Let me finish this fight, he tried to think to whoever it was, but it was just no use. *Pick up the stone.* He could see and hear what was happening but could not control anything. Not even thought. He reached down and picked up the stone off the gleaming tile floor where he had dropped it.

And now he could feel the power to resist. To assert himself. Apparently the stone itself gave him this power. And in fact, while being controlled like this was an odd experience for Franco, it was not totally unique. On the contrary, it seemed to him that he, as well as everyone he knew, with the possible exception of Drusilla, was always partially under the influence of someone or other. Someone with charisma, power, call it what you will. Some dumb movie star. If he wore it, then you had to wear it too. Under control of someone smarter than you. Or television commercials. The only difference was that this was more direct. But when the stone they were all squabbling over gave him the power to resist that control, it also gave him an idea. More than just an idea. A glimpse into a whole new level of thinking. Would the stone give him the power to resist not only this but *all* attempts to control him; could it finally set him free? Really free? And after all, why shouldn't he have the stone? Why should he continue to be a pawn?

Okay, then, let's get started. He struggled afresh with whoever it was in there, and somehow managed to force his body back over to the bathtub. But even with the help of the stone it was hard work going against those commands pounding inside his brain. It made his head ache. Besides which, his eye was swollen shut, his nose too. He couldn't breathe out of it at all. That really saps your strength, he thought. Tough old fart after all. Hard head. Best not to take any chances. Drown the mother.

He knew better than to let loose of the stone now. It was hard enough to concentrate even with it in his hand. Let go of it, and you could just forget about surviving here. Let alone winning.

Time for your bath, you old fart, he said to himself. If you're not dead, well, a little swim and you will be. But he certainly looked dead. Didn't he?

Bring me the stone. The idea kept surging through his head. More of an impulse than an idea. Wrecking his concentration. And it hurt. It throbbed.

First things first. Deal with the old man. Concentrate. Don't lose track of that. Then deal with whoever it was inside his head.

He kneeled down and leaned over to start the water going in the tub. Keeping a careful eye on the old man, of course, but not careful enough, because as soon as his right hand closed on the hot water handle, a nightmarish thing happened. The old man, who had obviously been playing possum (here on Maui, more likely playing mongoose), suddenly came to life, darted up, and snared Franco's hand, holding it there clamped onto the handle while his other hand locked Franco's elbow and shoved. There was nothing for Franco to do but plunge forward headfirst into the wall, very hard; and dazed, ears ringing, some little part of him far away was aware that now the hand was seized with both the old man's hands and twisted, wrenched, even, and—oh God, what was happening? The pain brought him out of it, and he came to with his face pushed sideways up against the tiles to see out of the corner of his eye the old man ram his left elbow into Franco's, which being all twisted around that way simply could not take the blow, and broke with a horrible cracking sound. Pain followed. Unbearable pain.

But while this stopped Franco, it did not stop the old man, who slammed his elbow in there again and again, just to be sure.

Screaming, Franco simply lurched backward, oblivious of what that would do to his arm. Another loud crack here, but Franco could no longer distinguish one pain from another. Franco's weight as he fell threw the old man back over in the tub, causing him to hit his head on the side of it again, so that as both men scrambled for their feet, Franco easily got there first. Lurched up, swayed dizzily, but managed to stay there. Waited until the old man had almost made it up, and then suddenly unleashed a short vicious front kick right into the poor old dude's belly. Franco didn't kick much, but when he did, he kicked hard. And this one was hard enough to slam Corbo backward into the wall and snap his head into it hard; then he just sort of crumpled up.

Franco, who was going through the kind of pain he had never even imagined, managed to keep control and force himself to throw another kick, catching the old fart in the ribs this time. More head on wall before Corbo flopped back down into the tub. Limp as a bowl of Franco's special spaghetti dish he sometimes cooked up for his friends, which was, contrary to popular ideas of stylistic excellence, decidedly not al dente.

Oh shit, Franco thought, allowing himself to stagger under that awful wave of pain. A broken fucking arm. In fact, he realized, I am going to be sick. He began to sweat. Staggered over and vomited in the sink. Sweat was pouring out of him now. His clothes were sopping wet. But he was not going to pass out. Yet.

Was the old man dead now? That was the $64,000 question. He sure as shit ought to be dead, and he sure as shit looked dead, but . . . And that was one big but.

Bring me the stone. "Will you fucking get out of my head and let me think for a minute?" he shouted out loud. "Otherwise this old fart is going to snuff me, and then who the fuck gets the stone, right?"

The voice in his head was silent. But Franco reeled from a fresh wave of nausea and dizziness. He just wanted to go over and sit down on the toilet seat and close his eyes, just for a moment, but he knew better. Not yet.

Don't blow it, he said to himself. You've still got the upper hand here if you just don't blow your cool. Hey, you know what, he said to himself, surprised with the thought, this is the championship bout. The world championship. Win it and you win it all. Lose it and . . .

"Hey, you know what, you old fart? All I need here is a weapon. That's all. And then I got you, you dig? No answer? You dead? Tell you what. You either dead, or you dying. Wait here, don't run out on me, okay? Fun's just beginning."

Staggering from time to time, but mostly walking slowly but under control, Franco left the bathroom, went through the hallway and out into the den.

"All right," he said enthusiastically, putting the stone in his shirt pocket (no reaction from the voice in his head—good!). Then he picked up the wooden chair that belonged to the old rolltop desk in the corner, quite gingerly, with his left hand. He was surprised at how heavy it felt. And to a man of his strength. (Strong, but getting weaker fast?) Let's finish this job, okay?

It was obvious to him now that his right arm was not only broken but broken in two places. Clean at the elbow, but not so clean at the forearm. Ruined, probably. But what the hell, this was the world championship. Win this one and he could always buy himself a new arm, right?

It seemed like a herculean task for him to lug the chair back into the bathroom again.

"Still dead?" he muttered. Then, "Shit, I knew it."

The old man was standing up in the bathtub now. Sort of. Clearly too weak to stand on his own, he had propped himself up against the wall, leaning against his right shoulder. But he was all scrunched over. And wheezing something awful when he breathed.

"Broken ribs," Franco suggested helpfully, setting his chair down a safe distance across the room and leaning on it to sort of rest up for the final surge. He figured all he had to do was hold the chair up with the legs pointing at the old man and lunge into him, rather like a lion tamer, except that, unlike a lion, the old man had nowhere to back off to. Then, once he got him off his feet, just bash his head in with some part of the chair, any part at all would do. That way he never had to touch the old fart at all. I've won, he thought. There's no way out of this one, you treacherous old son of a bitch.

"Except," the old man wheezed. "Except for . . ." He started to cough from the effort.

"Hurts, does it? Good. 'Except for . . .' You reading my mind? All right, I'll bite. Except for what?"

"The, the ceiling," the old man choked out. At least

that's what it sounded like he was trying to say. Franco patiently waited out another wave of pain and dizziness, leaning on the chair, and then cautiously glanced up at the ceiling and then quickly back at the old man again. Hadn't moved.

"What, the ceiling?" Franco said, surprised how high-pitched and reedy his voice sounded to him. Better get it over with, he thought. Shit, his eye was swollen shut, his cheek was gashed open, and his arm, his poor throbbing arm.

The old man choked again and couldn't speak—good! Just pointed up at the ceiling. What was with this ceiling shit? A pail full of water that would dump on him? Ha ha. But still, he couldn't resist it. The old man was clearly too far away to reach him. Couldn't even walk, probably.

Franco looked up over his head at the glistening blue tiles, but could see nothing. Held onto the chair for balance and tilted his head farther backward, just for a quick glance, that's all, when suddenly he was aware of a frantic twitch of movement from the old man. He had a brief sensation of something winking toward him and was aware that Corbo had fallen over the edge of the tub onto the tiled floor.

Good follow-through, he thought ironically, as all at once he felt what seemed like a terrible lump in his throat, a lump that was growing and growing and then suddenly exploded into pain. In blind panic, he tried to get to it with his right hand, more pain. Can't breathe at all, he realized, and reached up with his other hand and jerked the lousy little Swiss Army pocketknife (same one the lying little mother had never bothered to learn to throw) out of his throat and tossed it. Blood welled out, but he held his left hand over the wound and managed to partially stanch the flow.

Got to get out of here. Get some distance before,

before . . . Somehow he managed to stagger out of the bathroom and down the hall. Bleeding. Too much blood: had he severed the jugular? No way. Not that much blood. So he might make it yet. He was breathing now; great gasps, not enough air, but still, breathing nonetheless.

He found himself outside on the wide wooden front porch with the built-in hot tub where the rich could splash about nude in the sweet warm Hawaiian air. He ought to know. He had made use of that Jacuzzi himself. Perks. Perks were ninety percent of this job. Dream job. Dream. Visions of nude flesh, splashing in glistening water. Fragments. Sound of laughter, glasses clinking. Red haze.

Suddenly he swam up through a sea of pain to the surface once again. Opened his eyes. What was he doing sitting here on the wooden deck next to the hot tub, clutching his throat? So much blood and pain.

He watched in amusement as something scuttled across the wooden floor toward him: he thought he was hallucinating. It wasn't until it swarmed up over him and caught hold of his thick curly hair and dragged him down onto his stomach that he recognized what it was.

The old man, he thought. And then, sadly, as his head was thrust inexorably into the Jacuzzi: the champion of the world.

He could see his own hair flowing outward. Strangely beautiful, like seaweed. I should have cut it short, a crew cut, he thought. He could not breathe. He could not think. He could not . . . not . . . not . . .

"Well, I told you my little knife could fix up anything, didn't I?" the old man wheezed. Then, amazingly, tried to laugh. Which hurt. Coughed up a little blood. Broken ribs were the least of it. Broken everything, was what he figured. No getting around it, Achmed had trained Franco well. Too well. Who should know better than Corbo, who was also known as the Shadow, as well as by many other names. For hadn't he trained Achmed? And his father before him? And all of the chief bodyguard instructors back through the ages, for too long to remember. For despite all this modern-day folderol about oriental martial arts, none of it came close to the gladiatorial training of ancient Rome. Only the useless embellishments were new. The fancy empty stuff.

"Congratulations, Achmed," he hissed. And tried to laugh again. Which hurt even more. But served the purpose of waking him back up.

And there was the stone, right there. Must have fallen out of Franco's pocket. Careless of him. Question is, could he get it back to the others before he died?

So he gritted his teeth and hunkered down and began to crawl across the wooden platform toward the stone. It wasn't so bad if you didn't mind torture. And it wouldn't take too long, he figured. Only the rest of his life.

Somehow he managed to get to the stone and scoop it up. At once he felt its healing powers, subtle but strong. A few days, maybe a week, and he could heal himself, live on. And on. But he did not have a week or a few days. He did not have anything at all except right now.

He had adopted a crawling style that dealt him the least amount of agony. How ironic that the last thing I ever teach myself, like the first, is how to crawl, he thought. Down the steps was the tough part, but then, none of it was easy. And it took so long. He headed around the side of the house toward the back again, an endless journey, through endless pain.

But I'm going to make it, he thought. By this time he had worked his way into the backyard and almost halfway around the pool. On top of everything else, he was shivering and shaking. It was freezing cold. Was that an illusion caused by his physical condition or a side effect of the work of Germanicus and Popillius?

And the sky was so bright. Then he sensed clearly that something in it was watching him. Not rushing in to attack, but taking its time, enjoying his misery. He rolled over on his back and looked up. It came for him then, flashing across the sky, blazing like a meteor.

It fell on him from out of the night and perched on his chest; peering into his eyes, drinking in his pain. He perceived it as a giant eaglelike creature, with the cruel ice-blue eyes of Germanicus.

Its talons penetrated his body, but at first he felt nothing. Suddenly, just for an instant, its wavery form solidified, and finally, in an explosion of pain, Corbo died.

The astral eagle shrieked in triumph. Then, enormous wings spread wide, it hopped over to try and pick up the stone and fly off with it. But this, it could not do. For a moment it would become solid and its talon would close around the stone, but as soon as it took to the sky it would lose its solidity and the stone would fall through its grasp. So it flew off, and back to the roof of one of the other bungalows, where the figure of a very big man was seated cross-legged. The two figures merged, and the man rose up and stretched his massive limbs. Then walked over to the edge, turned around, and lowered himself onto a ladder positioned there. Made his way down the ladder and along the gravel path that led toward the main bungalow. In less than three minutes he was kneeling down next to the lifeless body of Corbo and the stone was in his hand.

Silently he stood up and raised both hands into the air, a stone in each. I have won, he thought. From a distance, from the skies. The Aryan way. The air: victorious over fire as it would be over earth and finally over water. For the New Age, he felt, was to be the age of air, and also the age of Aryan.

For a moment he pondered what step to take next. Considered changing his battle plan, for was the air not flexible, not open? But in the final analysis he felt it best to go with his original approach. Climb back up on the roof and prowl the skies in his astral form, watching and waiting until the time was right, everything perfect, then strike from the skies. The great Aryan eagle, loosed at last upon the final crumbling, crippled defenses of the old world.

So he climbed back up onto the roof of his bungalow, settled into his cross-legged position, palms of his huge hands up, resting on his knees, with a stone in each palm. Closing his hands over the stones, feeling the power flow through him, he began the necessary mental preparations for the reemergence of his astral form.

12

THE LITTLE GROUP inside the circle watched with various mixtures of awe and trepidation the smoky form floating in through the doorway. As it neared them it took shape, as if it existed only for their eyes and only through their awareness of it. But the shape it finally assumed was not one that any of them expected. Least of all Brice.

Brice blinked and shivered; the temperature of the room seemed to have dropped another notch with the entrance of the creature, but it was not the cold that made him shiver. And it was not the cold that made the tears stream down his cheeks.

"Conal," he choked.

"Might as well call me Quinn, Bricey boy, I died as Quinn. I guess it was as Quinn that I lived too. Really alive, I mean. In the fire. Oh, it's really Quinn that I am, and not Conal. Quinn the clown. Quinn the killer. Quinn the ghost. It's no fun being a ghost, Bricey. I can't honestly say that I recommend it."

"I don't believe in ghosts," Brice said in a hoarse voice.

"Oh, but that's what I am, all right. Belief or no belief. I'm dead. That bitch Mary Jane did me in. And you her, ain't that the truth, Bricey? Okay. That was the way to go, all right. Revenge. I can dig it. It had to be done. You did it.

"But this . . . ? What's the point, Bricey? Believe me, you can just walk away from it. Live your life out. Let them squabble over the fucking stones, the power. Just walk. Now. While you can."

"Don't listen," Drusilla said. "That's not your brother. Just an apparition, a tool of Germanicus or Popillius. Do you think they'll really let you walk away from this?"

The children were no longer thinking about sleep. They weren't even blinking. "He killed Mary Jane?" Violet whispered in disbelief to William.

"*Au contraire,* Dru—you are the famous Drusilla, I presume. With my uncanny knowledge from beyond the grave. Shit. There is no knowledge beyond the grave, Bricey, no nothing. Just dark. Not even that. Don't try it. Avoid it as long as you possibly can. Take your sage older bro's advice and get thyself away from these weirdo mystics sitting around like marbles just waiting for Boris and Pop to come strolling in and shoot them out of their circle. You stay alive. Live long and prosper. But if necessary, don't even prosper. Just live long. Die of a heart attack brought on by oral sex at the ripe old age of one hundred—but hey, choose a little better partner than Mary Jane this time, won't you?

"Jesus." Impersonating Groucho: "I told you his girlfriend would be the death of me, didn't I? Yuk, yuk, yuk." Then solemnly, "Some joke!

"Remember all your promises, Bricey, O honorable one? You were going to master the guitar for Dad, master tai chi for me? Master Boris and Pop for the old man? Who are you kidding? Break all promises, bro. Just live. Get out of here and live for yourself. But go, now . . ."

The form wavered as if it were a pond a leaf had fallen into, then cleared again.

"Ah shit, Bricey. They're calling me back. Back into

the dark. Or lack of dark, or whatever you choose to call it. Don't follow. I repeat, do not follow me there."

He began to fade.

"You were the only thing I ever loved, Bricey. Just do me one last great big favor and keep yourself alive. *Adiós, hermano.*"

And he blinked out like a light.

Brice screamed, a high-pitched, inhuman cry like that of a cat, crumpled up in a ball, knees to his chest, and wept, bringing up huge wrenching sobs from deep down in his diaphragm.

"I'm telling you it's not true," Drusilla said in a calm, sure tone of voice. "It's a trick, it wasn't your brother. They are just probing for a weakness. Like a couple of smart boxers in the first round, *capisce?* That was not your brother."

"Then how," he sobbed, "then where did they . . . ?"

"From you," Drusilla said. "Where else but from you?"

But even as she was talking, new figures were floating into the room, formally, through the open doorway, as if they actually came from the outside.

13

AT FIRST NO one seemed to recognize them. The tall slender man with the dark glittering eyes and the rakish goatee; the small, delicate Oriental woman, not much more than a girl, really. They rather resembled a pair of beatnik extras from a television series of long ago. Perhaps stand-ins for a coffeehouse scene on *Peter Gunn,* maybe even *Dobie Gillis.* Too beautiful to be the real thing.

Suddenly Violet whispered in an awed voice, "Daddy? Mom? Daddy, Daddy, Daddy!"

Brice came out of his fit of misery long enough to grab Violet just in time to keep her from running into the apparition's arms.

"Oh, for Godsake," the man said petulantly, "they are my kids, not yours. Listen to me, Vi, William. I want you out of this. You understand? Oh God, how I miss you two. The both of you. You think it's been a long time for you? You know how long it's been for us? An eternity, that's how long. Umpteen million years from that automobile accident. Some accident. Same kind of accident that's just about to occur to all of you. Unless you just give it up and get out of here. Now.

"Listen to me. Not just the kids, but all of you. I can save all of your necks if you'll just let me. All you have to do is stop. Just stop. They'll let you go. I guarantee it. You think they care about you enough to kill you? Don't give yourself airs. You're no more than gnats to them, once they have the stones. William, I'm ordering you and Vi, get out of here. These fools can't hold onto you forever."

Drusilla took hold of William's arm, but he shook his head. "He's not my daddy," he said.

"How do you know?" Violet shouted, still struggling with Brice.

"I just know, Lettie."

Violet's struggles subsided.

"Are you denying your father?" the dapper man exclaimed exaggeratedly.

But at that point, another form suddenly materialized in the room, behind the handsome couple. At first it was smoky and indistinct, then suddenly it too took on a familiar form.

"Corbo," Elena said in astonishment. "But you're not dead."

"Wrong, as usual, Elena," he said, chuckling. "As to you two phonies, be gone. Now. Vanish." He waved his hands disdainfully at the two phantoms.

The pair began to fade. The woman said in a high, sweet voice: "As in life, I never got to say anything," then disappeared.

"Listen close, Elena," the ghost of Corbo said, "because I'm cheating here. Hitchhiking. I'm stealing some of the power Popillius is dealing out, in order to hang around a little while longer, but he'll catch on soon. Too soon."

"You're dead?" Elena gasped in disbelief.

"Oh, I'm dead, all right. And soon I'll be gone forever. Not like those phony ghosts he's been tormenting you with; those are only phantoms. But I'm a real ghost, which means—guess what, Elena—yes, they now have Drusilla's stone. So you can't just sit around here on your asses in a protective circle and wait for me anymore. Because . . . I'm . . . not . . . coming . . . Wait a minute. Pop's onto me already. I've only got a moment left to be me. Then I've got an eternity to be everything.

"So you know what you got to do, don't you? You just do what I would do. That simple. Go bring back the ally of the yellow cloud. Then head straight for Pop. He's the weak one. Ignore Germanicus and deal with Pop. But hurry. The only reason you have any chance is that I suspect he's scared to death and trying to protect himself from Germanicus at the same time. Even Pop's not stupid enough to trust that bastard. Thank God. And don't look at me like that, Elena. You think you can't do it, but let me assure you, you have within you the power to control Yellow Cloud."

He began to laugh and fade at the same time. "Always leave them laughing," he choked, and blinked out.

14

YOU'VE GOT TO give me the stone. Can't you see that?" Drusilla held out her long slender hands. Which were trembling.

"Fat chance," Elena said.

"Then you've got to do something," William said. "Do what the old man told you to do."

Even in the dim candlelight, everyone could see Elena blanch.

"What is it?" Brice said. "What's wrong?"

"I can't," Elena said. "I'm just not strong enough."

"Tell us what you're talking about," Drusilla snapped. "If you can manage that much."

"There is a world where he sometimes goes. An astral world, some horrible place of power, where he goes to seek help. He brings back with him an ally that he, somehow or other, to some small degree, manages to just barely control. A terrible fierce ally. It almost kills him every time he does it. I know I'm not strong enough. It isn't a question of courage, you morons. It's just a simple fact that I know I'm not that powerful."

"Okay," Brice said, after a brief pause. "I'll try it. If you can get me there and back out again. I'll do my best. It's better that way anyway. At least if I get killed you'll still have the stone."

"You can't! Believe me, you're not strong enough either," Elena stammered. And could not help adding, "And a half."

"What have I got to lose?" Brice said bitterly. "Now hurry. It's been quiet around here for a couple of minutes, but I have a feeling that won't last. So how do I find this yellow cloud thing and what do I do to control it?"

Elena's grimace grew more exaggerated. "Don't worry, he'll find you. It's his turf. He'll find you and attack you; try to drain the psychic energy out of you. You just keep concentrating on me; on yourself, who you are, what we're doing here. And bring him back. But it just won't work, Brice, because believe me, you're not Corbo."

Brice nodded. "I can believe that, but let's get going. We're just wasting time here. And we don't have the time to waste."

For several years now, Elena had been practicing what the old man had called the art of opening the doors. She had been good at it; the old man, in fact, had remarked that it was the only thing she was good at. Big laugh here.

At first she had started by just holding the stone in her hands, closing her eyes, and quietly watching.

"I don't have nothing to watch," she had complained.

"Then watch nothing," he had answered.

Typical! Well, he wouldn't be making that kind of remark anymore. Or any others. The thought sobered her.

Now she looked down at the stone, closed her eyes, and descending swiftly and effortlessly into the vast darkness which was herself, she formed the thought "Yellow Cloud," which carried within it the seed of an image. Instantly she could feel the stone pouring energy into that image, igniting it into a flame of light. Then, as if it were somehow a concrete thing, she moved away from it. Leaving it pulsing there alone, moving of its own accord, struggling to dissolve back into the dark whence it came. But in some way that she could never explain to anyone, using the energy flowing from the stone, Elena took hold of that image and thrust it outside herself. Now she opened her eyes, almost as soon as she had closed them.

A doorway—really something more like the entrance to a cave, but what the old man had always alluded to as a doorway—began to appear inside their circle of protection. At once it grew clear, real, here, now. Through Elena's will, and the will of the stone.

To Brice this eerie vision seemed almost as if it were somehow manifesting to him—to him alone. For a moment he looked away from it and stared intensely at Elena. With his little raccoon eyes, as she saw it. Looked like he was going to say something. But no, without a word, he turned and went through the door. Elena watched until he was gone and then closed her eyes again.

15

FOR THE FIRST time Brice believed, really believed. Oh yeah, astral realms, other dimensions, ghosts, the tooth fairy, you name it, he believed it. Up till now, he had stubbornly held onto his system of rational disbelief in some corner of his mind. If he couldn't figure it, it wasn't happening. Not really. Not all the way. But he had been given no choice. Everything had simply swept him along like a piece of driftwood in a tidal wave, and it had been too fast a ride for him to examine, think, accept, or even argue with any of it. I'm having weird dreams about ancient Rome—okay. You're practically two thousand years old—okay. We're being attacked by some kind of were-creatures—okay. Oh, by the way, you four are the guardians of the world—sure, well, let's get a move on.

The ghost of his brother, or whatever it was, the other phantoms, the old man's ghost, they had been just more weird experience he had not yet had time to analyze, to accept or reject.

Hallucinations, visions, dreams, hypnotic reveries—these were all possibilities. So when Elena had calmly closed her eyes and opened up a door for him to go through, right there in thin air, sure he had gone through it. To pick up the old man's ally, Yellow Cloud, and bring him-it back. Of course, why not?

But once through the doorway, a strange and wonderful thing had happened. He believed. And found not just belief, but understanding; new reality. He understood now what it meant to be born again into a fresh new world of unimaginable possibilities.

For he had just stepped from the bare wooden floor of a room in a luxurious spa in Maui onto the soft, foliage-carpeted floor of a jungle. But a jungle unlike any jungle Brice had ever heard of.

The first thing that struck him, in midstep, while he still thought of himself as being "in the room," was the cloud of hot moist air, impregnated with the myriad heady odors of growth and decay and the screams of death and lust and defiance.

Monkeys screamed. Birds screamed. Insects screamed, copulated, struggled, died, killed.

Brice noticed, even as his foot sank into the thick jungle carpet, that the group of creatures moving with such lovely fluidity through the trees, screeching insults and threats at him, were definitely not monkeys.

One of the smaller ones, perhaps a youth, perhaps not, scrambled partway down onto the trunk of the tree just in front of him and bared its teeth, which were sharper than any monkey's teeth. Its round eyes glistened with an odd maleficent intelligence, and in its little clenched fist it held out toward him a weapon of sorts, what appeared to be a crudely made stone ax. It retained its threatening pose long enough for Brice to notice its little pointed ears, and most of all, its luminous soft blue fur. Long enough for Brice to start to give serious consideration to flight, before it panicked and ran back up the tree again.

And, in the manner of monkeys everywhere, when it panicked the whole tribe panicked with it. They erupted out of the tree in all directions, screaming, screeching, and even uttering long ululating moans. Before Brice had time to run away, they were gone. Only the defiant answers of distant birds remained.

And the trees themselves, while similar to jungle trees that Brice had seen before in photographs and movies, nonetheless were obviously not of this earth. Jungle trees are green and simply not every color in the rainbow.

The hot wet air, redolent with heady scents, made Brice reel. Made his thoughts reel.

This is another world, he thought, and I am in it, here, physically. Totally. Mentally and physically. This was not visiting an astral world in your astral form, because how could you trust that, because after all, an astral form is an altered state of consciousness. But this was just . . . just real.

And there were other worlds, planes, whatever you call them, many others—he had picked up that much from snatches of conversation between Elena and the old man. He had not believed it. Or disbelieved it.

But now, looking around in awe at the many-colored jungle, drinking in its layers of odor, light, and sound, he asked himself a new question: is life about love of family, or is life about exploring myriad new worlds of consciousness? He did not know the answer.

He began to move through the jungle, looking behind him from time to time to reassure himself that the doorway, strangely enough, was moving right along with him. Sure, it stayed in the center of the circle back in the room, but here it followed him around. Why not? It only figured that time and space did not have the same meaning here as it did back there.

Time. How much time was passing back in that room? What really was his role in all this? It was not to wield the stone. He had sensed that clearly when he held it in his hands just a short while ago, before it had gone to where it belonged. In fact, he had even known it in ancient Rome, or in his dreams of ancient Rome. So the old man could be wrong. Dead wrong, in fact. But what part was he to play?

He stopped moving. What had Elena said, Yellow Cloud would find him? Consciousness was the answer, not movement. He closed his eyes. He had noticed how effortlessly Elena had created the doorway. It had not escaped him that she had shifted into an altered state of consciousness as quickly and easily as snapping her fingers. He could imagine how much time and effort it had taken her to attain that level of control. And he knew he could not hope to equal it. But he was a gifted musician. He had years of practice at merging with music. And that was also an altered state of consciousness. At least it was when it worked.

Yellow Cloud, he thought, I'm here. Then he tried simply saying "Yellow Cloud" to himself over and over.

For a moment other thoughts, a bundle of nervous impulses, interfered. Then, surprisingly, the words seemed to sail into clear space. Stretch out, elongate. Change into little things. The little things stretched out. Changed into other little things. And . . . Suddenly he snapped his eyes open. The jungle was deathly silent. Something was coming. Something of which everything else lived in fear.

All of his enthusiasm abruptly fell away. What was the matter with him? They were all simply on the losing side of a war. What was he doing here? The ghost of his brother, or whatever it was, had been right. Run away. Live as long as you can. That was the only meaning of life—just hang on.

He turned and started for the doorway. But as he did so, he was buffeted by a cold, wet wind, so that he actually staggered, and something glided onto him, something liquid and clinging. Something like death.

Too late, he thought. I'm too late. He was so weak, so tired. Tired of it all. Who cared anyway? To sleep. To forget. No more struggles. No more dreams. No more nothing.

But he was still on his feet. And the doorway was so close. Concentrate on who he was, Elena had said. On the group. Back there in the center of the circle, so far away and yet so near. They needed him.

Perhaps he could make it yet. He felt the creature's tendrils of cold so swiftly draining him of energy. Inexorably sucking out his soul. Not eagerly or excitedly, but with the certainty of a predator who is dominant over everything it ever encounters—except the old man. The old man had tamed it—to some degree. What an awesome, impossible feat that had been.

But Brice knew now what Elena had known all along. That he did not have the strength to carry the yellow cloud. No one did, except the old man. And that was simply that.

He reached out of his agony toward the doorway, so near . . . yet not near enough. He sank down in a heap on the jungle floor. Fading away into the cold. Don't kill me, he thought. And then, true to the folktales of drowning, for he was drowning here, scenes from his past popped up out of his subconscious, flared, and fizzed out.

Daddy, Mommy, long ago. Here was Mommy all dressed up in her going-out-to-dinner clothes, carrying a watchacallit-thing that you put all your clothes in.

"Bye-bye, honey, I'm going to be gone forever, so be a good boy."

She couldn't have said that, could she? Funny little scenes. Here and gone in an instant. Were they true or just hallucinations? Was anything on this bitch of an earth, or off it, true? One thing, and one thing only.

I love you, Conal. You were the only one I ever really loved, he thought as he died.

16

ELENA'S GREEN CAT eyes blinked open. Drusilla had the kids chanting something now. Nothing else was happening here yet. He's gone, Elena thought—knew for certain. It had only been a few seconds since Brice had entered the doorway, but Elena knew that time was different in these astral worlds. They were closer to the edge of manifestation. You could spend a month inside and yet be back out in an hour or two.

But whatever amount of time had passed, it had been enough for Brice to have failed. She knew that.

She had always "known" things, as the old man had put it, but she had never had the courage to accept that knowledge before. As long as the old man had been running things. But now there was no one left to turn to. Unless she trusted Drusilla. Drusilla's big, black, earth-mother eyes were on her now, as a matter of fact.

"He's dead," Elena said to her in a low, emotionless voice.

"Of course he's dead," Drusilla answered. "That's why I want the stone."

"Not Corbo," Elena said, "Brice. They're both dead."

Drusilla swallowed; the kids had stopped chanting whatever it was they had been chanting.

"Which is why I want the stone even more," Drusilla said. "You know, we're not exactly winning here. Have you figured that out? Huh? Now, quit acting like a fool and give me the damn thing before it's too late for all of us."

Elena looked into her eyes for a moment and then shook her head. "Not ever," she said.

For the first time since they had met, Drusilla exploded into a rage. "You bitch," she shouted. "You silly vain little bitch, you'll be dead and dust and forgotten while I live on and on."

Again Elena searched her eyes and then shook her head. "No," she said. "I don't think so. I think you've just about run your race, old girl. And you're not ever getting this stone, you see. So I'll tell you what you're going to do. You're going to stay right here and take very good care of these kids, and protect the circle, while I go inside and try to drag Yellow Cloud back out here with me."

"Fine! And what happens to us if you don't make it?"

Elena nodded, thinking it through. "You better hope I make it," she said finally. But as she rose to her feet she could not block out the fact that Violet was crying again. Both of the kids' eyes were fixed on her.

"You kids have got to fight with everything you've got. Do you understand?"

Both of them nodded solemnly.

"That's all you can do, so just do it." I'm starting to sound like the old man, she thought.

Well, it's just you and me, Yawtlée. Shall we give it a try? Was she mistaken or did she feel the stone pulse in answer to her question? I'm even starting to think like the old man, God help me.

She walked through the doorway and disappeared.

17

WHILE IT WAS true that Elena had visited several astral worlds before, she had never done so without the protection of the old man. The last few times he had coaxed her into accompanying him on his "mystic journeys," she knew that what he had been really waiting for, planning for, was for her to take the reins, stretch her little wings, and fly away from the nest. Grow up. Move out. Take charge. But not Elena. No way, Elena. How could the old man have ever put up with her? Somehow—and this struck Elena as the most mystic element in their relationship—somehow the old man had more patience than she had fear, anger, reticence, stupidity, you name it, and he had more than enough patience to wait it out. But now he was dead, so here she was. Shaking in her Sauconys, as he would surely have pointed out.

On the other hand, no matter how often you came here you were never going to be prepared for the bizarre experience waiting to greet you. Maybe that was another thing the old man had understood. Sooner or later Elena would have had to do it on her own, so why rush? Well, later was now, unfortunately.

Yellow Cloud. She started to project the image that would bring him-it to her, and then a strange thing occurred. Without any conscious volition on her part, some deeply buried mechanism of her subconscious mind reached up from below and snuffed it out. She took a deep breath and slowly expelled it. Tried again, with the same results—or rather, lack of results. It was like getting ready to scream out a name, then getting it caught in your throat and having it come out a whisper. Or even less than a whisper. Something inside herself would not let her call the old man's terrifying ally to her side. (To her side? On her back, was more like it.)

What I need is rest, she thought. About ten years' worth. She sat down beneath a tree (where else?) and closed her eyes. What difference did it make, anyway? She knew how slowly time was moving back there in that room. In the center of the circle. The center of the cyclone. The eye of the hurricane. They probably hadn't taken two breaths since she had left them. So what was her hurry? She felt herself sink into the cacophony of jungle noise as if it were an ocean. And she slept.

18

AS SOON AS Elena had gone, Drusilla started the kids in chanting the protective mantra she had given them earlier. Did the word itself really do anything, or was it just a focus to aid your concentration? After all these years, practically two thousand of them, Drusilla still did not know the answer. For some reason, and to some degree, the procedure worked. That was all she knew and all she needed to know.

I'm the only one left here with that kind of experience, she thought, and that foolish baby, that insignificant ephemeral female, barely out of her teens, won't even trust me with the stone. Yet if we are to win this one, come out of this alive in any way, it will have to be because of me. There's got to be a way out of this, and I'll find it. I always have.

How many times had she escaped from the barbarians' teeth? Germans, Huns, Turks, Mongols—they were all the same to her. And she had not only escaped, but she had controlled them when necessary. All four of the Guardians had, and that had not turned out to be such a bad deal for mankind after all, had it? Where would civilization have gone had the churches not been nudged into sponsoring the universities of Europe, an idea that would hardly have occurred to them on their own?

And how would England have developed culturally had that great oaf Harold won out over the Normans? They would probably still be whacking each other with broadswords in the middle of the main thoroughfare.

But of course there had been some little mistakes. Like the black plague. That was one of hers.

China, 1333, one of the few really nice places to live around that time. In fact, although Drusilla hated to admit it, even with her bias toward European culture, she had to agree with Popillius on that one. But, as always, the barbarians were frothing at the gates. Between 500 and 1500 the Chinese seemed to be constantly fighting off invaders, only this time it was not merely Mongols, but Mongols under the influence of Germanicus.

As it had for all of them, the power of the stone had opened up doorways to many worlds for Drusilla. It had also protected her from disease. But not before she had experienced the first onslaught of symptoms from the virulent bubonic plague in one of those myriad worlds.

It had been an obvious way out for her to return there, taking with her a terrified servant of the Emperor, and then right back again with him as a carrier of the disease. How could the poor ignorant army of Mongols have guessed the danger lurking in the whimpering little coolie sent out the gates for them to play with? Well, they hadn't. Even Germanicus hadn't until it was in fact too late. And his army had been decimated. But then, the plague had also decimated China. And who would have guessed that in a few years it would spread all the way to Europe? Three threes—1333—she would have guessed it to have turned out a year of great luck, and in a way it had been, for her. But not for the rest of the world. She shook her head, as if to clear it of memories—so many memories—and brought herself back to the here and now.

"Keep chanting, you kids. Remember what Elena told you: you've got to fight with everything you've got."

She was right about that one. Wrong about everything else.

"Why aren't you chanting?" It was the boy, William. Staring at her in that disconcerting defiant way of his.

Am I reduced to this? she thought. I, who have lived out so many lifetimes. I, whom emperors and kings have bowed down before. Taking flak from two little hybrid children. Mongrels. How like Corbo to have dragged in a couple of Eurasian orphans and their Mexican nursemaid and then put them in charge of me.

"You just do what I tell you to do or you're going to be real sorry, do you understand?"

But the boy didn't flinch at all. "So what?" he said. "We're all going to be real sorry anyway."

She reached out to slap him, but he still did not flinch.

Get control of yourself now, worry about revenge later. "Okay, okay, just please keep chanting. Concentrate on the circle. Remember to see it as a dome, and keep chanting. I've got other things to concentrate on. But it's important for you to chant." Billy Bunny wants you to chant, she almost said.

Even without the stone I have powers. There is no way anyone can break into this circle while I'm guarding it. At least not for a while.

"Why are you looking at me like that? No, don't answer, just keep chanting."

But both of them were staring at her, with astonished expressions.

"What is it?"

"You look older."

It's just a trick. "Keep chanting."

Still staring, they continued their chanting.

Another figure floated in slowly through the open door, and this time Drusilla almost welcomed it. Whose ghost would it be this time?

When she made out who it was, she gasped.

"How can you be the ghost of me? I'm still alive."

"All things grow old and die, Drusilla," the beautiful ghost said. "Some just take longer than others. One day everything will be a ghost."

So pale and eerie, floating here in the room. So ephemeral, but then, aren't we all?

"Ah, but you don't look like this anymore," the specter of herself told her. "You look more like this now." A small network of wrinkles crawled out from the corners of her lovely eyes and the edges of her sensual mouth, as the ghost's silky smooth, firm skin visibly loosened. The ears and the nose appeared to grow (or had the face simply shrunk?) and the flesh formed little pockets under the ghost's eyes. Then she began to laugh, in a cracked, dry version of Drusilla's voice.

"Old, and every second getting older."

The ghost floated backward, hovered and waved, said "Bye-bye, dearie," in its horrible scratchy voice, and abruptly disappeared.

No, no, no, Drusilla thought, the word pounding in her head like a headache, the supreme mantra. "No, no, no," she chanted out loud. It's only a trick. A trick.

The kids, strangely enough, were still chanting. They were really hanging in there now. But at the same time they were staring at her—was it her imagination?—in bug-eyed horror.

"You stay here, you understand? You keep chanting. You'll be okay."

Don't do this, she said to herself. You can't do this. Whatever you do, you can't break the circle.

There were mirrors in the main bedroom, weren't there? An entire wall of them. Don't do this. Oh God, don't do . . .

She rushed out of the circle and immediately staggered under the onslaught of some devastating attack she could not name. It left her on her feet, but diminished somehow. Disorganized. Disorganized outside and disorganized inside.

For some reason, she coughed. At the last moment she remembered she had to at least try to close the circle before she left the room. And she did go back and go through the motions, only it was so hard for her to concentrate. The kids just kept on chanting. Bug-eyed.

Then down the hall and into the bedroom. Mirrors, mirrors on the wall, who's the fairest of them all? Not you, Dru.

"Oh no, no, no," she wept in her hoarse voice. Couldn't even stand up straight anymore, so it was an effort to look at her face in the mirror, where—oh no, no, no—further changes were taking place at lightning speed. Wrinkles were weaving a myriad of new expressions, each more hideous than the last. And now she recognized the disorganization for what it was: it was entropy. It was old age. Only in her case, it was ancient age.

As she sank down onto the plush carpet in all her many-mirrored forms, she thought bizarrely: All I ever wanted was to be young forever. Was that too much to ask?

She had to laugh at that—cackle at that.

And the war was over, she realized. With a strange awful surge of relief. She no longer cared in the slightest who won or lost. What happened to the kids, or even to herself. The only thing she ever cared about was gone forever. Her own fair beautiful youth.

She tried to picture herself that way and was shocked to find that she could no longer even remember what she had looked like a few moments—an eternity—ago. Only a vague image in her muddled old brain, of a pale face, dark hair; but the features, she could not get them right. Still . . .

"You were the fairest of them all," she cawed out

loud as another wave settled over her and left her vacant and drooling, curled up on the rich-red-carpeted floor. From time to time she had a thought. Whoever owns this place will be mad at me.

19

AFTER A WHILE Elena stirred. Swam back up, through the myriad cries and screams of insects, birds, and other jungle dwellers, to the surface, and opened her eyes. This time she did not even try to call Yellow Cloud. He would find her anyway, wasn't that what she had told Brice? But deep down inside, she recognized with a start that not only was she muffling her conscious attempts to call the ally but in some manner unknown to her she was casting a protective camouflage over her thoughts, and even her physical existence. He would not even know she was here. I have more power than I thought. Just like the old man always insisted. Well, no matter. What's the hurry? Why the rush to die?

She began to slowly make her way through the jungle. I could live here forever, she thought. Like Jane, only without Tarzan. Even without Cheetah.

Again she asked herself, What's the rush to die? In her mind's eye, a snapshot of the two children appeared with amazing clarity. Would not go away.

Elena was crying now, still stubbornly trying to forge her way through the incredibly thick underbrush.

Suddenly she stopped and said to herself, Oh shit, what am I doing? I've got no choice. I've never had one. I've got to call Yellow Cloud quick, before it's too late. If it's not already too late. Oh God, don't let it be too late.

"I never had a choice," she said out loud, still crying. And as if in answer, a sad wailing call not unlike that of a loon drifted to her through the hot moist air from a great distance. Followed by a sudden silence.

She could feel something primeval and stultifyingly lethal swiftly drawing near. Unbidden. She hadn't even called out to it. Somehow, without knowing it, she must have simply given up hiding herself. Oh my God. Rushing to her.

A ghastly cloud of some pulsating, almost liquid substance spilled through the trees and foliage and swirled toward her. Yellow Cloud, the old man's fierce ally. She had witnessed it before, only then the old man had been there to bear the brunt of its awful attack.

Now, as it flowed toward her, she suddenly glimpsed psychically, through the sickly yellow sheen, that the ally was not the same as it had been then, that something had been added to it. A presence, a core of emotion and consciousness, that was somehow familiar to her.

"Brice," she shouted out in fear and confusion.

The cloud paused, swirling and billowing before her, and was it only her imagination or could she make out Brice's features pulsing, forming, and then fragmenting again, somewhere inside of the thing?

Suddenly, with astonishing grace and speed, it rolled onto her like a breaker at the beach, and she felt herself drowning in it. Dissolving, her thoughts fragmenting and her energy draining away—as it fed. Even now, within the terror that was engulfing her, she could still feel awe: no one but the old man could have withstood this onslaught and lived.

But now she sensed a change taking place. Something within the creature began struggling to hold it back.

Elena. It was only a thought, but she felt it like a whisper, a caress. Somehow Brice, who was dead, partly lived on within the yellow cloud, and was fighting to control it.

Elena realized she was lying down on her back on the damp jungle earth. She forced herself up onto her knees and waited out a wave of nausea there. Then she made it the rest of the way up onto her feet.

Still engulfed in the hideous predator, she forced herself to stagger toward the eerie glowing doorway that had followed her through the jungle. Movement was agony. She was so weary. The creature was not deliberately trying to harm her now, she knew that. She could clearly feel that the part of it that was Brice was in control. But nonetheless, carrying it, moving inside of it, breathing it in, was causing her to pay a terrible price.

Through the doorway and back into that other world, the room, the circle, seen through a film of sickly yellow, chanting heard through liquid. Drusilla's gone.

The two children, chanting, still in the center of the circle. But now the circle was broken. Elena could see that clearly through the mystic cloud, and a concentrated angry force was pouring steadily in through the break and pressing onto the smaller protective dome the children had formed over themselves. Everyone has more power than they realize, she thought.

For a moment she reeled dizzily, forgetting what to do, just watching through the fog. Then, with a mental push of will, she unleashed the cloud, which rolled hungrily off her and across the room and surged onto whatever was forcing its way into the circle. And fed.

The moment it left her, Elena felt a wonderful wave of giddy relief. Nothing will ever get me to do that again, she told herself, watching the yellow cloud consuming and draining the enemy's psychic force field.

But as soon as it was over and she saw the cloud billowing backward away from her, she cried out:

"Brice, come back here! Please, don't go yet. I need you. We need you."

For a moment the cloud seemed to be hesitating. Then it flowed back onto her again.

"Hurry," Brice warned her somehow. "I can't control it much longer. It— We have to go back soon. To where we came from. To where we live."

The children had finally stopped chanting. They both stood now with their arms around each other. Their expressions were somehow slack, as if even fear had lost its ability to move or change them. They look like I feel, Elena thought.

"Elena?" William said. "Drusilla's gone somewhere. I think she . . . I think . . ."

"Later," Elena said. "Follow me. Stay close."

Outside. Except that nothing was outside anymore, not when you were inside the cloud. Stop. Look around. She could see so much more. Sense the whirlpool of psychic energy that was the life that ignited the profusion of Maui foliage in its explosion to reach the sun. She could see everything she wanted to see.

But at the same time, her brain was sizzling. I'll never be the same, she realized. Followed by: Who cares, Elena?

She could see the two nuclei of power, the tremendous blazing one on the rooftop of the bungalow to her right, and the less virulent but more complex one to her left. What had the old man said? Take out Pop. He was the weak link.

So she took the path to the left. Noticed she was staggering from one side of it to the other. One more step, she told herself. Then one more step, she told herself again. And so she moved on. Slowly and painfully, but on and on through a psychic sea.

At one point she felt something flashing toward her and the children from out of the sky, perceived vaguely what it was, and at the same instant was aware of the yellow cloud which enveloped her, hissing, drawing itself in, getting ready to pounce.

But at the last moment it swept aside and circled back the way it had come. Germanicus, she realized, and struggled on until finally, a million years later, she reached the door of Popillius' cottage.

20

NO CHOICE, POPILLIUS was thinking wearily from the center of his own protective circle, I had no choice at all. What else could I have done? What did they want me to do when Germanicus came to me with his big idea? Just say no? *Mais certainement,* Nancy, that's the fucking answer, all right. Just say no to Germanicus. Of course he'll kill you, but what the hell. Or you can just say yes like I did. Then he'll kill you later if the others don't manage it first. None of us had any choice here, except Germanicus—who in typical Western fashion so impulsively took it. Unfortunately, it turned out to be the wrong choice, but what the hell, aren't they always?

Watching the door. Knowing he was lost. Thinking, Don't bother with me, I'm all juiced out. My heart's not in it. Go take on Germanicus, okay? He'll give you a great fight, he's stark raving mad. The flaming bloody Nazi eagle of the Maui skies. By choice, of course. Another one of his great choices. Have you ever seen one of his paintings? By Zeus Pater, for your sake I hope not. Just take my advice and go after Germanicus.

But they came after him.

"Shit," he said out loud as Elena struggled through the doorway, enveloped in a sickly cloud of yellow. Corbo's ally. Popillius had never been sure whether he was more afraid of Germanicus or of Corbo. It was a toss-up. But luckily Corbo had left him alone. (Or was that unluckily?)

"I'll make a deal with you. Too many dead here already."

"Sorry," Elena said in such a weary voice. "You've got to die."

Oh shit, Pop said to himself. I've got to concentrate on the circle. If I can just keep that thing outside the circle, she'll wear out and it'll go back to whatever hell it comes from. I can win this race yet. And with two stones, maybe I can even hold out against the mad Nazi. Look at her, she's practically out on her feet here. Just hold on, Pop old boy, focus your psychic energy.

As Elena trudged inexorably toward him, step by painful step, he said: "Come on, Elena, you know I'm never going to let that thing inside the circle. Let's talk." (Let's stall.)

But to his astonishment, Elena never slowed or faltered; she simply stalked right into the psychic circle (which peeled the sickly yellow cloud off her like the skin off a grape) and tried to wrestle him out of the chalk lines. It would have struck him as comical had he not been so terrified.

The act was so totally unexpected that it almost worked, forcing Pop to give ground with her initial surge until he was practically standing on the chalk line. But then he was able to reverse her momentum and easily trip and throw Elena flat on her back, hard. Outside, where she belonged.

"Oh, come on, woman" (deliberately using the dreaded "W" word here), "surely you don't think you can take me in a wrestling match? For Godsake, I outweigh you by forty pounds, and I'm a master of the martial arts." (Chop suey, maybe, he amended to himself.)

Elena sat up silently. Blinked. Don't lose concentration here. That yellow cloud thing was slithering all over the protective dome, frantic to get at him. And here comes Elena. Stubborn as superglue.

But this time he was ready for her. Punch in the jaw, which she took with surprising resignation, and again tried futilely to wrestle him outside the circle. The stone! By Jupiter, she's got to be carrying the stone, probably wearing it around her neck. Yes! It's all been such a shock, I forgot. Come to Pop, baby.

He now wrestled her around so that he could get a stranglehold around her neck from behind. Clamped down, when suddenly he felt something hit his right leg hard. Looked down. Good Jupiter, now it was the little girl, clinging to his leg like a monkey. He tried to maintain his choke hold on Elena and kick Violet loose, and at the same time stay in the circle. Miraculously, somehow he managed. Clamped down harder. Elena was still struggling, but she had to pass out any moment here; meanwhile, where was the boy?

The girl not only managed to hold onto his leg, but she—oh shit—she was actually trying to bite him. Luckily his thigh was fairly big, and her mouth was very small.

"You little bitch," he snarled, "I'll skin you for this." Germanicus ought to be pleased by that image, he thought.

Then he spotted the boy. He was just coming out of the kitchen, where he had obviously gone looking for a weapon of some kind. He was carrying a broom.

Cautiously, standing on the outside edge of the circle, the boy poked the broom handle at Pop's knee, missed, moved around the circle looking for a good angle, then stepped in and poked again. Connected. Pain shot through his left leg. Desperate, Pop threw himself down flat, but over backward, maintaining his choke hold on Elena and taking her down on top of him, but immediately he rolled over, losing the girl somewhere in the process and now really clamping down on the choke. The boy jabbed him painfully in the ribs, but he just ignored it. Broken ribs would heal. And yes, Elena went limp. He had won after all.

He looked up to see the boy, just out of reach, staring into his eyes. Smiling, the kid was smiling! "Your foot," he said. And then Pop felt something take hold of his left foot, which, oh no no no, had wound up somehow just outside the chalk circle. Slowly his body began to slide along the wooden floor and out of the area of protection.

He let loose of Elena and tried to claw his way back in. Tried to kick his leg loose, but couldn't move it at all. Couldn't feel anything in it. It was dead. Just like the rest of me's going to be, he thought.

And now it had him by the other leg, and all at once all of the fight went out of him. Why bother? he thought. I've lost. I lost right from the start. But at least I dragged it out.

Suddenly his body was whipped out of the circle as if it had no more weight than a rag doll, and something cold and moist enveloped him, eagerly draining everything out of him at once. He hadn't even had time to be aware that it was he who was screaming. He only registered the sound along with the pain, the cold, the weakness, and the final plunge into nothing.

Elena came to and crawled painfully outside of the circle and somehow or other, with Violet's help, managed to stand up.

Satiated, the ally of the yellow cloud was floating back away from them. Elena knew she could not hold it here any longer. "Brice," she said in a hoarse, tired voice, not really knowing what she wanted to say. Once more the cloud flowed toward her, and stopped and floated there in front of her, swirling and waving as if it were treading water. It seemed to want something from her. Want to say something to her. Or want her to say something to it. But what was there to say? She searched it wearily with her newly developed, or perhaps newly discovered, psychic sense, and yes, somewhere inside, hidden within the fierce predatory hunger, the longing to return to its own environment, she could feel the awful aloneness that was Brice.

One of its tendrils spiraled out and touched her gently, perhaps even tenderly, on her stomach, just the slightest touch. Then, with astonishing speed, in some manner which she could never explain, even to herself, it flowed out of her dimension. Was gone.

Overcome with weariness, Elena sank down to her knees again on the wooden floor.

"I'm sorry," she said to no one in particular. "I've done all I can. I can't do any more."

William came over to her, carrying something in his outstretched hands. The stone: Popillius, like her, had worn it around his neck in a pendant.

She shook her head. "You keep it. I'm sorry, I'm just too tired. Here, Violet, take this." She removed the stone the old man had called Yawtlée from around her neck and handed it to Violet.

"You two take the stones and run for it. Maybe they'll protect you enough for you to get away, somewhere, anywhere. I can't fight anymore. I can't walk, I can't even think. I'm sorry. We did our best but it . . . Just get out of here, will you?"

She stopped talking, lay down on the hard wooden floor, and closed her eyes. Immediately her breathing deepened. She slept.

William turned and walked out the door onto the porch, stood there looking up at the sky. A moment later, Violet followed.

"I think this one's almost out of power," she said.

"Let's try this," William said. "Hold them together. There—do you feel it? I think it's charging up the other one."

For a few moments they stood in silence. Then Violet said, "That Germanicus guy is up on the roof of that bungalow there. He's doing something real weird, Will. I don't know how to say it, but he's flying out of his body and all over the sky. But he keeps going back, to the stones. Then he takes off again. I think he has to keep going back to the stones for some reason."

"Maybe he's afraid he'll get lost," William said.

"I think it's something or other like that. Anyway, that's what he's doing. He's going around and around like a hawk or something, then back to the body on the roof. Watching from the sky and waiting. He's not going to let us get away from here, is he?"

William didn't answer.

"Have we lost, Will?"

His small delicate features were set in an expression of intense angry determination.

"Not yet, we haven't," he said.

21

LET THE OTHERS sit in protective circles and shiver in fear. Let the others flock together like sheep bleating out in the night. Germanicus will climb to the highest rooftop and fling himself upon them from the skies.

I'm starting to think of myself in the third person. Fine. Wonderful. So much the better, for I am changing from myself into something purer, stronger, aren't I? The new man. The ruler of the New Age. The man eagle. Germanicus the astral avenger.

The distance and the purity of the skies. Only he had thought to pursue them and the power contained within them. All that power. Only he was capable of providing a worthy vessel for it. Only he, with his giant body, his clear, pure mind. Only he wanted it. And only he deserved it. For that, of course, was the great secret of the universe. You got exactly what you deserved.

The others had been a dead end, Pop the pimp and Dru the mother-whore; even Corbo, killer Corbo. They had all been a dead end, and now, as dead ends should be, they were all dead.

Only he had experimented in new directions. Only he had been drawn to the skies.

Whereas they had been satisfied to explore the astral worlds, only he had painstakingly developed an astral body of his own and learned to use it right here, in this world. And in fact, he had lately reached the level, undreamed of even by himself, where he could actually solidify his astral form for a brief moment and make contact with matter. It was this unexpected talent that enabled him to kill while still in his astral form: the astral claws inserted so effortlessly into the physical body suddenly hardened, tearing asunder whatever flesh they touched. This was the way of the astral eagle. The sky ruler of the new world. And his powers would grow and multiply, he knew that. Once he had all four stones, to what new, unimaginable heights would the astral eagle soar then? He would find out soon enough.

This approach had its drawbacks, of course, as does any approach, but the strengths far outweighed the weaknesses.

It took time to achieve the astral form, for whenever he wanted to use it he always had to build it anew out of pure concentration. He had to envision it, harden it with will, until it was a diamond of consciousness, and then, using the stone (stones, now!) as an amplifier, channel his life force into it.

Then he would surge, screaming, into the sky, returning again and again to the stones to amplify his power.

Too bad his powers had not been developed enough to enable him to pick up Corbo's stone while still in astral form and carry it to his waiting physical body on the roof. It had cost him time and effort to have to go back down and physically retrieve the stone, climb back up onto the roof again, and then to have to forge a brand-new body of consciousness and finally build up enough psychic power to launch it.

Also, soaring through the skies in his magnificent astral form was always just too ecstatic. You were tempted to fly too far from the stones. (Who knew what would happen then?) You were tempted to make rash decisions, to lose control. The very thing which had got you there in the first place.

As when he had seen Elena carrying the ally called Yellow Cloud to poor Pop's bungalow. He had been so filled with ecstasy, circling way up there above everyone, that he had almost been unable to resist mounting an all-out kamikaze attack. But at the last moment, as always, he had regained control, done the right thing. Left them and Pop to fight it out. Whoever wins, fine.

The ally of the yellow cloud was a being of great power, but it had its drawbacks too. It was just plain too powerful. It wound up exhausting itself and half killing whoever used it. All you had to do was wait it out. Which he had.

And now for the final battle. Ragnarok. The twilight of the old gods, the birth of the new. All that was left was to dispatch the two children and poor helpless Elena, and gather in the reward. Precious stones. The only precious stones, of which all the other precious stones of history were mere symbols.

Waiting here, watching from the skies, he sailed out again and again, wheeling around and around, simply waiting. Making no mistakes. No old-fashioned Roman close-quarter short-sword type thinking. Waiting to kill from afar. Germanicus, the ruler of the skies.

22

I GUESS IF he can do it, then so can I. Don't you think so, Lettie?" William was frowning, looking down at the stone he held in his hands as if expecting to find the answer there.

"I don't know, Will. I guess so. I guess you can do just about anything, only don't ask me to go flying all over the place like that."

"Can you tell how he does it, Lettie?"

Violet closed her eyes for a few moments and stood very still. Her hand was stretched out toward Germanicus' bungalow, as though reaching for his thoughts. Then she opened her eyes again.

"I can feel how he does it, but it's kind of hard to describe, Will. I don't think I can do it, but maybe you can. You have to think real hard about another body, you know, imagine it. And then you use the power in the stone to shift your thinking over to that body. Then you can do anything that body can do. It's very hard, though, it takes him a long time."

William looked skeptical. "It doesn't sound that hard to me," he said. "It's just because he's a grown-up. Everything's hard for grown-ups, Lettie. Remember when Uncle George tried to play Super Mario Brothers 2?"

Both kids started to laugh, but Violet quickly held her finger to her lips and whispered, "He'll hear you."

"Okay, Lettie, you listen here. I'll do whatever-you-call-it, the thing he does, and I'll get him to chase me. You can see what a big dweeb he is, right? Then I'll ditch him and go back to his body on the roof and try and see if there's some way I can hurt it."

"Oh yeah, like how?"

William spread his arms in exasperation. "Like how would I know, okay, Lettie? I haven't tried yet."

Violet shook her head. "Okay, okay, I'm sorry. What do you want me to do, Will?"

"You have to guard my body here, if he tries to get at it. You can do that better than anyone. You know, make up another circle, like you did back inside there when Drusilla ran away."

"I wonder if she's dead," Violet said.

"We don't have time to worry about it," William pointed out insistently. "So can you or can't you? Come on, Lettie."

"Sure, I guess so. Only what about the candles and chanting and all that? Don't I need to . . . ?"

William shook his head: "No way," he said. "That's just 'cause they're grown-ups, Lettie. I told you, grown-ups need all kinds of stuff to help them because . . . they're . . ." He waved his hands as if conducting, and both of them said in synchronization, drawing the word out, ". . . dweebs."

Again they started to laugh, and Violet silenced both of them by holding her finger to her lips.

"Okay, okay, we'd better get going. —And Lettie?"

"Yes, Will."

"Do you believe in heaven?"

She shook her head. "You?"

"I don't know, Lettie."

For a moment they were both quiet. Then William

said, "Okay, let's go. Can you start on the circle, Lettie?"

Violet closed her eyes and said, "It's done."

"Okay," William said, "you just keep it up, Lettie." And then he too closed his eyes.

23

AS THE TWO children wandered out onto the front porch, Germanicus was immediately aware of them from his position in the sky, as he was aware of everything in the vicinity all at once. The higher you flew, the more things were included in your eternal now: the other bungalows hiding in the profuse Hawaiian foliage, the blazing patches of bougainvillea, his own body sitting cross-legged on the roof there, the children on the porch, even the insects and birds. For the air meant vision, psychic and otherwise.

The children had the stones with them. There was no doubt of that; when you were in astral form the stones sent out powerful radiant emanations that you could pick up more clearly than sunlight. In fact, they were rather like small psychic suns, he thought. From his astral viewpoint, it seemed to him almost as if they were controlling the flow of phenomena he thought of as the universe. Stop, stop, he told himself, don't start thinking like Corbo. They're just power. Your power.

Once again he had to hold himself back, keep himself from just falling on the kids from out of the sky. Perhaps it was a trap of some kind. He put out psychic feelers, but could not find any sign of Yellow Cloud. Or Popillius or Drusilla, for that matter. But Elena was still around; he could sense her presence inside the house. Why, then, were the kids carrying the stones?

Still, what kind of trap could it be? Perhaps he was being too cautious here. Circle and swoop, circle and swoop. Just when he had finally decided to throw caution to the winds and attack, a psychic circle of protection sprang up down below around the kids on the porch. A strong one. Could the little girl actually be doing that, as his senses seemed to be telling him she was? Circle and swoop, circle and swoop.

Suddenly, astonishingly, a small form exploded out of the psychic circle and blasted upward through the sky right at him.

Germanicus shrieked and dodged; the small sparrow-type shape streaked by and now turned and hovered there, staring at him defiantly—at Germanicus, the ruler of the skies, defiantly!

With a scream of rage Germanicus lunged at him, but the boy's astral form turned and sped away.

It flew darting and swooping, twisting and turning, like a bird's version of a small boy on a skateboard maneuvering the ocean of air. But Germanicus followed close, moving steadily and confidently. Kill the boy's astral form and the physical body would die.

And he was the king of the skies. The boy had made a fatal mistake in challenging him here in his own element. For already Germanicus was mastering the peculiar flight pattern, not so much emulating the boy as just knowing when and how to cut him off, straighten him out. Soon it began more to resemble a dog herding sheep than a bird of prey chasing a victim. In fact, Germanicus realized, it was fun. And the boy was tiring now, there was no doubt about that. It would soon be over.

Nevertheless, as they flew on and on, Germanicus felt a grudging admiration for the boy. The cool reasoning mind, the courage to try something new, rather reminded him of himself.

And he flew so well for someone who was flying for the first time. Desperation, of course, was a wonderful teacher, but even so, there was something special happening here.

Still, what had the little fool expected to accomplish? Once or twice already the boy had tried to dodge and turn around, but Germanicus had effortlessly cut him off and driven him onward. Did he think he could outwit the king of the skies and circle back around him? Costliest of errors!

As they flew on and on, Germanicus realized two things. One, that he could have caught the boy several times now, but was deliberately driving him on, just toying with him. The instincts of the predator came along with the form he had chosen for himself. The other thing he realized was that he had been lured into flying farther away from his body than he had ever flown before.

In this, the boy had done him a service. Now for the first time he understood that all his fears about flying too far from his physical body had been illusion; there was no limit. He knew exactly where his body was, could even feel the stones throbbing in his hands; he did not need to see them at all. The stones were a psychic beacon reaching out to him wherever he went; the boy had freed him from his own self-imposed limitations.

"Thank you," he shrieked as, finally tiring of the game, he surged up to strike the boy from behind. Closed his talons and turned around in the air.

They were somewhere over the ocean now, and the island called Maui was not even so much as a dot in the blue. He had never realized before how fast one could fly in an astral body. I'll fly all over the world, thanks to you, dear boy. Can you hear me, or are you dead?

No, the creature was wriggling in his grasp. Hurt, but

not dead. Yet. As much as Germanicus prided himself on his efficiency, he couldn't help wanting to drag things out just a bit more. After all, was there anything as sweet as gazing down at the helpless form clutched in your merciless talons, then killing it? But now the boy was limp, unconscious. Well, there was really no such thing as unconscious; Germanicus had learned that much for sure. When you were resting in that blessed state people called unconsciousness, you were simply someplace else, perhaps the dream realm or the astral, active as ever. Even the boy here, just somewhere else. The only real mystery about consciousness that remained for Germanicus after all these years of mystical experience was what happened after death, and he had no intention of ever solving that one.

Still, speaking from a predatory viewpoint, it wasn't much of a thrill killing someone who wasn't here to experience it.

"Wake up," he said to the boy. "Come to Poppa." —Kid wouldn't listen.

And what about the girl? Germanicus knew better than to slack off at this late stage of the game. But no, the girl was no problem, he could sense her down there using all of her energy to protect the boy's body. How like a woman, always on the defensive.

Germanicus didn't have much use for women. He felt nature had clearly fashioned them to be servants to the bigger, stronger males of the tribe. Then there were the freaks of nature, like Drusilla. Even his astral form shuddered at the thought of that aberration. Leave it to the overcivilized Romans to elevate their women's status and then be forced to grovel before them. By the gods, no healthy barbarian tribe would ever consider such an arrangement. No, let Pop the pimp take care of the whore, as he apparently had. But the boy here was another matter. He deserved the warrior's death.

"Wake up."

No use. There was a way to reach him, though. Germanicus merged his consciousness with William's and forced the boy back into the astral form squirming in his claws.

"Now you die," he said, savoring the moment of final victory. The boy showed no fear. Eyes cool and appraising, staring up into his. Unnerving in one so young.

"But you will not be able to go through the door," the boy said calmly.

This was so weird Germanicus could barely register it. Was that really what he had said?

"What door?" Germanicus demanded. "The door to what?"

But there it was, an ordinary door. In the sky. And the funny thing was the feeling he had that it had always been there. Near him. Waiting for him to open it. Go through it. But . . .

"Because I am the door," the boy finished patiently.

Silence. Close the claws and shatter this glowing consciousness. Just a twitch. But he did not twitch.

"The door to what you want," the boy said.

Right there. Within easy reach. Germanicus reached out and, changing one of his wings back into his arm, took hold of the knob, and it was round and cool and pleasing to the touch. He was delighted to see it was made of agate. For some unaccountable reason, he shivered. Was he really afraid of a mind so young, so new and inexperienced?

He turned the knob and opened the door and entered, immediately transfixed by the singing. The pure golden voices of the Aryan men blended together in a fine old drinking song. The clinking of steins. And the swastika. Everywhere, on the flags, the armbands, that moving, crushing wheel. The big brawny golden-haired brotherhood that nature had created to rule the world were gathered here together.

"I don't hate the Jews," the man next to him said.

"That was one of *his* mistakes. They are so useful. They could have helped us. They are so clever. I believe they could have developed a bomb that would have blown up the world. Such clever little servants."

Germanicus turned and stared into the man's beautiful blue eyes. It took him a moment to recognize himself.

He raised his stein and drank a big swallow of the beer. "It is so sweet here," he said, gesturing with his hand to take in the room, the men, the singing, and the beer.

But the man who was himself shook his head.

"No," he said, "it was better with the swords. Such cleverness was not necessary then. Only strength, and the purity of energy. Only the swastika. Before the Romans. The swords and the snow. And the swastika. But then"—the man stared lovingly into his eyes—"that's another door."

The man set down his stein on an old-fashioned coffee table and put one hand on each of Germanicus' cheeks. Then slowly and luxuriously moved forward and kissed him long and lovingly on the lips. Why, this is who I have always loved, Germanicus realized with a start. No wonder I have achieved such ruthlessness. It was all plain to him at last, that formula, as accurate and meaningful as Einstein's: pure narcissism equals pure ruthlessness. This was the energy that fueled the journey through endless time.

"I am the swastika," he said blissfully to himself.

"But I am the door," the boy repeated from wherever he was, "the only door to what you want."

And sure enough, there it was, right in front of his eyes, in the middle of the room. And as much as he wanted to stay here with his comrades . . .

He opened the door and went through it.

He had forgotten how cold it was. And how terrifying. How lonely. How painful. How could you remember things like that, things that woke you all the way up and balanced you on the edge? You drowsed, you fell!

He had forgotten the snow and ice, the howling of the wolves. Everything so white and pure, except for the blood. There was his father and his big brother, Arn of the One Eye. His whole tribe. His tribe of giants. His little tribe (no more than a few families) of men so big they could not ride the little European ponies the rest of the Germans rode into battle, and so had to fight on foot. Men legendary among the other Germans, men who chose only the biggest of women to bear their children.

"We must hurry. They are after us with horses," his father said. And, in answer to his questions: "Other men of the North, like us, only lackeys of the Romans. They've hired them to hunt us down."

Germanicus howled, because it was true. The clever little Romans with their impudent sharp-tongued women and decadent, *civilized* lifestyle were hunting them down. Were organizing other Germans to do it. And his father and his brother, feared and legendary as they were, would be killed, and he would be accepted into Roman civilization and educated as a Roman and would one day earn honor and even fame in her army. Would become a general. But in his heart . . .

There was no salvation here. He knew where this was heading. But the door! "To what you want," the boy had said, and what he wanted was the past. He knew that now. The doorway went against the grain of time. It took you back and then back again, instead of driving you forward like life. And that was what he wanted. The only thing he wanted.

There it was again, wavering in the icy air. Then becoming clearer and clearer. He reached for the beautiful agate knob longingly, because he knew where it led. Back before the beginning, to the time of Titans, where the purity of the will burned untainted by the corruption of thought, of restraint. Back to paradise—or chaos. Call it whatever you want, it was the time of raw power. What did it matter if you won or you lost? He was turning that knob, opening that door into sweet chaos, when he paused.

Something that was not thought stopped him. What did it matter if you won or lost . . . what? He smiled. The boy was clever, offering him happiness. But what did he want with happiness? What he wanted, had to have, was the triumph of his indomitable will, not happiness. What he really wanted was simply to win every battle.

And now, filled with new admiration for his clever little opponent, he rushed back through the imaginary worlds the boy had created, and crashed through the barrier back into the world we call reality.

24

FLASHING ACROSS THE sky, zeroed in on the bungalows way down below, off in the rapidly diminishing distance, the astral eagle screamed triumphantly. For he had won, had escaped the illusionary world the boy had created for him, rejected the last temptations, as had that other, weaker savior; and now he was heading back more powerful than ever, with the squirming body of the boy still clutched in his talons. For throughout the hallucination that boy had created for him, he had somehow unconsciously held onto the little bastard.

And now he had decided to kill him in front of his sister. The idea, after such a struggle, was enough to make him practically swoon with ecstasy. What delicious irony: there she would be, wasting all of her energy trying to protect her brother's physical body, while he would be crushing the life out of his astral form right before her innocent eyes. From there it would be a simple act of mercy to dispatch her.

But she was not on the porch. The circle of protection was gone. The helpless body of the boy just sat there all alone, waiting . . . Where was she?

25

Crying steadily but softly, the two amulets hanging around her neck, bouncing inside her shirt against her belly, Violet ran along the gravel path. Partly she was crying from an onslaught of fear that was almost too intense to bear, and partly she was crying because she felt she had made the wrong decision. After all, no one was protecting her brother's body now, and wasn't that what he'd asked her to do? Wasn't that the right thing to do? She didn't know.

But the moment the two astral forms had flown out of sight, she had made her decision. Not really knowing what she was going to do (what could she do?) when she got there, she had broken her magic circle of protection and headed for the bungalow where Germanicus' physical body waited on the roof.

Now, still crying, she climbed the ladder. Peeked over the edge of the roof, and almost choked in fear to see his enormous muscular body seated there.

He had taken off his shirt, and his flesh was strangely pink, like that of a baby.

And he was huge. Like a giant in a fairy tale. It took a few precious moments for her to unfreeze her body and force herself to go up there on the roof with him. All of the bungalows were built with long low wings on either side of the main structure, and while the main structure had a peaked roof, the wings were both flat on top. A nice place to come and sit, she thought. Bet Will would really love it up here.

The thought of William prodded her to move closer to the sitting figure.

"Knock knock," she whispered. "Anyone there?" No answer, thank God.

Now what do I do? Unbelievable as it was, the awful wave of fear she was suffering intensified, and for a moment she just stood there, shaking. Unable to go forward or back up.

Try to get the stones, she thought. Oh please, please, pretty please, Lettie, move your bod here.

But it took a few more precious moments to bring herself to actually touch his hand. The flesh was strangely cold.

And he was so big, and his hands were fists around the stones; she could not pry those fingers open.

Now fear was thudding in her head. Pounding in her chest. Be quick, oh be quick. Because he's coming back, because Will's body is just sitting back there empty, without any protection, because he can't outfly Germanicus. Oh, be quick. Be quick and do—what?

Suddenly she felt, rather than saw, the two forms flashing through the sky toward her, the one struggling in the clutches of the other. Do what?

She did the only thing she knew how to do.

26

THE ROOF, HE realized, as his eagle senses pinpointed the girl. She's on the roof. A shock wave of fear hit Germanicus for the first time.

Dropping the victim that had been so eagerly clutched in his talons, he twisted around and with frantic strokes of his giant wings sped toward his bungalow. He did not even see the released form wriggle back into the boy's body, the body crawling painfully back into the house, where it collapsed.

The roof! He dropped from the sky and streaked toward his physical body with the most speed he had yet attained. Only to bounce off . . . what? Tried again, only to bounce off again. The girl had constructed another psychic circle of protection. Stronger than the last. Stronger even than he had believed possible. And this one was around his own body, keeping him outside.

Frantically he tried again and again to penetrate it. With no success.

"Let me in, you little bitch, or I'll tear you to pieces, slowly. Do you hear me?"

Could she hear him in his astral form? He was not certain. But apparently shc could, because now she did something new to the circle. He watched it grow cloudy and dark, as if smoke were swirling around inside of it, until he couldn't see her or his own body or anything in it. And at the same time she must have done something else to further strengthen it. Because the mystic power of his stones was no longer penetrating it and pouring its psychic energy into his astral form.

Don't panic, he thought. No need to panic. She doesn't know what she's doing here. She's a child. A girl child, at that. Soon she'll tire of this and quit. All I've got to do is stall. Concentrate and last it out. As always. Just hang in there.

But it was the first time he had been in astral form without the aid of the power of one of the stones. And it was not all that easy to concentrate. His thoughts disassembled, scattered, flew away like birds.

Don't panic, he thought again, when he managed enough strength to order his thoughts momentarily. What difference does it make? How can I get lost if I don't go anywhere? Just stay here.

Even as he said this, he flew up in the sky and hovered. I'll just circle and wait, he thought.

He began to sail around and around. Then once again the ecstasy of the air struck him, and his thoughts scattered, blew away like leaves in the wind. Bliss! Bliss!

Another momentary burst of clarity, and he looked down in panic; but there was the roof of his bungalow, same as before. Only wasn't there something different about it? He marshaled his powers of concentration and focused on the rooftop. As if looking through water, he was able to perceive strange creatures moving upon it, gesturing to him. At first he did not find this odd at all. Almost as if he had been expecting it. But then he realized where he was.

I'm in another world, he thought. An astral dimension. The power of the stones must have been what kept me from drifting here before. These creatures seem to have been waiting for me here.

Circle. Circle. He could hear their faint cries down below. Imploring him to land. Whining. Begging.

I'll never get back, he thought with a sharp stab of anxiety. Then: Back where? He fought for it. Dredged it up. Clumsy oaf, somewhere sitting on a rooftop. Had he really wanted to go back to that? But why?

Down below, the shambling earthbound creatures on the roof were reaching up their heavy, hairy arms toward him, as if he were a flower to be plucked from the sky.

"Please," they cried out. "Oh please, please land, Oh magnificent creature of the sun."

But he screamed back at them in defiance: "I'll never come down." And now, deliberately, he flew off with strong, sure strokes. And whether it was the loss of the stones or whether it was his own mutated consciousness, he was moving faster and farther with each sure swift stroke now, into strange, new, unimaginable realms. On and on.

"I'll never, never go back," he shrieked ecstatically into the air—his air now. Forever.

27

IT WAS HOURS later when Elena came up on the rooftop. The sun was shining now. It was early morning, but already starting to grow hot. The body of Germanicus was sitting cross-legged, eyes open, vacant, staring off into the empty air. Not moving. Violet lay in front of him, limp as a dishrag. Like an offering.

"Good morning," Elena said as the girl stirred.

"I must have fallen asleep, I guess," Violet said. "Oh no, no, I must have . . . must have . . ."

"It's okay," Elena said. "It's okay now."

She went over to Germanicus and started prying at his fingers. "Come on, open up here, you don't need them anymore."

Like Elena, Violet could sense the emptiness in the body of the giant.

"Are you going to hurt him?" she asked.

"I don't think he can be hurt anymore, Violet. I think it's over now. Come on, damn you, open up."

A loud cracking noise.

"You broke his finger. —Will! What about Will?"

"William's all right. He was hurt. But who wasn't? He'll be all right. He's sleeping. I carried him back to our cottage. Somehow," she added wearily. "He's young, resilient. The stone will heal him fast. No, he'll be fine. —Ah yes, come to Elena." She held out her hand triumphantly; one of Germanicus' stones was in it.

"Come on, one more here."

Crack!

"You broke another finger."

"Only what I have to break. Okay? Got it. Got both of them."

They climbed down from the roof. Walked slowly along the path together.

"We ought to call someone. I mean, about Germanicus."

"We'll call someone later, after we've gone and I've had a chance to contact some of our people."

"We ought to cover him up. He'll get sunburned." The girl looked so tiny. Just eyes, Elena thought.

"Honey, he doesn't care about his skin anymore."

"And Drusilla?"

Elena shook her head: "Drusilla too. Drusilla doesn't care about anything."

At the door to their cottage, they paused.

"What will happen . . . What will . . ." Crying again. You'd think she'd be all cried out by now. Elena put her arm around her.

"We stay together. You and your brother and me. That's all. Like the old man said, we're family here. All that separating and struggling and squabbling and wheeling and dealing, it's over. No need for it anymore."

I guess it must be some kind of New Age after all, she thought, or maybe an even older one. Like something that happened before, happening again. Who knows? Who ever knows?

Violet had stopped crying now, but her expression was confused: "But Elena, who will . . . The fourth stone? Who will be the fourth Guardian?"

Elena closed her eyes. And smiled. It was maybe the first time that Violet had seen her smile. Or realized just how beautiful she was. Even beat-up, she was beautiful. Now Violet had to smile too, because Elena was always beat-up, right? One of her beautiful eyes was always black. She always limped. But she kept going. So fragile, yet tough as nails.

Behind closed eyes, Elena captured the necessary memories and put them together. The old man assuring her that the power to control the ally was within her. Yellow Cloud–Brice tenderly touching her stomach. And one other memory.

The Sea View Motel—an eternity ago. The old man had been preparing her to go next door and perform her seduction scene with Brice. When all of her arguments had broken against the steely calm of the old man's will, she had snarled exasperatedly: "I don't have any birth control. What the hell do you think I do, carry around rubbers?"

The old man had laughed his crazy, crazy laugh (she could hear it now, from somewhere far away, yet inside herself) and then he had said: "Why, don't worry, Elena, I have perfect control over these matters."

She opened her eyes, still smiling her weary smile.

"I'm pregnant," she said.

About the Author

Ronald Anthony Cross's short stories have been featured in *Isaac Asimov's Science Fiction Magazine, The Magazine of Fantasy & Science Fiction,* and *Pulphouse.* His first novel, *Prisoners of Paradise,* was published in 1988.

Cross practices meditation, tai chi, and dream control, all of which helped prepare him for writing *The Fourth Guardian.* He is currently writing *The Lost Guardian.* He lives in Santa Monica, California.